SHE was walking toward him. Twelve years. She looked much as he remembered her. Tanned. Healthy. Confident.

He didn't move. Corinne faced him from a yard away. The slender thread linking them across time was an electric wire charged with the voltage of shared and unforgotten passion.

"What are you doing here?" he asked.

"I need to talk to you."

Old aches, like young wounds, reopened, disrupting his world. "Fifteen minutes. No more."

"I want you to find my son," Corinne said. "I—I can pay you, if that's the way it is."

Maguire finished his brandy and put down the glass. His eyes locked with Corinne's. "I have all the money I need for now, thank you. What else can you offer?"

MATANZA

a novel by

Peter Gentry

FAWCETT GOLD MEDAL • NEW YORK

MATANZA

Published by Fawcett Gold Medal Books, a unit of CBS Publications, the Consumer Publishing Division of CBS Inc.

ISBN 0-449-14117-9

Printed in the United States of America

10 9 8 7 6 5 4 3 2 1

1

Mexico City, February, 1913

Maguire had eaten well, drunk moderately and checked the card tables and roulette wheel. Now a faint, rambling melody concocted by the piano player followed him across the alley behind his casino, *El Madronito*. The winter night was brisk at this altitude and the music sounded more brittle than it really was. As always, he stopped halfway to the door. There the music and the raucous banter of men balanced finely. Another step and the music would fade completely, obliterated by shouted bets and cries for more tequila. Always more tequila.

The step taken, he listened carefully. The voices were muted tonight. The men were waiting. Good. There would be plenty of excitement in a few minutes when Fuentes arrived. Maguire checked his clothes. He flicked an ash from the arm of his heavy pin-striped coat, which was

5

beginning to make him sweat. The creases in his trousers, black and straight as a pipe, were knife sharp. He pulled a strip of cloth from a rear pocket, reached down and dusted the hand-tooled black leather boots made by a craftsman from Oaxaca. Polished to a fare-thee-well, the boots literally glowed in the faint light.

His coat parted, Maguire touched his good luck amulet and checked his watch. Two minutes to midnight, the appointed time. Pensive, he considered Fuentes's arrival and the challenge it presented. Trouble followed Jesus Fuentes like a mongrel pup its bitch.

Maguire snapped closed the lid of the watch and dropped it into his vest pocket. The gold chain drooped across the black silk vest stitched with silver thread in configurations of Aztec origin. He smiled. This was a Maguire who would surprise Fuentes. The last time they'd met, Maguire was dressed for the mountains. He had been a *gringo* mercenary then. Now he bore the manners of a gentleman of stature. The change was reflected in his dress, an elegant mixture of Mexican and Anglo, much like the man himself.

It was time. Casually he strode to the door, opened it and stepped inside. Immediately an expectant hush spread over the crowd. Heads turned and necks craned. Maguire had arrived.

Maguire touched the silver grip of his walking stick to the brim of his bowler in informal greeting. "And where is this *gachupine* and his hen?" he said, slowly and clearly.

The insult was received with hoots of good-natured laughter. *Gachupine* was a term of derision for the upper class pure blood Spaniards born in either Mexico or Spain. The *gachupines* remained aloof from the masses. Supported by the blood and sweat of those they deemed to be less valuable than animals, they lived luxuriously in Mexico City, Paris, London or New York, and rarely visited their vast, magnificent *haciendas*, the uncounted acres over which they ruled with the haughty disdain of absolute monarchs. A hundred years earlier the bond with Spain had been broken. A hundred years of revolution and counter-revolution had followed, and still the chosen few, well served by hated lackeys, retained their positions of authority. If there was a middle class at all to fill the yawning gulf between the supremely wealthy and the innumerable utterly destitute, it was composed of men like those who crowded the triple circle of seats around the clay ring in the center of the room. All were marginal entrepreneurs like Maguire, moving between two worlds and earning a precarious living in the midst of impermanence. There were more of them now that Porfirio Diaz was gone and Francisco Madero was president, and their existence was a little easier. For this, no one was more thankful than Maguire. He had known good times and bad, but none better since the day Madero became Mexico's president. Since then things had been looking up. Riding high with his own casino, money in his pocket and, if not the affection, at least the tolerance of those in power, Maguire was determined to see the present state of affairs continue. When a man hits a string of good luck, he'd better play it to the bust. An old warrior and soldier of fortune he had known in the Philippines had offered this advice and Maguire had adopted the credo.

The crowd parted and Maguire made his way to the pit in the center of the room. Dark, oily smoke from hand-twisted, stumpy *puros*, the cheap cigars manufactured from the dregs of Valle National's export crop of tobacco, darkened the air. Gray white coils of smoke from cigarettes writhed upward to the rafters, glided snakelike over the weathered beams and seeped through the thatched roof. Hands clapped Maguire on the back with rough familiarity, offered him earthen jugs of tequila and pulque. The men liked Maguire not so much out of friendship, but because they admired his success and identified with him. He had known the devil hunger, as had they. He too was of mixed blood—a half-breed. His light coppery skin and thick black hair now tinged with a sprinkling of silver allowed him a freedom *norteamericanos* seldom found south of the border. A six-foot frame and sharp blue eyes recalled an Irish father who had enjoyed a brief liaison with his mother. The Irishman disappeared after discovering she was with child. When Maguire was nine, his mother took him across the border into Mexico to her father's scrubby little farm. There, until her death, when he was thirteen, he slaved in the fields. Then he ran away for good. The men around him could read it in his face—Maguire had learned survival the hard way.

"Aaaieee!" A piratical-looking figure sprang upright at the far edge of the pit. Stretching to his meager five-foot height, he flapped his hand in pain and cursed. "Damned *gallo*! I'll give you to Rosita to make enchiladas with! She'll stew the meat from your worthless bones."

"And we'll be out a casino, my friend." Maguire laughed, making his way forward. Riciotti Lucca sucked the blood from his wounded palm and spat onto the clay floor. "Here is a man who I've seen fight with three bullets in him," Maguire said to the crowd, "and he howls when a chicken pecks him. Some great warrior, eh?" Lucca snarled a reply. "What happened?"

Lucca pointed to the crate, then held out his hand. A chunk of skin a quarter-inch wide and deep and four times as long was missing. "Some bird," he growled, grinning with pride, for he himself had trained the rooster.

Maguire squatted by the box and peered through the slats at the fighting cock within. "Ah, Torrito. You forget your size when you bite Lucca. That rooster is no match for you. Save your anger for Fuentes's hen."

An orange beak snapped at his fingers but he snatched them away just in time. As for Lucca, everyone enjoyed themselves at his expense. In retaliation, he grabbed a bottle of tequila from the nearest reveler. The *mestizo* cursed and started to take back his bottle, but Lucca's eyes narrowed and his hawklike bearded face hardened. The other man pulled back and watched silently while the Italian took a long draught. There was a point beyond which the feisty Lucca would not be pushed. Slowly he drank. Slowly he returned the bottle, then flashed the donor a wicked grin.

A door at the other end of the room opened. The crowd quieted much as it had when Maguire entered. A voice muttered against the chill wind and several men gained admittance. Others shivered, but whether from the night air or the presence of the men who entered, it was hard to tell.

Jesus Fuentes paused, allowing the drama of his entrance to reach those who had yet to discover his presence. When the room was sufficiently quiet, he strode through the quickly opened lane of men. He could sense the hostility of those he passed among and enjoyed it all the more because he knew they feared him. Fuentes's features were those of the high born Castilian: aquiline, lightly olive-toned, almost white. Light blond hair bleached by the sun hung to his shoulders. His sombrero of brown felt trimmed with gold rested on his back, held there by a leather cord tied about his neck. His dress, which was showy and gaudy—a short jacket and tight riding pants, both laden with heavy gold trim—contrasted sharply with that of the motley arrayed crowd that surrounded him.

Most chilling was the black patch covering Fuentes's left eye. On it a perpetually open, staring orb was emblazoned in gold—an evil eye to chill the hearts of the superstitious and weak-willed. Compounding the horror of his disfigurement, a jagged line of scar tissue started above the bridge of his nose, disappeared under the patch and reappeared to run halfway to his ear. What lay underneath was left to the imagination. As a result, few mistook him

9

for the fop he appeared. Those unfortunate enough to miscalculate his prowess seldom lived long enough to regret their error. Jesus Fuentes had killed his first man at the age of fifteen. A dozen more, not counting those who fell in revolutionary battles, followed over the years.

Fuentes's men, dressed in black *sombreros*, jackets and breeches of colorless gray, entered behind him, heightening the dangerous mood. Mottled black and gray blankets rolled into thick, ugly snakes hung over their left shoulders and met below their belts behind holstered pistols. Coiled snakes stitched in white on the holsters stood out in bold and terrifying contrast.

Los Serpientes, as they were called, were in the pay of Gregor Bortha, the political and military force in Chihuahua. Officially designated *rurales*, the rural police force, they were in reality a private army of fifty efficient and ruthless murderers. Though Bortha paid them, Maguire knew *Los Serpientes* owed their allegiance to only one man—Jesus Fuentes.

Fuentes reached the edge of the pit and, hiding his surprise, smiled at Maguire. Maguire smiled back. No one mistook them for friends. "Good evening, Maguire."

Maguire nodded in return. At the same time a voice from the edge of the crowd called out, "One-Eye." The crowd tensed as Fuentes searched the sea of impassive faces for the source of the insult. One Eye, in spite of the macabre decoration on his patch, was the one name that could shatter his icelike composure and bring him down to the elemental level of those around him. The five *Serpientes* accompanying him moved toward the sound but he stopped them with the slightest movement of his hand.

"I have waited, Maguire." He touched the patch. "One year, ten months and four days. If I had known where you were, I would not have waited so long. But no matter. I say this to your face. Tonight is the beginning of my revenge. First your casino, then . . . Perhaps an eye for an eye."

"You talk too much, Fuentes," Maguire said. There would be time for words later. Perhaps by that time he would know why Fuentes had brought his *rurales* to Mexico City.

Fuentes stared in disdainful silence. "Adolfo," he finally said. One of the *Serpientes*, a burly, flat-faced man, stepped forward and jumped into the pit. A second man set a box made of pine slats fastened with leather on the edge of the ring. Adolfo opened the lid and lifted out a black rooster.

The crowd sighed in admiration. The bird was magnificent. Jet plumage, shaved at the breast and the back of the neck, gleamed richly. What had once been a proud, high comb had been cut low to the skull so it would offer no purchase. Still, the bright red was a slash of color that drew the eye to the proud head. A third *Serpiente* brought forth a small chest and set it on the rail enclosing the ring. When Fuentes nodded, the man opened the chest to reveal a glitter of gold coins. A greedy stirring rippled through the spectators. None had ever seen such a fortune.

"Twenty thousand," Fuentes said in a near whisper. "One thousand twenty-dollar gold pieces, *norteamericano*. If you wish to count?"

Maguire shrugged. "I trust you." He ran a finger along his moustache and stared at El Negro, the fighting cock Fuentes had brought; then he reached inside his coat and pulled out a white envelope. Inside was the deed of ownership to *El Madronito*. He placed it on the edge of the fighting pit. "Take him out, Lucca."

The Italian nodded, took a final swig of tequila and jumped into the pit by the box. "You bite me again, *gallo*, so help me . . ." he muttered. Torrito had smelled his adversary, though, and no longer gave thought to the man's hands. Already brain and blood were aware of one overriding fact: another cock was nearby.

11

Fuentes and his men knew the valor of a fighting rooster was not measured by his appearance. Still they laughed when they saw Torrito, for he was a ratty-looking beast. Rust-colored feathers extended in every direction from his scarred, battle-worn body. One eye was permanently cast to the left, the result of a previous close encounter. His comb, a mass of hardened scar tissue, was a mottled knob of indeterminate color. The initiated observer looked past Torrito's ugly exterior and appraised the strength of his legs and the musculature of his breast.

El Negro and Torrito, king and knave. Both had been shorn of feathers at the breast and the back of the neck to make them equally vulnerable. Both waited—tense and expectant. They would fight *natural*, meaning using only their own leg spurs and not the razor sharp metal spurs in vogue in some places. El Negro's spurs were a full quarter inch longer than his opponent's, but not as thick as Torrito's, which were stubbier and less likely to snap.

Personal feelings among the spectators toward Maguire and Fuentes disappeared. Like Maguire or not, the issue now was a cockfight, and the bets shouted across the ring considered only the relative strengths of the birds. The crates were removed. Maguire and Fuentes stepped out of the ring, leaving Lucca and Adolfo alone. The official, a silver-haired man by the name of Anselmo, climbed into the pit. Old enough to make the two-foot descent look an ordeal, Anselmo's feebleness was far outweighed by his experience and the legendary fairness of his decisions. Landowner or *campesino*, Anselmo played no favorites and would abide no infractions.

"It is understood," the old man said, "there is to be no handling. This is a fight to the finish. I will see the birds, now." He inspected the black first, checked the bird's eyes, wings, breast, legs, spurs and vent, and wordlessly handed him back to Adolfo. A similar minute inspection of Torrito followed. "The roosters are acceptable," he announced to owners and crowd, "but . . ." A rising murmur of expectation faded. He turned to Maguire. "Your red is a quarter kilo lighter than the black, *señor*. You understand the black has the advantage."

"I understand, and accept the disadvantage," Maguire said flatly. A dozen new bets followed the announcement.

Lucca and Adolfo wasted no time. Adolfo poured tequila into his hand and wiped El Negro's neck and breast. Lucca accepted a proffered bottle, filled his mouth and sprayed the red's head and breast, then flipped him and spat more of the fiery liquid onto his vent. Torrito struggled, angry at last.

Anselmo waved the two men together. The crowd stilled, anxious to watch the billing. Lucca and Adolfo stopped at arm's length, and with a firm hold on their birds, extended them toward each other. Black and red, at close range at last, pecked viciously at each other. When a spot of blood appeared on the black's stubby comb, Anselmo signaled again and the handlers stepped back and knelt at opposite sides of the ring. In dead silence Anselmo raised a bandana and held it high in the air. When it fell, the fight would begin.

The crowd was roaring before the flag hit the clay. Lucca and Adolfo loosed the cocks and jumped out of the ring. The birds needed no urging. Without hesitation, they charged, rose into the air and, feet extended forward and slashing, crashed into each other and fell to the floor. A blurred flurry of feathers later, they backed away, initial contact over.

The crowd held their bets. Legs stiff, wings extended down and back, the roosters circled, heads low, bobbing and weaving. The black, heavier, stronger and with the boldness of relative inexperience, lunged, leaped into the air and raked downward with his spurs. The red rose a fraction of a second too late and fell backward with a gash across his breast.

"Three pesos for one on the black!" a voice screamed.

"Five for three, the black!"

"Done. One for two, the red, anyone?"

Los Serpientes were cheering and betting as profusely as anyone and, though they did not wish to anger Fuentes, trying to keep the odds on the black as low as possible. One for one, after all, was much better than three to one. Brown faces looked worriedly to Maguire, who remained impassive though his booted toe edged forward to cover the envelope.

The birds were in the air again. Neither gave ground willingly. Generations of breeding and weeks of arduous daily training made each seek the advantage. The black, by virtue of his weight, continued to gain. Torrito was bleeding from comb and breast. A drop of blood had formed at the corner of his beak. Again the black attacked, rising high in the air. Torrito anticipated and rose higher. Both birds slashed and beat at each other, fell and rose again in quick, feinting hops. They were panting now, out of breath with the fury of battle. The black fluttered into the air but the red, too tired, side stepped. When El Negro came down, he staggered to one side. By common consent both birds crouched, resting.

No killing blows in the first three minutes meant a prolonged fight. The winner would be the cock with the most stamina. The betting swung heavily to the black.

No animal in the world is as game, or has so much courage, as a well-bred fighting cock. No animal, pound for pound, will battle so tenaciously or so viciously. Maimed, bloodied and lamed, a valiant fowl will fight until his strength is utterly depleted, or he is dead. The black and the red, beaks open, bodies heaving, staggered to their feet, ready to fight again. Spurs raking, beaks stabbing, holding and tearing, they circled, closed and traded punishment like two old prizefighters, finesse long forgotten, standing toe to toe and trading brutal blows with no pretext of defense.

Pesos changed hands, voices offered new bets. Maguire

ignored them all. Even Lucca's hand, tight on his arm, went unnoticed. The world had receded and he was alone, strangely detached and aloof. Sweat was running down his sides and, for reasons he couldn't identify, he wished he were in the mountains again, far away from the noise and bustle of Mexico City. Then his eyes met Fuentes's across the ring and he looked back to the fight. There, in the battle on the clay floor, lay the determination of his fate. There. With a battered, losing rooster.

His spirits sank as Torrito fell to one side, wings flapping feebly, from what seemed the worst of wounds. "He's finished!" Fuentes bragged, echoing the sentiments of everyone else in the room.

The black seemed to know. Strutting, he circled the red, arched his neck and let loose a ragged crow of triumph. Torrito lay without moving, panting so fast one could not count the breaths. But slowly he struggled to his feet, game to the end, and the black was forced to acknowledge that his adversary was not yet dead. Determined, he raced toward his stricken prey.

Suddenly, what had been a wounded, helpless victim erupted straight into the air. Torrito was not finished fighting. His heart would not let him. Faster than the crowd's imagination, his stubby, sharp spurs flashed downward on the black, whose momentum carried him underneath the red. There was a cry, drowned out by the excited babble of voices.

Only when both roosters fell to the ground could the spectators see what had happened. One of the red's spurs had stabbed into the black's left eye and caught there. Frantic, both birds struggled to free themselves. The crowd was going mad. Those who had thought themselves sure winners cursed; those who thought themselves losers howled with glee.

Torrito finally jerked his leg free and stumbled to his feet. One wing dragged in the dirt. Immediately he retreated, too tired for the moment to follow up and kill the black. El Negro fluttered to the center of the ring. He was bleeding from the beak. His left eye was gone and he was disoriented, still wanting to fight, but confused.

The crowd pressed close around the ring, waiting for the red to finish off the black. No one knew who sent up the first cry, but immediately a second voice joined. Then the whole throng, winners and losers, with the exception of *Los Serpientes*, were shouting the name. For both El Negro and Fuentes, it certainly fit.

"One Eye. One Eye. One Eye!"

Building, crescendoing. "One Eye. One Eye. One Eye. One Eye!"

Suddenly it was quiet. Fuentes had drawn his pistol. The Colt .38 raised slowly and the crowd swayed backward, unable to run, uncertain as to what would happen. A thunderous report filled the room and the black rooster's head exploded. In the stunned, ringing silence that followed, El Negro, spurting crimson streamers of blood, danced a death's jig and then collapsed.

Maguire tensed as the revolver swung to cover him. Holding his breath, he knelt and picked up the envelope. Slowly, he opened his coat to show he carried no weapon, then tucked the deed into his pocket. Every eye around the pit was focused on Fuentes who, sensing the time was not ripe, slowly holstered the gun in the brown sash around his waist. "Another day, Maguire," he said softly, his real eye gleaming with hatred. "Another day." Thin lips tight, he spun on his heels and left the arena without another word, leaving the box of gold behind. Though *Los Serpientes* followed without paying their debts, not a man stood in their way. Nor would they have, for all of Moctezuma's treasure.

Maguire leaped into the pit and crossed the bloodied floor. He ignored the wet, red gamecock picking at the corpse of his opponent and headed for the ornate mahagony chest. The crowd sighed. Maguire closed the lid, grabbed the handles and heaved. Gold is heavy, but

16

to the owner, light enough. Grinning triumphantly, he raised the box high over his head.

The spectators went wild. Money was money, but defeating the hated *gachupine* was worth infinitely more than mere pesos. Jugs and bottles of sour-smelling pulque and sweeter, potent tequila were passed freely as toast after raucous toast filled the thick air. Caught in the fervor of the moment, Maguire sat down and opened the chest, removed a fistful of gold coins and tossed them among the delirious celebrants. Fuentes's threat forgotten for the moment, he struck a pose, hands on hips, and roared with laughter at the pandemonium that followed.

2

Blue preferred to be called Patrick Henry, but folks somehow always used his last name. Blue sounded less important, less prestigious than Patrick Henry. He would have settled for Mr. Blue, but had ceased taking issue. What was the use?

Feeling bored and sorry for himself, he followed the blaze of the train's single headlight as it stabbed across the *jacals* of yet another tiny settlement nestled along the tracks. Beyond the light, hidden by night, were the hills and mountains, plains and tortured gullies of the state of San Potosi of Old Mexico. They'd be in Mexico City by the next afternoon if their luck held. Ahead, a shrill whistle blew and the locomotive started around a right-hand turn. The headlight disappeared. In its place was his own reflection, and a further cause for dismay. A wry, boyish face, complete with freckles, peered back at him from under a shock of violent red curls. He looked younger than a man of twenty-one should, even though he packed over two hundred and twenty hard pounds into a gangly six foot, four inches. Oh, the girls back East had liked him well enough, but here in the Southwest, a tougher, weathered exterior seemed in order.

The train slowed, then shuddered on an upgrade. Up and down through Mexico. He could file a hell of a story on that, boring as it was. On the summits, the train would gather speed and then plunge downhill. Groan going up, quiver and shake going down. Either way portended peril to the faithless, for if the train broke down or flew off the tracks the passengers would be stranded and afoot with Mexico City a grueling hundred-mile hike away. But of course they wouldn't stop. Even if they did, only the *norteamericanos*, with their affinity for maintaining schedules, would mind.

As usual, the train paused at the crest and started back downhill. Blue sighed in relief and then tensed, his knuckles white on the edge of the seat. They were slowing! And then stopping. The silence was uncanny, weird. After two days of pounding noise, there was nothing. "Damn!" Blue said. "Damnation!"

Darkness. He pushed up the window and poked out his head. Utter darkness, still, and then the winking light of a swaying lantern. No one seemed very concerned. As nearly as he could tell, they were on a siding. The lantern went out. The train slept.

Well, that's it, he thought. Here we are in the middle of nowhere. Wind kicked down from the foothills and moaned around the cars. Somewhere high in the eastern mountains lightning flickered eerily. Shadows in the fields took on lifelike aspects. God only knows what was creeping up on them. Writing would help. Anything to keep from dwelling on what might be out in the strange, almost barbaric country so different from the manicured farmlands of his native Connecticut. The train would move soon enough. He'd tidy up a paragraph or two, relax and get some shut-eye.

The story of Alpine Ranch lay scattered all over the seat. Harvard Van Allen had assembled the original acreage back in 1840. His son, Harvard, Jr., had increased the holdings. By the time Lee Van Allen married Corinne Madison, more than 2 hundred thousand acres of prime West Texas cattle land were inside his barbed wire fences.

Lee Van Allen was known as a proud, driven man. Bad leg or no, he was a hard worker who expected no less of himself than the lowest paid man on his ranch. Blue's association with Van Allen had been brief: the rancher had rejected him out of hand and then ignored him, making it difficult for Blue to remain as objective as a good reporter should be. As a result, Blue had to keep reminding himself, the rest of his information was based on rumors and whispered, whiskey tales. Trouble between Lee and Corinne Van Allen. Bad blood between Lee and Maguire, the man Mrs. Van Allen had vowed to find in Mexico City. The relationships were murky, but of two things Blue was sure. There had to be a story, and he'd get it.

Blue began to write, and had grown accustomed to the preternatural silence when someone tapped at the door. He jumped. Another knock. "Yes? I mean, *si?*" Maybe it was the porter. He hoped so, even if his faltering Spanish was disastrous. The door opened to reveal a mass of disheveled, golden hair.

"What happened?" Acting as if she were an old friend, Mrs. Van Allen slipped into his compartment and closed the door behind her.

Blue blinked rapidly and tried not to stare. He'd seen peignoirs before, and Lord knows he'd seen Mrs. Van Allen a lot during the last week; but this was different. Far different. He cleared his throat. "I don't know. Nothing important."

Hoofbeats thundered nearby, followed by a cannonade of shots. Blue slammed down the window and closed the curtain. When he turned back, Mrs. Van Allen was at his side, trembling. "It's all right," Blue said, trying to convince himself. Cries of "*Viva Madero*" rang through the night. "See? Just a bunch of Mexes carrying on. Here. Let me, uh, let me . . ." He stacked the papers, closed the typewriter and shoved the whole pile under the seat. "You want to sit down?"

"Thank you."

Blue stood, anxiously wondering what *was* happening. He had bet his last two hundred dollars this would be the story that would vault him to success, and so, with Corinne Van Allen's grudging concession, had bought a ticket and joined her. To date she'd avoided him as much as possible without being rude. Now here she was in his compartment, and in a nightgown and peignoir, no less. The combination was unnerving. "I, ah, I've been working. A little something for my editor. Train travel through Mexico. Inspiration, you know." The lie sounded flat.

"Oh? May I see?" Mrs. Van Allen reached for the pile of papers.

"Later," Blue said, kicking them farther under the seat. "It's only a first draft, and I'd rather . . . "

"I understand."

The silence was deafening. Blue waited, unsure of what to do or say. Up until now Mrs. Van Allen had been uncommonly circumspect. Always dressed properly, a lady of manners. But the way she was sitting caused her peignoir to part and fall away from the bow at her throat. Underneath the light nightgown revealed and accentuated trim, rounded breasts swelling above a slender waist, and molded itself to her thighs.

Blue forced himself to look at her face. She met his gaze without a trace of coyness. Blue was the one who blushed.

"You are a handsome boy." She leaned forward, eyes glistening with playful wickedness. "There was a time, dear Mr. Blue, when I would have . . . " She sighed and sat back. "But those days are long past."

Blue gulped as quietly as he could, gingerly sat next to her and crossed his legs in the hope she wouldn't notice what she was doing to him. "Well, I wouldn't say you're decrepit, Mrs. Van Allen."

"I am thirty-two years old."

"And one of the most beautiful women I have ever met." That was better. He'd found his tongue again.

"For that, Mr. Blue, I shall buy your breakfast. If morning ever comes."

"And if there's anything to buy."

"Yes. That's right, isn't it?"

Silence again. Blue wanted to start a conversation, but didn't know how to begin. The air in the compartment was close. What did the woman want? Why had she sought him out? Comfort? Protection? He was big enough, to be sure, but it rankled to be noticed only because of his size. He wished he knew what time it was, for some reason. Wished his stomach wouldn't growl. Wished he could think of something brilliant to say. Wished he didn't feel like a bump on a log.

Suddenly the night exploded as another train, unheard as it had rushed down the hill toward them, rocketed past, whistle blowing. Blue wasn't sure how she got there, but Mrs. Van Allen was in his arms, huddled against him, her head pressed to his chest. She was quivering with fright, like a small animal, only infinitely more soft and warm.

"It's all right," he said awkwardly when the train had passed. "It's all right. We'll be moving now." Proving him right, the faint sound of their own train's whistle piped down the tracks and the car jerked into motion.

Timidly Blue let his hand touch, then stroke her hair. Mrs. Van Allen stirred against him. He could feel her breasts through the thin silk of her gown and the thicker cotton of his shirt. When she raised her head to look at him, he thought her eyes the bluest he had ever seen. Her fingers touched his jaw and a jolt of electricity passed through him.

He couldn't help kissing her back when her lips touched his. Again they met, and a third time. Her tongue parted his lips and she moved against him, a soft moaning deep in her throat. Blue's hand found her breast, caressed the soft flesh until it began to swell and harden.

"No!" She struggled to free herself. Blue tried to ease her back onto the seat. "No! Please!" she repeated angrily, pushing him away.

She meant it. Face burning with shame, Blue stood abruptly, and, forgetting his height, cracked his skull on the ceiling. Stunned, he dropped into the seat.

"Oh, dear." Mrs. Van Allen laughed, then realized he'd really hurt himself and sympathetically reached out to touch his head.

"Ang foo rit . . . " Blue garbled, brushing her hand away. "I'm all right." Completely embarrassed now, he just wanted her to leave.

Mrs. Van Allen pulled her peignoir together and adjusted her hair. The silence returned, grew intolerable. "Do you know what loneliness is?" she finally asked in a small voice. "I don't mean the word you write on some silly page. I mean the awful kind you live."

"Ma'am?"

"It was mean of me, the way I've behaved. Mean and just not very nice. I'm sorry. I suppose at thirty-two a woman begins to wonder, but that's no excuse."

"Mrs. Van Allen . . . "

"Corinne. Call me Corinne."

"You don't have to apologize for anything."

"But I do. Well, maybe not apologize. Let's call it an explanation."

"I don't think . . . "

"Really," she interrupted, the words rushing out of her. "What else have we to do? Dark night, long journey, fellow travelers. The perfect time for stories, isn't it? And you're a writer, after all. Perhaps you'll understand me a little better." She paused awkwardly, hands clenched at her sides. "Maybe I will, too."

His head ached. He wasn't at all sure he wanted to understand, but the snug compartment and gentle, rocking motion of the train were conducive to revelation. And once begun, Corinne could not stem the tide of pain, betrayal and love that spilled from her.

The story began in 1897, in Washington, D.C. Corinne Patricia Madison was a vivacious, willful girl of eighteen suffering from naïveté and ennui, and when Lee Van Allen happened along, she fell in love with him. Six months later, blissfully married against her parents' wishes, she accompanied her new husband to Texas.

Shortly after their arrival, Lee's father died and the ranch was hit by the recession of '98. As the hard months passed, Lee was transformed from the cheerful, relaxed companion Corinne had married to a harried, work-ridden shell of his former self. Lee rarely smiled. He had few words and less time for his wife. He disappeared for weeks, driving himself mercilessly in an attempt to save the ranch. Lonely and depressed though she was, Corinne forced herself to hope for better times, and fought to save their love.

Then Maguire arrived. Maguire and Lee had been friends since 1885 when Harvard Van Allen, Jr. took in the wiry, work-hardened orphan from across the border. Five years later, eighteen years old and bridling at the bit, Maguire left to see the world and become a soldier of fortune. Ten years passed, the last one spent fighting the Moros in the Philippines, before he returned, haggard, pale, and suffering from unhealed wounds of both body and spirit. Since the Van Allen holdings demanded the bulk of Lee's time, the task of caring for the prodigal soldier of fortune fell to Corinne. As was inevitable, they became friends.

Unspoken memories, indelible, pressed into the fabric of her soul like a leaf caught between the pages of a book. The memories flooded back and Corinne grew silent, listening to past yearnings and never-forgotten pains. She remembered a rainy day.

> Rain . . . Rain singing to the ground.
> What a lovely sound.
> Drop by drop through the dark.
> I can't tell them apart.

Poetry amused Corinne, filled the lonesome hours and painted over, more than once, the drab days with a special mantle of acceptability. Rhyme and meter whirled her away on flights of fancy from the harsh West Texas landscape.

The messenger from Alpine had left an hour earlier. Now lightning glimmered and the muddy ground shone electric blue before succumbing to darkness once again. A particularly violent crash of thunder sent her reeling from the window. "Oh!" she screamed, backing against Maguire. She spun, saw it was him and regained her composure.

His hair hung in thick tousled lengths, black as the stormlit sky. Firelight danced on his naked torso. A shiny black belt encircled his midriff and hugged the soft doeskin trousers to his slender waist. "I couldn't find my shirt. Didn't mean to frighten you."

"I just wasn't expecting you to sneak up behind me," she said.

"I called to you twice."

Corinne softened. "I'm sorry. I didn't mean to sound shrewish."

"Lee is staying the night in San Antonio?" he guessed.

She nodded. "He sent word. A rider from Alpine delivered the telegram. I should be used to it. The ranch. Always the ranch. Ever since Harvard's death Lee has driven himself, put this damn . . . "

She blushed. Maguire stood with his back to the fireplace. Golden light outlined the sloping muscles of his shoulders. His hands were spread to the flames. Corinne and a Mexican servant had nursed him back to health, and had vanquished the shroud of weary illness that had draped him on his arrival almost two months earlier. He had filled out since then. Color had returned to his flesh. Corinne suddenly grew aware of the pressure of the wind against the outside walls of the house. And though the wind was whining out of the north, the room felt warm. The simple calico gown she wore felt heavy and close. She stepped close to Maguire, then past him to a nearby seat. Chess pieces carved of horn were neatly arranged on a checkered field of battle. Maguire sat opposite her. Had that been a glint of desire in his eyes as she moved past him? The thought provoked her, led to other, more forbidding conclusions.

She moved first, a familiar queen's pawn. He caught her hand before she could withdraw it. Lightning crackled down the sky. It darted through her blood and quickened the already rapid beating of her heart.

"I'm sorry," he said, removing his hand. She looked at him, puzzled. He stammered an excuse, "You've cared for me, tended my wounds. I was so damn weak I figured I'd be dead by now. And I would have, if it hadn't been for you."

Golden curls spilling forward, Corinne lowered her face. Maguire reached out and loosened the ribbon in her hair. But then he stood and stalked to the fireplace and leaned against the mantelpiece. "What the hell are we doing?" he asked in a tension-filled voice.

Corinne rose. Slowly, her legs and feet acting without

27

conscious will, she went to him. Hand trembling, she touched his back. "I think we're about to make love," she said.

Loneliness. That was the excuse they clung to. Loneliness . . . To betray a husband. To betray a friend. Loneliness . . . But the word rang hollow. She had bathed him in fever and had watched over his delirium as he relived some awful agony. She had brought him food and sat with him. Even fed him until his strength returned. And laughed as he entertained her with stories of the Orient, San Francisco, Peru and the Philippines. She had never known a man like him. Never known a man with whom she could share the loneliness.

Both of them knowing, yet both needing each other. Their bodies moved together, and he carried her into the inner room. There, caught in slow, entwining passion, he swept aside her clothes.

This is wrong. Wrong wrong wrong . . .

Both of them knowing; both incapable of stopping. At last they were one—two bodies caught in the timeless motion—and loneliness became love.

"Friends," Corinne said. "And then more than friends," she added, her voice catching as she recalled their first time together, and the sweet aftermath she'd never known with Lee. From that moment there had been no turning back.

"And then one night Lee returned a day early and found us together. He had a gun."

Corinne leaned against the seat. As vividly as yesterday she could see herself twelve years earlier, standing in the doorway to her bedroom and watching the two men struggle in the firelight. She would never forget the animal sounds they made, nor, more horribly, the roar of the gun and Lee's scream of pain. Nor would she forget the look of anguish on Maguire's face as the awful realization of what he had done struck him with full force. Once again she relived the wild, careening ride, Maguire driving while she cradled her husband and wondered how her world could crumble so.

"Lee's shattered knee was beyond repair," she whispered. "He has been a cripple ever since."

"And Maguire?" Blue asked when she hadn't spoken for a long moment.

"I stood on the porch of the doctor's house the next day and watched him walk down the street to the train station. The train was a half-hour late. He had been standing alone on the platform, I remember. When the train left, he was gone."

They had stopped again. Blue opened his eyes one at a time, reached out with his left hand and pulled back the curtain over the window. The train had stopped on another siding. It was still dark, but dawn couldn't be far away because the tops of the mountains were silhouetted against a faintly gray sky. Corinne, as Blue had finally gotten accustomed to calling her, slept sitting up and leaning against him, her peignoir pulled tightly around her. Her hands looked tiny in her lap. Blue realized he couldn't move without waking her. "Corinne?" He touched her arm, gently shook her. "Corinne?"

"Mmm?"

He liked the feel of her weight against him. "It's almost morning. We've stopped. You'd better wake up."

Eyes not yet open, she stretched. The peignoir pulled apart and Blue swore not to look, then decided to hell with it. Corinne opened her eyes and closed the peignoir. "Just friends, remember?"

"Maybe you better get dressed. I can't stand too much of being just friends. At least not when you're dressed like that."

Vendors outside the train were hawking food. Corinne laughed and kissed him on the cheek. "Very well. I owe you breakfast, remember? Give me two minutes to dress."

29

"Yeah."

Corinne stopped at the door to the compartment. "I wish you could see yourself. You really do look funny," she said. The door closed with a soft click.

Funny? Hell, crap and damn. Three hours of sleep, at the most. His mouth felt like someone had let in the desert. His eyes burned. The knot on his head hurt and he was stiff as a board from sleeping sitting up. Funny!

Blue groaned, hauled out a canteen from under the seat and drank a few swallows of tepid water before splashing some on his face and checking himself in the mirror. He looked weary, but passed it off. Who wouldn't be bone-tired after spending half the night listening to a beautiful woman in a nightgown tell all about the man she loved. Men she loved. Two of them. "Too late for complaints, Patrick Henry," he told himself. "Your last buck is on this and you'll have to stick with it to the end. Nobody ever said being a famous reporter was easy. Besides, at least she's friendly now. Shouldn't be any problem getting her to introduce him to this Maguire. He might have a story or two himself."

Determined to think positively, Blue locked his door and knocked on hers. It opened immediately. "We'd better move if we're going to find something to eat."

"I'm ready." Her hair was pinned up and she looked even more desirable in a simple, hastily donned ankle-length violet dress. A brightly decorated wool shawl covered her shoulders. "Blue?"

"Ma'am?"

"I led you on and then talked your ear off. I'm sorry. Will you forgive me?"

"Mrs. Van Allen, it's nice to be needed. And trusted." Every inch the gentleman, he offered her his arm.

They paused on the top step of the train. The station was in the middle of a plain that lost itself in the predawn distance. Three or four ghostly gray adobe houses reflected tremulous lantern light. Here and there cooking fires inside mud-wattled *jacals* leaked orange streaks of light. The air was pungent with the smell of cooking fires, of coffee and sizzling goat meat. Always the earthly odor of tortillas and frijoles. And soft voices, waiting patiently for the sun.

"It's so beautiful, don't you think?" Corinne asked. Blue's stomach growled. Corinne laughed. "A practical answer, sir. Shall we?"

Blue jumped down. Grasping her waist, he deftly lifted her to the ground. Most of the first-class passengers were still asleep, but the entire second-class section had scrambled out of their cramped quarters. Packed together more like animals than people, they took quick advantage of any excuse to escape the din and smell inside the tiny cars. To Blue the marvel wasn't that there were so many of them, but rather that he could detect no complaining or quarrelsomeness. He wouldn't have put up with what they were forced to endure. Not for a second.

They chose the largest fire. Corinne spoke fluent Spanish of the West Texas variety, and before long they'd drunk coffee and eaten some of the freshly cooked goat meat wrapped in tortillas. A strange breakfast, Blue thought, as he watched Corinne put a half-dozen more of the makeshift sandwiches into a colorful handwoven cloth she'd bought from the girl who'd served them. Not bad. Not at all.

The whistle blew and the second-class passengers dutifully trooped back inside. "Wait," Corinne said, stopping at one of the fires where a vendor displaying a few pots had set up shop. "*Hay café?*" she asked.

"*Si, señora.*"

Haggling quickly, they settled on a price. The vendor filled one of the pots, handed it to Corinne and accepted the coins she gave him without offering to make change. When at last she told him not to bother, his face, dark in the dull glow of the fire, revealed no trace of satisfaction.

31

Sullenly he doffed his hat and wished the lovely *señora* a pleasant day.

The conductor signaled once again and the steam engine inched forward. Corinne and Blue hurried to their car and jumped aboard. Blue remained on the platform in order to watch the first light of the new day spread cross the empty land.

3

A .38 wouldn't stop them. Not when they were worked up. Good advice, but worthless. Maguire yanked a small caliber gun from a dead man's belt. The .38 was all there was as the Moro leaped the barricade and, still in midair, cut down a man with his short-curved blade. Already bleeding from a half-dozen wounds, the native charged. Maguire held the revolver with both hands. He couldn't afford to miss. Not now. He absorbed the weapon's kick, brought it back into line and fired again. Practice makes perfect. Each shot scored. Flesh pocked where the bullets struck home. The Moro, knowing death was at hand, wanted to kill one last time. A primordial shriek filled the air. The Moro leapt, bolo raised, crimson steel describing a vicious, slicing arc. The .38 clicked empty.

Maguire bolted upright. A coffee-colored hand reached

out, touched his bare arm above the coverlets. "A dream *mon amour*. Nothing but a dream." The woman stroked his naked back. She loved the way the muscles fit snugly to his shoulders, marveled at the rippling layers across his scarred torso. "You were not with another woman?" she asked, jealousy barely disguised.

Maguire rose from the bed, crossed naked to the windows and threw open the shutters. Bright, clear light pierced the room. He breathed deeply and stretched until the bone in his shoulder where the horse had rolled on him popped.

So Dauphine had come to him. He didn't even remember her climbing into the bed. Too much brandy. Two days had passed since the cockfight, and during that time he'd allowed himself an unrestrained debauch of drinking and gambling. Every man needed a celebration now and then to leach his system of cares and tension. A small chest of coins, part of his winnings from Fuentes, lay open on the dresser. Dauphine would have pilfered a few. Squirreled them away in the hem of her gown, probably, or in the lining of her purse. He grinned. Well, why shouldn't she? If she was too proud to ask for money, the least he could do was let her steal some honorably. She wouldn't have taken much, in any case.

"Another woman? Hardly, Dauphine," he said.

Death was no stranger to him. He had faced it many times without undue fear. But the Philippine experience still haunted him, because of the sheer implacable insanity of the Moros. To be shot was one thing. To be beheaded by a maddened fanatic who wouldn't die, was quite another. Worse, he'd come away from the fiasco ill and penniless, and had to work his way home on a tramp steamer.

"You did not call." Dauphine pouted. "Three days I did not see you."

"Who let you in?" Maguire asked, facing her.

Dauphine chuckled throatily. "Riciotti would do anything for me."

"And you rewarded him," Maguire said sarcastically. "I can imagine."

She gave him a murderous look. "No other man for as long as I have known you, Maguire. Six months! Me!" she exploded, stabbing her chest with her finger. "Do not say such a thing again."

"All right, Dauphine. I'll even apologize, okay?"

She sighed and watched as he turned back to the window. His hips were narrow and his shoulders wide, showing little of his age. "I love you, Maguire," she said.

A mile away, the cathedral jutted above the drab reds and grays of the city. Maguire counted the tolling bells. Nine. Beyond the church the National Palace rose like an immense fortress island out of a red tile sea. Closer, the barren tips of a madrone tree in the courtyard below were silhouetted spikelike against the opposite wall. Never growing to great heights, the madrone's main distinction was an unusual shedding of bark that exposed patches of driftwood-smooth, flesh-colored wood. In summer, their rhododendron-like leaves provided ample shade. Madrones usually were found tucked away among the pine- and oak-covered slopes far from civilization. Why this one grew alone in his courtyard in the middle of the city was a mystery that fired Maguire's imagination. The tree was a renegade like himself.

"I love you," Dauphine repeated.

Maguire wondered if the brothel madam even knew the meaning of the word. He did, and found it synonymous with loss and emptiness. Crossing the room, he stood next to the bed. Dauphine's hair was cropped radically close to her head like a cap of tight curls. "Let your hair grow, Dauphine. You look too much like a man."

"*Chien!*" she cursed. "Like a man? Tell me truthfully.

You think Dauphine is a man?" She threw aside the covers to reveal Amazonian proportions. Breasts like massive dark fruits. Nipples and broad areolas dark as sweet chocolate. A waist only an inch thicker than six months earlier, and that because she'd allowed herself a touch of laziness since, for the first time in her life, she'd restricted herself to one man. Her strong *café au lait* thighs parted, and the triangular jungle of ringlets between them invited exploration.

"I must instruct you, Maguire," she said, reaching for him. "*You* are the man, no? I can tell by these . . . " a warm palm cradled him, " . . . and this . . . " Gentle, deft fingers circled him, tugged insistently until, rising and swelling, he knelt by her. Pulling him closer, Dauphine pursed her lips and, never quite touching him, blew soft puffs of air against him. "Tell me, Maguire," she repeated huskily. "You still say Dauphine looks like a man?"

Maguire, his hard length spear-straight, straddled her. "No."

Dauphine laughed earthily, rolled over onto her stomach and rose to her knees. "Prove it, Maguire," she said, swaying from side to side, rolling his manhood across her smooth, melon ripe buttocks, then poising and settling backward onto the engorged flesh.

Leaning forward, Maguire drove himself against her with increasingly savage thrusts. Dauphine cried out once, bowed her back and pressed against him. Sweat glistened along her spine. Locked in the copulative struggle, she said his name over and over from between her clenched teeth.

Now she wanted to see his face, but there was no stopping. Flesh against flesh, sliding easily, quickening, quickening. His hands on her hips, guiding her. Dauphine's elbows stiffened and her back arched, taut, as the roiling spasm started deep within her. At the same time Maguire grunted and, no longer capable of motion, held her tightly, shuddering at the force of the explosion that rocked him.

Dauphine moaned, reveling in the surge of energy and heat. The second his hands relaxed, she tensed to hold him in her and sank to the bed. "I love you, Maguire," she whispered, turning her face from the pillow. His mouth was close to her ear and she dared hope he would respond in kind. "You hear me, Maguire?" she asked when he didn't answer.

His lips moved and she could feel him stir inside her. "Say it, Maguire. The way I say your name. Over and over again, even when you're not with me."

The movement stopped. "No, Dauphine. There are only two things holding us together. As deep as you are, and as long as I am."

She felt him leave and roll to one side. Dauphine closed her eyes so he wouldn't see the pain she felt. When she opened them again his face was still, his breathing deep and steady. "You are a bastard, Maguire," she whispered, softly stroking his sweat-streaked hip. "You are a bastard, you hear me?"

He didn't answer.

Early afternoon, he guessed, judging by the narrow rectangle of light on the floor. The musky odor of their lovemaking lingered pungently in the room. Dauphine stirred, kissed him on the forearm. "Maguire?"

He swung his legs to the floor, rose and padded into the bathroom. A couple of minutes later, glistening wet, he stood in front of the window and toweled dry, then quickly pulled on work shirt, jeans and charro boots. Dauphine scurried out of bed, threw her arms around her lover's neck and kissed the bold plane of his cheek. "Maguire?" she whispered softly, challenging and tempting him.

He laughed, spun her around and slapped her ample bottom. Dauphine squealed in mock anger. "Wash up and get dressed," he said. "I'll see you downstairs." Not waiting for an answer, he grabbed a sheepskin vest and headed for the door.

He had known and loved many places. The balcony, he thought, was one of his favorites, the spot where he could stand and look out over a world in which he felt alive and completely at home. Mexico City. Fabled valley over a mile high and blessed with bright, clear air. The Aztecs had called it Tenochtitlán, he remembered, a name he loved to say for the sheer joy of hearing the syllables roll off his lips. The few books he'd read on the matter described it as a lush and beautiful garden replete with canals and towering pyramid temples. He would like to have seen that. It must have been more beautiful than the present sprawl of indigenous adobe brick and transposed European architecture.

But certainly no more exciting. A thousand scents. Food, animals, flowers. The fresh air curling in through the mountain gateways. A myriad of sounds, mingling. The clatter of iron-shod wagon wheels, the raucous intrusion of automobiles. The shrill whinny of horses, screech of horn and rippling crackle of electric trolley cars, joining the ever-changing, never-changing cacophony of goats and pigs and chickens. A dozen or more languages, native and European and oriental. Rich or poor, for better or worse, the city teemed and bustled with humanity. Maguire loved it.

The best of sound and smell came from immediately below. His boots clipping the stone steps, he descended into the courtyard. As always, he paused by the madrone tree and, for luck, brushed his hand across the velvet smooth wood before heading for the carriage shed under the balcony. There, sleek in the heavy shade, next to the tree and casino, sat his most prized possession.

The Studebaker limousine, his by virtue of three jacks over three nines at the end of a long, long night of gambling, was one of four in all of Mexico City. Brought in 1911 from South Bend, Indiana, the car had been maintained in immaculate condition. On the outside, the black paint had been buffed until it glowed with a deep luster, and its twin brass lamps, grill and decorative work shone brightly. Inside, the plush and luxuriously appointed back seat was completely enclosed. Spacious windows and heavy walnut doors protected the passengers from the elements. A speaking tube was supplied for instructions to the chauffeur, who sat in the roofed but otherwise open front seat. The auto's three mates were owned by wealthy *hacendados* who lived along the Paseo and Chapultepec Park. Maguire grinned. The fact that he, a soldier of fortune and not at all socially acceptable, should own the fourth, was a source of much consternation to the rich landowners.

Satisfied that everything was in order, he patted the hood and walked back across the courtyard to the rear door of his casino. "Aurora. Food!" he called, flinging open the door.

A host of mouth-watering odors enhanced by pungent wood smoke greeted him. He inhaled deeply and strode into the dimly lit kitchen. "*Buenos dias,* Aurora, wherever you are. Anything to eat?"

An elderly Mexican woman rose from behind a table and glared at him for asking such an insulting question. "*Sientate, chico,*" she snapped.

Maguire hadn't considered himself a youngster for many years, but he wasn't about to argue, and sat as told. "Never again, Aurora. I'm getting too old for these carouses."

Rapid Spanish emerged from inside the cloud of steam rising from the stove. Maguire stifled a laugh. Aurora. He'd looked up the name. Where the hell else in the modern world did the Goddess of the Sun appear as a Mexican cook? Thin as six o'clock, scraggly gray hair flowed down her back. Her left eyelid drooped from an old accident and a birthmark the size of an apple deformed her left forearm. She had, Maguire thought, the fastest hands he'd ever seen: when it came to making tortillas, her fingers literally disappeared in a blur of motion. When she wasn't busy preparing an assortment of delectables for the table Maguire kept laden for his guests, she was off on any of a dozen mysterious ventures. In the year she had worked for him, he'd discovered her hawking flowers from a pushcart, selling chances on local lotteries, matchmaking and caring for sick children in the surrounding neighborhood. As if all that wasn't enough, she displayed an encyclopedic knowledge of herbs and home remedies, the only sort of medical care the poor could afford. Every young man was her son, every young woman her daughter. What she did with the extra money she earned, he had yet to discover, for Aurora talked seldom, and never of herself.

"Eat," she commanded, slapping three *barbacoa* stuffed tortillas and a mug of strange looking liquid in front of him.

"What the hell is that?" Maguire asked, shrugging out of his vest.

"For your liver. And blood," she grunted, turning her back to him, a common enough tactic when she was disturbed by his excesses.

Maguire shrugged. The drink, a murky orange-brown color, looked terrible. Still he could read Aurora's mood and, since he had learned early on not to question her judgment if he wanted her to stay on, gulped it down. Not half bad, he decided. Fresh and fruity tasting. Next, he attacked the tortillas stuffed with shredded, barbecued meat.

The kitchen exited into a short hall that led to the casino proper. Stomach full, Maguire surveyed his domain. When Francisco Madero assumed the presidency, one of his first acts was to reward Maguire for military and intelligence services rendered. The alliance with Madero had been a gamble that had paid off and, for the first time in his life, Maguire looked around for a place to invest his money wisely. He recognized the prize placement of *Le Café Français*. Only a few blocks from Chapultepec Park, he was sure he could make it into a quiet, fashionable, slightly risque gambling club with a North American flavor. He bought it on the spot, taking over from a disgruntled Frenchman who wanted no part of the Madero regime.

Renaming the place *El Madronito* was the first step. Extensive remodeling was the second. The upstairs dining room went, to be replaced by his own quarters. Stained glass windows to give an air of class and privacy were installed. Plush, leather upholstered chairs, courtesy of a profiteering friend, surrounded lustrous mahogany tables from the same source. A small stage and a postage stamp-sized dance floor followed. Most impressive, a heavy, ornate bar complete with a soldier-of-fortune bartender friend were imported from San Francisco. And finally, to play the very latest American tunes, a piano and piano player had been imported from New York.

The effect was stunning and immediate. Within a week after it opened, *El Madronito* was making a profit. Drinks were priced high enough to keep out the un-desirables, even though, if Maguire was prejudiced at all, it was against the desirables who came to gamble and drink. Not a one of them, so far as he knew, had worked a day; rather they lived on the sweat and deprivation of scores of others. Still they were the ones with the money, and business was business.

At the moment, Payton, the piano player, was busy tacking a rousing flourish onto a catchy tune. Maguire threw his vest onto the bar and applauded. "Bravo. What is it?"

" 'When the Midnight Choo-Choo Leaves for Ala-bam,' " Payton answered, swiveling on his stool. "Irving Berlin. Came in yesterday's mail. Getting it ready for to-night. Like it?"

41

"Yeah. Why not? Anything else?"

"Little number called, 'Oh, You Million Dollar Baby.' Speaking of which . . . " He nodded toward the inside stairs.

Maguire turned to watch Dauphine descend the seldom-used front staircase. Wrapped in an expensive fox fur hanging open over a bleached muslin blouse and long, brightly colored skirt, she ignored the piano player's envious stare. "You'll come by?" she asked, pausing on the landing.

"Perhaps," Maguire said, noncommitally.

The front door opened and Riciotti Lucca entered. The Italian wore a flamboyantly striped woolen shirt, wool trousers and worn boots. A scarlet headband held back his thinning hair and a red sash circled his waist.

"You'll come." Dauphine smiled. "Bring the boy," she said, indicating Lucca. "I'm sure we can find some pot in which he can plant his little sprout."

"Anything and everything. They all remind me of you," Lucca growled.

Dauphine shot him a murderous glance and stalked out, slamming the door behind her.

"Place just oozes with camaraderie," Payton said with a laugh. "I'm off. Back at nine."

"See you then," Maguire agreed, stepping behind the bar and filling a pair of shot glasses with tequila.

"Careful, Lucca. Next time she'll chew off your head." The door closed again, and quiet settled over the casino.

"He's a prick," Lucca finally said, joining Maguire at the bar and downing his tequila.

"He's a damn good piano player."

"So he plays with his prick. What's the difference?" Lucca said as he examined the bottle for the telltale dregs at the bottom that indicated it was the best, from the town of Tequila itself.

Maguire poured a second round of the golden liquid. "What brings you out so early in the day?" he asked.

"You have become a man of prosperity and honor. A man of importance, sought out by men of national importance." Lucca raised his glass aloft—"I salute you!" —and downed the contents. "Just don't forget," he wheezed, "I know you for the bloodletter you are. We are cut from the same cloth, Maguire, madrone tree and pretty windows or no."

"Why are you here, Little Tiger?" Maguire asked for the second time.

"To drink your excellent, aged tequila, of course." Lucca rocked back on the barstool and roared with laughter. When Maguire didn't respond, the laughter died quickly. "But seriously, I bring a message from Gustavo."

"Madero?"

"None other. He wishes to speak with you in private."

Maguire frowned. He was trying not to get involved in politics and the president's brother wanted to see him. Every instinct told him to refuse, but he and Gustavo had fought together. "Where?"

"Outside. Begin walking west along the Reforma, on the right. You will be met." When Maguire sipped at his drink without moving, Lucca leaned forward, a twinkle in his eye. "Don't worry. I will take care of your beloved *El Madronito* in your absence."

"That's what I'm afraid of."

"Dishonor, now! You think Riciotti Lucca is a thief?" Cheeks flushed red as the sash tied around his waist, Lucca jumped to his feet.

Maguire flicked the tip of his finger against the bottle neck. The glass rang hollowly and the golden liquid trembled, "No," he said, starting up the stairs to get ready. "I think you're thirsty."

Two o'clock came and went, and the waiting Maguire turned down the Paséo de la Reforma. A strong northerly breeze accompanied by a light, drifting drizzle

43

had driven the vendors and street people into doorways and under the makeshift shelters that choked the alleys. Only the purposeful, those with destinations, ventured along the broad walks or passed quickly in closed carriages or noisy, clattering autos.

Maguire kept his face forward, expecting nothing but ready for anything. Finally, opposite the Opera House, an ornate coach slowed and stopped. A door opened and a face peered out. "*Señor* Maguire."

"You took your time," Maguire complained, climbing into the coach and sitting next to Gustavo Madero, the president's brother. "I would have worn a slicker."

His host raised his palms in a gesture of helplessness and struck the ceiling once with his walking stick. The coach started with a jerk. Gustavo let down a panel on the partition and brought forth a decanter and two crystal glasses. "Brandy, for the cold and wet. You will survive, no? I was detained. There have been difficulties."

Maguire accepted the libation and apology and settled back, patiently waiting for his host to make the first move. He had met Gustavo two and a half years earlier in San Antonio. Four months later, they were fighting together in the revolution that toppled the dictator Porfirio Diaz and drove him, ill and aged, into exile. Gustavo Madero, the *hacendado* turned political reformer, looked gaunt, tense and older than his age.

Warming slightly, Maguire unbuttoned his coat and dropped his hat onto a cushioned stool. Gustavo reached over and lifted the loose flap of Maguire's vest. A .45 automatic Browning rested snugly in its shoulder holster. "It is my brother's wish that men feel secure enough under a system of honest government to walk the streets without bearing arms."

"Your brother is an idealist," Maguire replied flatly. "I'll join him just as soon as Jesus Fuentes leaves the city."

"Fuentes is a good soldier who has served us well.

I am sorry you two do not get along." Gustavo chuckled softly. "I heard he recently donated a couple of months operating expenses for *El Madronito*."

"You might say that."

"Five thousand American dollars, no?"

"Give or take," Maguire said. If Gustavo didn't know how much was involved, there was no sense in offending him by suggesting he was wrong. If he did, which was probably the case, no comment was necessary.

"To old times, eh, my friend?" Gustavo raised his glass. "And continued embarrassment to the multitude of generals with whom God has seen fit to test our will." Their glasses met and both drank. "*Por Dios*! I am glad you were on our side. Else I would not be the brother of the president of Mexico, eh?"

"The brother of so eminent a man ought to have a fine motor car like the families along Las Palmas."

"Not for me. I have never fed a motor car a lump of sugar, Maguire, nor had the pleasure of stroking one's neck while it nuzzled me in gratitude. Listen, what do you hear, my friend and comrade?"

Maguire looked out the window. They were turning into Chapultepec Park and leaving the main thoroughfare for a lesser traveled, cypress-lined avenue.

"I will tell you," Gustavo continued. "The creak of leather. The singing of little bells attached to the harnesses. Hooves striking the good earth. If you listen closely, you will hear the horses blow, and remember that their breath is sweet." He lapsed into silence, listening to the sounds he'd known and loved all his life.

"And an automobile?" Maguire asked quietly, knowing the answer.

"Bah! Old soldiers coughing and trying to spit. And smelling worse. No thank you, Maguire. I shall keep my coach and geldings. They suit me."

Maguire took the liberty of pouring more brandy. It

was time to get down to business. "You didn't ask to see me to talk about horses, Gustavo."

"No." Considering his words, the younger Madero sipped his brandy. "My brother Francisco is a compassionate man," he began.

"He is a fool," Maguire snorted.

"But my brother," Gustavo warned.

"Enough, Gustavo. North American bluntness, now. You mentioned difficulties. I can believe that. It once took Francisco four days to travel the seven hundred miles to Mexico City. Thousands gathered to greet him, cheer him and touch the clothes on his back. 'Little work, lots of *dinero*. Beans for all, Viva Madero!' they cried. Only twenty months have passed, and I do not remember when I last heard those words. Am I deaf? Am I blind? The *federales* we chased into the desert at Juarez have new arms and uniforms. The same assassins bully the people behind your back. The *rurales'* power is undiminished. They enforce the law only for the rich landowners, which the *peones* remember you once were. The same Diaz sympathizers who once threw your brother into Belem prison mock him even today. Does Francisco kill or exile them? No. He forgives them and allows their fat asses to soil the seats of his cabinet."

"My brother may be lenient," Gustavo countered heatedly, "but that was the point of the revolution: Mexico must be ruled by law. Not men. The violence and killing must come to an end or else we fought in vain and are no better than Diaz himself. Who else is to set the example?"

"Ideals, Gustavo. Ideals. Not even greed kills so many."

"Bah. What do you care. I waste my time!" Madero blurted angrily. "Your allegiance is to money. Nothing else."

Maguire sighed. Things changed. A man's reflexes slowed a little bit every year. Forty years meant too many little bits had been accumulating. Forty years meant he was no longer young enough to chase other men's ideals. Death had ceased to be a laughing matter. "That's right," he said simply.

Harness, bells and hooves. The clatter of wheels. Gustavo swallowed the last of his brandy and set down his glass. His hand on Maguire's forearm was tight, squeezing the flesh. "Come back with us, Maguire. We need you. With your help we can reform the *federales*. You will be commissioned and appointed second in command, with only me over you."

Maguire shook his head.

"But why? The money will be . . . "

"It isn't just the money! Damn it, Gustavo, a revolution is like digging a bullet out of a wound. You can't just pierce the skin and then quit because there's a little blood. You have to keep after it until the slug is out, no matter how messy it gets. And then heat the blade and cauterize the wound. Francisco opened a great, gaping wound in Mexico's side, but refuses to finish the job. Now the wound will fester, and the patient . . . " He did not finish.

"We have made a start. There can be no counter-revolution without a figurehead, and Felix, Porfirio Diaz's nephew, is the obvious choice. And we have him in prison."

"Not good enough, Gustavo. What about Huerta, just to begin with?"

"Francisco trusts him completely despite my objections, even though his name has been linked very recently with Diaz and others who seek to overthrow us. The man is completely amoral. His loyalty is like the dust devil. Who knows what course he will take? Not unlike yourself, eh?"

"You know my course, Gustavo. Whatever benefits me."

"No man can remain in the middle, Maguire. Not now. You can't remain neutral."

So trouble was that close. Maguire stretched his legs and stared at the toes of his boots. Lucca had told him of increased activity at the National Palace. Other friends had whispered of unusual troop movements. Try though he might to ignore them, the signs were there to see. A general thinning of *El Madronito*'s clientele over the past week. The arrival of Jesus Fuentes. Still Maguire was determined to remain uninvolved. "We'll see. There'll always be a need for a casino where the fashionable can drink and gamble in comfort. Tequila and cards are apolitical, Gustavo. I intend to keep them that way."

"And that is your answer?"

"Yes."

Gustavo stiffened in his seat and nodded sharply. "Very well. There is nothing more to say then. I will drive you back," he said, rapping sharply on the ceiling.

The carriage turned in a tight circle and started back the way they had come. "Perhaps you'd better let me off here," Maguire said. "The rain has stopped and the walk will do me good."

"Very well," came the curt reply, followed by two taps.

The carriage rolled to a stop. Maguire opened the door and stepped out. "I'm sorry, Gustavo."

The handsome younger brother of the president turned. For a short moment, Maguire thought Madero would reiterate his plea. Instead, an icy veil dropped over his eyes. "So am I."

"Right. Well, good-bye."

"Yes." Once again, his walking stick tapped the ceiling. The door closed of its own accord as the coach clattered off.

Pensive, Maguire strolled across the still wet grass, climbed a hillock and paused. Mexico City lay before him. A quiet Mexico City from where he stood. In the distance, the thin piping of a train whistle cut through

48

the silence. That would be the Eagle, from the border. Maguire sighed. Whatever North Americans were aboard, they had chosen a difficult time to visit. Maybe one hell of a time.

4

"Now they will be convinced, by hard experience, that the only way to govern our country well is the way I governed." Victoriano Huerta's deep voice rumbled like thunder in the enclosed room. He ·turned bleary eyes from the portrait that adorned the place of honor behind his desk in his private study. "Those words were spoken to me by President Diaz in Vera Cruz. His last words spoken on Mexico soil. We embraced, and then our leader marched aboard the German ship, *Ypiranga,* which waited to carry him into exile."

Jesus Fuentes listened respectfully, the perfect example of an attentive guest. He allowed no doubts to cloud his expression. If the tale was embroidered, or Huerta's importance exaggerated, little harm was done.

"He was right," Huerta said, sitting behind his desk and pouring his third brandy since Fuentes's arrival. "But he is also gone. He has had his day, and reminiscing accomplishes little. So how is Bortha?"

"Well enough, General," Fuentes replied, taking the switch in subjects without a blink.

"Satisfied?"

Fuentes shrugged. "Who can describe satisfaction? One always seeks to rise."

"And why not?" Huerta leaned forward. The wrought-iron grilles over the windows split the light and cast a latticework of shadows over the old warrior. "No troubles, then?"

"Only one." The truth was best told on the assumption Huerta knew it already. "A minor nuisance. Bandits under the leadership of a *soldadera* who calls herself *la Halcón*. She and her followers will eventually hang. And there was a *norteamericano*, a *Señor* Van Allen, who tried to interfere in our affairs by offering support to troublemakers farther north, but he has been taken care of. Discreetly, of course."

Huerta nodded. "Bortha is a good man. And soldier. I am pleased."

Hiding his jealousy, Fuentes pretended accord. Nothing concrete had been said yet, and he waited patiently to learn why he had been summoned from the north. Surely not to philosophize. He and Huerta had both served Madero during and after the revolution, but the general was still an enigma. As always Fuentes found himself ill at ease trying to analyze and plumb the depths of the man who sat in front of him. Physically, Huerta was unimposing. Sparse hair clung to an almost bald, mottled skull. His face was that of an Indian, coarse and chunky and ill-proportioned. A pair of dilapidated, wire-framed glasses gave him the look of a dislocated owl. Already half drunk at ten in the morning, his eyes, set close to the heavy, veined nose, were bleary. His uniform despite rows of medals and bright buttons, was stained and slovenly. None of this fooled Fuentes for a second, for he knew too well the native cunning that lay below Huerta's unimpressive exterior.

"Power!" Huerta's fist slammed on the table. "The force of arms. The military must rule. Only then can a semblance of order be maintained. Madero is worse than useless. He is a weakling who panders to the *peones* and fills their heads with promises of land and what he calls individual freedom. Pah! There are the rulers and the ruled. Any man can see that. Those who hold power must rule with firm hands. How else is our country to grow and prosper? How else to win the respect of our neighbors and friends across the ocean and to the north? But Madero simply does not understand this. Why, even *Señor* Wilson, the North American ambassador, considers him a mountebank, and has said openly he should be replaced." He paused and cocked an eye at Fuentes. "And you, Captain. What do you think?"

So there it was. Fuentes would have to be very careful. "The winning and wielding of power often are two unrelated talents," he answered adroitly. "A man who is capable of one is not necessarily equipped for the other." He paused to choose his words. "General Bortha, I think it is safe to say, shares your concern, General."

Huerta beat on the table and, when a servant answered his summons, demanded another bottle of brandy. "You display admirable restraint, Captain," Huerta said the second they were alone. Unwilling to commit himself further, Fuentes nodded in gratitude. "A noble trait for one of noted recklessness in battle. A noble trait." A knock sounded on the door. "Come in," Huerta barked.

"Colonel Serrano is here, General."

"Give me a moment and show him in. Say nothing of the captain, here."

"Yes, sir."

Huerta eyed Fuentes sharply. "A good general likes to think he knows when to gamble, Captain. I am going to gamble with you. I am going to wager that you value your tongue, and would not jeopardize the head in which it rests. Wait behind that screen," he ordered without further explanation.

Outwardly calm, Fuentes obeyed. No sooner had he sat in the chair placed behind a screen than the door opened and closed. *"Buenos dias,* General Huerta," an unknown voice, evidently Colonel Serrano's, said.

"Sit down," came the rough rejoinder.

Fuentes leaned forward and peeked through a crack. By shifting from side to side he could see both General Huerta and his guest, who was forced to wait while his superior shuffled through a pile of documents. The man's face was unfamiliar to Fuentes. Short, thin and dapper, he had the look of a lawyer or politician instead of a military man.

"So you've come then. Is everything ready, as I ordered?"

"My troops are waiting south of the city."

Fuentes shifted to his left. Huerta was pouring another brandy for himself. How he functioned with so much alcohol in him was a mystery many men had tried and failed to solve. "And Diaz? What has he concluded?"

"He accedes to your demands. Those men loyal to him will support you until the trouble is ended and you have placed him in the palace."

Huerta leaned forward and peered over his glasses. "I must be able to rely on them completely. Drastic days lie ahead."

"You will be the power in Mexico until the situation has calmed. Then of course, we will proceed with the formal election of Felix Diaz, which will make both the *hacendados* and *norteamericanos* happy."

"You think so, eh?"

"Yes, General. We do. And of course you will be amply rewarded."

Huerta sipped at his brandy. "As will you, Colonel. So we are agreed."

The visitor smiled condescendingly. "One thing more. *Señor* Diaz is most anxious not to languish for too long."

"No. And I don't blame him." Huerta slapped his hands on the desk and rose. "Well, then, Serrano," he said with jovial familiarity. "A toast, eh? To success?"

"I prefer to drink after the fact, General," Serrano said primly. He stood, pulled on a pair of gleaming white gloves. "And now, if you will be so kind as to excuse me?"

"I am at your service, Colonel," Huerta replied affably. "Good day."

The interview over and Colonel Serrano gone, Fuentes emerged from behind the screen to find Huerta nearly purple from rage.

"*Señor* Diaz is most anxious not to languish for too long. I prefer to drink after the fact, General." He spat out each word as if it were poison. "Toad! Dog! Simpering idiot! Does he think me a complete fool?" Huerta downed a half tumbler of brandy with no more effect than had it been water. The drink helped, and he soon calmed down. "Well, all for the better. What do you think, eh?"

"I'm afraid you've taken me by surprise, General Huerta," Fuentes said, genuinely perplexed. He prided himself on his own cunning, but the general's duplicity was overwhelming.

Huerta handed him a tumbler half full of Hennessy. "Then I will speak plainly. There will be a coup, of which I will officially disapprove, and during which I will be placed in command of the government troops. Directing Diaz's rebels as well, I will use one force to destroy the other. Those in reserve, loyal only to me, can then come forward. Tell me, Captain," he said, leaning back and looking out the window, "can I count on General Bortha—and you, of course—for your support?"

Fuentes smiled thinly. "I think I can promise that. Yes, sir."

"Your unconditional support, no matter what happens?"

"Yes."

"Good." He sat silently for a long moment. "The action will begin Saturday night."

Surprised, Fuentes sucked in his breath.

"Yes. Three days. That soon. We will do nothing to impede them until Diaz has been freed and his men have committed themselves. After that . . . " He trailed off, swiveled back to stare intently at Fuentes. "You can arrange to be in the National Palace Saturday night, can't you?"

"I have an interview with Francisco Madero himself that afternoon. Staying will be no problem."

"Good. Diaz intends to occupy the president's office early Sunday morning. With Colonel Serrano's help. If Serrano were to be killed—if he were to die a hero's death—I would be pleased."

"Serrano? But he—"

"—is revered by his men. Madero will bear the responsibility for his death. And what then, do you think, will happen?"

"*Matanza*," Fuentes replied with a knowing smile. "A bloodbath."

"See to it then," Huerta said coldly. "This I swear. When this matter is concluded, Mexico will see a new president. Neither Madero nor Diaz, but a strong man the nation can turn to in time of discord."

"Yes, sir." Fuentes stood, took a quick last look around. The walls were lined with leather-bound volumes Huerta had never opened. A painting of the National Palace, official home of the president, hung over the door where the general could see it from his desk. There was no need to ask who General Huerta planned to seat in the palace. After the bloody and destructive clash of two armies within the city, the people would accept the devil himself as president if he promised peace.

"We will not see each other again for a few days," said Huerta. "When we do meet, during my heroic attempt to save the country from chaos, perhaps you will be willing to serve in other ways, eh?"

Patrick Henry Blue meditated on the luxury of a real bed, even if it was a foot too short. Anything was better than a train. Anything. Waking slowly, he wriggled his toes, cast aside the covers and stretched mightily, flexing his shoulders and legs to work out the kinks left from the long train ride.

Remembering where he was, Blue jumped from the bed and ran to the window, only to stare in disappointment. Where the hell was Mexico City? he wondered. All he could see were trees, lawn and, in the distance, rising, snow-capped mountains. The room itself bordered on opulence. Paintings of European origin hung on the walls. A mammoth English wardrobe carved and faced with walnut burl filled an entire corner. For that matter all the furniture was English—dresser, chairs, bed and writing desk. He might as well not have come to Mexico City, by the looks of it. Still he *was* in Mexico City. He'd seen parts of the city when they arrived.

Suddenly anxious to get out, wander around and take in all the sights, he looked about for his clothes. Everything was gone. Worried, he threw open the doors to the wardrobe and sighed with relief. His suit, cleaned and pressed, hung neatly on a rack with his coat and extra trousers. His duffel bag lay on a shelf near the floor next to his boots, both pairs of which had been shined.

A quick check of the dresser showed the extent of the unknown servant's meticulousness. His hair brushes and cufflinks rested on top next to his penknife. Two handkerchiefs and three pairs of underwear had been placed in one drawer, folded shirts in another. The desk held his typewriter, pens, pencils and pads, all neatly arranged. His shaving and toilet gear rested in a neat array on the lavatory in what evidently was his very own private bathroom. There was even hot water. Humming, he worked up

57

a lather and shaved; then feeling like a king, he stepped into the tub to scrub off the layers of dirt accumulated in five days of travel.

It took a moment to decide what to wear, but he finally chose clothes suitable to the hardy environment. Moving quickly from wardrobe to dresser and back again, he donned a khaki shirt, army pants, wool socks and battered but wearable ankle high lace boots. A canvas belt and shiny brass buckle completed the outfit. Working swiftly, he plied the twin brushes and inspected himself. Not bad, he thought. Not bad at all. Whistling gaily, he dropped notebook and pen in his pocket, grabbed the peaked campaign hat he'd bought at the border and stepped into the hall.

Nobody was in sight. Boldly he started down the stairs, but when he got to the bottom, wasn't sure of which way to turn.

"Good morning. I trust you slept well."

Blue turned to see an ebullient, rotund gentleman emerge from a side room. "Yes, sir," he answered brightly, trying to remember the face.

"I am Anthony Drexler. Afraid we missed each other yesterday afternoon."

"You are very gracious, Mr. Drexler. I'm Patrick Henry Blue," the reporter said, shaking hands. "Mrs. Van Allen explained we were to be your guests."

"My pleasure. My pleasure. I am only sorry I was previously committed last night. Corinne's father-in-law and my father were friends for many years. Partners too, once, shipping cattle across the border, selling them in Kansas City and splitting the profits. I often visited Harvard's ranch in Texas during the latter years of his life. Lee and I took a liking to each other and have remained friends ever since. When Corinne wired that she wished to visit . . . But see! Already I am ungracious. You must be hungry." His eyes twinkled. "Will you have coffee with me?"

"Well, ah, yes sir. Coffee sounds good."

Drexler guided Blue down the hall past delightful pastoral settings painted in oil and set in rococo frames. They stopped in front of a Grecian pedestal holding a bust. "My wife is an artist," Drexler explained proudly. "The scenes in the paintings are of Chapultepec Park which, as you may have been told, we border. This is an example of her sculpture."

"Caesar?" Blue asked, glad to be able to identify the subject.

His host chuckled. "Juarez. His memory is as precious to the Mexican people as Abraham Lincoln's is to you. The olive leaves are gratuitous, I admit. Benito Juarez was the simplest of men. And thereby a great man."

"Beautiful," Blue said, closely inspecting the bronze with what he hoped looked like an experienced eye. "A magnificent piece of work. You have every right to be proud of her efforts." He wondered what had happened to Mrs. Drexler, but decided it wouldn't be polite to ask.

"I'm sorry that my wife can't be here to receive your praise in person. I sent her to Vera Cruz to visit her father's estate." He opened a door and gestured for Blue to precede him.

"And where is Mrs. Van Allen?" Blue asked.

"Sleeping? Bathing? Gazing out the window? Who knows what the ladies do with their mornings. But never mind. Since they do not ask us what we do with our evenings, we will return the courtesy. In any case, you will see her at the *comida* this afternoon."

"*Comida*?" Blue asked, itching to take notes but afraid it would be impolite.

Drexler laughed good-naturedly. "You will find out, my friend. And be delighted, I hope. Ah, David."

A lean whip of a young man sitting at a large dining table looked up from a newspaper. The youth, not yet eighteen, stared at Blue's pseudo-military garb in openmouth astonishment. The elder Drexler coughed discreetly

59

and the young man rose to his feet. "David, Patrick Blue, our guest. Patrick, my son, David Florio Drexler."

"Good to meet you," Blue said, grinning and extending a hand, then awkwardly dropping it when the gesture wasn't returned.

"Yes," came the stiff reply. The young man stared with cold contempt at Blue. "And now if you'll excuse me, please?" he said in impeccable English. He inclined his head in a formal bow. "Father." And stalked through the French doors leading to the grounds beyond.

Drexler was clearly embarrassed. "I beg you to pardon my son's manners, Patrick," he said in a subdued voice. "I'm afraid David's Latin blood is more powerful than his English heritage, for he professes to share his mother's distrust of North Americans. At any rate, he models his behavior after, shall we say, more colorful figures than I would choose as companions. Do you have children?"

"No, sir, I don't," Blue admitted, as embarrassed as his host.

"You will one day, God willing. And know the joy and pride of being a father. Unfortunately," he smiled ruefully, "there is an age at which they come to believe their fathers are fools, as Mark Twain has observed. David seems to have reached that age."

Blue wished he were someplace else. Corinne had warned him that there were those in Mexico who harbored a seething hatred for Americans, but he'd expected it to come from the poorer classes. To find it in Drexler's family, with their close ties in the States, was a surprise. In any case, being an object of such animosity wasn't a pleasant experience, even if he could live with it. "That's all right, Mr. Drexler," he said a little too heartily. "I don't mind. Really."

"You are kind, my boy. But come!" He rang a small bell sitting on the table. "One shouldn't be too morose. Rebellion is a natural trait of the young." A maid entered and curtsied. "*Café por dos, por favor,* Amaranta.

Y pan dulce con mantequilla. Please sit down, Mr. Blue. Do you know *pan dulce*? Similar to sweet rolls, only lighter and more delicate."

His host chattered on, but Blue found it difficult to concentrate. Ravenous, he drank coffee and devoured *pan dulce* dripping with fresh butter. And he thought to himself: If he had ever acted the way David had in front of a guest, his father would have taken a razor strap to him.

Corinne settled into the soapy depths of the tub. Hot water from a tap was a luxury she always associated with the Hotel Menger in San Antonio or the Baker in Dallas. She had sworn they'd have the same at Lee's ranch one day, but that day unfortunately kept getting delayed. Idly, she stretched one leg and turned on the hot water until it came up over her breasts.

She hadn't slept well at all. The bed was too soft, the room unfamiliar. A thousand questions plagued her as she tossed and turned. Her son, Christopher. Was he unharmed? What had happened to Lee? Where was he? Was he even alive? And Maguire. Would he help? And when they met . . .

Half dazed, exhausted, finally lulled by the heat and relaxed by the water she felt herself slipping into sleep.

"*Señora?*"

"Oh!" Corinne's eyes flew open. "You . . . you startled me," she said in Spanish. "I'm afraid I went to sleep again."

The girl apologized for waking her, and said, "I have brought coffee."

"May I have it in here, please?"

"Of course, *señora.*" The girl curtsied, left the room and returned a moment later with a tray which she placed on a chair by the tub. "If the *señora* wishes . . ."

"That will be all, please," Corinne said, more sharply than she'd intended.

"Yes, ma'am." The girl started to leave, but turned in

the doorway. "Oh. *Señor* Drexler wished me to tell you. There will be a *comida* this afternoon. He has invited the gentleman you wished to see."

"Tell him I am in his debt, please."

"Of course, *señora*."

The girl left. Corinne was alone. Carefully, she poured a cup of coffee, added milk and sugar and sat back in the water.

Would he accept Drexler's invitation?

He had to.

The notion of meeting him again after all these years filled her with apprehension. But Christopher's life was at stake. For better or worse, there was no turning back.

5

The Studebaker limousine careened down the Paseo de la Reforma and, nearly missing a street cleaner, turned onto San Pedro. It skirted the eastern tip of Chapultepec Park before barely managing the turn onto Constituentes. Maguire, who sat in the back, gaped at the other auto approaching them. Was Riciotti blind? He reached for the speaking tube, only to be thrown against the side door as the limousine swerved sharply and straightened. A dark blue metallic blur passed within inches. Maguire shouted for Lucca to slow down, then turned in the seat. Behind him, the Nash had been forced off the road and the chauffeur was standing by the curb shaking his fist at the idiot who had almost killed him.

Maguire slid across the seat again as the Studebaker made a sharp turn, tore up a drive and skidded to a halt in the long circular drive winding in front of the Drexler residence. Lucca jumped out of the front seat, opened Maguire's door and doffed his chauffeur's cap. Maguire wondered how many gentlemen's drivers sported a gold ring through their earlobe. "Put that back on."

"*Si, padrone*."

"Didn't you hear me say slow down?"

"I was concentrating on the road."

"Well concentrate on this. If there are any dents in this car when I get back, I'll personally wrap your ass around the radiator."

Lucca appeared mortally wounded. "You do not trust your friend, Riciotti. Such indignity." The Italian cast a disapproving eye over Maguire's short black jacket, tight black trousers and lace shirt showing above the ornate vest. "And from such a fine gentleman!"

Maguire adjusted the flat-brimmed felt hat on his head, checked his boots and the ruffled lace shirtfront. "Look okay?"

Lucca snickered. "You are beautiful. The ladies will swoon, the gentlemen guests sputter with envy. I myself think I am madly in love with you. Especially your lace shirt."

"Damn it, Lucca!" Maguire rapped Riciotti's shoulder with the heavy, artfully crafted silver panther's head grip of his cane. "Just remember what I said about the car."

"When do you want me back?" Lucca asked, gingerly rubbing his shoulder.

"I don't," Maguire said, starting up the front steps.

"But—"

"I'll walk."

Lucca blanched. "But you didn't bring a gun!" he shouted. Maguire ignored him and disappeared inside the house. "Damned fool," Lucca muttered. "Get yourself killed. Fine with me." Still grumbling, he climbed into the limousine, eased it into first and drove cautiously away from the house, down the magnificent drive and onto the broad boulevard.

The engine throbbed beneath the hood. He could feel the power waiting, the tap of a foot away. Still he continued to be the most conservative of drivers until well out of sight. Then, head tilted back, he roared with laughter and jammed down his foot on the accelerator.

Comida. Maguire liked the sound of the word. Musical. Welcoming. One of the reasons he enjoyed being in Mexico. He paused in front of a full-length mirror. The servant escorting him dutifully waited while he adjusted his tie and straightened his vest.

Comida. So this was how the rich lived. The invitation had taken him by surprise for, though many men of wealth frequented *El Madronito,* he had never been invited to their homes. And now this. He'd spent the morning at a tailor having the suit and shirt altered to comply with the invitation, which stated the dinner would be formal. Maguire scowled. He'd had mixed emotions. The whole affair reeked of affectation, and he felt a little out of place in such regal surroundings.

Respectability, he told himself. You're a grown man, Maguire. Time to leave the world of guns and violence and enter that of the velvet glove and whispered influence. Accept what you've been offered. Even if Lucca laughs. What the hell does he know?

The servant coughed discreetly. Maguire nodded, manufactured a dazzling smile and dutifully followed the man past a bust of Caesar, through a large dining room and outdoors to the garden.

"Mister Maguire!" Anthony Drexler rushed to greet Maguire and shake his hand. "I am honored you could come. Welcome to our simple little party."

Simple? The garden was decorated to look like an idealized and romanticized peasant village. The servants were dressed in brightly colored Indian garb such as few Indians had been able to afford for decades. Thatched *cabañas* to protect visitors from possible rain were supposed to represent animal sheds. A quintet of musicians dressed in white linen carried instruments whose value outweighed whole villages. A bevy of brightly dressed women chattering among themselves in a native dialect ground corn in *matates*, stone upon stone. Their companions patted out circles of the finely ground meal and cooked fresh tortillas on special stoves set up at either end of each of three groaning tables. Nobody ate the tortillas, which were there for effect only, but rather concentrated on other more elaborate dishes. The most extravagant replica was the village fountain: instead of water, a trio of spigots poured imported chablis, rosé and burgundy.

Maguire accepted a glass of chablis. He'd heard of such parties, of course, but the reality was more than he'd imagined. Any real peasant would decide he'd died and gone to heaven. What intrigued Maguire most, though, was Drexler. A self-proclaimed egalitarian who announced his belief in the equality of men at every opportunity, yet was capable of such obscene excesses.

Maguire sipped the wine. "Delicious," he said, careful to sound unimpressed. "Your invitation honored me."

"I have missed *El Madronito* and our weekly game of chess," Drexler lamented. "Alas. There has been trouble in my family."

"Trouble in all of Mexico," Maguire said, noting silently that Drexler, of all people, should know. His newspaper, *Verdades*, took care to scrupulously chronicle the nation's multitudinous ills.

"And magnified by the hour." Drexler gestured to the guests, the majority of whom were men whose wives and children were away from the city and the present unrest on what were euphemistically termed vacations. He sighed. "I'm sure you've heard there are those who say I am in part to blame. I admit my little paper taxes the patience of our lenient president, but what am I to do? Only the truth will save us."

"Or destroy you," Maguire heard himself saying. "Unfortunately, this isn't the United States or England."

"I know," Drexler answered sadly, as he led Maguire into the garden. "I am painfully aware of the destructive nature of truth. A year ago there would have been over two hundred guests at any party I gave. Today?" He gestured. No more than fifty stood in small clusters of three or four. "It has touched my family as well," he said. Maguire followed his gaze in time to see David Drexler stalk out of the garden. "My son burns with *Porfirista* zealousness. He, too, has turned against the truth. His mother's doing, I fear."

Maguire knew an ulterior motive when he saw one. So that's why the invitation, he thought. He wants something from me. "Mr. Drexler, I had hoped the games we play were restricted to the chess board. I am a half-breed *gringo* who owns a casino. More than most, I may be approached openly. Now why did you invite me to your *comida*?" he asked, dreams of social acceptance by the affluent fading rapidly.

His host laughed. "You are too suspicious, Mr. Maguire, although I confess I gave you cause. No, no. I am not that devious. You were invited to eat and drink. And, of course, to meet some of my guests." He glanced toward the house. "Ah, I see *Señor* Boaz has arrived. If you'll excuse me? Make yourself at home. My house is your house." Without waiting, he hurried off to greet the newcomer.

Across the yard the musicians serenaded a young couple. Maguire snagged a full glass of wine from a passing waiter and, trying to decide if he believed Drexler or not, stopped in front of one of the tables. There'd be some additions to the menu at *El Madronito,* he swore, tasting a *conchito,* a puffed tortilla stuffed with suckling pig. A servant girl with a shy smile handed him a plate.

Steam rose from an enormous platter of beef strips

spiced hot enough to turn the palate into an inferno. *Quesadillos,* fried tortillas stuffed with cheese, sausage or squash blossoms. Tidbits of squid, baked in their own ink. Chunks of papaya and mango brought from the south. Huge boiled shrimp from the Gulf of Mexico. Delicate *flautas,* cornucopia-shaped pastries filled with whipped cream laced with brandy and chips of sweet chocolate.

Maguire greeted acquaintances, men who had been to *El Madronito.* Beyond rapid comments on the weather, there seemed little to say. The dearth of conversation confirmed his belief that all was not well. Men in Mexico loved to argue politics. Now they were avoiding the subject like the plague.

Maguire found a secluded spot under a mammoth oak tree and took stock. He felt out of place. His clothes felt wrong. He wasn't adverse to having or spending money, but this was too much. Worse, he felt used. He hadn't been invited because he had finally been accepted, but because Drexler wanted something of him, and Drexler wasn't saying what. The more he thought, the angrier he got. A straightforward approach at *El Madronito* would have been acceptable. This was patronizing, and Drexler could go to hell, *cochinitas, quesadillas,* chablis and all.

Then the atmosphere changed subtly. A light buzz ran through the guests. Maguire stepped away from the tree and looked toward the house to see what had attracted so much attention. A woman, her back to him, stood in the midst of a small knot of men. Something about her piqued his curiosity, but he couldn't decide what. The color of her hair? The way her American-cut gown hung on her shoulders? One of the men made an unheard comment, and she laughed.

Maguire stiffened. Across the lawn, Corinne Van Allen turned and posed, motionless. Maguire found it difficult to regain his composure. It couldn't be her. Impossible.

She was walking toward him. Twelve years. She looked

much as he remembered her. Not so much older as more mature. Tanned. Healthy. Confident. At ease. The years had agreed with her, treated her kindly.

He didn't move. Corinne faced him from a yard away. The slender thread linking them across time was an electric wire charged with the voltage of shared and unforgotten passion.

"Maguire," she said. His gaze lifted from her and darted toward the house beyond. "Lee isn't here."

"Oh." He couldn't think of anything more appropriate.

"I saw you from my window. For a moment I considered not coming down. But I knew I had to talk to you." She glanced shyly down at her hands. "May I have a drink?"

Maguire looked around. The nearest servant with wine was on the far side of the garden. "There isn't a glass right now."

"I can share yours." She drew his hand toward her, tilted his glass and sipped.

His hand felt inflamed where she touched him. "What are you doing here?" he asked, more disturbed than he cared to admit.

"I am Anthony's guest. Just as you are," she said, nodding amiably to a passing guest.

There was more, of course. Drexler had arranged their meeting. Why she wanted to talk to him after twelve years was a question that would have to wait until they were alone. The initial shock passed and Maguire began to think clearly again. Putting down his glass, he took her arm and led her toward the fringes of the party. They smiled and exchanged pleasantries until they reached an opening into a smaller, secluded garden. There, protected from prying eyes by a hedge of ornamental Italian cypress, Maguire spun her around.

Corinne stifled a cry of surprise. His hands were cutting off the circulation in her arms. She was powerless in his grip, unable to prevent him from drawing closer.

Her cheeks were icy with fear, though burning with hunger. Suddenly he pushed her away and turned to leave.

"Maguire. Wait!"

He stopped, back tense and shoulders hunched. "How did you know I was here?"

"Your name was in the papers during the Revolution. Then, a month ago, I was in San Antonio and met a friend up from Mexico City. You were mentioned in the conversation."

Maguire had to admit he was curious, but being so close to her brought back too many painful memories. "Well," he shrugged, "you've seen me."

"I need to talk to you, too. Please."

Maguire looked at the sky. He felt as if he were at the bottom of the ocean, a drowning man watching the underside of the water and knowing there was no escape. "We have nothing to talk about, Corinne." His voice shook as he said her name for the first time in a half-dozen years.

"It's been a long time, Maguire. Twelve years. I'm not a silly young thing anymore." Her voice hardened and a note of bitterness crept in. "I won't force myself on you, if that's what you're worried about, but I do need to talk. Fifteen minutes. In Drexler's study. It's all I ask."

She seemed assured, but an undercurrent of fear and desperation tinged her words. Against his better judgment, Maguire relented. "All right," he replied half-heartedly. "Fifteen minutes. No more."

Watching her walk. Remembering the cool touch of her hand that had broken his fever—and begun another. No other woman among the many he had known had been remotely like Corinne. Old aches, like young wounds, reopened, disrupting his world. Their footsteps echoed as she led him up the stairs and along the hall. He felt as weak-kneed and eager as a youngster. To hold her would be a miracle. Fifteen minutes, and then he'd leave as he had before. She opened the door and he followed her inside. Where will I find the strength to leave? he asked himself.

As they entered the study, someone was standing behind the door. Maguire sidestepped, slammed the door and swung his cane up to thwart any possible assault. A tall, burly, red-headed young man danced back and almost fell over a chair.

Corinne grabbed Maguire's cane arm. "He's a friend. Please."

Maguire lowered his cane. The youth wore a shiny dark suit with too short jacket arms. He looked uncomfortable in the white shirt, starched collar and tie. "Who the hell is he?" Maguire asked.

"I'm a reporter on assignment for the *New York Times*. My name is Patrick Henry Blue."

"Well, Patrick Henry, you shouldn't stand so close to doors. Makes some people nervous."

"You gave me quite a start," Blue said, tugging on his collar.

"I meant to." He glared at Corinne. "I thought you said you wanted to talk in private."

"Mr. Blue shares my complete confidence."

"Good for him," Maguire said sarcastically. "Goodbye."

"Maguire!" Her voice was sharp and took him by surprise. Maguire watched as Corinne crossed to the window. The tortoise shell comb in her hair caught the sun and split it into undulating blues and reds and yellows. Her hair shined like spun gold. "I have a son," she said quietly, almost as if to herself. "His name is Christopher Van Allen."

"Congratulations," Maguire said dryly.

She whirled to face him. "Will you stop it!" For a moment Maguire thought she would burst into tears.

Instead, with great effort, she composed herself and sat, hands folded tightly in her lap. "Three weeks ago, while riding fence with our foreman, he was kidnapped. The foreman was killed. I want you to help me get him back."

"Oh?" It was Maguire's turn to be surprised. Corinne's ice-blue eyes cut into him and Maguire regretted opening his mouth. For something to do, he helped himself to a decanter of brandy. "Who took him?"

"Gregor Bortha," she answered.

"He's Madero's man," Maguire said.

"Was. He's his own man now. He has grown corrupt and greedy."

"How would you know?"

"A year ago Lee talked to some fugitives from Bortha's so-called justice. Lee caught them stealing cattle—not for profit, but for food. As time went on, conditions in Chihuahua deteriorated and more and more men were swimming the river. Finally Lee got fed up with the whole mess and offered support to any man who would cross back to fight Bortha."

"That's illegal, you know."

"Yes. But we couldn't feed half of Chihuahua, and nobody in the government would help us. At any rate, Lee was supplying weapons and ammunition to those who wanted them. Bortha found out, of course." She could barely be heard. "His men crossed the border and took my son. We received word that should the kidnapping become widely known, Christopher would be killed. We were instructed to pay a sizable ransom and agree to stop supporting what had become a near rebellion."

"And so you came to me for help."

"Not right away."

"Oh?"

"Only after Lee disappeared. He went to the border to hire men to help him get Christopher. When I didn't hear from him after a week . . . " Corinne stifled a sob.

"I didn't know what else to do, Maguire. I couldn't just sit there."

Maguire shifted his attention to Blue. "What's the reporter got to do with this?"

Blue cleared his throat and answered. "I was heading for the Van Allen ranch to do a story and happened on the kidnapping. The foreman was already dead, so they used me as their messenger to the Van Allens."

"You didn't try to stop them?"

"There were three of them. They were armed; I wasn't. I tried to go with Mr. Van Allen, but he wouldn't have me, so I came here with Mrs. Van Allen."

"To help or write a story?"

"Both," Blue answered defensively.

"Jesus!" Maguire shook his head in amazement. "I can't believe you people. You sound like a bad dime novel. A brave but determined mother accompanied by a boy reporter set out to . . . "

"I want you to find my son," Corinne broke in. "I can pay you, if that's the way it is."

"I have all the money I need for now, thank you. What else can you offer?"

"Look, friend," Blue said, obviously angry.

"I'm not your friend," Maguire snapped. "Sit down."

Blue thought about that. He figured he was as brave as the next man. His massive build usually settled arguments before they took a physical turn. Still the craggy features, hard eyes and cold-blooded way Maguire spoke gave Blue pause. He stepped around Maguire and helped himself to Drexler's brandy. He didn't sit down. But he didn't stay in Maguire's path, either.

Maguire finished his brandy and put down the glass. His eyes locked with Corinne's. "I'll see if I can talk to Madero. No promises, but I'll try," he said, a little more gently. "Go back home, Corinne. All you can do is make it worse. For Lee and your son." Not trusting himself to stay longer, he walked across the room and out the door.

Blue watched him go, waited until his footsteps faded. "So that's Maguire," he said.

Corinne reached out and took the brandy snifter from his hand. Her voice was bitter, but she was determined not to give up. Not yet. "That's Maguire," she said.

6

El Madronito, Maguire's casino, was named for a tree whose gnarled velvety flesh-colored limbs twist and climb their way upward, to fall far short of heaven; a delicate shy tree that usually hid among high mountain pines, but, by luck, was here lending its rare beauty to the courtyard of a casino.

Inside stained glass windows reflect brilliant rainbows and subdue the noise of passing automobiles, the clatter of iron-shod carriage wheels, the shouts of friends or enemies. A girl, Cecilia, moves among the hushed tables and takes orders. She is dressed in high heels, mesh hose, short black skirt and revealing white silk blouse held open by widely spaced, firm breasts. The men look at her, but no one touches her, for that is Maguire's rule. Behind the bar, Seifert, a German alchemist, dreams of past wars and mixes, with meticulous care, creations of gin and rum and tequila and scotch.

Payton, the piano player, holds forth, playing gentle tunes of his own concoction mingled with the latest hits from New York. His music reflects the cosmopolitan flavor of the city, for on any given evening one can hear songs of Spanish, French, German and even Irish origin.

Friday nights conventionally are for men only. Here a pair of American businessmen sit and discuss the price of the *peso*. There a trio of young men exaggerate their latest exploits. In a third corner, a dapper gentleman ponders a chess problem and sips Grand Marnier. His son-in-law arrives to join him. The gentleman returns the pieces to the board while the son-in-law bewails the fact his wife has discovered his mistress and is making stubborn, unreasonable demands. The gentleman's advice is clear and succinct: paddle her bottom first, buy her a new dress second. He discovered this formula years ago, and it still works. "Come. Let's play," he says, the matter resolved. "Black or white?"

The walls are pocked with niches holding wood carvings from the mountains of Oaxaca and fine black pottery vases glazed in the kilns of San Bartolo. From Guadalajara, pitchers with fluted necks and crystalline bodies fashioned of blue glass capture a thousand images in their jeweled depths.

There are flames everywhere. Flickering, amber flames blossom from candles or wicks protruding from oil-filled bases. Dancing flames reflect back on themselves from thick, whitewashed walls, from crafted wood and pottery, from blown and stained glass. *El Madronito* shimmers with the pulse of life.

An extension of a man.

Maguire.

Glass held in front of a candle, he stares into the dusky amber of Sauza Especial, the only tequila worth drinking. Concentrating, he touches a dab of salt to his tongue, sips from his glass.

Everything had been going so well, Maguire thought.

He'd played both ends against the middle, and won. Mexico City was a good place to live: he enjoyed its varied faces and the constant hum of excitement flavored with a hint of adventure and danger. When he was tired, or needed a quiet niche in which to sit back, he could retreat to *El Madronito*. There was peace, and a sense of accomplishment and possession. And then Corinne had to show up and revive all the old memories. . . . He stared at the candle, and the dancing flame became the pulsing afternoon sun of twelve years ago.

Underneath the sun a train pounded across the bare land. Inside the train the jolting rock-a-bye motion lulled a Maguire too weary to ponder the consequences of this trip. Flushed with fever, bones aching, empty pockets sweat-clamped to his thighs, all he cared about was that the trip end while he still had the strength and determination to walk. Then, if old Harvard didn't take him in, the hell with it. He'd just collapse right there in the yard. Make Harvard and Lee do the burying, if nothing else.

He stared at his satchel on the opposite seat and wondered where the strength would come to carry it. Stared at his shoes—city shoes. Stared at his hands, still blotchy from too long in the jungle. Christ! Two years in the wet Philippines, and now the dry, desiccating air of West Texas. The bottle of mineral water he'd bought in El Paso was long gone. Should have bought two, he told himself. Should have bought two, in time to the clickety-clack of steel wheels on steel rails. Should have bought two. And the sun burned through the open window. And the sun burned through his skull and drilled into his brain.

The train eased to a stop. Somehow, Maguire found the fortitude to stand, reach for and grab hold of his satchel. Right arm weighted painfully, left hand supporting him from seat to seat, he lurched down the aisle, past an irate minister's daughter and down the steps to the platform where the dry planks sounded hollowly under

77

his feet. Walking carefully, he stepped onto the dusty road that led, a block away, to the center of Alpine, Texas. Luckily the first person he met had a buckboard and looked hungry. "Hey, you!" he called.

The farmer shaded his eyes, gave the impression he didn't like what he saw. "You talkin' to me?"

"Name's Maguire."

"Don't know you."

"I need a ride out to the Van Allens'." Maguire threw his satchel into the back of the buckboard.

"Say, now. Look here, mister. You can't just . . . "

"They'll pay what you ask. I'm a friend of theirs."

"Never saw or heard of one of their friends lookin' like you."

"Guess you'll just have to trust me, then," Maguire said, awkwardly climbing aboard and easing onto the hard wood seat.

"Why?"

"Because you can use some extra cash." He summoned a smile. " 'Sides. Harvard'll raise holy hell if I die right here in your wagon." And then he passed out.

There was a hand on his forehead when he woke up. Maguire thought it was the coolest, gentlest hand he had ever felt. The wrist beyond it was pale white, laced with delicate blue veins. To one side the skin moved up and down slightly in time to an unheard heartbeat. Maguire forced his eyes to focus beyond the wrist, and discovered the most beautiful woman he had ever seen. Uncertain as to how he managed to come under her care, he let his eyes slide to one side in an attempt to find out where he was.

"You're at the Van Allen Ranch. Luckily for you, Lee was here to recognize you, or I might have had old Mister Tibbs drop you somewhere along the road back to town." She smiled. Cherry red lips opened to reveal even, white teeth. A wisp of pale golden hair fell over her left eye, which was as blue as cool water. Maguire tried to say something to her, but her image shimmered like a puddle stirred by a fallen leaf, then faded completely.

She was still there when he woke for the second time. The room was quiet, wrapped in darkness glowing with lantern light. How she knew he had awakened was a mystery, but he had no sooner opened his eyes than she lay down the book she'd been reading and reached for a nearby washbasin.

"You're still with us then," she said in a musical voice that hinted of laughter. "You gave us quite a scare, Mr. Maguire. Feel better?"

Maguire tried to wet his lips but his tongue was too dry. When he did manage to get out the single word, "Yes," it sounded hoarse and scratchy.

"You've had quite a fever, but I think it's broken now. Here." She wrung out a cloth, folded it and placed it across his forehead. Maguire winced at the coolness of the water. "Can you sit up?" He struggled to get his elbows beneath him and raise himself. "Never mind. Let me help."

Stronger than she looked, she put her hand under his head and lifted it, then held a glass to his lips. Maguire sipped. The cool, tart sweetness of lemonade was excruciating, and for some unfathomable reason, he almost felt like he was going to cry. "Just a few sips for now," she said. "That's right. There you are."

She lay his head down again, took the cloth from his forehead and replaced it with a new one. Maguire couldn't get over the taste of lemonade, the touch of her hands. Silent, he watched as she dipped the cloth in the basin again and began washing his shoulders and chest. Sensation piled on sensation. He couldn't remember feeling so much. Curious he looked down at himself, recoiled at the sight of his gaunt and wiry arms. The Philippines had almost done it, he thought. Almost finished him for good. He'd left with his life, though. That was more than many

of the others who had accompanied him on the fool's
venture that had promised gold and delivered death.

The cloth paused. The woman's fingertips were tracing
a jagged line of scar tissue that streaked his side where
he'd fallén on a bamboo spike. Suddenly she noticed him
watching her and quickly drew away her hand. He could
have sworn he saw her blush before the darkness descended again.

"Good morning!" Sunshine, dappled by a mesquite tree
outside, streamed through the eastern window of the room.
"Think you're ready to eat something?"

Maguire blinked, yawned. He was propped up on
pillows. A blanket covered his legs and hips, but he was
naked from the waist up. He felt as weak as a mouse and
his mouth was so dry he wondered if there was water
enough in the world to slake his thirst. By the time he wet
his lips to speak, she was sitting at his side and dipping a
spoon in a cup. "Who are you?" he managed to ask, just
before she slipped a spoonful of warm broth past his lips.

"I'm Lee's wife. My name is Corinne. Here. Take
another swallow. It's broth from last night's stew. A
strange breakfast, but just what the doctor ordered."

Maguire swallowed. The broth tasted a little salty, but
good. He let her feed him another spoonful. "Where is
Lee?"

"Working. He's come to see you when he could."

"I don't remember."

"No doubt, the way you've been the past week."

"Week!" Maguire croaked, jerking up from the pillows.

"Relax," Corinne scolded, reaching for the washcloth.
"Look. You made me spill this." Frowning, she handed
him the cup so he could sip some more, then set to work
wiping the luekwarm trickle of broth from his chest.·

Maguire lay back on the pillows and let her sponge him
off. Try though he might to reconstruct the missing days,
they were utterly lost. A whole week, he thought. My

god! That means she'd probably been . . . Embarrassed, he dutifully worked at the soup, feeding himself at last and trying at the same time to swallow his pride.

Appearing pleased with the result of her nursing the woman watched him drink. "Do you recognize where you are?"

"This room used to be mine," Maguire said after a moment's hesitation.

"That's what Lee said. His father gave it to you when he took you in. Lee thinks of you as a brother, you know."

"Yes." He handed her the cup and their hands touched, a half second longer than necessary.

Corinne blushed again and glanced around the room, focusing on everything except Maguire's eyes. "Harvard thought a great deal of you, too."

"Thought?" Maguire asked, a sinking feeling in his stomach. "I didn't know. I . . . " He stopped, and a sense of loss poured through him. Harvard had been the closest thing to a real father he could remember. Gruff and demanding on the surface, in reality he was slow to anger and a loving, born teacher who cared more for his sons—natural and taken in—than anything on earth. Without Harvard's influence, Maguire knew he would have been a poor and miserable good-for-nothing itinerant working for forty a month and board. "When did he die?" he finally asked, his voice subdued.

"Two years ago. Lee tried to get in touch with you, but his letters were returned. If there'd been a permanent address—"

"I never had one. Except maybe here."

"That's what Lee said." She went to the dresser, returned with an ebony cane with a silver head and handed it to Maguire. "He also said you'd recognize this. Harvard wanted you to have it."

Maguire's eyes misted. The old panther head cane he'd admired as a boy. And Harvard had left it for him. Corinne forgotten for the moment, he closed his eyes and

81

remembered the love he'd felt for the man who had raised him. Harvard Van Allen dead. Maguire had been a damned fool for leaving. He'd never had a chance to say good-bye. Never even a chance to let the old man know how he felt.

"Mr. Maguire? Are you all right?"

"Yes." He looked at her, handed her the cane. "Thank you. Harvard never used it. He was going to tell me where it came from and how he got it, but I wasn't here." The words were slurred, and sleep was creeping into his muscles. The last thing he remembered as he closed his eyes was her face, over his. Too damn beautiful, he thought, fading quickly. And too long alone. Lee always was lucky. He could feel her hands as she pulled the extra pillows from under his head and then rearranged the cover —feel them linger longer than necessary. There was a loneliness in her. And he told himself, get well. Get well, and leave.

Muscles, healed beneath the sun, flexed and left a line of fence posts in the wake of healthy sweat and hard labor. The weeks had been kind to Maguire. Rest and plenty of simple food and clean water had erased the ravages of the jungle. Each day had seen him out a little longer until, this day, he'd stayed the morning and into the afternoon. Lee Van Allen, his wry, boyish face resisting thirty years of wind and sun, sauntered around the house toward the corral and Maguire. "You're gonna kill yourself," he said, grinning widely.

Maguire dropped the shovel. "When did you get back from Fort Worth?" he asked, grabbing and shaking Lee's hand.

"Just now. What the hell are you doing?"

"Earning my keep." He kicked the last post he'd put in, felt with satisfaction that it was solid. "Couldn't stay in bed any longer." Which was the truth, he decided. He inadvertently glanced toward the house, caught a glimpse of

Corinne in the doorway and looked away again to hide the look in his eye that said she was the real reason he was here beneath the sun. Not for the therapy of work, but to be away from her.

"Corinne's treating you all right, isn't she?"

Maguire laughed. "Like a mother hen. I think she's trying to feed me all of your stock."

"Good. I was hoping you'd become friends."

They had. Maguire had found he could talk to Corinne as he had been unable to talk to anyone in his life, and the hours they had spent talking in the quiet desert twilight had solidified the bond that had grown between them. In addition, the solitude of the Alpine Ranch—and for all the scattered activity around the place, there was indeed solitude—was forcing them closer, however unwillingly. Realizing he wasn't yet strong enough to leave, Maguire also understood he wanted very much to stay. Because of this he had begun to feel uneasy about his and Corinne's friendship, and he had already decided that, difficult as it would be, he would have to leave the day his health permitted.

Lee noticed Corinne, turned and waved to her. "Washington's finest," he said proudly. "Lucky, aren't I." A look of concern turned his face serious. "Come on. Let's get you out of this sun before you have a stroke. Pa always said you worked too hard."

"He'd be saying that of you right now," Maguire countered. What he was saying was none of his business, but he said it anyway.

Lee patted the dust from his western suit. He was beginning to sweat, and loosened his string tie for comfort before waving a browned hand to indicate the rolling sweep of yellow-brown land that swept to the horizon. "It takes work. Growth always does. Alpine Ranch is bigger and better than Pa ever dreamed."

"It was big enough for Harvard. He never could see the need for any more than he had."

"Well, I do," Lee snapped, the warmth gone from his voice.

"You're hardly ever here," Maguire said, knowing he was overstepping himself. "A man shouldn't leave his home so damn much."

"And what in hell do you mean by that?"

Maguire could read the ominous tone in Lee's voice. The man who was once almost a brother to him had changed. He was no longer a simple, diligent rancher. The two years he had spent in the East had taught him what a man could grasp if he tried hard enough, if he worked and extended himself. But then again, maybe he hadn't changed. Maybe he had always felt thwarted in his father's shadow. Well, no longer. It was plain to see that Lee Van Allen was a determined man. And to stand in his way invited trouble. "Nothing, Lee. It's only something I think Harvard would have said. Or would have thought, certainly."

"Pa's dead, Maguire. Alpine Ranch is mine now," Lee said harshly, sounding like a man who had said the same thing more than once before. His anger dissolved immediately and he clapped Maguire on the shoulder. "Hey, listen to me. What the hell? I'd like you to stay, Maguire. I need a good right-hand man and there's no one I trust more than you."

"No." A little too quickly, Maguire mentally scolded himself. "No. I've been out of ranching for too long. Anyway there's some business waiting I need to take care of," he improvised. "Soon as I can, I'll be moving on."

"Don't refuse too soon. Think about it at least. Will you do that?" Maguire looked dubious, dug a bootheel into the dirt. "This is 1900, Maguire. The Twentieth Century! There's no telling how far we could go."

"I don't know—"

"Just think about it, okay? Come on. Let's go inside."

The sun overhead was a brilliant molten white ball

84

sliding across the sky. Maguire pulled his shirt from the fence rail and started after Lee. Suddenly the world was spinning. He staggered and grabbed for Lee's shoulder in order to steady himself.

"Easy," Lee cautioned. Maguire's face was white as a sheet. "Here. Damned fool, working in this sun. Corinne shouldn't have let you. Let me help you to the house."

Through reeling vision Maguire watched the ranch house draw closer. Corinne, concern evident on her face, came to the doorway and helped Maguire into the kitchen. And he wanted to warn her—to warn them both.

The night of rain, that night of nights when first they lay entwined together, lay far behind. Weeks had passed, turning summer into autumn. Lee was gone most of the time. Recently elected a key member of the Cattlemen's Association, he was spending most of his time running the cattle lobby in Austin. Maguire had let himself be persuaded to stay at Alpine Ranch. Healthy from long hours of work in the open air, he was in the process of taking over the daily operation of the ranch as Lee's second in command and trusted friend.

The words were like a heated branding iron on his soul. Each time he saw Corinne, the guilt cut deeper, yet he was incapable of stopping or leaving. No amount of self-incrimination was great enough to tear him away from Corinne's laughter, or her touch. For better or worse, he loved her. Loved her more than honor, more than the free wild life he had known. No matter how much he disliked the idea, he was firmly enmeshed in a trap that, with each liaison and each lie, held him tighter and tighter. Clearly he saw that the whole situation would end one day. End tragically, perhaps, for them all. They could not hope to go undiscovered forever.

They had made love that night with unusual urgency, for Lee was due to return from Austin the next afternoon. Afterward, while Corinne's breath slowed, waves of guilt—and anger, for the thought of her going to bed with Lee had begun to plague him—rolled over Maguire. Unable to sleep, he slipped from the bed and pulled on his trousers. The room was dark, but he needed no light to find his way to the window.

A procession of images, of moments and places each more treasured than the one before, traipsed across the night sky. Sunset atop Sleeping Lion Mountain. Arm in arm, he and Corinne had watched the alpen glow settle on the distant mountain ranges to the west. In that evening light he had admitted to himself how much he had come to love her.

A furtive, shy tryst under the pines on the ridge of a hidden valley secreted from inquisitive eyes. Their horses had arrived from different directions. Maguire remembered her dismounting and shedding her clothes. Her skin had been incredibly white and pure, there in the mountain air. They lay together all the lazy afternoon. Even after she left he could sense her presence.

Stolen nights during Lee's absences. Hungry for her and torn by his friendship for Lee, Maguire counted the days and waited for the nights. He had known many women, but had fallen in love only this once. Because he couldn't bear to think otherwise, he persuaded himself that Corinne had to feel the same way as they lay wrapped in each others arms.

Once, at the grave of Harvard Van Allen, the man who had taken him in, had taught him and become a foster father to him. There, secluded by the juniper grove that shaded the tiny cluster of white stones, Maguire had tried to pray for the first time since he had been a child, to somehow communicate with Harvard and ask his forgiveness.

Behind Maguire, naked beneath the draped and touseled blankets, Corinne slept. Outside, the norther that had blown in that morning swept beneath the eaves with a world-weary moan. The minutes of the night were spinning away as he stood at the window and watched. Maguire did not hear the door open, was hardly aware of the soft lantern glow spilling into the room from the hall.

"My friend," Lee said.

Maguire glanced up, saw the figure in the doorway reflected in the window pane. Corinne sat upright, startled awake, not yet fully aware enough of what was happening to be frightened.

"My brother," Lee said flatly. "I heard a story in a bar in Austin. I didn't believe it until I learned what the gossips in San Antonio were saying. Everyone who knows me knew, I suppose." His voice was calm, betraying neither sadness nor anger. "Everyone but me."

"I tried to tell you, Lee," Corinne pleaded, pulling the blankets tight around her.

"The hell!" Lee roared. His face contorted and he slammed his fist into the wall. "The hell!"

"We both did," Maguire said, turning to face Lee. He inched away from the window and worked his way toward a small chair he knew he could use if need be. "But you were never here. Or never had the time to listen. You've got to . . . Lee!"

He was gone. "You've got to stop him," Corinne whispered to Maguire. "He—"

"Get dressed," Maguire snapped, and ran out of the room in time to see Lee disappear into the study where the gun rack was kept. Run or fight. The thought flicked through Maguire's head. Either way, he was a loser. There was no doubt Lee would follow him. Better to face him now, get it over with.

They met in the lantern-lit hallway just outside the door to the study. "Lee, don't!" Maguire warned when he saw the handgun.

"The hell!"

The gun swept up. Maguire's arm shot out and the edge of his hand struck Lee's wrist. The gun fired and the bullet buried itself in the wall. Not waiting for another shot, Maguire swung with his right. His fist hammered against Lee's jaw. The rancher staggered, bounced off the side of the door.

Behind them, Corinne screamed for them to stop. Maguire held out his hands and shouted Lee's name, but might as well have saved his breath. Lee charged. Maguire caught his wrists and they struggled shoulder to shoulder. Work hardened and in his element, Maguire slowly forced Lee back and overpowered him, at the same time prying the gun from his hand. Suddenly Lee twisted and, with his back set against the wall, pushed forward and grabbed Maguire's hand and the gun. A second blast rocked the narrow hallway. Before the reverberations had time to die away, Lee, shrieking in agony, had fallen to the floor.

"Oh, my God!" Corinne screamed, her voice tiny in the deafening roar that filled Maguire's ears. Crying, she ran to Lee's side and knelt by him. He was unconscious. A ragged hole in his knee spurted blood. Maguire ran back to the bedroom and ripped a sheet from the bed.

"Get dressed," he told her for the second time, shoving her away from Lee.

"He's bleeding! O, my God, you've killed him."

"He'll be all right, damn it. Now get dressed. We'll have to get help, take him to town." Ignoring her, Maguire tore the sheet into strips and wound a tourniquet around Lee's thigh. When the bleeding refused to stop, he stuffed a piece into the wound and bound it tightly. While Corinne finished dressing, he ran outside shirtless in the biting wind to get the wagon ready. Luckily the team was still hitched to the buckboard Lee had driven from town. Pausing only long enough to move team and wagon to the side door, Maguire ran back inside, dressed and ordered Corinne to carry blankets to the buckboard. Finally he picked up Lee in his arms and carried him out the door and past the silent, accusatory stares of the hands. With Corinne holding her wounded husband, Maguire kept the whip to the horses all the way to town, a desperate, bouncing ride of five miles.

At eleven o'clock on a Saturday night, the town of Alpine was still wide awake. Word of the arrival of the wounded owner of Alpine Ranch, his wife and new foreman spread like wildfire. Moments after Doc Medoff washed his hands and dripped the ether into the sponge held over Lee's face in order to start surgery, Constable St. Vrain arrived. St. Vrain, a heavyset, stoop-shouldered man with a petulant face and a penchant for pin-striped suits and bowler hats, pulled at his sweeping silver moustache. "Fellow tells me you and Lee had a little argument," he said, after tipping his hat to Corinne.

Maguire watched the officer's gaze and yielded not an inch. "That's right," he said, thinking rapidly. He didn't like lying, but couldn't tell the truth. Not with Corinne there for everybody to talk about. "Ended up in a wrestling match, and he got shot in the knee. Doc's working on him now."

"Knee, huh?" St. Vrain glanced at Corinne, who nodded in corroboration. "Argument over what?"

Maguire grimaced. "Game of cards. Poker."

The constable raised an eyebrow. "Poker, huh? Thought you two was like brothers?"

Maguire nodded, hooked his thumbs in his back pockets. "Well, you know what they say, Mr. St. Vrain. Cards are thicker than blood. Especially when it runs hot."

St. Vrain stared at him a moment more. He glanced at Corinne again, and switched the toothpick he was chewing from one corner of his mouth to the other. "Uh, huh," he grunted noncommittally. "Lee's got a temper, all right. Well, you stay around until I can talk to him, you hear?"

Maguire told him he would, and then led Corinne to the hotel and got her a room. Too high-strung to sleep, he wrapped up in one of the blankets they'd carried Lee in and sat out the last hours of the night on the hotel porch.

Morning came and no one spoke to him. Bones slow with the cold, Maguire wandered into the New York Café and ordered coffee and steak. A half hour later he sat back and watched Constable St. Vrain come in the door and saunter to his table. "Well?" he asked, as the older man sat.

"Talked to Lee," the constable said shortly. "You mind bringin' me some coffee, May?" Maguire shoved his cup forward for a refill. "Just one will do," he added, looking Maguire in the eye.

Maguire leaned back and waited while St. Vrain poured sugar into his coffee. Whatever Lee had said, the lawman was in no hurry.

"I try to keep my nose out of other people's business, much as possible," St. Vrain finally said, speaking slowly. "Sometimes hard to do." He paused, blew on his coffee and tasted it. "Doc says Lee's gonna be a cripple."

Maguire tensed, unsure of what was coming next.

"Lee says you're free to go." The eyebrow shot up characteristically. "You got any better ideas?"

"No," Maguire said simply. He was being forced to appear a coward, but under the circumstances he could think of no better course.

"Good. Train from El Paso's due in a couple of hours." Finishing his coffee, the constable wiped his moustache with the back of his hand and rose from the table. "Guess you'll have time to ride out and get your gear."

He did; then he waited on the station platform as the braking engine shot steam at his boots. Wincing, Maguire thought of the pain in Lee's knee as he walked the last steps to the passenger car.

He could feel Corinne's burning gaze, and resisted the urge to turn around to see her one more time. He had done enough damage. Too damn much. He was a villain who had seduced a friend's wife and then crippled him. Leaving would end the matter, and maybe even permit Corinne to salvage her life in Alpine. No matter that he should have left long ago. At least he was leaving now. Better late than never, he told himself. It was little consolation.

Moments later the whistle blew and the train started out of the station. Maguire threw his satchel in the overhead rack, propped Harvard's cane against the seat next to him, and sat back. What came next wasn't certain—only that he would never see Corinne Van Allen again.

7

"Mind if I sit down?"

The real world intruded. Maguire swam out of limbo in time to sense a bulky shadow at his side and hear a dim thump. He looked down to see a big black metal case on the floor by his table. When he looked up again, a large hand jutted out of a sleeve in front of his face. Maguire refused the handshake and the shadow sat across from him and took the shape of a tousle-haired young giant dressed in a cavalry uniform from which the regimental identification had been removed. Maguire blinked.

"So this is your place. Nice. Had it long?"

Maguire tried to remember how to talk. Damn it, Maguire, you're only as drunk as you want to be, he told himself.

"You do remember me, don't you? Patrick Henry Blue?"

Maguire leaned back in his chair. Light played on the silver stitchings decorating his vest. "You need a forty-five. Anything smaller won't stop them."

"Beg your pardon?"

The kid talked in questions. Probably needed a drink. Maguire poured a tumbler half full of tequila and shoved it toward Blue.

"Oh. Ah, no thank you. I'm not sure I can handle . . . "

"You can take it, Patrick Henry. Big fella like you."

The youth colored angrily. He dumped some salt in his left hand and popped it into his mouth, took a massive bite out of a lemon and gulped down half the contents of the glass. Eyes watering, he gripped the edge of the table and waited for the temperature to drop. "Jesus!" he wheezed, momentarily unable to breath.

Maguire offered him the bottle.

"No thanks," Blue gasped.

"Didn't know you were in the army." Maguire winked confidentially. "On the lam, eh?"

Blue looked indignant. "Of course not. I use these as work clothes."

"Oh." That explains it, Maguire thought, leaning back and sipping from his own glass. "So what are you doing here?"

"Story," Blue said between breaths.

"What story?"

Blue stabbed a finger at Maguire and tried to talk, but his throat still wouldn't function properly. At that moment Cecilia walked past. Desperate, Blue lifted a pitcher of water from the tray she was carrying. Cecilia spun around in anger, but Maguire shook his head. Blue gulped down the water, not caring if he sloshed some on his clothes. The fire in his throat finally quenched, he placed the pitcher on the table.

"Hey!" Blue said, noticing for the first time the deep crimson color of the glass and the intricate patterns etched on its surface. "That's very pretty. This whole city is, too. Enchanting. Wonderful. A city of marvels."

"Yeah," Maguire agreed unenthusiastically. "That particular pitcher comes from a glassworks north of here, just below Chihuahua. But you didn't come here to admire my glassware."

Blue hunched forward over the table. His eyes shone eagerly. "That's right, Mister Maguire. I didn't."

"Maguire will do."

"Okay. Whatever you say. At any rate, I'm a reporter. I spent my last two hundred dollars to come here with Mrs. Van Allen to get a story. Now she's upset because you two didn't exactly hit it off, so the story may fall apart. You're my second chance. Mrs. Van Allen talked about you some, and frankly, you sound like quite a colorful character."

Excited, Blue thumped the table with his fist. Hell, with this kind of story, the *Times* would have to put him on the payroll. "This could make great reading for the folks back home. You're the kind of person my readers empathize with. Everybody is interested in Mexico. I can see it right now. 'An American Soldier of Fortune in Mexico City,' by Patrick Henry Blue. How does that sound? You'd be immortalized."

"That's a helluva idea."

"I thought you'd like it," Blue said, beaming.

"But the first thing we've gotta do is get you some local color. To know Mexico City is to know me. Or vice versa."

"Well then, tomorrow morning we can . . ."

"No. Now. Tonight." Maguire pushed himself erect, wavered a moment and used his walking stick to support himself. The room spun as he stood, but gradually it steadied, braking and grinding into place. He knew what he was going to do. And he didn't like it. But then he didn't much like Patrick Henry Blue. Nor the world. Nor himself.

"I don't think you ought to be . . . I mean, are you sure you aren't, well, you know." Blue stood, ready to catch Maguire in case he fell.

"Drunk? Afraid to say it? Afraid you'll hurt my feelings?"

"Well, no. That is, I just . . . "

"You want to write that story or not?"

"Yes, sir!"

"Good. You can leave the black case. No one will bother it in *El Madronito*. Come on. This way." Steadier with each step, Maguire led the way through the kitchen, past the disapproving stare of Aurora and into the courtyard.

The wrought-iron gate protested in rusted tones as the two men exited into the alley. Blue had trouble adjusting his vision. The glow from the electric street light in front of *El Madronito* failed to permeate the stygian gloom behind the buildings. Gradually, though, from stars and slivered moon and isolated candles and lantern light leaking from behind shuttered windows, a measure of sight returned.

The night was cold and clear. As they approached the next street where there was more illumination, Blue could see his breath clouding the clear air. He wished he'd worn a heavier coat, but hurried on behind Maguire without mentioning the cold. If Maguire could take it, so could he.

They moved from shadow to light and back to shadow, from spacious boulevard to cramped alley. They ventured into the depths of an unreal city where grotesque stone façades assumed ominous expressions. Makeshift stoves with coals burning like dragons' eyes glowed in the dark. Meat of questionable origin sizzled and popped. Clay bowls of beans and chili sputtered and bubbled. The provocative aromas mingled with the stench of excrement and rotting vegetation.

There were no automobiles in this part of the city,

only a jumbled commerce of teeming humanity. Grunting twosomes coupled openly in the wan glow of lanternlight oozing from cracked and broken shutters. Women laughed hollowly and men roared like cats and yowled like coyotes inside grim, dusty *pulguerias* that dispensed rotgut liquor and offered havens for poisoned souls.

"*Pelados*," Maguire said, slurring the word.

"What?"

"*Pelados*. The peeled ones. The skinned ones," he explained, indicating the surrounding poor.

Some men ignored them. Some stared in the manner of predators. Whether they were dissuaded from attacking by Blue's imposing size, or because they recognized Maguire, the reporter could not tell. Nor did he care, so long as he was allowed to pass safely. Still he hurried after Maguire, tagging in his footsteps, soaking up sights and sounds and smells, his mind racing with unasked questions. He was excited and frightened, but he wouldn't have foregone the experience for anything in the world. The story he wrote would be an unparalleled success.

"Three pesos. Three pesos," a voice whined to his left. A hand reached out to pluck his sleeve. Blue froze in surprise.

"Three pesos," the girl said, imploring eyes wide.

Fifteen years old at the most. Paper shoes on her feet. Heavily painted face more grotesque than suggestive. Mousy brown hair hanging tangled to her shoulders. Her dress was tied with a single bow which she quickly undid. The ragged garment fell open and she held both flaps and wobbled small, newly developed breasts with tiny, bruised nipples.

"Three pesos." Her belly was puffy above a nest of brown ringlets. She pursed her lips and made a soft sucking noise. Her meaning was obscenely obvious. "Three pesos."

Blue stood slackjawed, speechless, aghast. The girl pulled his hand to her mouth and began sucking on his

97

finger and moaning, at the same time touching herself with her other hand and pretending to climax.

"No."

Blue pushed her away. She stumbled and fell against the wall. Cursing in guttural Spanish, she jumped to her feet. Blue shrunk back, saw an impassive Maguire standing to one side. A pair of ragged *campesinos* called and the girl cast a contemptuous look at Blue and hurried to the men who waited across the street. Unable to move, Blue watched as they haggled momentarily. Suddenly one of the men dropped his worn, baggy trousers. The girl discarded her dress, folded it and placed it on the ground to cushion her knees.

Blue wanted to leave, but couldn't tear his eyes from the spectacle. He wasn't the only one. A scattering of men, women and children ready to be diverted by anything, gathered around to watch the fun. Oblivious to her audience, the girl took the first man while the second dropped his trousers and eagerly awaited his turn. A third, pants open and three pesos clutched in his fist, joined the line.

The girl's head bobbed back and forth, back and forth. Suddenly the man arched his back and cracked his skull against the wall of the cantina. The girl's head continued, faster and faster, the horrid sucking noises now drowned out by the man's long, lingering wail that faded in satisfaction. Everyone laughed. It was a good show. The girl began on the second man.

Blue bent double and heaved. His stomach walls contracted brutally as supper and tequila spewed onto the street. Clutching his belly, moaning, he staggered away from the sordid scene and grabbed Maguire's arm. "Out of here," he pleaded, white faced. "Out of here!"

"Enchanting. Wonderful," Maguire said through clenched teeth. He pulled Blue upright and spun him around to face the crowd. "A city of marvels."

Blue cringed. Half the spectators, bored with the girl's

performance, had turned to watch and laugh at the *gringo* giant heaving his guts over the curb. "Took me here on purpose," Blue gasped through the bitter juices that burned his throat and made his voice raw.

"Sure, Patrick Henry. Well? What about it? Think the New York *Times*'ll like it? 'Scenes from Romantic Mexico City,' by Patrick Henry Blue. Make us immortal. Here we are!"

"Bastard son of a bitch!" Blue twisted free of Maguire's grasp and bolted down the street.

"Hey!" Maguire shouted, the anger draining from him. "You'll get lost!"

The reporter bowled over a pair of protesting drunks, rounded a corner and disappeared.

"Run, kid," Maguire said softly. "Run. I don't blame you."

"Maguire?"

It was the girl. The crowd was gone. One of the children had stolen her dress. Her thin body shivered uncontrollably in the cold air. She wiped a skinny forearm across her mouth and, smiling, pinched her nipples in an attempt to make them erect. The shivering increased.

Maguire crossed the road and stood in front of her. "How do you know my name, girl?" he asked in soft Spanish.

"Everybody knows Maguire." She pursed her lips. "You like Remedios?" she asked boldly.

Maguire stared at her until she looked away. "No," he said, gently, slipping out of his heavy, striped suit coat. "Not that way. Stand up." He helped her to her feet, put the coat around her shoulders and buttoned it down the front.

The girl dared look at him again. Maguire searched his pockets, found a wad of crumpled pesos and a twenty-dollar gold piece and stuffed them in the coat pocket. When the girl started to cry, he put his arms around her and held her close, stroked her hair and rocked her. "Remedios," he whispered, glad the dim light hid his own red rimmed eyes. "Such a pretty name."

The girl shuddered. "Go to *El Madronita,*" he told her. "You know where that is?" Her head bobbed against his chest. "Go in the back door and tell the woman, Aurora, I sent you. She looks like a witch, but she is very kind. She will feed you, give you a bath and find a place for you to sleep. You understand?"

He felt her nod again, and then she broke from him and ran down the street in the direction of the casino. Maguire watched her go and wondered if he'd find her when he got back.

His vest provided little protection against the cold. He stared at the silver panther on his cane, into the inscrutable, blank-carved eyes that never offered answers. His forty years felt like a hundred. How many children like Remedios had he seen in the last year and a half? "Too many," he told the uncaring panther. "Too damned many."

Guilt his sole companion, he started walking again, aimlessly crossing the Avenue of the Owls. When he looked up, he found himself on the Avenue of the Virgins, home of a dozen prestigious brothels whose clientele were the city's dignitaries. A trio of well-dressed gentlemen, on their way home to docile wives, looked askance. "Who is that?" one asked.

"The *norteamericano,* the mixed-blood. Maguire. He is *loco.*"

"Speak softly," the third lisped a little too loudly. "He might hear. He goes to see his mulatto whore, the French woman."

"Would that she might lie with me." The second raised his hand and a carriage appeared out of the darkness. "It is said she . . . "

They passed beyond out of earshot. Maguire rushed up the steps and into the perfumed parlor.

"Is someone chasing you?"

"The world," Maguire said.

"Such an entrance. My guests were shocked."

"They'll get over it." Ignoring the obvious disdain of the gentlemen clients and the sidelong glances of their temporary paramours, Maguire had stalked through the parlor. The room he sought was at the rear of the house, down a paneled hall painted a lurid pink and embellished with nymphs and satyrs cavorting in Rabelaisian glee. Dauphine's room was tastefully furnished: filled with delicate wood and ivory carvings and hung with genuine European tapestries. Stern, comfortless furniture led one to the magnificent bed with matched, massive head- and foot-boards of intricately carved maple.

Dauphine wriggled out of her corset. Naked save for cotton hose, she lay down beside him. "Your coat?"

"I gave it to one of the little street whores. They'd stolen her dress and left her to shiver. She said her name was Remedios."

"Ah, yes," Dauphine laughed. "I have seen her. Remedios." She sucked her lips.

"Stop it!" Maguire snapped.

"You have softness for the little ones, Maguire." Dauphine slid closer. The large, round nipple of one caramel-colored breast touched his cheek. "And maybe something hard for Dauphine?" she whispered huskily, running her hand down the front of his trousers.

Maguire caught her wrist and held her hand away from him. Dauphine twisted free and, enjoying the game, caressed his mouth with her breast and rubbed her knee against the inside of his thigh. Uncharacteristically he sat upright with his back to her.

Dauphine leaped from the bed. "What is it?" she blurted, her features mottled with rage. Maguire attempted a puzzled expression. "Ooohh!" the mulatto shrieked, charging him. Maguire caught her by the wrists before she could rake his face with her painted talons. "Let me go!"

"Not until you promise to leave my nose where it is."

Dauphine struggled, but his grip only tightened. Slowly her outburst subsided. "Who is she?" she demanded again, her voice calm but menacing.

"What the hell are you talking about?"

"One of my patrons told me about the blond *gringa* at Drexler's *comida*. You cannot fool Dauphine."

"Ah," Maguire said. "That." He walked across the room and stood in front of the dresser mirror. The lines in his face had deepened in the last few hours, he thought. "A *norteamericana* from long ago. She has come to see me and asked my help. She wants me to find her son who has been kidnapped by Gregor Bortha. Gregor Bortha and Jesus Fuentes," he amended, wondering for the first time if that's why Fuentes was in town. Perhaps talking to Madero would be a waste of time.

"You will not go, Maguire." Dauphine threw herself against him and frantically tried to elicit a response. When Maguire remained passive, she stepped back, a pained look in her eyes. "I hate her. I will cut out her heart. Who is she? What is her name? Tell me. Tell me!"

"Never mind, it has nothing to do with you, Dauphine."

She began to pummel his chest. Maguire forced her to retreat to the bed. His arms pinning her, Dauphine fell backward. "Maguire," she whispered softly, her eyes slitting, her body undulating under him.

The change of tactics caught him by surprise. Heat radiated from her. An overpowering aroma of musk clouded his senses and awakened memories of unbridled passion. For a second he wanted her, but then the image of Remedios on her knees in the street struck him with such force he closed his eyes. "No." He sighed, stood and walked away from her.

Behind him, he heard Dauphine spring from the bed. A china pitcher crashed against the wall near his head as he touched the doorknob. He turned to look at her. One of the flying slivers had nicked his cheek. Dauphine stood with hands on hips, legs wide and formidable breasts heaving.

The whole world *was* chasing him. First Corinne, then Remedios and now Dauphine. Shouldn't have gotten drunk, he told himself. "I'm sorry, Dauphine," he said to her. "Not tonight." She threw the basin. He had to duck. Straightening, he opened the door. "Maybe tomorrow. I don't know . . . "

He shut the door just as something heavy and metallic clanged against the opposite side. A blond young man stuck his head out a side door. "*Vas ist?*" he asked, and seeing Maguire, hurriedly pulled his head back in and slammed the door.

The parlor was empty. Maguire searched in his vest pocket and discovered he'd left his watch somewhere. The hour was late, though, for the front door was barred and the lamps turned low. He slid back the bolt.

"Hey you!" Dauphine called from behind him. He whirled in time to catch his cane in mid flight. "I think you will be sorry," she hissed, making no effort to cover herself.

Maguire tilted the silver panther's head toward her in a silent salute, and left.

Dauphine ran to the door. "Very sorry!" she screamed into the night. Her voice echoed up and down the street. "You hear me, Maguire? Very sorry!"

Suarez nudged his companion, Hermann Elrecht, and pointed to the front door of Dauphine's. The German rubbed the sleep from his eyes and pulled his coat tight under his chin. The pair had followed Maguire since he left *El Madronito*. They'd watched Blue's hasty escape and snickered silently as they observed Maguire's tenderness toward the child *puta*. Such sentimentality on Maguire's part was a sign of weakness. Fuentes would be extremely interested, and probably reward them hand-somely.

"You got the name down?" Suarez asked. They'd in-quired about the girl's name, and Elrecht had scribbled it on a scrap of paper with a nub of a pencil.

Elrecht patted his belly. "In my belt. You worry too much."

"You should worry more."

"Why bother?" Elrecht poked Suarez in the gut. "There's enough of you to worry for a dozen."

"Mock me when Fuentes gives us gold for the name of the little street whore."

"Hey!" Elrecht frowned, concentrating. "Think. If our captain will pay gold for a name, what would he give us for something more?"

Adolfo Suarez scratched his bearded jowls. "What do you mean?"

"An ear," the German said with a wide grin, pulling a stiletto from his boot top.

Suarez flexed his beefy shoulders. "We must be careful not to kill him, though. Fuentes would peel our hides."

"And make a tent of yours," Elrecht added.

"An ear. An ear." Suarez tested the word. "A great deal of gold, I am sure. You have the sickly pale flesh of a true *gringo,* my German friend, but your heart is as fierce as a Yacqui Indian's."

"Shhh!" Elrecht hissed. Their quarry had set off down the street. Quietly, so they wouldn't warn their source of new found wealth, they followed Maguire through the sleeping city.

Chapultepec Avenue was all but empty of life save for an occasional motorcar or horse-drawn carriage hurrying its occupants to home and hearth. Barred, shuttered and draped windows stared blankly back at Maguire. The dimly-lit faces of the city buildings added to depression. He wanted to be home and in bed. Wanted sleep to still the muddled, contradictory voices that plagued his thoughts.

He took the shortcut down a side street that dead ended in a small park called The Grove of Saint Francis. The park was fringed with pines and a brick walkway wound among thickly planted maguey cactus radiating in intricate patterns from the saint's statue. The pines cut the wind, but the chill was still penetrating. Wishing he had his coat, Maguire swung his arms. Dumb, he told himself. Hell, the girl probably wouldn't even be there. She'd take the money and sell the coat. Be back on the streets in three nights, making those God-damned sucking sounds he couldn't drive out of his mind.

"Uncharitable, Maguire," he said aloud, just to hear someone talk. "She'll be asleep by the stove. Tomorrow I'll buy her a dress and see about school." Father Julio would help. The good padre—the only good one he'd met except for Father Moreno in the Philippines, and the Moros had sent him to heaven piecemeal. Father Julio ran a free shcool for the children of the city's poor. "Hell, he owes me." Aloud again. "Maybe have him find her a family, too."

Two figures detatched themselves from the shadows. Maguire pulled up sharply, the cynically benevolent monologue forgotten. Survival. The word clicked in his brain and his body reacted automatically. Cold, hot, drunk. Nothing else ever mattered. Only the threat. Which was why he was still alive.

He recognized Adolfo Suarez from the cockfight. Elrecht he could not identify, but the uniform of *Los Serpientes* told him all he needed to know. One thing more. Enough light from the boulevard filtered through the Montezuma pines to glimmer off the length of a double-edge steel blade held by the German.

Separating, the figures advanced slowly. "*Señor* One Eye allows his dogs to run free of their leashes," Maguire said tauntingly. "Lift your faces, dutiful mongrels. Let me see your collars. Does the butcher of helpless women and children wait behind you out of sight? Are you tethered to his wrist?"

The insult was too much to bear. Suarez charged, exactly as Maguire wanted. Poised lightly on the balls of his feet, Maguire waited and stepped aside at the last moment. At the same time, his cane lashed out to catch the heavyset *rurale* across the ankles. Suarez tripped and blundered full force into the stone Saint Francis. Bellowing with pain and rage, he bounced off the immovable object and flattened a cactus.

Maguire heard the whisper of steel through air and spun, bringing the cane around to block Elrecht's initial slashing attack. Hoping to sever his opponent's fingers, the German skidded his blade along the length of the cane. Maguire twisted and leaped back too late as the point of steel sliced open his knuckles.

Painful but superficial. Ignoring the pain, as he'd taught himself, Maguire tried to concentrate. Search until the inevitable weakness was found, and then strike—decisively and without mercy.

Both *rurales* carried guns. Why didn't they use them? And then he realized. Fuentes, his sworn enemy, was in this case his protector. So great was Fuentes's desire for revenge he probably would allow none of his men the opportunity to rob him of his one, all-consuming desire. Whatever the cause of their attack, these men would not dare to kill him. Small comfort. Maybe they only wanted a piece of him.

Heavy footsteps to his right gave sufficient warning. Head lowered and arms open to engulf his victim, Suarez charged again. Maguire danced aside as Elrecht, using his bulky companion as a diversion, leaped through the air. Once again the cane turned aside the stiletto. But not the man. Attacker and victim fell to earth and rolled into the punishing embrace of a maguey cactus. The blade lashed out and over. Maguire kicked free and sprang to his feet. His vest was slit up the middle, his shirt in tatters. "Damn!"

Suarez charged again, determined more than ever to crush the impudent *bravo* in his bearlike embrace. Maguire ducked and jabbed the tip of his cane into the *rurale's* Adam's apple. Suarez stopped dead in his tracks, hands clutching his throat and choking for breath.

Again the German charged, this time low and with knife held wide. Moving easily now that he had found the rhythm, Maguire whirled and spun the cane, slapping it across Elrecht's wrist. The stiletto skidded into a cluster of cactus. The cane continued moving, changing direction as Maguire stepped sideways and, grasping the tip, swung the weighted panther's head into Suarez's crotch. The fat *rurale's* eyes bulged. Breath rasping through his throat, he rose on tiptoe, bent double and collapsed.

The hell with Fuentes's orders, Elrecht decided, fumbling at the dust cover over his holster. The Mauser was half drawn when the cat's-head knob of silver whistled through the air and rapped against the German's skull. His whole body went numb. Nerveless fingers dropped the automatic. Elrecht crumpled to his knees and fell face forward.

Cut knuckles, tattered vest, skinned cheek. Worth it. Damned well worth it to feel alive and in control again. The weight of the long night lifted, leaving Maguire exhilarated and charged with new life.

"Thanks for the help," he said to Saint Francis.

Cane twirling, breathing deeply of the sweet, fresh air, Maguire left the park and headed for *El Madronito,* and home.

8

The captain of *Los Serpientes* listened impatiently while Suarez talked. Elrecht sat, with permission, and contributed an occasional moan. He seemed to have trouble with his vision and from time to time gingerly touched the plum-sized bruise over his right eye.

"Enough!" Fuentes interrupted, snatching the scrap of paper with Remedios's name scribbled on it. "The rest of the story is evident." He stared with disgust at Suarez. The man was an uncouth braggart and bungling idiot. His prowess in battle was the only reason he was allowed to remain with *Los Serpientes*. Gunfire and the shrieks of the wounded and dying transformed the lout into a juggernaut worth a half-dozen ordinary men.

Fuentes lifted the machete from the table by his side and, holding the scrap of paper, sliced it into three ribbons. A beatific smile lit his face as the strips fluttered to the floor. The heavy blade, three inches wide and thirty inches long, reversed and pointed at Suarez's belly. Suarez gulped nervously. Fuentes's skill with the blade was legendary.

"I detest that *gringo*," Fuentes said, his good eye glittering dangerously. "One day I will have Maguire's head. With this." The point touched his lieutenant's belly, pressed in until the skin almost broke. Beads of sweat popped out on Suarez's grizzled balloon of a face, but he did not back up. "However much I hate him, though, I do not underestimate him. You must be more careful, Adolfo, do you understand?"

"Yes, Captain." The blade withdrew and Suarez sighed with relief.

"Good. Now get out." The gold eye flashed in the morning sun streaming through the balcony windows. A grateful Suarez exited rapidly.

It was Elrecht's turn. Head throbbing and stomach churning with nausea, the lanky German stood. Fuentes picked up a stick of white marble and slid it along the already razor-sharp machete blade. The sound hurt Elrecht's ears, but he knew better than to complain.

"I am disappointed in you, Hermann. To have become involved in such foolishness isn't like you. I hope it doesn't happen again." Glad to have his part in the fiasco dismissed so lightly, the German shrugged and mumbled an apology. "If you can find one, have a doctor see to your head and get some rest. I will have need of you later, for it begins tonight. And as for Maguire—I will think of something. Go."

Elrecht wobbled from the room. Fuentes replaced the machete on the table and leaned back. So the girl's name was Remedios. And she had been sent to *El Madronito*. Perhaps she would be useful after all.

A servant placed at his disposal by the manager of the Hotel Christobel entered and set a tray on the table. Fuentes watched as the silent Indian poured hot chocolate from a china pitcher into an equally delicate cup, smiled faintly as he uncovered a silver platter of hot *sopapillas*. The Indian stepped back and waited, as the manager had instructed him. Fuentes dipped one of the sugar-dusted puffs of frybread into the pot of honey and plopped the morsel into his mouth. His languid wave of dismissal signaled approval. The relieved Indian padded out of the room.

This was the life he deserved, Fuentes thought as he sipped the chocolate. He leaned back and gazed out across the city. The sky was a limpid, bright azure through which distant snow-capped Popocatepetl cut a jagged line. Here was a fit setting for one of his caliber and ambition. How much better to contemplate these vistas from afar, where their beauty could be appreciated.

He was entitled to more than a captaincy, of course. The second son of a Castillian-born Sonoran slave trader, he had been raised in luxurious surroundings. As a young man, he had traveled in Europe, lived in Paris, studied in Spain. His features darkened as he recalled the disruption of the life to which he had become accustomed, and the subsequent theft of his birthright. The message had come on a morning much like this one. "Come home immediately," the letter said. So he had, to find father and family slaughtered during a Yaqui uprising.

His life fell into a shambles. The two-month interim between their deaths and his arrival had been sufficient time for his father's enemies to carve up his estates. Jesus Fuentes, at twenty-one, was penniless. President Porfirio Diaz, who had allowed the rape of his rightful inheritance, took pity on him and made him a lieutenant in the *rurales*. Nearly incoherent with rage, the young Fuentes held his tongue and accepted the appointment. But at that moment he vowed revenge on those who had wronged him.

Three of the four landowners died mysteriously in their sleep. The Yaquis he decimated and drove into out-

111

lawry or slavery. Eight years later he accepted a transfer to Chihuahua on the condition that the by then famous *Los Serpientes* could accompany him. Two years passed, during which time the Tarahumaras and raiding Comanches felt the sting of his growing madness. Finally, almost a decade to the day after Diaz betrayed him, he returned the favor and allied himself with the *Maderistas*. There, under the command of an exiled Boer general, Gregor Bortha, he met and fought alongside the *gringo* mercenary named Maguire.

The vision of the flicking motion of Maguire's wrist and the snaking, snapping bullwhip that had sliced Fuente's eye from his head had plagued him for two interminable years. One more day, he thought, his fingers tracing the jagged line of tissue running from eye patch to temple. A mere twenty-four hours. Maguire, too, would be repaid. Fuentes's good eye closed as he contemplated the sweetness of revenge.

The sound of hoofbeats outside drew him from his reverie. "Diego!"

His orderly was already on the way in. "They've arrived, Captain," he said, throwing open the doors to the balcony.

Fuentes rose. "My chocolate is cold, Diego. See to it, please."

Fresh air. Sunshine. Fuentes posed at the balcony railing. Below, the remaining forty-five *Serpientes* trotted into the courtyard and raised their American-made Springfields in salute. All forty-five were armed with at least three revolvers for fighting from horseback, a bolt action Springfield for long-distance work and such edged weapons as each chose for hand-to-hand killing. There existed no better fighting unit in all Mexico, Fuentes thought proudly. His heart raced at the sight.

"Diego!" he called. The orderly rushed back in. "See that rooms for them are readied."

"The manager has protested, Captain. They say they

can accept twenty men and no more. The rest of the
rooms are taken."

Fuentes smiled thinly. "Tell the manager to look out
the window. Inform him that my men have ridden a long
way. They are tired, irritable and easily angered." His
lips tightened. "Perhaps he will reconsider."

Diego grinned. "At once, Captain." He started out,
ducked his head back in the door. "Oh, yes. The one
who sent you the message last night is downstairs."

"Good. Send him up. And don't forget my chocolate."
Diego disappeared. Fuentes watched as the *Serpientes*
dismounted and tied their horses. He had just settled into
the massive wicker chair brought him the night before
when the door opened and boots clicked across the tile
floor. "I'm on the balcony," Fuentes called. "Bring the
plate of *sopapillas* with you and join me. There will be
fresh hot chocolate in a moment."

"The chocolate, Captain," Diego called from the door.

"*Si?* Out here." Fuentes hooked his boots into the
wrought-iron railing. "Ah, be seated *Señor* Drexler. Be
seated. You were kind to come. Chocolate?"

Dutifully, David Florio Drexler removed his silver-
trimmed sombrero, handed it to Diego, and sat down.
He had first seen Fuentes three days earlier and, on
learning his history, was suitably impressed. The captain
moved with confidence, acted with flair and was obviously
a gentleman. When it was whispered that he, too, hated
Madero's egalitarian nonsense, David Drexler could hardly
contain his excitement, and he had sent a note requesting
an audience. Here was a man of action. Here was the man
he would emulate, and follow.

The fresh chocolate poured, Diego withdrew. "You
witnessed the arrival of my men?" Fuentes asked.

"Yes, Captain Fuentes."

"Some die, of course, but new ones always join. Have
a *sopapilla*. Their taste lingers on the tongue. I only
accept men of great courage." He gazed at the moun-

113

tains. "Are you and your friends such men?"

David Drexler proudly raised his head. "We are."

"Then you shall have the opportunity to prove yourselves. How is your father?"

"Well enough, I suppose." Young Drexler found it difficult to disguise his disgust. "I have not spoken to him for two days. He thinks more of the *peones* than his own son."

"Your father has always been known as a generous man—with other men's property," Fuentes added. "He and our current president have much in common." He paused. "Tell me, David—I may call you David?—who is the woman?"

"The woman?" Drexler asked, impressed anew. Fuentes knew everything.

"Your father's guest. There is a woman, is there not?"

"A *gringa*." His voice dripped with contempt.

"Her name?"

"Señora Van Allen. A friend of a friend, Father says."

Fuentes bolted upright in his chair. "Van Allen, did you say?"

"Yes."

"Her husband is here, too?"

"No. She's escorted by a *gringo* with hair the color of a carrot. A big-footed soldier masquerading as a reporter."

"A soldier?" Perplexed, Fuentes paced the balcony.

"Yes. I do not know how she became acquainted with my father. Perhaps through the *gringo* Maguire. They seemed to be old friends."

Fuentes leaned on the table. "What does Maguire have to do with this?" he asked, his mind racing.

"They talked together privately at my father's *comida*."

"Ah." Why was Van Allen here? To see Maguire? Maguire had lived in West Texas. Maguire knew Bortha. He knew Chihuahua as well as any *norteamericano*. Who better to send for her son? The possibility existed, which meant he had to warn Bortha as quickly as possible.

Unless. A nub of an idea. A surreptitious glance at David Drexler. It just might work. "Diego!"

The orderly hurried onto the balcony. "Yes, Captain."

"The case under my bed. Bring it." He popped a *sopapilla* into his mouth. "The chance to prove yourselves," he said around the bread.

"Sir?" David Drexler looked puzzled.

"The chance to prove yourselves has come sooner than I expected." Diego entered and placed a polished wood case on the table. "Thank you, Diego."

Fuentes opened the lid. Inside were three double action .38 caliber revolvers. Young Drexler stared at them, then at his host. "One for you," Fuentes said, "one for each of your two companions."

Reveling in self-importance, the youth picked up the nearest weapon. "Think you are capable of capturing a man and bringing him to me?" The plan just might work. Maguire would never suspect three pampered aristocratic brats.

"Yes."

"And you have been to *El Madronito?* Know where it is?" Fuentes went on.

"Yes."

"Good. Here is what I want you to do."

9

He'd known she would come. Felt it in his bones. Maguire peeked over the edge of the balcony wall. Corinne was standing at the base of the madrone and looking up into the twisting branches. Pealing church bells signaled the eighth hour of the day. A train wailed in the distance. The train to the north. If Maguire had had his way, Corinne would have been on it.

"Maguire!" Aurora shouted. "There is a *señora!*"

He ducked back inside so they wouldn't think he'd been watching. "I hear you," he called. "Give her some coffee and send up some hot water. I'll shave and be right down."

Damn! She was wearing the same sort of outfit when first he saw her—Levis and embroidered work shirt. He'd told her then she did something special to men's clothes. Almost thirteen years ago, he reminded himself.

Icy water waited in the basin. Maguire scrubbed his

face with cupped hands, wiped dry on a fresh towel and inspected himself in the mirror. Thirteen years. Best not to count the wrinkles, he thought with a grimace.

Remedios entered with hot water. Aurora had altered one of her dresses for the girl. The effect bordered on the ridiculous, but at least she was covered. "The woman is your *querida?*" the girl asked, handing him the steaming pitcher.

"No." Maguire worked up a lather. "If she were, it would be none of your business."

The girl pouted, sat on the edge of the bed and watched him strop his razor. "Aurora says I must go to school," she said, testing the softness of the mattress.

"If you want to stay here, yes. And after school, you will help in the kitchen and sleep in Aurora's room until I can find a better place for you."

The springs creaked. Remedios stretched out on the bed and tried to look irresistible. "I will stay with you. I do not need school."

"You heard me, girl. Now downstairs with you. Father Julio will be free after his ten o'clock mass. You're to wait for him at the rectory. Tell him I sent you and want you to start school next week."

Eyes blazing, Remedios jumped to her feet. Maguire was shaving and paid no attention to her. The anger disappeared, replaced by a crafty look. "We will see, Maguire," she purred, and hurried from the room.

Corinne tapped a nervous finger against the coffee cup. Aurora, the cook, had told her she could wait in the courtyard if she wished. A strange place for Maguire, Corinne thought. He was a man who loved open spaces. Not the darkness of the nightclub. But her memories were thirteen years old, she reminded herself, and people change. She had. Everytime she passed a mirror she noticed and was reminded. Time had marked her. Not that it showed to the casual acquaintance. Her beauty was still undiminished. For that she was grateful, for she might well need it before the day was ended. But the laughing, winsome, carefree girl who had won and broken the hearts of Washington beaus was gone. And thankfully so. Corinne possessed a determination that Washington belle had never thought existed. And yet, there was a sadness to the passing of youthful illusions. But that's what they were. And realities needed dealing with now. Realities like the loss of her son. Realities like being in Mexico, here at long last with Maguire. It frightened her. But not enough to leave.

Footsteps clattered on the stone stairway. "You look like a wealthy Texan," she said, rising.

Maguire tugged at the cuffs of his coat, a western-cut affair of brushed doeskin. Dark striped trousers, white shirt and string tie completed the image. He doffed his flat brimmed hat. "Thank you, ma'am," he drawled.

Was he making fun of her or happy to see her? No doubt he knew precisely why she'd come. Corinne smiled and posed. "And will I shock the natives?"

Intricate stitchery coiled down her sleeves. Hair radiant as spun gold caught the early morning light and brightened the shadowed courtyard. Tooled fawn-colored boots peeked out from under tailored and crisply pressed, brass-studded men's pants. "I doubt it. They will decide you are the wife of a wealthy *gringo hacendado.*"

Corinne winced. "Is there someplace we can talk? Privately?"

"Again?" Maguire asked sarcastically.

"If I'd known Blue's presence was going to upset you, I wouldn't have asked him to be there. I'm sorry now that I did."

"Okay, Corinne. Okay. But no more protestations of innocence. Wait here." Five minutes later he emerged from the kitchen with a picnic basket over his shoulder. "Flour tortillas and chicken. And coffee. I haven't eaten since last night." Corinne followed him into the shed.

"Studebaker," he said proudly, throwing open the doors leading to the outside alley. "Here. Take the basket and get in."

Corinne climbed into the front seat and watched Maguire check the tank and add gas from a drum against the wall. He reached inside to set the spark and the throttle. "Like it?"

"It's beautiful. Wherever did you get it?"

"Card game." Without further explanation, he headed for the front of the car. A moment at the crank and the engine kicked into life. Maguire hopped behind the wheel.

"Here we go." With practiced ease, he backed out of the shed, down the alley and onto the busy Niza.

As they drove through the heart of the city Corinne managed to forget, for a brief span, why she'd come so far. No American city offered sights to compare with Mexico City. The shop-lined streets were crowded with wagons, carriages, automobiles and pedestrians. Beggars were stationed on each corner. In front of the cathedral, the poor and afflicted hobbled on bended knees toward the open doors to seek dispensations and favors from a presumably attentive God.

The *zócalo*, a vast square facing the ostentatiously ornate National Palace, was packed with humanity. Indians and mestizos—Spanish-Indian, Spanish-Negro, Indian-Negro and Anglo mixtures of them all—mingled with a cosmopolitan flux of Europeans, Scandinavians, North Americans and Japanese. A confusion of languages filled the air.

They drove on past overturned carts surrounded by swirling, heated arguments, and through flocks of sheep and herds of bleating goats. Everywhere crowds of half-dressed children appeared as if by magic and, all smiles and laughs in spite of their obvious poverty, gawked at Corinne and begged pennies from Maguire.

The Studebaker eased past a bicycling boy carrying baskets of bread piled high on his back and a sixth balanced on his head, then waited for a heavyset man crying,

"Tripa, tripa!" as he pushed a rickety cart full of pungent, steaming entrails across their path. A proud Indian, with a dozen brightly plumaged wild birds in individual cages attached to his back by an elaborate tangle of string and rope, strode alongside them for nearly half a block. Mournful piping accompanied his passage through the streets.

On one corner, a girl balanced a huge circular platter of delicate white cakes and tried to avoid a quartet of impatient six-year-olds bent on mischief. A smiling priest ignored their presence, as did a hawk-faced entrepreneur prowling the streets and looking for unwary tourists. Outstretched arms draped with an array of brightly colored *serapes* and heavy woolen *rebozos*, the hawk-faced man resembled an unlikely merchant Christ pulled from his crucifix.

The fringes of the city were bleak, festering sores of humanity housed in makeshift huts made of any available material. The road deteriorated rapidly into a series of water and mud-filled ruts and holes. Children dressed in rags, pregnant mothers and out-of-work fathers stared dully at the car as it passed. Embarrassed but intrigued, Corinne found herself staring back in fascination.

Finally the city lay behind them and they were speeding along Tlalpan, the main road between Mexico City and Puebla to the southeast. The road climbed gently and the air in the open front of the Studebaker became chilly. When Maguire realized Corinne was uncomfortable, he stopped to get a blanket from the enclosed passenger seat. A half mile farther up the road they came to an abandoned truck with two putty-flat tires. On the back, painted in brilliant crimson, was the slogan, "What has been." Corinne turned as they passed. "What will come," she read aloud.

Maguire shook his head. "That's Mexico for you. What *is* would keep the damned truck running."

Corinne settled back, let the fresh air wash over her. The blanket was warm, the throbbing sound of the motor pleasant. She dozed off and suddenly the car was tilting and they had turned onto a side road leading to a long winding shrub- and tree-lined lane. Ten minutes later, Maguire guided the auto between a pair of giant cedars and shut off the engine.

Neither moved for a moment. Then Maguire jumped down, crossed to the passenger side of the car and helped Corinne out. As he reached for the blanket, his coat fell open and she caught a glimpse of the polished wood grip of a Browning automatic jutting from a leather shoulder holster. Corinne had abhorred guns ever since the night Lee was shot, yet she could say nothing. The irony of the situation struck her. A gun had crippled Lee: only a gun could effect Christopher's return.

Side by side, they walked through the hushed gardens overrun with creepers and vines and roots. Cypress, oak and pine towered overhead. Berried juniper and dormant mimosas growing willy-nilly broke the path into a maze. Leaves, spear- and fan-shaped, elongated, clumpy, elephantine, reedlike and lacy, wove a tapestry of green that sequestered them from the outside world. Maguire took her hand and helped her climb onto the trunk of a giant, fallen Ponderosa pine. Below them a lake lay jewel-like among the trees. Mirrored islands drifted on the surface. As they watched, a single flat-bottomed boat poled by a young man in white drifted into view. His companion reclined gracefully in the bow and trailed her fingers in the crystal clear, amethyst water. "It's beautiful," Corinne whispered.

"Xochimilco," Maguire said, emphasizing the Z sound of the Mexican X.

Corinne jumped off the tree trunk and sat on the sloping bank. Maguire hesitated, then sat next to her and opened the picnic basket. "It means 'field of flowers,'" he explained between bites of tortilla smothered with a fiery aromatic sauce and wrapped about slices of chicken. "The islands were once immense woven baskets filled with earth and planted with crops. The roots eventually grew down into the lake bed. By the time the baskets rotted away, the islands were established."

"You know so much about the place."

"I come here often." He poured two cups full of coffee. "Sometimes alone, sometimes with a friend. Coffee?"

"Thank you." He was being spiteful but she refused to be jealous. "You haven't asked about Lee."

"I figured you'd tell me when you were ready."

"He uses a cane. As long as he doesn't overtax himself, he manages."

"Old Harvard Van Allen took me in. Gave a scrawny thirteen-year-old half-breed a home and a family. Raised me as his own." Maguire shook his head sadly. "And how do I pay him back? By sleeping with his daughter-in-law and crippling his son. Isn't that a hell of a note?"

"Mr. Van Allen is dead."

"I know. But some things even death doesn't erase."

"I like to think what we felt needed no forgiveness." Corinne lay back on the soft grass. Rearranging, redefining themselves, lofty cumulus clouds drifted behind Maguire's battleworn face. How easy for clouds. "I'm sorry for what happened, but I can't condemn us, Maguire."

Maguire poured more coffee and changed the subject. "I talked to one of Madero's aides yesterday afternoon and I don't think it will help to talk with Madero himself. He's too preoccupied, to begin with. More importantly Bortha would probably refuse to comply for the simple reason he detests taking orders. If that happened, Madero would have to do something drastic, and right now he's in no position to do anything more drastic than blow his nose."

"You really don't care, do you?" Corinne said wearily.

"What am I supposed to do, Corinne?" Maguire asked in exasperation. "Call up the army? Storm Bortha's *hacienda*, grab the boy and shoot my way out?"

"Yes. If that's what it takes."

"I can't."

"I can pay. In any currency you suggest." Her eyes were soft, gazed frankly into his. Her lips, moist and slightly parted, beckoned. More than anything else, he wanted to catch and hold her to him. "Any currency, Maguire," she emphasized in a husky voice that recalled shared intimacies.

Payment. She could talk so callously about payment. And to Maguire, who had had so often been accused of cynicism, if not downright cold-bloodedness. The one woman he'd ever loved was offering her body in payment for his ability to fight. He pushed away from her. "No. Not by a long shot, lady. Not that way. Forget it."

The light in Corinne's eyes changed from passion to anger. Maguire stood and started back for the car. Corinne rolled onto her stomach. "Maguire!" He didn't stop.

"Damn you!" Her fingers dug into the earth. Then she was on her feet, racing after him and catching him in the middle of the enclosed glade. She planted herself in his path and took a photograph from her shirt pocket. "Look at him."

"Corinne . . . "

"Look at him!"

Maguire looked. Wide, sensitive eyes stared back at him. Dark hair. High cheekbones. A lean kid, tough and ill at ease in coat and tie. A touch of the hellion. Maybe ten, eleven years old.

Mesmerized, Maguire raised the picture and tilted it so the sun wouldn't glare off the paper. His pulse was racing and the back of his neck felt clammy, because he knew. There had probably been others over the years, but he hadn't given them much thought because he'd never seen them, never cared. Now, looking into those eyes . . .

"That's right, Maguire. Christopher is your son."

I didn't want to tell you, she explained to herself only. Corinne sat alone in the Studebaker and watched

124

Maguire move among the trees. She had imagined him often during the years of their separation, tried to analyze while remembering what had drawn her to him. The aura of suppressed violence, first, she was forced to concede. Next, the contradictory gentleness. Why hadn't she told him earlier, at Drexler's *comida*? But how was she supposed to? How admit she'd kept his son a secret from him until the boy was in danger?

Time had forged its own answers long before Corinne asked the question. Lee had taken her only a few times, passionlessly, after Maguire left. After that, though she still loved him, their conversations became short and to the point, utilitarian and sterile. They no longer shared a bed. Corinne could not blame Lee and, as a self-imposed penance, drove herself to become a model wife. When the child was born, she found herself incapable of telling the truth, for the truth would have been too painful. A man like Lee needed a son, and she could not deny him. Not after Maguire. As a result, Corinne remained silent and pretended, to herself and the rest of the world, that her marriage was complete and wholesome. Only at night, alone in the bed large enough for two, did she dare recall Maguire. Sometimes, when her body ached for him, she wept because he was gone from her life and she would never see him again.

Until the *rurales* stole Christopher and Lee disappeared. Only then did she break her vow and seek out Maguire, for the debt he owed her was greater than the debt she owed Lee.

A shadow fell across the seat as Maguire reached inside to adjust the throttle and spark. "I wasn't pretending, Maguire. I admit I was trying to use what we once had, but the need was there. I wasn't pretending about that." He didn't answer. A moment later, when he turned the crank and the motor coughed into fitful life, a flash of birds scattered in fright from a nearby juniper. Funny, she thought. She hadn't even noticed they were there.

"Your things are at Drexler's?"

"Yes," she answered.

"I'll let you off there." He stared at the field of flowers he might never see again. "Monday morning we will catch the train north."

"Maguire, I . . . "

"We'll be together as far as Chihuahua. You'll continue on to Presidio."

"And you?"

He put the Studebaker in reverse, backed into a tight arc and guided them out the winding path over which they'd come in. "I'll need a week, maybe ten days. If I haven't brought him out by then, you'll know I failed."

He concentrated on the road. Corinne sensed the change in him. Tight-lipped, sober, introspective. He had not returned the photograph. Wisely she refrained from asking for it. At last they emerged from the trees. The sky was bright and clear. No shadows darkened their path. To right and left, slumbering fields lay on slopes eager for spring and hoe and maize.

When the Studebaker topped the last rise before the junction with Tlalpan, they saw the soldiers. How many on horse and foot was hard to say, for the file extended beyond the quarter mile of open road. A flurry of activity indicated the car had been seen. By the time it reached the junction, an officer riding a brown mare blocked the way. Maguire loosened the Browning and braked to a stop a few feet in front of the horse. A dozen rifles were pointed at him.

"Your names, please," the officer demanded.

More horses approached. Maguire considered fabricating an identity but quickly gave up the idea. The chance he might be recognized was too great. "Maguire. What is happening?"

"This road is closed to all traffic," the officer said.

What outfit this was, and why it was marching on the city, Maguire was not sure. Something was afoot, though. There was no legitimate reason for their being denied passage. "But we are expected back in the city for a dinner party," he lied.

"You will have to forget your party for today, I think."

A thin reed of an officer, arrow straight in the saddle, guided a high-stepping stallion toward the car. "What is the problem, Major Quirozco?"

The major snapped to attention. "Colonel Serrano. These two seek to pass. I believe they should be taken into custody."

"Now, see here, friend," Maguire protested. "My companion is Muriel Elaine Hearst of the California Hearsts. Surely you have heard of them, Colonel. Mrs. Hearst is a guest of Ambassador Wilson. I'd hate to think of what would happen if the ambassador's guest were kidnapped on the road. Why, a colonel could lose his . . . "

"That will be enough." Serrano inspected Maguire closely, leaned over to peer at Corinne. "Your name, madam?" he asked.

Corinne glanced at Maguire as if she didn't understand. When he translated, she smiled broadly. "Mrs. Muriel Hearst, of California," she answered slowly, and with a charming smile.

Colonel Serrano bowed low, swept his hat across his chest. It was necessary to remain in Ambassador Wilson's good graces. Especially when the magic name of Hearst was mentioned. "My humblest apologies, madam," he said in school-book English. "A grave error has been made. Please accept my most humble apologies."

"You are very kind, Colonel," Corinne said with a gracious, even regal, inclination of her head. "I will remember to mention your gallantry to Ambassador Wilson."

"The pleasure has been mine, madam." The colonel twitched the reins. The stallion, magnificently trained, pawed the earth, tossed his head and backed away. "Let them pass, Major," Serrano commanded, reverting to Spanish.

Quirozco knew he would be reprimanded, but his face

was impassive. "Let them pass!" he ordered, at the same time wheeling his horse out of the path.

Maguire drove onto the main road and, at top speed, roared past the troops. When they had left the column a safe distance behind, he exhaled slowly.

"What was that all about?" Corinne asked shakily.

"I don't know. But I've seen that colonel before." He grinned. "How'd you know Muriel Hearst had a southern accent?"

Corinne looked aghast at him. "You mean there's a real? . . . You didn't! What if . . . "

Maguire's laughter cut her short. "Hell, I don't know. I just made up Muriel Elaine and tacked on the most impressive last name I could think of. Hearst seemed to fill the bill."

His laughter was infectious, and soon Corinne had joined him. "You're impossible, Maguire. Really, Muriel Elaine!" She stopped laughing. Maguire's face was creased with a new set of worry lines. "What is it?"

"That was Colonel Hebert Juliano Serrano. He and his men are supposed to be garrisoned in Puebla."

Corinne stared at him. They had enough troubles without Maguire inventing more. "So?"

"Puebla is one hundred and fifty miles away," he said. Snatches of his last conversation with Gustavo Madero raced through his head. And more. The silent men and missing women at Drexler's *comida*. The rumors carried by Lucca and others. Fuentes's presence in Mexico City. Maguire's hands gripped the wheel and he drove with renewed concentration. "And I can't think of a single good reason why they're only twenty miles outside Mexico City."

They approached the broken-down truck on the road. The scarlet letters emblazoned on the front bumper took a new and ominous meaning.

What will come.

10

The woman cajoled, the woman pleaded in strident, emotion-packed Spanish. How could the *norteamericano* be so heartless? Did he not see how poor she was? Could he not see the destitute misery in which her children were forced to eke out their wretched lives? She yanked on his sleeve until he followed her behind a rickety stall to a patched and ragged tent over which a crude roof of salvaged boards had been erected. Restrained from more extensive exploration by a rope partition, a host of yapping dogs and squalling children played inside. The oldest child couldn't have been more than four years old.

"Thirteen!" Blue muttered, counting again to make sure.

The woman nodded vigorously, as if he'd uttered a pearl of wisdom, and held out her hands in supplication.

"Thirteen?" They couldn't all be hers.

Tears streamed from the woman's deepset eyes, pooled

129

in the dark hollows beneath her lower lids and over-flowed onto the flood plains of her cheeks. Her voice, broken by sobs, wailed and wailed and wailed. Blue finally surrendered. Digging deep in his pockets, he found a single peso, hurriedly slapped it into her palm and ran. The woman followed him, shouting his praises.

Blue plunged through the marketplace, the woman close behind, holding aloft a soda bottle doll with a straw head. Red-faced, wanting only to escape the amused expressions of the other vendors, he ducked around a corner and into a tiny coffee shop. Not to be denied, the woman followed and placed the doll on his table. Satisfied at last, she disappeared.

The hot, sweet coffee cost him his last centavo, but he didn't care because he was so tired. He had no idea of what time he'd run from the nauseating scene with the little whore, less of where he'd gone afterward. Sometime before dawn, near collapse with fatigue, he'd found a sheltered corner in a park and slept a few hours. When he woke up the sun was high. Half starved, mouth tasting as foul as the littered streets, he found a small café. A half hour later, belly full and spirits restored, he set out in earnest to explore. Luckily the morning passed without incident. He didn't think about getting back until he heard bells chiming noon, and then he got held up by the crazy woman with all the kids.

Unfortunately news of his munificence had spread, and when he finished the coffee, four little boys waiting outside the door preceded him backward down the street. Each extolled the superiority of his shoe-shining ability. When Blue couldn't take their incessant pleas any longer, he stopped and yanked his pockets inside out. The boys stared at the empty linings, then down at his boots. Their faces turned angry, as if each had been suddenly robbed of a fortune. Showering him with a dozen scornful epithets, they scurried off like a pack of dogs searching for new game. Blue shook his head in despair, turned to leave and ran smack into the corner of a vending table. Bending double in pain, he watched, horrified, as a half dozen hog heads rolled into the dusty street.

The vendor raced out of his stall and called on his patron saint to smite the lumbering *gringo*. "Ten pesos! Ten pesos!" he demanded, snatching one of the bloodless heads by the snout and shaking it in front of Blue's face.

Blue stared at the severed neck. Suddenly he was angry. "No," he said, tired of being a victim of a bunch of crazy Mexicans not a one of whom could speak English except to demand money. He grabbed the head from the vendor and slammed it onto the table, knocking off another two or three in the process.

A crowd gathered. Someone laughed. The butcher's pride was at stake. Howling with rage, he reached for a long iron meat hook. A woman screamed. Blue whirled and clamped his hand over the vendor's. The vendor tried to raise the hook, tried to budge the makeshift weapon, but couldn't.

Face grim, Bue pulled the offending hand away and took the hook. Gripping it in both hands, he exerted his full strength. His neck swelled, blood drained from his fingers and the muscles along his arms knotted. Slowly the hook straightened and Blue stabbed the spike into the table.

The butcher stared slack-jawed at his new ice pick. Thoroughly cowed, demands forgotten, he kneeled and began picking up the other heads and placing them back on the table. He wanted nothing more to do with the awesome giant. Behind him the tortilla woman, the man with the birds, the sombrero woman, the potion and herb woman and all their friends began to cheer. When Blue realized they were cheering him and laughing at the butcher, a momentary sense of elation seized him and he clasped his hands over his head.

The sight of a hunchbacked, toothless, one-armed old woman brought him to his senses. The elation evaporated and he hurried from the market. To hell with the story. It had been a bad idea in the first place and wasn't working out anyway. What he'd do is use his ticket back to the good old U.S. of A., find a job and build up another bankroll. He could pick up his gear from Drexler and . . .

"Damn!" He stopped dead in the street. A passerby collided with him from the rear, mumbled an apology in Japanese and hurried on.

He'd left his typewriter at Maguire's. He toyed with the idea of asking Drexler to send someone for it, but quickly decided not to. Patrick Henry Blue wasn't going to hide behind anybody. Not anymore. "The hell with Maguire," he said out loud. Shoulders hunched and fists knotted, he set off to find *El Madronito*.

The Studebaker protested a tight turn. Hard rubber wheels clipped the curb and bounced the automobile into the middle of the street where it almost sideswiped a trolley. Corinne grimaced and shied away from the door as the car sped past a gaggle of gawking villagers from outlying areas. Landless peasants, they had come to the city to carve for themselves a piece of the promised pie of prosperity. Their hopes for a new life waited behind wide, frightened eyes; waited in awestruck children; waited in the protruding bellies swollen with unborn sons and daughters; waited in meager sacks of ragged clothing and bags of parched corn and dried beans.

Maguire played the car down the center of the street, weaving between and narrowly missing a steamed-corn vendor and a pair of frock-coated gentlemen. A hard right onto San Juan followed by a swift left brought them to Avenida Juarez.

The encounter with the soldiers weighed heavily on his mind. Of course there might be a perfectly innocent explanation for Serrano's presence. Madero could have ordered him to ride north to bolster the capital's security. But that didn't wash. Serrano had been a confirmed

Porfirista, an outspoken opponent of the Revolution and all it stood for. Other men of unquestionable loyalty— Pimiento in Oaxaca and Guzman in Durango, to name only two—were available.

Speeding alongside Chapultepec Park, following the winding, tree-lined narrow road he and Lucca had taken the day before, Maguire headed for Drexler's home. If anyone would have some answers, Anthony Drexler would. The iron gates at the end of the drive were uncharacteristically closed. Maguire stopped and squeezed the horn bulb. When no one arrived to admit them he climbed out of the car.

"I can walk from here," Corinne offered.

"Stay put," Maguire said, opening the gate. "I need to talk to Drexler." The car sped up the drive and skidded to a gravel-rattling halt at the bottom of the broad front steps. No one answered his knock. Trying to appear casual, Maguire peered through the iron grillework that protected the front windows. "Not a soul," he said, perplexed.

"But that's ridiculous," Corinne protested.

"I know. Come on. We'll look around some. Stay close."

"Maguire, I . . . "

"Just stay close," he ordered curtly. The wrong smell. The wrong feel. Twenty years of danger taught a man to know. As unobtrusively as possible, he unbuttoned his coat and drew the automatic.

All the downstairs windows were shuttered. No sign of gardeners. No activity on the lawns or in the garages. The side doors were closed and locked, as were those in back. One shutter swung free. Maguire lifted Corinne so she could see in. Nothing.

"He couldn't have just left," Corinne said, a little scared. "That doesn't make sense. My clothes, Blue's. No. He must have stepped out for a while."

"And released the servants?" Maguire asked, waving his arm in an all-inclusive circle.

133

"Possibly. Maybe he gave them a special holiday. What else could have happened?"

"He could have been taken."

Corinne took a step backward. "But by whom?"

"Come on. Let's get out of here."

"Maguire . . . " He grabbed her wrist, pulled her along with him and helped her into the auto. The drive sloped down. Maguire let the Studebaker roll and let out the clutch. The engine turned over, started. They picked up speed rapidly. Royal homes, shaded and cool, flitted past. Little boys and girls in stiff suits and flowery print dresses strolled with dark-skinned nannies whose job was to guard, wash, feed and often times provide parental love. Corinne gripped the handhold. "Maguire?" she asked again, frightened as much by the look on his face as by Drexler's disappearance. "What's happening?"

"I don't know."

They headed for *El Madronito*. The normal procedure was to drive straight into the shed. But because he was disturbed by Serrano's presence and Drexler's absence, Maguire took the precaution of backing down the alley so, if the need arose, he could drive straight out. Before they left the shed, he slammed shut and barred the heavy timber outside doors.

Aurora's shrill voice spilled into the courtyard. Maguire didn't envy whoever had incurred her wrath. He and Corinne hurried through the kitchen and into the casino proper. "Blue!" Corinne exclaimed, rushing across the room to give him a friendly hug. "What happened? Have you see Anthony Drexler?"

Blue paid her no attention. Looking as imposing as a colossus, he stabbed an angry finger in Aurora's direction. "She works for you, Maguire. You talk to her. I'll be damned if I can."

Scrawny and scrappy as a gamecock, Aurora blocked the stairway. Even with Maguire in the room she refused to move. "It is a matter of principle now!" she proclaimed in rapid Spanish. "This big-footed *gringo* can't tell me what to do!"

"What'd she say?" Blue asked.

"That you have big feet and can't tell her what to do," Maguire translated.

Blue glanced down. "Big feet? I'll big feet her," he yelled, thoroughly exasperated. "You tell her she's . . . "

He got no further. Hands on hips, head thrust forward, Aurora assailed him with a string of imaginative curses so complex Maguire failed to catch them all. The important ones were enough, though, and he began to laugh.

"Laugh!" Aurora's eyes blazed and she turned her anger on Maguire. "You leave me to protect this miserable *pulqueria,* and then laugh? A big-footed, red-haired *gringo* calls me a blackened cookstove and threatens to cut off my hands and you laugh?"

Maguire looked at Blue. "Did you say that, Patrick Henry?"

"What?" Blue suddenly looked worried. "What'd she say?"

"That you said she was a blackened cookstove and you were going to cut off her hands."

Blue stared at Maguire, then at Aurora, and back to Maguire. "Did I really say that?" he asked plaintively.

"Must have."

"I *thought* I asked her where my typewriter was."

"In Spanish?"

"Well, yeah. That and English. You said it would be safe, and I need it, and . . . Now look here!"

Maguire chuckled. "It's upstairs. I put it there for safe-keeping. Go on and get it."

"I will." Blue started for the stairs and stopped. Aurora still blocked his way. "Do you think you could, uh, tell her it was a mistake?"

Maguire translated, explained that the *gringo* admitted he had big feet, was sorry that his Spanish was so bad, and wanted to get his typewriter.

135

"No!" Aurora yelled, stamping her foot and refusing to be placated.

"Move!" Maguire said, getting tired of the whole mess.

"No."

Maguire took three steps, grabbed Aurora by the waist and threw her over his shoulder. "Get your damned typewriter," he said between his teeth. Aurora was pounding on his back. Maguire crossed the casino, deposited her in the hall and shut the door. When he turned, Blue was staring at him. "Well? What are you waiting for? It's under a chair to the left of the door."

Blue hesitated as if to speak, then stomped up the stairs.

"Jesus!" Maguire stepped around the bar and drew a cold beer from the keg chilled by ice carted from the mountains. "What're *you* laughing at?" he asked Corinne. "Never mind. Don't say it." He blew the foam off the top of the mug at the same time a shot rang out from upstairs.

"Jesus!" They heard Blue bellow.

Maguire tore up the stairs and kicked open the door in time to see Blue toss Dauphine onto the bed and wrest a derringer from her hand. Dauphine fought back, kicking and trying for his eyes with her nails. Blue pinned one wrist, missed the other and fell flat on top of her. Dauphine changed tactics. Dress riding over her thighs, she wrapped her legs around him and, mimicking copulation, thrust her pelvis against him.

"Hey! What'd'ya' . . . "

Dauphine all but swallowed him in a kiss. Totally confused, the reporter released her, freed himself from her embrace and, in full retreat, scrambled from the bed. Dauphine laughed triumphantly. Her eyes riveted Corinne with a hateful stare as the blond woman entered the room. "The gun was for her," she hissed at Maguire. "Or you. I'm sorry I missed!"

A trickle of blood ran down Blue's face where the

bullet—or one of Dauphine's fingernails—had nicked him. "Christ!" he repeated, dabbing at his cheek and staring at the blood on his kerchief. "Everybody in this goddam city is crazy!"

Dauphine dug inside her bodice, tore a key from its chain around her neck and threw it on the floor. Head tilted imperiously, she adjusted her skirts and stalked out via the balcony.

"You okay, Patrick Henry?" Maguire said after the door slammed.

"I guess so," Blue responded, touching his cheek again. "She's crazy. Just shot without warning."

"You're alive." Maguire yanked Blue's typewriter from underneath the chair. "Here."

"Thanks." He stared from Corinne to Maguire and back. "Well. I guess I'd better get back to Drexler's place."

"I wouldn't advise that," Maguire said.

"I'm not sure I'll ever follow your advice again, Maguire," Blue countered belligerently.

"He's right, Blue," Corinne, said, emerging from her shock at Dauphine's behavior. And at Dauphine.

"Why?"

"I'll explain downstairs," Maguire said. "Come on. You look like you could use a beer."

A mystified, intrigued Blue, prodded by Corinne, had decided to stay at the casino. Maguire, impeccably attired in pin-striped coat and trousers, a black silk ascot at his throat and ever present cane in hand, took them later in the evening to dine at a Japanese restaurant owned by a friend. As they ate Maguire told Corinne they'd head north on the Monday morning train. He would leave the train in Chihuahua and Blue could accompany Corinne the rest of the way to the ranch. Blue decided then and there he'd be with Maguire when the action started, but wisely refrained from saying so until a more propitious time.

They returned to *El Madronito* before midnight. Corinne scolded Maguire the length of the journey for dressing so elegantly while she was unable to complement his attire with something from her own wardrobe still at Drexler's. Maguire's excuse, that Mexico City was a city of diversity, only made her more displeased. Eventually he apologized. She wasn't sure he meant it.

At *El Madronito,* a small but subdued crowd gathered around favorite tables. *Señor* Sanchez and his son-in-law continued their marathon at the chess board. A fat German sat alone in a corner and stared into a glass of *schnapps.* A pair of young bloods impressed with their fathers' wealth and their own growing importance, sipped Napoleon Five Star and conversed in hushed tones. The door opened and the aging but still active owner of Court Haven, one of Chapultepec Park's most distinctive mansions, entered, flanked by a lovely *señorita* on each arm.

"Good evening, *Señor* Danton," Cecilia, the waitress, purred, immediately guiding the threesome to a table near the piano. Payton quickly segued into the wealthy Englishman's favorite song and received an appreciative nod that bespoke a handsome tip later on.

DuClerc was having a bad evening. Fully aware that when the cards were bad they were very, very bad, he had left the table when the five hundred pesos with which he started each night ran out. A consumptive cough racked the Frenchman's body as he approached Maguire's table and bowed. He dabbed his lips with a lace-bordered handkerchief. "Your pardon, madam."

"No sheep to be sheared?" Maguire asked.

"I am afraid I was the lamb tonight." The gambler shrugged eloquently. "Another night. The cards always turn." He fingered the gold watch chain hanging across his vest.

They went through the watch chain ritual every time DuClerc ran out of cash. "Forget it," Maguire said. "Your credit is good. Have Seifert fix you up."

DuClerc brightened. "You are sitting," he said gallantly to Corinne and Blue, "with the last of a dying breed, *monsieur et madam.*" Nodding his thanks to Maguire, he started for the bar. Seifert was already filling a glass.

"Poor Maguire," Corinne said, a little tipsily. "Gone the way of the buffalo."

"Not yet, Mrs. Van Allen." He stood to greet three newly arrived couples who headed immediately for the roulette table. The table was strictly for the clientele, and operated by whomever chose to play. Maguire could never be accused of cheating because he never lost or won—except for the handsome profit on the drinks the players invariably bought.

"It doesn't work, you know," Corinne added as soon as Maguire sat.

"What?" he asked absentmindedly.

"The tailored coat, fancy shirt and pin-striped trousers. Not to speak of the bowler."

"Bad manners," Blue chimed in, his tongue loosened by fatigue and one too many whiskey sours. "Shouldn't wear your hat inside."

"It's called building a tradition. When Maguire's hat is on he's the host and you're in good hands." All of which would be interrupted by the trip north, he thought. Seifert would have to take over. Two or three weeks—three at the most—and he'd be back.

"In your case, clothes don't make the man." Corinne sighed. "The real you shines through."

"I can only try," Maguire said dryly, his mind on what would happen during his absence. Seifert and Aurora got along. Lucca might be a problem—he'd drink the place half dry—but could be depended on for protection. Unless the Italian could be talked into keeping him company. A word to one of Gustavo's aides might be a good idea, in that case.

The door opened and David Florio Drexler entered. "David!" Maguire called, rising and hurrying to intercept him.

"*Buenos noches*," David said formally.

"Your father. Is he ill?" Maguire knew damned well he wasn't, but a polite inquiry seemed appropriate.

"No."

"I drove *Señora* Van Allen to your house this afternoon, but no one was there. Not even the servants. I hope nothing is wrong."

"My father orders his household as he pleases. He does not confide in me. Now if you'll excuse me, I have friends waiting." David stepped around Maguire and crossed to the table where the two rich young men rose to greet him.

Maguire turned to the bar and signaled Seifert. "Three fresh ones for my table. And cut theirs a little," he added, nodding toward Drexler's table. Every kid was entitled to a few years of ingratitude before time taught him the meaning of responsibility, but Maguire was in no mood for insolence or misleading answers. The afternoon's worries pushed in on him, then faded as Seifert set the drinks on the table.

"Here we are," Maguire said, trying to recapture his optimism. "Gin and tonic for the lady, whiskey sour for the gentleman and straight tequila for the one whose light shines through. How about a toast?" Corinne and Blue dutifully raised their glasses. "To a successful journey," he said.

"And the reunion of loved ones," Corinne added, meeting Maguire's gaze.

Blue drank. "Don't worry. We'll get him," he slurred.

"We?" Maguire's shoulders tensed.

"Well, yeah," Blue stammered, wanting to kick himself for letting the cat out of the bag. Nothing to be done but press on, though. "I'm going with you."

"Right. As far as Chihuahua."

"Wrong. To Bortha's ranch."

"The hell you are." Maguire's voice had turned cold and dangerous.

"There's a story and I mean to have it. An opportunity like this comes once in a lifetime."

Corinne hadn't moved. Maguire leaned across the table. "You only die once in a lifetime, too. Now you listen to me, kid. I pick the men I fight with, and I base my choice on a hell of a lot more than how capable they are with one of these." He tapped the typewriter case Blue kept in sight at all times. "What the hell good is that thing anyway?"

"You're being too hard on him, Maguire," Corinne interrupted. "I've traveled with Blue and found him a most resourceful companion."

"Oh, Christ!"

"I can speak for myself," Blue whispered hoarsely.

"Sure. Out of ignorance. The men you'll meet would as soon open your throat as look at you. I've seen Fuentes and his *Serpientes* do it. Tie a man down, slit his throat and dance on him just to watch the juice spurt." Blue paled but Maguire didn't relent. "So what are you going to do if they corner you? Throw a damn typewriter at them?" He snorted derisively. "I'll take Lucca and his shotgun every time."

Blue lowered his eyes and stared at the cherry in his whiskey sour. Maguire's logic was overpowering.

From the dim past, Maguire recalled a time when an older man had said much the same thing to him—and every bit as brutally. Hurt and ashamed, he'd hung his head as Blue did now. "Look, Blue, I know how you feel, but this water's hotter'n you're used to. If I have to rub your face in the truth, I will. I have to have confidence in the people around me. I can't afford to spend time worrying about how they'll react or when they'll break. This isn't a training expedition. A boy's life is at stake." His eyes met the unplumbed depths of Corinne's. "Ah, hell, I'm too sober." He sighed.

Maguire pushed away from the table and headed for the bar, then stopped dead in his tracks as the sound of distant explosions cut through the hum of conversation. All talk stopped. Mexico City had felt that trouble was imminent, had waited and watched for it as men who expect a storm cast their eyes skyward. There would be no more waiting. The storm had come at last. Everyone paused, frozen in place as he or she listened to the deadly reverberations. Payton, fingers poised above the keyboard, at the piano. Danton, the English Lord, one hand raised to summon Cecilia. His companions, the beauties, false smiles lighting their faces, leaning toward him. The gamblers, eyes slitted as they peeked at a new deal. Cecilia, lifting a tray of drinks. The chess players, old gentleman and wife-weary son-in-law, in studious concentration. Seifert polishing a glass. Maguire reaching over the walnut bar, hand closed around a fresh bottle of tequila.

The cannon fire died out, replaced by the fading hum of the roulette wheel and the final click of the ball. In the ensuing silence, David Drexler and his two friends rose, yanked identical .38 revolvers from under their coats and pointed them at Maguire.

Blue reacted automatically. Grabbing the typewriter case, he hurled it at Drexler. In the same instant, Corinne screamed, "Maguire!"

Maguire spun away from the bar just as young Drexler fired. The shot was wide of the mark because the typewriter case slammed into his side and knocked him sprawling over a table. Seifert hit the deck. Maguire leaped over the bar. A second bullet whined past his head and shattered a bottle of crème de menthe. Blue flipped over the table, grabbed Corinne and pulled her to the floor. Drexler's friends, seeing their leader down, backed toward the door, emptying their guns into the casino as they went.

Frantic patrons screamed and crawled for cover. Bullets shattered glass vases from Chihuahua and pottery from Oaxaca. One or two found and mangled living flesh. Outside, easily heard through the now open door, a thunder of cannons erupted again.

Hoofbeats sounded in the street as the killers fled. Panic-stricken, the casino's remaining patrons ran for safety. Only two remained. Danton, the Englishman, lay dying of a heart attack. His companions, before exiting, stripped the rings from his fingers as he had stripped them of honor. A bullet had freed *Señor* Sanchez from his long-suffering son-in-law. The old man lay, in death, across a chess board strewn with knights and bishops.

Maguire threw David into a chair and splashed water on his face. He nudged the dented typewriter case that had saved his life. "I guess it was good for something after all. I've been wrong before. Thanks."

Pleased, Blue nodded and reached down to help Corinne to her feet.

David Drexler sputtered awake. Suddenly aware of his plight and abysmal failure, he tried to run.

"Sit down." Maguire pushed him back into the chair and held the .38 in front of him. "Stay down. Where'd you get this? Whose idea was it?"

The youth gave him a mute, murderous look and shook his head, no. "Seifert! Throw me that bottle of ninety-five." A bottle of clear grain alcohol sailed through the air. Maguire caught it, knocked off the neck on the edge of the table and sloshed some of the alcohol in Drexler's lap. The youth watched as Seifert set a pitcher of water just out of reach, lit a match and handed it to Maguire.

"For the last time," Maguire said. "Whose idea was it?" Rifle and cannon fire rolled across the city.

David Drexler stared at the match. "You wouldn't . . ."

Maguire dropped the match in Drexler's lap. The alcohol caught fire immediately and the boy shot out of the chair. Maguire held him away from the water. "Whose?"

143

"Fuentes! Fuentes told me to bring you to him!" Maguire let him get the water. The youth doused himself. The coarse texture of his clothes had kept him from permanent damage. "Pig! Swine!"

Ignoring horrified looks from Corinne and Blue, Maguire shoved the youth into the chair again. "Now. What about your father? Where is he?" Drexler spat at him. Maguire picked up the alcohol and reached for a match.

"Fuentes has him!" he blurted.

Maguire shook his head in disbelief. "You let Jesus Fuentes take your own father? What kind of an animal are you?"

"It was for his own good. I let them in, and *Los Serpientes* took him into custody until the revolution is completed."

Serrano. All the other signs he'd ignored. "What revolution?" Maguire asked, dreading the answer.

"Ha! Are you deaf?" David Drexler's face shone with excitement.

Maguire cocked the pistol, held it a bare three inches in front of Drexler's nose. His finger tightened on the trigger.

"Don't, Maguire!" Corinne whispered in a shocked voice.

His finger loosened and he lowered the gun. "Get out. Because of your father, I'm giving you your life." He stepped back.

The youth stood shakily. The front of his trousers was scorched. Blisters showed through on patches of naked thigh. He backed toward the door and, finally convinced Maguire wasn't going to shoot him, turned and fled.

Maguire handed the .38 to Seifert and took a swallow of brandy. "Is everybody all right," he asked calmly, almost clinically. "Corinne? Patrick Henry?" Both nodded. One by one the others answered. Seifert. Payton. Cecilia. Duclerc. "What about Aurora?"

"She went to find the girl," Payton said from the hall

door. "I tried to stop her. Might as well have saved my breath."

"Remedios?" Maguire asked. "I thought she came back this afternoon."

"No."

"What time is it?"

"Two-thirty, three o'clock."

Maguire brushed remnants of shattered glass from a table, went to the door and listened. His movements seemed different, graceful, almost feline.

"Better plan on spending the rest of the night here," he said casually, and closed the door. Somehow, the gunfire seemed louder.

11

Remedios ran down the Street of the Owls. She was always running. First from a drunken uncle, who shamed her. Then when the others mocked her, from the village at the base of Malinche, the mountain named for a mistress. Or running from cold, from starvation, from horror. From the men she knelt before, or squatted over, in the Street of the Owls. And now down an unknown, ragged alley in a city torn by strife.

The lumbering nightmare who chased her guided his horse between and over stalls. Remedios had eluded his two companions but the horse was proving more difficult. If she took to the wide streets, the horse would surely run her down. If she kept to the alleys, she might run into a closed trap at any moment. She tried to think, but fear and fatigue clouded her brain, leaving her no option but blind, headlong flight.

Hoofbeats behind her. She rounded a pyramid of barrels and leaped a pile of shattered bottles. A hand caught her ankle and sent her tumbling against a nearby building. When she tried to get up, pain knifed through her left knee and she collapsed onto the filth-covered bricks. Panting, sobbing, she tried to crawl. Rough hands caught her, threw her to the ground and pinned her shoulders.

"In here, Suarez!" a man with a strange accent called.

Remedios could not see, only heard the horse enter the alley and the sound of boots crunching broken glass as the rider dismounted. "That you, Elrecht?"

"*Ya*. Be careful. He wants her unharmed."

"I know. Tie her." A coiled rope hit her buttocks. Rough hands grabbed her wrists, tied them together and then rolled her over. Eyes wide with fear, Remedios looked into the faces of her captors. The one named Suarez leaned over, reached beneath her blouse and squeezed her breasts. "She feels firm," he muttered, a loathsome light in his eyes.

Remedios tried to bite his wrist. Suarez slapped her face, caught her jaw and forced her lips into a pout. "Ah, a real little alley cat. My friend and I have seen you on the Street of the Owls, no? Maybe I let you drink my milk also."

"She'd probably bite it off," Elrecht snorted in disgust. "Out of the way." He lifted Remedios, carried her to the horse and flung her over the saddle. A face appeared in the window above them. Suarez cursed and fired at the observer. No one else cared to see what was happening in the alley.

Helpless, Remedios cried out against the pain that washed through her body. One of the men hit the sole of her feet with something hard. She knew then that she must remain still.

The night blurred and she shut her eyes in order to drive away the pain and the cold. She tried to think of Maguire. She had heard he was cruel, but that was not true because she had seen his gentleness. He gave her his coat, and money. He took her into his house. The talk of schooling and of the Padre had frightened her and she ran. Now she begged the baby Jesus to let Maguire rescue her as he had before. She would take baths and go to school. Even go to mass. Anything he said she would do, and more.

She was grateful for the warmth, but the bright lights of the hotel lobby blinded her. Soldiers dressed in gray stared hungrily in her direction as Suarez carried her draped over his shoulder. She was glad her hair fell forward to cover her face. His shoulder dug into her belly as he carried her up some stairs covered with red carpet stained with mud. She tried to pass out again, but couldn't.

At long last she heard a door open and a sharp command to enter. A pair of shined, black boots preceded them into a second room where she was thrown on a bed and retied, wrists to the headboard, ankles to the foot. She did not recognize the man who entered then, nor did she dare look at him for more than the briefest of seconds. A scar disappeared beneath a patch over his left eye. On the patch—a scream caught in her throat—an evil eye of gold glittered in the candlelight. He reached down, ripped the skirt from her waist and handed it to Elrecht. "Keep this until tomorrow, and then deliver it in person," Fuentes ordered. "Outside now and tell the men I will be out soon."

The door closed. They were alone. The man picked up a machete. Remedios caught her breath as the blade slipped under her blouse and ripped upward. The cotton cloth parted with ease. Never touching her, the blade whisked from right to left. The torn blouse fell away to either side, leaving her breasts exposed.

She could hear a voice, a coming storm sweeping through the city, through the open windows to gather over her. The man ran a practiced, gentle hand along her

149

neck and down her stomach to the dark triangle of curls between her legs. Remedios winced involuntarily as he leaned forward, but all he did was kiss the nipple of her right breast.

She began to hope. Why he wanted her above all the others he could have had was a mystery she couldn't begin to appreciate. At least he was gentle. Many others she had known hadn't been. She had never been tied before, but men were strange creatures. Perhaps he would release her if she pleased him. Concentrating, she raised her chest so her breasts were closer to his mouth, felt her nipples swell into hard buds.

His fingers entered her, moved back and forth, up and down. Remedios closed her eyes, moaned and gave herself to him. He would let her go. Release her. Perhaps pay her. Send her back to Maguire.

A surge deep within her. Remedios strained against the ropes holding her, arched her pelvis against his hand. When the contractions stopped, she opened her eyes and smiled at him. He leaned forward, brushed a sweat-soaked tendril of hair from her forehead and kissed her. He would free her, she knew.

Her captor appeared pleased. "Do you know my name?" he asked softly.

"No, *señor*."

"Have you heard of Jesus Fuentes, the Captain of *Los Serpientes*?"

She hadn't, but was afraid to say so. "Yes," she lied. "You let me go now, yes?"

"No." He pulled a black cloth from his pocket and wiped his hands while staring into her eyes.

Fear welled in Remedios's heart. His smile was no longer friendly, but as evil as the gold eye he wore. "Please, *señor*," she pleaded, trying not to panic. "I . . . "

"You must wait here for Maguire. He will come get you, I think." Laughing to himself, he walked away from the bed and opened the door. As soon as he stepped outside the room, the men who had been waiting crowded in.

The one named Suarez was the first. Remedios tried to make herself invisible. Horror filled her eyes and she twisted against the ropes that held her. More men filed into the room. She could hear others in the hall. The fat one climbed on the bed and kneeled between her legs. He was grinning. Slowly he unfastened his belt and slid his pants down.

Someone laughed.

Maguire would rescue her.

A hairy body smelling of sweat and pulque covered hers. The pain was like a sharp knife between her legs.

The others prepared themselves.

Remedios began to scream.

12

A half moon ducked in and out of racing clouds. Save for an occasional burst of gunfire, the silence was oppressive. Lights burned prematurely in the windows of the great houses along the shaded paths where the lineaged wealthy, protected by armed servants, stood anxious vigil. Keeping a respectable distance from those houses, young Drexler worked his way along hedges and around shrubs and trees. He had seen patrols of militia. They would be nervous at a time like this, and perhaps shoot before asking questions. It paid to be careful.

When he reached the corner of the wall that surrounded his father's estate, he proceeded an extra twenty paces north, found the boulder where he'd played as a child and jumped onto the top of the wall. An eight-foot drop and he was inside. Ahead, a meticulously manicured lawn sloped upward to the back of the house. Panting and out of breath, he sprawled on the cool grass to rest a moment.

The back lawn was comforting. Here he had picnicked with his mother. Here as a child-general with tiny, brightly painted tin soldiers for brave *compañeros*, he had led invincible armies to brilliantly executed victories and received tumultuous acclaim from kings and presidents. Unfortunately he was no longer a child. Rather a humiliated fool in charred trousers. Unable to face Fuentes, he had left word with an underling that they hadn't been able to capture Maguire after all. His request to see his father was accorded only a curt, "You'll find him at his house. We released him."

The moon disappeared again. David rose and felt his way uphill until he could see the house. A single light burned in the upstairs back hall. He calculated quickly. Almost four hours had passed since the guns had first sounded. His father should have been returned a couple of hours ago. He was probably asleep after a long and harrowing day. David hoped Anthony Drexler hadn't been told of, or discovered, his son's role in his detention.

He followed a second, lower wall of smoothed brick past the gazebo and under a trellis of dormant wisteria. The back doors would be bolted from the inside. No matter. He had the key to the front door. Once in his own room, he could remove his shameful apparel without waking his father. There would be questions to face the next morning, of course. He broke out in a sweat at the thought of having to explain to his father where he'd been and what he'd been doing during the fighting. Unfortunately a lie wouldn't do. Too many people had witnessed his ignominy and his father would, in due course, hear the story. Under the circumstances a full confession might be his only resort. Everyone made mistakes, after all. Well, that's just what he had done—but in the process saved his father's life. His father would be angry, but would ultimately forgive him. He always had before.

The side of the house was dark. He followed the low brick wall he'd learned to walk as a boy. The memory beckoned like a path waiting to be explored. Little David's first attempt to walk on the wall had failed. He had lost his balance and cried out. Papa had been there to catch him. The memory was bittersweet. Poor Papa, with his heart aching for the *peones*. Why couldn't he face reality? The *peones* were meant to suffer. Their subjugation was proper and essentially just. The ignorant poor, *campesinos* and *peones* alike, were incapable of managing their own land or of administering a government. Madero and his associates were criminally mistaken, and therefore, needed to be replaced. The revolution was necessary. Salvation lay in the hands of men like Felix Diaz and Jesus Fuentes: strong, capable men of character who would rule with an iron hand.

David's mood darkened. Force was necessary, of course, but he would be happier when the violence came to an end and *Los Serpientes* and the others of their ilk were relegated to their proper function of enforcing the law. He sighed in new-found awareness. The raging street battles and twisted dead he'd seen would haunt his dreams for the rest of his life. In that respect he was like his father. He had no stomach for killing; not after brushing so close to death.

Seven steps up to the porch. Twelve more to the door. "Damn!" He tripped, fell forward and skinned the palms of his hands. The cold air stung like a thousand tiny needles. One of the servants had left something lying across the porch. David cursed again and, groping in the dark, discovered a foot, then an ankle and leg.

"My God!" David fumbled in his pocket, pulled out the key and managed to unlock the door and push it open. Light from the foyer streamed out to reveal the frock-coated torso and rounded face of his father. A tiny black hole marred the broad, even forehead.

"Papa!" Stunned, David sagged to the porch floor and knelt by his father. Who could have done this? And why? "Why?" he shouted in anguish. "Why?"

The door behind him slammed closed. The bushes on either side of the porch steps rustled. Terrified, David crouched over his father's corpse and squinted into the darkness. A dark shape separated itself from a shrub. Another. Outlines of men in dark clothes blended with the night. A brief flash of moonlight. Gray jackets and trousers. Black *sombreros*.

Los Serpientes. Fuentes had lied. A cold rage beyond his meager experience engulfed David. Lied! And now, a more horrible realization. His own father. My fault, a voice screamed from the depths of his soul. Mine!

"He said my father would not be harmed!"

The men in black did not speak. Behind him, the door opened and closed.

Still they did not speak. Two more stalked him from either side.

David closed his father's eyes. His murdered father's eyes. He had been lied to. Fuentes was a villain, worthy of no more than contempt. A child no longer, David Florio Drexler rose and faced the two men who stood in front of him. His voice was calm and clear. "Fuentes is a liar and a murderer. Take me to him immediately, do you hear."

"*Si, padron,*" a mocking voice behind him said.

David turned.

The knife that slid in under his ribs made a hideous sucking sound as it was withdrawn. David twisted free. A second fanglike dagger sank deep into his vitals. A third, and a fourth, dispassionate lightning. Glistening blades turned dull and sticky. David staggered off the porch, turned away one blow but stepped into another.

Step by step, the men, arms punching in and out like methodical butchers, kept pace.

Suddenly he was alone. Fingers tangled in the vines, he fell against the low wall of his childhood. Strangely the pain receded. A lethargic numbness crept over him. He felt . . . wet.

The whitewashed brick wall, stained and slippery, loomed above him. He blinked in surprise. Arms outstretched for balance, a child stood there.

"Watch me," he rasped. "Watch me, Papa."

The child, concentrating on each move, placed one foot in front of the other. His toe caught in the vine and he lost his balance and fell. But he was not afraid, because his Papa was there to catch him . . . .

"That's it."

"Check to make sure."

A dark figure stepped forward, nudged the corpse with his boot. The crumpled, lifeless form didn't move. "I told you."

"It's always better to make sure," the leader said. "Finish the job, Diego."

A match flared. By the dim light, Diego scratched *Viva Diaz* into the wall above David's body.

"Hey," one of the others joked as he found a dry spot on David's coat and started cleaning his knife. "The *Maderistas* have killed Colonel Serrano. Now Diaz's people have commited this atrocity on a just man and his son. These are terrible times, no?"

One of the men chuckled. Diego finished his task. "*Vamonós*," he said. The men ran to their horses, still securely tethered at the back of the house, and a moment later were gone.

13

Church bells played a joyful melody of brass to heaven's glory against a punctuating, throaty background of bass cannon fire. Corinne opened her eyes. Once, years ago when she was a child, she had waked to this same music. Then the orchestration was more perfect, for the U.S. Army Band was playing Tchaikovsky's "1812" Overture. Strangely enough she had been more frightened then. A ten-year-old, she had fallen asleep in her father's lap and awoke with a confused and startled shriek when the artillery barrage began. The incident became known as "the-time-Corinne-thought-the-Redcoats-were-shooting-at-her," and laughed about for years.

The Seth Thomas clock on Maguire's bureau read almost one o'clock. Corinne felt sluggish and tired. No one had gotten to bed or sleep until well after daylight when the heavy cannon fire had finally slowed. Yawning, she rolled from the bed and pulled on one of the shirts Maguire had left her. The shirt fell just midway to her thighs, making a perfect nightgown.

Dark, ominous clouds blotched yesterday's blue sky and sheets of metallic-gray water puddled on the stone floor of the balcony. To the east a black haze drifted over the city where the downpour was smothering the flames that had reduced whole blocks to smoldering skeletons. As she listened, the barrage slowed and the church bells, plaintive appeals for peace, ceased.

The door opened and Maguire entered. Corinne clutched the front of the shirt together. Their eyes met over the awkward silence. "Good morning," Maguire finally said. "Or afternoon."

"Good morning." Corinne cleared her throat.

"You sleep well?"

"Yes." Why did she sound so awkward? "You?"

He shrugged. "A little." His eyes dropped to her legs, swept up her body, paused at the soft hint of breasts under the cotton shirt. "You'd, ah, better get dressed. We're going to get out of here while we can."

Corinne stiffened in alarm. "Is it that bad?"

"Looks like it." He leaned against the door. "Let's go."

"Is there someplace I can dress, or do you want to watch?"

Maguire pretended surprise. "Sorry. You can go behind the screen."

"Thank you," she said, with exaggerated sweetness. Corinne grabbed her pants and shirt from the chair beside the bed and disappeared behind an ornate Japanese screen in the corner.

"I'll have to see about rounding up some more clothes for you later on," Maguire said. "Aurora should have something tucked away."

"I'll manage, thank you." She slipped out of his shirt, tossed it over the screen and bent to pull on the pants. Maguire concentrated on wicked thoughts. After she had buttoned her own shirt and was tucking it in, Corinne noticed the mirror against the opposite wall. In it she could see Maguire, which meant . . .

Temper boiling, Corinne rounded the screen. "Why didn't you tell me that mirror was there?"

Maguire flashed a good-natured leer. "I was struck dumb." The smile disappeared. "At one time you wouldn't have minded. In fact you would have been pleased."

Confused, unable to define her own emotions, Corinne turned away from him. "That was a long time ago, I wish you wouldn't . . . "

"Maguire!" someone downstairs called, interrupting Corinne. A pistol appeared in Maguire's hand. In one fluid motion he spun and hurried out and down the stairs. Boots in hand, Corinne followed.

Someone was beating on the door and cursing in what sounded like Italian. DuClerc stirred on his tabletop bed. Payton blinked awake. Blue stared at the barred doors as the words came through it. "Maguire, you son of a Greek whore! You offspring of a goat's turd and sheep dung, open this door!"

"Sounds like a whole army," Blue said, hurriedly pulling on his shirt.

"It is," Maguire replied, lifting the heavy timber bar. "Of one."

Riciotti Lucca burst into the room and slammed the door behind him. A rain-wet circle of shiny, sun-browned scalp was surrounded by short, springy curls of sparse hair that continued down his jaw to flower into a full, grizzled beard. A small brass ring pierced his right ear. A soiled crimson sash tied around his waist held up torn and muddy trousers. Twin bandoliers crossed his chest and knife handles jutted from his boots. He carried an enormous Parker-Hale twelve-gauge pump shotgun which was almost as long as he was tall. Blue hadn't been far off the mark. What Lucca lacked in height he made up for in ferocity. He certainly looked like a whole army.

"Nice day out there." He grinned. Wicked, narrow

eyes traveled from an instant appraisal of Corinne's merits as a bedmate to a cynical judgment of Blue's towering physique. The ones he knew—Maguire, Payton and DuClerc—Lucca ignored. Inspection over, he lunged across the room, placed the shotgun on the bar and leaped over, landing catlike in front of a bottle of rum.

"Be careful. It's from Vera Cruz," Maguire cautioned.

"Best kind." Lucca bit the cork, spat it onto the counter and raised the bottle. The only muscles that moved were in his throat. Bubbles rose into the bottle to replace the rapidly disappearing liquor. Blue and Corinne watched, spellbound. Finally Lucca lowered the bottle. His eyes glazed for a moment. "Better," he said, swinging himself up to sit, legs dangling over the edge, on the front of the bar. "Good stuff." He looked for all the world like a mad, pixie schoolteacher about to conduct a class.

Maguire leaned on a table, crossed his arms and allowed Lucca his moment of drama. "Well, *piquito*, little bird," Maguire said dryly, "you've drunk your water. Now will you sing?"

DuClerc sat up, awake at last. Payton moved closer.

"I have seen it. Ah, Maguire. Men like us will never be out of work. Felix Diaz, cousin to the late great Porfirio, has allowed himself to be convinced that his rightful place in this world is where his uncle sat, and is determined to oust Francisco Madero. The *Maderistas,* for their part, naturally have refused Diaz's magnanimous offer to assume the presidency." He drank again to fortify himself. "So. The loyalists are concentrated around the National Palace, for protection so they say, and around the barricaded Ciudadela where the rebels are holed up. The loyalists—General Huerta has been placed in charge, I am told—are shelling the Ciudadela, but their marksmen . . . Ha! That they should be called such a thing! . . . are shooting like blind men and their shells fall everywhere.

"Colonel Serrano was killed last night by a *Maderista* bullet as he advanced on the palace. Others have fallen to Diaz's assassins. Each side accuses the other of atrocities. To complicate matters, shells struck the walls of Belem prison this morning and the prisoners—mad dogs without allegiance to Diaz or Madero—wander the city stealing and looting and killing. Few of them have guns, but it's best to be wary of them."

"The trains?" Maguire asked.

"What trains? The rebels hold the station and the tracks have been cut by shells. Or so I am told."

"No!" Corinne said plaintively.

"Don't worry," Maguire snapped, then more gently said, "This can't last forever."

"But can get much worse," Lucca said, sounding as if he hoped it would.

Corinne slumped into the nearest chair. Blue moved to her side. Maguire perched on a bar stool and digested Lucca's information. The Belem prisoners were the worst threat in this part of the city, he reasoned. Still, with the doors barred and window grilles in place, they should be reasonably safe. Unfortunately Seifert had slipped out moments after David Drexler left the night before to check on his family and hadn't returned. That left Lucca, if he stayed, Payton, DuClerc, himself and Blue to stand watches and thwart any attack.

What else did he need to consider? The water cistern should be full, with all the rain they'd had. If not, they had plenty of beer. Thre was enough food in the kitchen and pantry. Which reminded him of Aurora and Remedios. Remedios, he assumed, was safe at the Padre's. And Aurora? The old woman had left with no explanation. Still, with her encyclopedic knowledge of the city and her numerous relatives scattered throughout, she shouldn't need Maguire to look out for her.

"We'll stay here," Maguire announced, startling almost everyone. "This ought to blow over in a couple of days.

If Diaz's only strongholds are the Ciudadela barracks and the train station, Huerta shouldn't have much trouble wiping them out."

"But Christopher . . . " Corinne faltered.

"The train is still our fastest way north, even if we have to wait a few days. The first thing Madero will do is see the trains are running. Trust me."

"I have to, don't I?" she said, standing.

"Yes."

Lucca leaned forward to watch the swing of her hips as Corinne ascended the stairs. When she disappeared, he sighed longingly and switched his attention to Blue. "Exactly what army does the kid belong to?" he said.

"You can ask me direct." Blue was tired of being talked around. "I'm not in any damn army. I bought these before crossing the border because they're excellent, appropriate desert wear."

"His name is Patrick Henry Blue." Maguire made the name sound ridiculously pompous. "He's a reporter. And this," Maguire waved a hand at the cocky Italian, "is Riciotti Marcello Lucca."

"Nephew of Guiseppe Garibaldi," Lucca added proudly.

"Also to wolves, jackals and rattlesnakes. And reputed to be an eater of *carne crudo*."

"That's raw meat," DuClerc wheezed by way of explanation. He ambled toward Lucca, who offered him the rum. Declining, DuClerc stepped around the bar and pulled a bottle of Bordeaux out of the wine rack.

"I'm keeping tabs," Maguire grumbled.

Without warning, three windows shattered. Irregular, arrowhead-size fragments of rainbow-colored glass flew through the air. Lucca flipped backward over the bar, and Payton dove behind his piano. Maguire brushed Blue aside and snatched Lucca's shotgun from the bar. More rocks, small enough to pass through the iron grille-work but large enough to obliterate whole panes of glass bounced off tables and skidded across the floor.

Elbows raised to protect his eyes, Maguire ran through a shower of splinters, poked the forty-two-inch barrel through the remnants of one bright red pane and fired once without aiming. The hail of rocks stopped. A shrill voice shouted in alarm and footsteps receded.

His mind gradually freeing itself of images of criminals and thieves come to plunder and murder, Blue released a deathgrip on a table leg. Lucca emerged from behind the bar and returned a stiletto to his boot sheath. A frightened Corinne appeared on the stairs. "My God!" she gasped. "What happened?"

"Kids," Maguire snorted. He tossed the weapon to Lucca, who caught it with practiced ease and immediately reloaded.

Everyone stood about, not knowing what to say, staring at the broken glass and the rain pouring in. "Shit," Maguire said. He'd spent a lot of money on those windows and had been proud of them.

Lucca cleared his throat. "Ah, hell, Maguire. You can always buy . . . "

"Don't say it," Maguire warned. He stalked to the window, picked out a piece of yellow glass and squinted through it. The world looked murky. "Well?" he asked savagely, turning on them. "What are you looking at? So they're broken. You never see broken windows before?" Rain darkened his shirt. His eyes darted around the interior of the casino. "Dark in here. Get lanterns lit. Payton, there are spare ponchos in the garage. Get some. Hammer and tacks, too. Let's get the place cleaned up. And something to eat. Who wants to cook?"

Corinne noticed heads turning in her direction, but she studiously ignored them. She was damned if she was going to play servant. Next they'd be after her to do the wash.

Lucca wiped his hands on his trousers, looked at them and tried his shirt. Still they were streaked with mud. "Well, hell. A little dirt never hurt anybody," he said, starting for the kitchen.

"All right," Corinne said with a sigh. "You win." She hurried across the room and into the hall leading to the kitchen. Behind her, eyes twinkling, Lucca righted a chair.

DuClerc swept. Payton and Blue stretched and nailed ponchos over the broken windows. Maguire and Lucca arranged tables and chairs in defensive positions designed to cover each entrance in case of a better planned or more determined attack. Work finished and a semblance of order returned to the casino, Maguire stepped behind the bar and twisted a decorative piece of woodwork. A concealed gun rack swung into view. "Guess there's no sense in keeping secrets any longer," he said, laying a pair of rifles and four bandoliers full of ammunition on the bar. "Winchesters, model 1895," Maguire said, feeding six shells into the box magazine. He worked the lever once to crank a round into the breech and handed the rifle to Blue. "These are military loads. They'll bring down just about anything you can hit."

"Me?" Blue asked.

"That's right, Patrick Henry." He turned his attention to the second rifle. "DuClerc?"

The gambler coughed. Several wracking coughs later, he stuffed his handkerchief back in his pocket and pulled out a deck of cards. "These are my weapons."

"Payton?"

The pianist struck a dark chord. "Leave it on the bar. I'll use it if I have to."

Maguire reached into the rack and pulled out a Browning .45 automatic in a belted canvas holster. "Here you go, Patrick Henry. Matches your uniform."

"I already have a rifle. Why do I need . . . "

"Put out fires before they start and you won't get burned. Strap it on." Maguire dropped belt, holster and gun on a table in front of Blue. "Be careful. It's loaded. You know how to work it?"

"I don't intend to kill anyone."

"Listen to the pup," Lucca hooted. "You never do until

the day when your ass is on the line. Before you know it," he pointed a finger at Blue, "Bang! And there you are."

"This was already on the stove," Corinne interrupted. "I just mixed in some beans and rice and warmed it up. Be careful. It's hot." She stepped between Lucca and Blue, casually shoved the .45 out of the way and set a large cast iron pot on the table. "Wait a second and I'll bring some bread."

Lucca leaned over the pot, lifted out a ladle full and tasted. His face brightened. "Beer, anybody?"

Corinne reentered carrying a tray piled with sienna-glazed clay bowls, a fistful of spoons and a huge loaf of bread. "Eat up," she said, serving herself first and tearing off a chunk of bread.

Lucca plunked down a mug of beer and helped himself to a bowl. DuClerc patted his stomach and declined. "My thanks, madam, but my doctor has restricted me to a liquid diet." He lifted his wineglass and toasted her health.

There were worse places in the world. Outside the rain and cannons bombarded the city. Inside the cavelike atmosphere of *El Madronito* it was dry and relatively safe. The smell of food revived everyone's spirits. They were under siege along with the rest of the city, true, but the nonsense would end in a day or two and life would return to normal.

Seeking light, Corinne headed upstairs. A moment later, chili and bread in one hand, a schooner of beer in the other, Maguire followed her. As the door closed behind him, Corinne turned in the chair she'd placed in front of the window. She looked as if she'd expected him. "I can't tell which is thunder and which is cannon."

Maguire set his food on the bedside table, pulled over a chair and joined her at the window. The city stretched out before them, bleak and gray under a solid layer of flat-bottomed clouds. "That's thunder," he said between

167

spoons of chili. "Old Harvard Van Allen used to read to us from the *Iliad*. He said Alexander the Great knew it by heart. Why, I could never figure out. The only part I really liked was where Zeus held his scales and weighed the fate of the Greeks and the Trojans."

"You're like one of them. The gods, I mean."

"I've been called a lot of things, lady, but never a god."

"It's true, though. Ares."

"The god of war?" He tore off a chunk of bread, dipped it in the sauce. "What about . . . "

"Maguire!" A shot rang out. At first he thought it was trouble downstairs, then realized the sound came from the alley behind the courtyard. Two more shots. "Maguire!"

Keeping low, he ran onto the balcony. The rain pelted him with furious, stinging drops that drenched him immediately. A man on horseback waited by the gate. "Maguire!"

"Up here!" Maguire shouted over the hissing rain.

The man looked up, held a bundle over his head and dropped it outside the gate. "She's at the San Cristobal! Ask for Captain Fuentes!" Not waiting for an answer, he wheeled his horse and galloped off.

Puzzled and increasingly apprehensive, Maguire took a chance and raced down the steps to meet Lucca, who had come out the back door, shotgun in hand. "Cover me," he called, indicating the gate.

Lucca moved unhesitatingly to the madrone tree. Maguire unlatched the gate and glanced back at Lucca, who released the safety and nodded. Swiftly Maguire swung open the gate, grabbed the bundle and ducked back inside, slamming and bolting the gate behind him.

"What is it?" Lucca asked, joining him.

Maguire held out a soggy piece of material. "A skirt," he said flatly. "Aurora's."

14

The Le Mat was an over-under handgun of French manufacture. The top barrel consisted of eight inches of octagonal steel rifled to .45 caliber. Underneath a six-inch smooth bore barrel took a single .60 caliber shotgun shell. Maguire fed nine .45 cartridges into the upper cylinder, slipped a shotgun shell loaded with double-ought into the lower chamber and closed the gun. The weapon had been given him when he was in the Philippines. Lessons in the art of survival accompanied the gift. His teacher, a scarred and weathered mercenary by the name of Tom Leach, in the end failed one of his own exams. But not before he'd saved Maguire's life. Maguire always regretted the fact that he'd never had the chance to thank Leach. That, too, was a lesson of sorts.

The Le Mat had played an important role in hounding the *Porfiristas* out of Mexico City during Madero's revolution. Once the fighting was over and Maguire had bought and remodeled *El Madronito,* he switched to a lighter handgun. The Le Mat, too heavy and bulky to be concealed beneath city clothes, was wrapped in oiled cloth and hidden out of sight, much as its owner's rootless, mercenary past. A short-lived calm, Maguire reflected. Hardly two years.

The brushed leather holster had been designed and made for the Le Mat. Maguire slipped the belt loop over his left arm, shrugged into the harness and back out again. The easy life of a casino owner had made him beefy. Scowling—he'd let himself ignore the extra ten pounds he carried—he loosened the buckle a notch and tried again. A quick turn, a crouch. Arms overhead, reaching to right and left. Satisfied at last, he slipped the gun in the holster. Some things never changed. The weight of the gun felt reassuring.

Almost dark. Almost time to go. Corinne quietly entered the room, closed the door behind her and watched Maguire finish. Pockets empty, belt buckle blackened. The knife secure in his boot. He tucked a pair of gloves in his belt and checked in the mirror. A dark knit cap hugged his forehead. His jeans were faded but still dark enough to look like a shadow. A thickly woven black wool sweater against which the dull black leather harness and holster all but disappeared completed his outfit.

"I came to ask you not to go."

"I know." He threaded a rawhide loop over the hammer of the gun.

"If something should happen to you, I . . ."

"It won't."

She moved closer. "Have you forgotten your own son? What about him? You're risking his life, too." He started past her. "A skirt! A simple skirt! It could be anyone's."

"But isn't."

"Okay, so it isn't. She's an old woman. They're baiting

you. Can't you see that? She's probably already dead!" she blurted, each syllable whispered more intently than the one before. The strength of her anger faded and she slumped into a nearby chair. "I'm sorry," she said, barely audible, and held her jaw to keep from crying. "But why, Maguire? Damn it, why?"

He walked toward the door. "If it's any consolation, I've tried to convince myself it's a wild goose chase. Hell, I know why they took her. I wasn't born yesterday. But I can't let them get away with it."

"But she's . . ."

The balcony door opened and closed. Maguire slipped down the back stairs and stood a moment under the madrone tree. Slowly his eyes adjusted to the darkness. At the same time another change came over him. It had been a long time since he'd gone out like this, but as he waited the old feelings came back. Survival, his brain whispered. Survival, his body responded, loose, relaxed and ready.

For a brief second, he wished he'd let Lucca come. That would have been like old times, too. The pair of them, a team, each sensitive to the other, each knowing almost instinctively what the other was doing and thinking, where he'd go, how he'd act. But no. Maguire wanted the Italian to stay where he was. Lucca would defend *El Madronito*, and therefore Corinne, with his life. Not so much out of loyalty, Maguire reflected, but because the diminutive warrior had a well-developed sense of property. Riciotti Lucca considered the liquor supplies of *El Madronito* his own personal treasure.

Time to go. The rain had stopped over an hour earlier. Water still dripped from the tile overhang and gathered in a myriad isolated pools. *El Madronito* was a dark shadow behind him. Ahead the alley was pitch black. Blending with the shadows now, a part of the night itself, Maguire slipped across the courtyard and unlatched the gate. The soft scurrying sound of rats foraging told him the alley was clear. Moving quickly, he swung open the gate and stepped out.

The night, moist, chilly and secretive, flowed over and around him. The alley was a blank, dull cavern of rain-washed brick and rotting fences. Squat, fetid barrels of garbage and rubbish waited in ambush. Maguire passed among them as unobtrusively as a shadow until he heard the faint pad of footsteps. Black against black, knife in hand, he flattened against the nearest wall. Whoever was following him was as stealthy as a water buffalo. Lord save me from fools, Maguire thought, pulling the Le Mat from its holster. When the figure passed, he grabbed a handful of *serape,* jerked backward and jammed the muzzle of the Le Mat against a pale patch of neck. "Move and you're a dead man."

"Jesus, Maguire, it's me!" Blue croaked, involuntarily grabbing at his neck where the *serape* was choking him. Off balance, he almost fell backward.

Marguire let him go, spun him around. "What the hell are you doing here?" he hissed.

"My job."

"Getting me killed?"

"You? Christ, you almost choked me."

"Keep your voice down. What happened to your face?"

"Lampblack," Blue whispered. "Lucca said it would . . . "

"Lucca! He sent you out here?"

"Not really. I talked him into letting me go."

Maguire snorted. "I'll bet. Must have taken you all of three seconds."

"More like a minute. Then he gave in and said I couldn't stay a virgin forever."

"That son-of-a-bitch!"

"Well, maybe he was right. You ever think about that?"

"I don't have to think about that. You're not going."

"Look, Maguire, I may be the only American journalist in Mexico City. This the chance I've been waiting for. Besides, if I'd wanted to get you killed, I sure as hell wouldn't have bounced my typewriter off Drexler's chest. The damned carriage is bent. Ruined. You know how much a typewriter costs?"

"I didn't do anything to deserve this," Maguire lamented.

"So you owe me," Blue went on. "Now, we can stand out here and argue about it, or we can move on—together." Blue pulled up the *serape*. The Browning automatic was holstered on his right hip. "I brought this if it makes you feel any better."

An exchange of gunfire several blocks away rattled the stillness. "A virgin, huh?" Maguire said, remembering a similar night, years ago, in San Francisco. He'd been scared shitless, but was just as boldly determined as Blue seemed to be. "You sure you know how to use that thing?" he asked, tapping the .45.

"I cocked it inside so there'd be no noise. It's on safe."

A night in San Francisco. 1892. Tong killers and opium and a wealthy silver miner. And Maguire, still wet behind the ears, a .44 tucked in his coat pocket, youth and speed and strength his only assets. Stealth and street-wise savvy wouldn't come until later. "What the hell. Come on. But you do exactly what I tell you, when I tell you. Understand?"

Blue seemed to grow an extra two inches. "Perfectly." He trailed Maguire out of the alley and into the street. "Hey? Where we going?"

Maguire's face was a frightening mask in the sickly mustard-colored light. "To the devil," the mercenary said, without a trace of mirth.

Fires that had raged through the morning still smoldered, filling the night with acrid smoke that hung low in the heavy air. The streets were virtually deserted, for with darkness, those with sense had retreated to home or hovel. Maguire led the way. Blue, completely disoriented after five minutes in the twisting alleys and streets, followed a few cautious paces behind. Only once, when they paused in the Street of Owls, did he get his bearings.

Maguire raised a hand and ducked into an alcove. Blue wedged in beside him. A few seconds later, a motley crowd of at least a dozen men, shivering in ragged cotton trousers, baggy shirts and bare feet, trotted past. Three of the men carried rifles, the rest an assortment of knives, machetes and makeshift clubs. One paused in the middle of the street and stared directly into the alcove. Blue swallowed, felt a movement beside him as Maguire drew the Le Mat.

A voice called in guttural *Poblano,* a dialect more Indian than Spanish. Instead of replying, the man took a tentative step toward the alcove, then jerked backward as Maguire cocked the Le Mat and said two low, indistinct words Blue couldn't understand. The choice was obviously the Indian's. Years of pent-up hatred vied with the certainty of death. The Indian glanced down at his machete and decided. Arms swinging, he turned, broke into an easy stride and vanished.

"Jesus. I thought we were finished. What'd you say?"

"Just asked him if he wanted to die, is all. He didn't."

"Lucky for us. Hey!" Blue was alone in the alcove. He hurried out to join Maguire. "Give me some warning . . . "

An angry glance cut him short. They were standing in the shadows at a corner. On either side, dark buildings loomed against the sky. Ahead street lights tore the shadows apart and left the pavement exposed. Blue waited, uncertain. Suddenly Maguire stepped out of the shadows and walked openly down the street. Blue had no choice but to join him.

"What if someone is watching?" he asked, his heart in his throat.

"They'll shoot big holes in us."

Feeling naked, vulnerable, fear pricked at Blue's neck. They went a half block and nothing happened. Blue lost all sense of reality. Two men were walking an empty boulevard, that was all. A feeling of euphoria enveloped him. Everything was quiet, peaceful, tranquil, calming.

The wind shifted, ambled down the boulevard like a Sunday stroller. Blue sniffed, wrinkled his nose. "Jesus! What's that smell?"

"Meat," Maguire replied laconically. "Burnt meat."

San Cristobal. Each letter had been carved into the wood and then painted peacock blue. Now amid sad destruction, the sign lay broken on the ground. One-half was obscured in a puddle; the other, smeared with mud, balanced on the crumpled hood of a Chevrolet and bobbed up and down like a seesaw.

"There it is," Maguire whispered. "San Cristobal. First-class hotel. Just the place Fuentes would pick."

"Is there a back door?" Blue asked. The dark, ornate façade looked as uninviting as the face of death.

"Suppose so," Maguire answered. "Usually is." The building was a quarter block down the street. A few seconds' sprint.

"So what do we do?"

"What they don't expect, I hope. Coming?" Maguire was through explaining. He stepped into the street and headed for the hotel. Broken glass crunched under his feet.

"What are you doing?" Blue whispered, near panic. The man was crazy, just like all the others.

"He said ask for Fuentes's room."

"Jesus! What happens if . . . "

"If you say 'Jesus!' just once more, Patrick Henry, I'm going to tear out your tongue. You understand?"

They stepped around the submerged half of the sign and ascended marble steps pocked with bullet holes and strewn with trash. Maguire lost count of broken windows.

175

He used to know one of the desk men. His mind raced into the narrow past and found a name. He paused at the door. "Okay. Keep that hat down over your ears. One look at that red hair and some trigger-happy fool will shoot you."

"But why?"

"All *gringos* are rich. Take the left side of the door when we go in. That way we'll be spread apart. Ready?" Hand poised near the Le Mat, Maguire shoved the door and stepped in quickly. Unsnapping the flap on his holster, Blue followed.

The foyer looked like a refugee camp. Candles glimmered feebly from behind overturned tables and chairs, throwing huge shadows across Maguire and Blue. Men and women lay on scattered piles of suitcases and hastily bundled clothes. No one paid attention to the two armed men.

The check-in counter was deserted. Maguire searched the cavernous room, finally waved Blue to his left and headed for an oversized sofa and a thin, pale man with wisps of white hair. Knobby fingers folded in his lap, the man stared into space. He was dressed in a dark brown, meticulously tailored suit, but where the cuffs of his trousers rode above his ankles, pallid flesh showed. He had forgotten to put on his socks.

"Mr. Chambliss?" The man noticed Maguire for the first time. "Mr. Chambliss, do you remember me?"

"The guests," he said in a quavering voice. "I'm responsible. If they can't find . . . find . . . Ah. Maguire." Blue detected an English accent.

"That's right." Chambliss closed his eyes. "Listen to me. I need a room number."

"Fuentes was his name. He brought his men here. By order of Huerta, he said. Drove out my guests. No time to pack."

Maguire squatted in front of him. "Where is he now?"

"Gone."

"When? A half hour ago? An hour? This afternoon?"

"Sometime. Just gone."

"Which room was he in?"

"Room?"

"Which room? What number?"

"Oh." Eyes closed, Chambliss moved his index finger in short lines as if following the writing in the hotel register. Maguire waited. "Fuéntes. Three twenty-seven, sir."

"Are you sure?"

"Yes, sir. Quite positive, sir." His expression changed from shock to fear. "They brought a girl to him. Right through the lobby. The fat one and the German with the bandaged head."

Maguire raced across the lobby to the main stairs. Images of St. Francis's statue and the two *rurales* who attacked him. The fat one. The German. Damn them. Hand on the rail, two steps at a time. Girl? Should have killed them. Girl? Should have slit their throats where they lay. Fuéntes, too. Shouldn't have stopped with his eye.

The top landing was deserted and the hall dark. A trap? Probably. He hoped so. "Back to the second floor," he instructed Blue, sneaking down the steps. A lit match showed the way. Two twenty-seven was the fifth door on the right. Maguire turned the knob and entered. A large and spacious front sitting room opened onto a balcony. To the right, one door led to a closet, another to a bedroom, which opened onto the same balcony as the living room. With luck, the room above would be similar in design. Maguire spent a minute whispering instructions to Blue, then led the way back up the stairs.

No one challenged them. All indications led them to believe they were alone. Maguire pressed against the wall, nodded his head. Blue backed off and hit the door running, knocking it completely off the hinges. He was still rolling when Maguire, Le Mat in hand, stepped inside,

177

moved quickly to his right and kicked shut the closet door.

Silence.

"You all right?"

Blue's head popped up from behind a chair. "Yeah."

"Check the balcony. Crawl, damn it!" Maguire edged toward the dull light from a candle burning in the bedroom.

"Clear," Blue whispered. He began to rub his shoulder. "Shit, that hurt."

"Good. Bedroom."

A dark shape slithered across the floor and stood on the opposite side of the doorway. Maguire, pistol at ready, nodded his head. "Now!"

A single blurred motion carried Maguire through the door. Crouching, searching for waiting targets, he swung the Le Mat in a wide arc. Behind him, Blue peered around the door frame. "Oh, my God!" the youth said, choking.

Her hands and feet were black from lack of circulation. The skin was swollen, almost closed over the cruel leather thongs. Her poor bruised little breasts raised and lowered with each shallow breath. The coverlet and sheets were caked with dried blood. Her genitals were engorged and clotted with blood.

Blue couldn't stop staring. "My God!" he repeated. "My God."

Maguire silently crossed the room. Remedios. Not Aurora. The girl. Remedios. His left hand pulled the knife from his boot. Through veils of madness, her eyes followed him. He reached across her and cut the thongs. She didn't move.

"You'll be all right," he whispered, his throat constricting. He pulled a cover over her nakedness. She wouldn't, but he repeated it anyway. "You'll be all right."

Remedios stopped breathing. She was dead.

Maguire felt her throat. No pulse. For a brief moment

more he gazed down at the lifeless remains, then gently lowered her arms and pulled the cover over her face. "Nothing more we can do here," he said hollowly. "Let's go."

"For the love of God! Doesn't this affect you at all?"

Maguire spun, slammed into Blue with such force he propelled the reporter against the wall. The Le Mat bore into the soft skin under his jaw. Blue didn't breathe. Didn't try to speak. Didn't blink. Maguire's face was bare inches away, his eyes black holes that burned away Blue's anguish and left nothing—not even fear—in its place.

Abruptly Maguire released him. Blue slumped against the wall. "I'm sorry," Blue gasped, near tears. "I didn't mean . . . It's just that . . . "

"We'll go now," Maguire said, taking a last look at the pathetic figure he'd been too late to save. "Out the back way. With luck, they won't be waiting for us."

They weren't, and the more Maguire thought about it, the more he thought he knew why. Fuentes had accomplished what he'd set out to do: teach Maguire a lesson. First David Drexler had been talked into wreaking havoc on *El Madronito*. Now one of Maquire's household had been horribly slain. The message was clear. Fuentes was having his revenge.

Silently they slipped out of the San Cristobal. Colon Avenue was deserted. Normally one of the more bustling areas of the city, the *Alameda* was a desolate no man's land. At last they were in front of the auto shed, then safely around the corner into the back alley, through the gate and safely inside the courtyard of *El Madronito*. Sweating in spite of the cold, Blue touched Maguire on the arm. "Maguire? I meant what I said. I am sorry."

Maguire stopped. "Fair enough." He looked up. The cloud cover was beginning to break. Remedios. Not Aurora. He cursed. "You did well," he said, turning to Blue, "for the first time. Learn anything?"

179

"Yeah. For a moment up there, I thought you might really shoot me."

The twisted limbs of the madrone tree cast a tortured umbra on the wet, bone-white walls and streaked Maguire with spiny shadows. "So did I."

It would be dawn soon. Not soon enough. Maguire sat on the stone steps leading to the balcony. The clouds were gone and the moon was low, almost buried.

If he had never taken Blue to the Street of the Owls.

If he had never given Remedios his coat.

If he simply hadn't cared.

"The others are asleep." Riciotti Lucca stopped at the bottom of the stairs. Maguire hadn't heard him come out the back door, which was a disconcerting notion. "But you and I, like two *gallos*, never rest."

Maguire drilled the stub of his cigar into the stone step, crushed the remaining embers under his boot heel. Lucca hooked his thumbs inside the sash around his waist. "Reminds me of a time in Sicily. A man, Carlo Piannici, owned a magnificent villa on the edge of a . . . "

"Please, Ricco. No stories. Not now."

Lucca slipped a knife from his boot, searched in his shirt and found a reed he had hollowed out. "As you wish." Concentrating, he smoothed one end and blew through the tube. Satisfied, he cut a notch near the thick end and, pausing frequently to check the pitch, began gouging out holes.

"What the hell are you doing?"

The Italian grinned, tried a trilling, off-key melody on his crude pipe. "Practicing. Not bad, eh? What do you think?"

"I think you're full of shit."

"And I think you, my friend, think too much."

"I killed her, Ricco."

"Jesus Fuentes killed her."

180

Maguire spit out a tiny piece of tobacco. "Fuentes, me—even you, Lucca. Three peas in a pod."

"No," Lucca retorted. "You are wrong." He held the dagger upright, spat on the blade and wiped it on the *serape* draped over his shoulder. "You are very wrong, Maguire. You and me may be bastards, but we are not sons of bitches."

"There's a difference?" Maguire asked sarcastically.

Lucca squinted at the crimson deck of clouds balanced on the summit of Popocatepetl. "Yes. Hard to find, maybe, but a difference all the same." He started back to the kitchen, and paused. "Hey, Maguire. If I were you I would not go off so much and leave behind all that gold you took from Fuentes. There are many robbers about. These are terrible times."

"I wasn't worried," Maguire said, rising and stretching. "Oh?"

"You were here, weren't you?"

Lips thin against pointed, yellow teeth, Lucca smiled.

15

General Victoriano Huerta studied the waitress. Her full breasts swelled against a thin cotton blouse and brought a gleam to his eyes. Perhaps, he thought, he would summon her one morning. A woman in the morning was good for a man. Especially a man who had drunk too much brandy the night before. The waitress leaned over the table to place a glass of brandy in front of Huerta and a cup of coffee in front of his guest. Huerta dismissed her with a nod and lifted his glass in salute to the man sitting opposite him. Gustavo Madero, determined to be polite in spite of the way he felt, raised his cup.

"So, Gustavo," Huerta's voice boomed in the nearly empty restaurant, "you and your brother, our esteemed president, need not concern yourselves with this ill-fated revolution. I will have Diaz yet. And perhaps bring you his ears, as we used to do with the Yaquis."

"The rebels still hold the Ciudadela."

"Of course. But we have them contained. They have little food and less water. As soon as I recapture the criminals freed from Belem and put a stop to the looting, I shall beard these foolish rebels in their den."

Gustavo leaned forward. "But why not both actions at the same time, General?" he asked.

"Alas! I have not enough men to scour the city and breach the rebel gun emplacements, too."

"You would have, had you not insisted on a foolhardy frontal attack with my brother's private guard."

Huerta drummed on the table with two fingers of his right hand. "Foolhardy is a strong word, Gustavo. Even from the brother of the president."

"You attacked in broad daylight across open pavement with the troops in an unprotected line. Under the circumstances their annihilation was inevitable."

"Under the circumstances, I almost captured the rebel machine guns. I took a calculated risk, to be sure, and one for which I accept responsibility. However," he slammed his fist on the table, "I am not totally responsible. Had I been given the few more men I asked for—"

"—there would have been that many more widows."

The two men glared at each other. At last Huerta shrugged. "I am prejudged then," he said, leaning back in his chair.

"This city has struggled like a wolf in a trap for five days. What these five days— and how many more? —cost Mexico will be the basis on which you are judged, General Huerta."

"I am willing to wait. In the meantime your brother is convinced of my loyalty."

"My brother," Gustavo countered, "is consumed by optimism."

Huerta chuckled dryly. "Surely you do not fear Felix Diaz will prevail?"

"No. But I do fear. I fear those who, by artifice

and subterfuge, would undermine our infant democracy. For them, I add contempt to my fear. Should they attempt to exceed their authority or betray the trust others show in them, I will do everything in my power to eliminate them. Do you understand?"

"Perfectly." Huerta's face was impassive. "As for my part, I promise you that by the time I put an end to this current bloodshed, you will entertain no more doubts about me." He stood, clicked his heels in the European manner and bowed slightly. "For now I am on my way to the Ciudadela. Perhaps you are right and there is a way in. Until this afternoon then." Huerta started to leave, then paused. "Oh, yes. A favor, *Señor* Madero."

"Yes?"

"The Ciudadela is well defended," —he patted his empty belt— "and I have no weapon. Perhaps you will lend me yours? I will return it this afternoon when we meet at the National Palace."

Gustavo stared at him. His aides had heard the request. To refuse would be to invite dishonor. Was Gustavo Madero, brother of the president of the Republic, afraid to be unarmed in front of Huerta? Was he any less a man than this Indian fighter? He slipped the Colt .38 from his holster and handed it to Huerta.

"Many thanks, *señor*. I trust your friends will see you safely to the palace." His smile was wide, and could have been interpreted any way Gustavo wanted. "But then, you have little to fear. The people love you as they love Francisco, your brother, no?" The room rumbled to an exchange of cannon fire. "Good day, Gustavo," Huerta concluded, eyes warm within his bullet skull.

Gustavo watched him leave, tried to shrug off his misgivings and motioned his aides to join him. The meeting with Huerta had left a bad taste in his mouth. Perhaps a drink would help. Even if it was only eleven in the morning.

185

Victoriano Huerta climbed into the rear seat of his requisitioned Model B Ford and grunted a sharp command. The driver nodded and eased the car into the empty street and around the craters left by the indiscriminate cannon fire that, according to Huerta's secret orders, plagued the city. They braked to a stop at the first corner where a ragtag crowd of convicts waited in the side street. Armed with makeshift weapons, they would have posed a formidable threat were it not for the line of horsemen behind them. Black *sombreros*, gray uniforms, creaking leather. *Los Serpientes* waited, menacing in repose.

Jesus Fuentes forced a path through the convicts and touched his hat with the naked blade of his machete. Huerta reached inside his coat, pulled out Gustavo Madero's revolver and tossed it into the street in front of Fuentes. One of the convicts rushed forward, scooped up the .38 and hurriedly rejoined his cohorts. A wild scuffle ensued as the convicts fought over the weapon. A brusque command from Fuentes brought an end to the contention.

"Any moment, now," Huerta said, his voice even and emotionless. Swerving occasionally to avoid obstacles, the Ford continued down the street. Pleased with the morning's work, Huerta settled back for the ride to the National Palace. He did not look back.

DuClerc took the three treys Lucca grudgingly surrendered and asked Payton for queens. The pianist winced and passed him one. He asked the same from Lucca. This time the short, cocky Italian chuckled happily and ordered the gambler to "go fishin'."

"Where's Maguire?" Blue asked, entering from the kitchen.

"I thought he was with you," Lucca said.

"No."

"Then try upstairs."

"He went out," Payton said, trying to remember what Lucca had asked for two turns ago.

"Out?" Lucca asked, closing his fanned cards and laying them on the table.

The pianist nodded. "I saw him leave."

Lucca's eyes darted about the room. "How long ago?"

Payton, knowing Lucca well, read his thoughts. "Don't worry, *gallito*. You needn't feel tempted. He took the money with him."

Lucca appeared thunderstruck, then insulted. "What do you mean?" he asked, his eyes narrowing dangerously.

"I am playing this ridiculous child's game," DuClerc interrupted, "because our Roman friend here says it's the only game he knows how to play. And now even this dubious pastime is denied me."

"Be quiet, gambler. Let the piano player talk." Lucca's voice was dark and threatening. "What do you mean, he took the money."

"Just what I said. He wore a money belt." Payton answered offhandedly. "Now, Give me all your sevens."

Lucca looked absolutely forlorn. "Outside," he grumbled. "Maguire went outside."

"Sevens," Payton repeated.

"Go fishin'!" Lucca retorted savagely.

Blue knocked, turned the knob when he heard her voice, and entered. Corinne stepped back onto the balcony where Blue joined her. "You know you're not supposed to be out here. Maguire says—"

"Maguire doesn't run my life," Corinne snapped, cutting him off.

"No. I can see that," Blue agreed.

Corinne looked askance at him, decided he wasn't being sarcastic. Sighing, she leaned on the balcony and gazed over the torn city. "I bet you wish you never even heard of the Van Allen ranch." A gust of clear, cold air

187

from the surrounding mountains washed over them and muted her words.

"No. I'm not sorry at all." He ran a hand through his tousled hair and perched on a wall. "That's quite a crew downstairs, though."

Corinne nodded. "Maguire attracts men like that. No. Not attracts—he's one of them. It's the life they lead. When he was at the ranch . . . " She blushed, remembering the night on the train and how she'd talked more than she really should have. "Sometimes men he knew would come by. They had heard of 'jobs', and wanted him to join them. He always refused."

Blue didn't need to ask why. He thought of the card players downstairs. "I don't know. Lucca and Maguire live an exciting life. I mean, people I knew back home in Connecticut—milkmen, bank clerks, dock workers —all kinds. Where was the adventure for them? What kind of lives did they lead?"

"Good ones," Corinne said, but the same mountain wind that stirred the golden lengths of her hair carried away her words.

"Maybe they know something we don't," Blue continued.

"They know how to kill." Distant machine guns punctuated her response. A rippling chorus of rifle fire took over where the automatic weapons left off.

"Sounds like an all out war," Blue said, turning toward the sound and stiffening as a movement in the alley caught his eyes. "Don't look," he ordered calmly, hopping off the balcony wall. "There's someone in the alley. Just step back from the wall."

Corinne obeyed without hestitation. Crouching, Blue pulled the .45 and peered into the courtyard in time to see the gate swing open and Maguire dart inside. What new horrors had Maguire seen this day? Unbidden, the image of Remedios returned. Four days had passed, and still Blue couldn't purge her from his memory. Black,

swollen hands and feet. Dull eyes, empty in death.
Brown, girlish body brutalized beyond belief . . .

"You can relax. It's just Maguire," he said, and rested
his forehead against the stone wall. The cold helped.
But not enough. Not nearly enough.

Maguire drank coffee strong, black and bitter, which
was how Lucca knew things were worse. Maguire never
drank liquor in a crisis. Only coffee.

"Gustavo Madero is dead," he began.

"Damn!" Lucca breathed. The Italian shoved a full
glass of rum away from him and reached for the coffeepot.
"How?"

"I ran into Mosca Bienevides, one of Gustavo's aides.
He was bleeding and almost out of his head with shock,
but I managed to wring some answers out of him. Gustavo
and Huerta met to discuss their differences this morning
at *La Luna* supper club. They had drinks and talked—
heatedly at times—mostly about Huerta's loyalty. When
Huerta left, he told Gustavo he was going to the Ciudadela and was unarmed. He asked for and received
Gustavo's revolver."

Lucca grunted in disgust. He would not give away his
only weapon, even to his brother.

"Gustavo and his men left a few moments later and
ran into a mob of escaped convicts. Gustavo tried to
run, but guess who was blocking the other end of the
street?" He paused, but the only response was silence.
"Fuentes and a dozen or so *Serpientes,* that's who. They
watched—didn't lift a finger to help—while the convicts
tore Gustavo limb from limb. Mosca managed to escape."

"Bienevides always was fast," Lucca said. Corinne
paled. DuClerc, seemingly absorbed in a deck of cards,
cut with one hand, thumbed the ace of spades off the top
and flipped it into the center of the table.

"I tried to reach the palace," Maguire went on,
"figuring Francisco needed to know what had happened

189

to his brother from someone other than Huerta. But Fuentes's *rurales* were guarding the main entrance."

"For the president's protection. That makes sense," Payton said.

"Right. But just in case it didn't make sense, I sent Mosca on ahead. The *Serpientes* opened up with a Lewis gun. They emptied a whole drum into him at twenty yards."

"Maybe they didn't recognize him. Maybe they just . . . " Blue searched for an explanation. His stomach felt hollow.

"All Mexicans may look alike to you," Maguire said, patting adobe dust from his sweater, "but I assure you they knew precisely who Mosca was. Lord knows what cock-and-bull story they told Madero. At any rate, that settles it. I have a feeling this thing is going to drag on. I'm leaving within the hour."

Lucca was on his feet immediately. "Leaving?" All that gold, gone, he thought. Maybe lost forever. "What do you mean leaving?"

"A little chore for the lady."

"You can't."

"I can't what?" Maguire asked, knowling precisely what was troubling Lucca.

"Leave, damn it. Leave." Lucca was fairly sputtering. "What about the woman. You can't leave her here alone."

Maguire shrugged. "We'll drop off her and Patrick Henry at the American Embassy. They'll be safe there."

"We?" The Italian leaned over the table. "You're crazy, Maguire. Why not stay here? We can make good money. They need us."

"Which side?"

Lucca threw up his hands. "Which side? Who gives a damn? What's it matter? Someone. Anyone. Hell, we have a reputation."

"I'm committed, Ricco. I told her."

"You told her what?" He hadn't cared enough about the woman's business with Maguire to ask. Suddenly he found himself wishing he'd done a little snooping. "What are you going to do for her?"

"That's between her and me. Now. You coming or not?"

Lucca looked at Corinne, then Blue, finally back to Maguire. "How much are you paying?" he asked.

"Corinne?" Maguire asked.

Corinne looked confused. "I . . . I don't know. Surely something worth your while, I suppose."

"It smells, Maguire. This whole mess smells like rotten fish in the sun. I'll tell you what." His mind was made up. "You go. I'll stay here. Keep an eye on *El Madronito* for you and pick up a little extra on the side."

"Suit yourself, Ricco." Maguire stood. "Be back in a minute."

A corner turned. A chapter ended, a chapter begun. An old ritual. Maguire folded a heavy blanket lengthwise and laid out an extra shirt, four pair of socks and a second pair of sturdy Levis and hard- and soft-soled boots. Next to his weapons, a man needed to take good care of his feet. Using his panther head cane for a stiffener, he rolled the blanket and tied each end with a length of rawhide.

The balcony door stood open. Maguire lit a cigar, leaned against the jamb and looked out over the city. A good place, Mexico City. As much like home as anywhere he'd been in the last twenty years. He turned, stood in the center of the room..

A closet full of fancy clothes that would be left behind.

The sweet taste of victory savored over brandy after a cockfight.

Dauphine—and other women—rising above him in the moonlight.

Waking to quiet, morning sun in his own bed, in his own room, in his own casino.

A chapter ended, a chapter begun. Unforeseeable episodes stretching over still blank pages . . .

The door opened and Corinne entered. Maguire tossed his cigar over the balcony. "Well, it was nice while it lasted."

"I'm sorry you feel that way."

"What way, Corinne?" he asked, sadness mixed with anger. He hadn't asked for a kid. Hadn't asked for Corinne to return and complicate his life. Hadn't asked for a revolution either. "What way do I feel?" She didn't answer. Maguire pulled open a drawer, took out a belt and box of shotgun shells. "Sorry. It's not your fault. I would have left sooner or later anyway."

"I'm going with you."

"So am I," Blue chimed in, entering and standing by Corinne.

Maguire started jamming shotgun shells into the loops on the belt. "The trains aren't running. I'll have to drive as far as I can and then make do the rest of the way. The embassy will be safer."

"I said I'm going," Corinne repeated in a determined voice.

"And so . . . "

"Okay. Okay!" Maguire buckled the belt around his waist, tossed the rest of the shells and three boxes of .45 cartridges in a leather pouch. "You'd better get ready then."

Corinne and Blue exchanged glances. "No arguments?" she asked. "No speeches about how a woman would slow you down?"

"And waste my breath trying to force some sense into you? Not me. Anyway you have a better reason for going than I have for asking you to stay."

Blue was skeptical. Maguire had something up his

sleeve. "No comments about inexperience or lack of trust?" he asked cautiously.

"Experience?" Maguire slung the ammunition bag over his shoulder, pulled a handful of cigars from a humidor and stuffed them in his shirt pocket. "Experience you'll get. Plenty of it, before we're through. The other night was a picnic, compared to this little jaunt. You might even get dead. Here." He tossed a box of .45 cartridges to Blue. "Stick these in your pocket."

Blue looked at the bullets and up to Maguire. "I think you're exaggerating."

"Sure." He pulled socks out of a drawer, extra blankets out of the wardrobe. "I don't know why you want to come along, but a man ought to be able to choose his own time and place to die without interference." He tossed everything onto the bed. "You better look through my stuff and see if you can find anything that fits. Then roll up a bundle for each of you. I'll be downstairs getting the car ready."

He left by way of the balcony stairs. The sun glinted for a moment on the sprinkling of silver hair as he paused to stare at the sky, then disappeared.

Coming into the dark shed from the bright sunlight left him momentarily blinded. Maguire groped until he found the car's left front fender, released the hood latches and lifted the hinged side flap. He pulled the LeMat from its holster and placed it close at hand on the fender. "I'd rather see it on the passenger seat, Maguire." Maguire froze as the shotgun barrel touched the base of his spine. Point-blank the 12 gauge would cut him in half. "The gun," Lucca said, nudging him. "Slowly, and very, very carefully."

Maguire moved as if through a sea of molasses. Using two fingers he picked up the revolver by the longer of the two barrels and flipped it through the open side onto the upholstered bench seat. "No sooner said than done, Ricco."

"Now the money belt."

"What was all this talk about bastards and sons-of-bitches, Ricco? I thought there were things you wouldn't do."

"There are."

"You would kill a friend?" Maguire asked.

"Only if he requested me to do so by making a sudden move," Lucca explained. "A friend I would rob but not kill unless I had no choice. An enemy I would rob and then kill as a matter of principle."

"I'm glad you make distinctions."

"I'm a man of distinctions, which is a very lucky thing for my friends." He took three paces backward. "And now the gold. Carefully, so I will not think you have a gun or knife in the front of your belt."

Maguire eased up his sweater, tucked it over the ammunition belt and undid the pouched money belt. "I bought American dollars with half of it. Nineteen thousand in gold was a little too difficult to handle."

"Nineteen thousand?"

"Spent a little, kept a little out. You wouldn't begrudge an old friend traveling money, would you? After all the rum you've drunk without paying?"

"Pass the belt behind you." Maguire twisted partway around, saw Lucca had stepped backward. "Too far for a play, Maguire. Just lay it over the barrel." He did. Lucca tilted the pump shotgun. The money belt slid down to the stock where he transferred it to the crook of his left arm. "I am truly sorry, my friend."

"So am I, Ricco."

"I think this will be a very bad time to be in Mexico. Especially for anyone Señor One Eye does not hold in high favor. The gold would have slowed you down."

"You're very considerate."

"What's a friend for?" Lucca grinned wolfishly. "This way you'll be able to move fast as lightning."

"While you slip off to Vera Cruz. And maybe to Sicily?"

"I'm not foolish enough to tell you where I am going, Maguire. Now please lead the way to the door." The pressure of the shotgun herded him across the garage. "We will step out and talk like old friends. That way our eyes will get used to the light. By the time you can see to get your gun, I'll be blocks away."

The door opened and Maguire, followed by Lucca, stepped out into the brilliant afternoon sunshine. They stood quietly, neither speaking, Maguire tense but calm. The gun was lowered, unobtrusively pointed at Maguire's legs. "Well, it's time. So long, Maguire. Maybe we meet again someday."

"Sure, Ricco. As friends."

Lucca started down the alley at a slow trot. Maguire stepped back inside, closed the door and waited for his eyes to adjust. When he could distinguish the black of the car from the surrounding darkness, he retrieved his gun and, with an almost laconic air, resumed preparing the Studebaker for the long journey ahead. The ground shook underfoot. Dust settled from the rafters. A shell had fallen uncomfortably close.

Riciotti Lucca kicked in the already battered door of a plundered and abandoned pharmacy emptied of medicines and remedies. All he wanted was a den, a retreat, a safe hole until nightfall. He swung the shotgun to cover the empty interior; quickly and professionally he checked the back room and the single closet. Perceiving no threat inside, he hurried to the front window, ducked below a jagged border of ruined shutters and peered up the street.

"Don't follow, *amigo*," he said apprehensively, then snorted in disgust at the Spanish word. He'd been in Mexico City too long. He was turning Mex. "Last thing I

195

want," he grumbled, vowing to get out as soon as possible.

Something moved. The shotgun swung up effortlessly. Lucca held his fire. A cluster of old women dressed in drab black widow's garb entered the street from an alley and started to search for booty. Harsh voices shooed them off from the occupied buildings. One of the crones found the crumpled body of a *federale*. The others, seeing her picking at the corpse, descended like the birds of carrion they resembled. Within seconds the dead *federale* had been dragged into the middle of the street and stripped naked.

Still no Maguire. Good, Lucca thought, heaving a sigh of relief. He really didn't want to shoot Maguire. They had been friends for too long. But all that money! And Fuentes, to boot. A bad combination. After all, Maguire wouldn't want Fuentes to get his money if he were captured and killed. Better his friend Ricco had it. He lay aside the shotgun. "You guessed it, Maguire. First Vera Cruz," he said, unfastening the belt. "But Sicily? No, thank you. Paris! Oh, I will have lovely, tall women. Beautiful ladies for the taking. And a little château, maybe. And perhaps . . . perhaps . . . "

His voice trailed off. He ripped open a second pouch. A third. All of them, until a pile of gray metal washers and strips of torn newspaper lay on the floor at his feet. Outside the old women froze as an unearthly wail floated from the looted pharmacy less than ten yards away. Blessing themselves, they clutched their booty, lifted their long black skirts and ran off as fast as age-brittle legs could carry them.

16

The frenzied vengeance of the dispossessed mob was a lethal storm that raged up streets and down alleys. Windows were shattered. Broken doors and shutters swung free on their hinges. Cries of frustration and rage preceded the mob like a tidal wave of fear. Maguire listened and peered out of a slit cut in the poncho covering one of the front windows. A small, two-storied, brown adobe brick hotel stood across the street. Neither shabby nor elegant, *Los Nieves del Invierno*, the Snows of Summer, was described as quaint by the *gachupines* who took their paramours into the hotel's shaded, fern and flower bedecked and wholly discrete interior. It was the only undisturbed building on that side of the block.

"He has someone up there all right," Maguire announced, stepping back from the window.

"You really think you are that important to One Eye?"

Payton asked, trying not to sound worried, "that he would send one of his men to watch the place?"

Maguire slung a bandolier across his shoulder. "He's a good hater. What I can't figure out is why he's held off so long. Only reason I can think of is Mrs. Van Allen. She's prominent enough across the border to warrant caution on their part." And maybe to be our ticket out of here, he added to himself, not without some feelings of guilt. The fact that the mob outside wouldn't be as discriminating put him in an untenable position. With Lucca gone, he couldn't hold out alone. Not even with Blue and Payton's help.

"Where do you want the water keg?" Blue asked from the hall doorway.

"On the floor of the passenger compartment. Get the mattress from Aurora's room to wrap around it. That water may have to last us." Blue nodded and withdrew. "Well? What about you?" Maguire asked, leaning over the rows of cards decorating the tabletop.

DuClerc shook his head, coughed into his handkerchief and folded it so the flecks of blood couldn't be seen. "I have no stomach—or lungs—for adventure, *monsieur*," he said, playing a black ten on a red jack.

"Listen." Shouts. Glass breaking. Gunfire. Unleashed madness coming closer. Looters. "When they finish with *El Madronito,* there won't be a drop left to drink—or an unbroken glass to drink out of."

"I have no quarrel with Captain Fuentes." DuClerc smiled wanly. "I was smart enough to lose to him the one time we played. The three tens I dealt him beat my aces and jacks."

"The crowd out there couldn't care less," Maguire said, a note of pleading in his voice. He didn't want to leave DuClerc behind. "The only sensible thing to do is get out. Like your five-hundred peso limit. Live to play another day."

DuClerc played the ace of hearts, followed by the two

and three. In the same motion, he unfolded the handker-chief to expose the clots of blood. "You know better, Maguire."

Maguire stared down at him. Eighteen years, they'd known each other. The fastest rapier on the Gold Coast. "Yeah. I guess I do." Maguire held out his hand. "See you around?"

"Sure." They shook hands and Maguire turned to leave. "Maguire!" DuClerc fumbled at his waist and a bright gold chain flew through the air. "Here. Pass it on someday. Be careful." He played a king on an empty space and turned up a new card.

Corinne waited in the courtyard. The shadow of the madrone tree draped her like a mantle that covered the spun gold of her hair. "Would you like to be alone for a last look?" she asked.

Maguire stared at her, his face like weathered granite. "Why?" he asked, harshly. "Why the hell should I?"

Twenty-five pounds each of flour and beans. Five pounds each of coffee and sugar. One pound each of salt and baking powder. Cooking pots, coffeepot, spoons, tin cups and plates. One bed roll of clothes for each person. For the car, toolbox, three spare tires and patch-ing kit, two hundred feet of stout rope, a tarp, oil, six five-gallon cans of gasoline wrapped in blankets and placed in a makeshift box tied securely to the rear bumper. Three machetes, two Winchesters, a twenty gauge birdgun, two .45s, a .38, the Le Mat and enough ammunition for a small army.

Blue tucked the tattered mattress taken from Aurora's room around the water keg on the rear floor of the Stu-debaker. Everything Maguire had mentioned was packed. For something else to do he unbarred the shed door and eased it open.

The first boy landed with enough force to propel Blue

into the back alley. He flung the weight away. A make-shift club thudded off his shoulder. He saw a brown face—then two and three—and struck out blindly with both fists.

A blade glittered. Blue sidestepped, ducked and grabbed for his .45. A woman screamed and dove for his hand, pinning it to the holster. He slammed his free arm down across the back of her neck. She dropped. His hand free, he pulled the automatic and, holding it too tight, fired two rounds into the air.

The pack retreated a few paces. Blue held the gun in front of him and started backing toward the shed door. "Stay back!" he barked. "Just stay back! All of you!" Not a one of them understood a word he said, but they heeded the message that needed no translation—the gun.

"I don't want to shoot any . . . " The edge of a brick caught his heel. He tripped, fell backward and saw the warped tines of a wooden pitchfork coming toward him from the side. The recoil of the Browning surprised him: he could not remember pulling the trigger. The man with the pitchfork was caught in mid-leap, twisted and flung back against the courtyard wall. Blue watched, horrified as the man hung there a second and then, leaving a crimson streak behind him, slid to the ground.

The rest of the howling pack fled as Maguire appeared. Gun in hand, he dragged Blue to his feet. The man against the wall did not move. He looked to be all of eighteen. Blue stared at the automatic.

"Come on, Patrick Henry. Let's get out of here."

"Jesus, I . . . "

"Hurry." Maguire shoved Blue toward the shed door. "That bunch was only for starters."

"Leave me alone!" Dazed, heartsick, Blue squeezed his eyes close. "I killed him. I killed him . . . "

Maguire's hand stung Blue's cheek with three rapid slaps. "You listen and listen quick. It was him"—he pointed to the prostrate man Blue had shot— "or you with a wooden pitchfork in your gut and twelve hours to think about it. Now get in the car or stay here." Spinning on his heel, he left Blue, trotted around the corner and into the shed.

Corinne was in the back seat, Payton in the front. Maguire cranked and the engine caught. He rounded the fender and jumped into the driver's seat. "Where's Blue?" Corinne asked, worried. Maguire advanced the spark and put the car in gear.

"I don't know about this," Payton said, one of the Winchesters uncomfortable in his hands. Perspiration beaded his forehead and his cheeks were pale.

Maguire eased out the clutch. "You rather stay here, too?"

An explosion shook the alley. "No." The piano player adjusted the rifle in his lap. Out of town, he told himself. He'd be safe. Find friends who appreciated his talent. He'd just keep thinking of that. Keep thinking . . .

The car nosed forward into the side alley. Maguire hesitated. If he went to the right and the street in front of *El Madronito*, they'd have to run the gauntlet of the mob gathering out on Niza. Possibly even some of Fuentes's men. He spun the wheel to the left and the back alley just in time to see Blue round the corner and fling himself onto the running board. "You'll have to go right," he panted, jumping down again and running ahead of the car.

Maguire gunned the engine, shot into the alley. Blue preceded him, throwing out of the way garbage cans, old wagon wheels, pieces of timber and any other obstacle that would have slowed the Studebaker. Maguire glanced in the rear-view mirror. A crowd of men dressed in prison garb surged up the alley and halted at the rear gate to *El Madronito*. The first one was already climbing over the wall. Soon the gate would be open and the crowd of looters inside. Maguire forced DuClerc from his mind and concentrated on escape.

"Road's clear near as I can tell," Blue shouted, jumping into the rear seat with Corinne. The shock that had so unnerved him moments earlier seemed to have passed.

"Hold on!" Maguire called back. "Here we go!"

No one saw the woman until it was too late. One of the party that had attacked Blue, she stepped out from behind a fence and hurled a large rock that struck Payton on the temple. The Winchester went off, shooting out part of the windshield. Payton slumped over onto Maguire, who swerved and pushed the injured man away from him. The car jolted. Behind them, the woman howled and fell. Maguire spun the wheel right. The Studebaker missed the edge of a building by a hairbreadth and emerged onto the street.

"I don't know about this," Payton groaned, holding his head.

"Hang on," Maguire said, accelerating. "We'll get you fixed up as soon as we can." The car lurched from side to side as he tried to avoid the worst of the chuckholes. At last they found a clear stretch. Maguire speeded up, squealed around a corner and angled north. Ahead two groups of men on opposite sides of the street were exchanging shots. "Get down!" Maguire shouted, sliding down in the seat.

Hot lead whined through the open windows, ricocheted off the hood. Just barely able to see over the dashboard, Maguire made himself as small a target as possible and then, realizing the dazed Payton still sat erect and exposed, tried to pull him down. Suddenly a tire blew and the car swerved. He jerked the wheel, fought to bring them under control and straighten them out. The right-hand side of the car darkened as a man leaped onto the running board. Maguire wrestled the wheel and reached for the Le Mat, knowing he would be seconds too late. A .38 revolver in a woman's hand appeared over the back seat and two shots rang out. Struck in the wrist and arm, the boarder howled and tumbled to the pavement.

The street battle lay behind. Maguire found a quiet side road and pulled to a stop. "Cover me with the rifle," he told Payton. "You all right?" he asked Corinne.

Her face was white as she reloaded the .38. "Yes."

"Thanks."

"I've learned a lot in the last dozen years," Corinne answered.

"Yeah." He opened the door. "Let's get that wheel changed," he called to Blue. They were prepared for just such an emergency. Blue pulled one of the three spares out of the back seat and started undoing the lugs while Maguire hurriedly jacked up the car. Within minutes the new wheel was in place, the old, shredded one lay discarded in the street, and they were ready to move. "Let's go." Blue jumped in the back, Maguire in front. "Payton."

No answer. The piano player lay slumped in the seat, head tilted back, mouth hanging open. "Damn!" Maguire jumped out again, ran around the car and dragged Payton onto the sidewalk in front of a bookstore and propped him against the wall.

"Excuse me," a voice said.

Maguire looked up. A narrow face encumbered with thick glasses and a scraggly goatee peered at him through a splintered window. Maguire could make out a hunched, crooked form wearing a shiny black coat and a bowler hat pulled down almost to his ears. "Are you the owner?"

"Yes. I'm Mr. Priest. Rare books. Antiquities."

Maguire folded a ten peso note and tucked the money into an open crack in the glass. "Will you see that he's buried?"

A clawed hand plucked the money from the glass. "The book business is bad these days," the merchant said.

A stray shell from a distant artillery piece smashed into the façade of a gallery across the street, exploded

203

and showered them all with debris. A hunk of masonry obliterated Priest's remaining window. Cursing whoever had ordered the deliberate ravaging of the city, Maguire ran back to the car. "Ride up front!" he shouted to Blue as he dove behind the wheel. "You stay down," he told Corinne over his shoulder.

Blue climbed into the seat still moist from Payton's dreadful head wound. Maguire shifted, let out the clutch and advanced the spark. As the car leaped forward a shell scored a direct hit on the space they had just vacated. Hot shrapnel thick as bees filled the air around them. Maguire gritted his teeth and prayed for the tires. They couldn't afford to lose another one so early in the game. As for the extra cans of gas, he could only hope the combination of wood and blankets would be enough protection against stray bullets.

The shelling stopped as abruptly as it had begun, but thick, choking dust still clogged the air. Maguire slowed to a crawl to avoid potholes and then suddenly swerved to one side and stopped. A pair of horses dragging a half-destroyed trolley car emerged out of the dust. As they passed, the stink of long dead passengers assailed the nostrils. Maguire, Blue and Corinne stared as horses and charnel wagon, like ghosts, faded from sight in the cloud of dust.

They backed, started again. The farther they went, the thicker the dust, until they were moving blindly. Grit and acrid gray smoke stung their eyes and filled their lungs. The road became lumpy and the car bucked and heaved. Sighs and groans accompanied them. The stench of putrefaction increased. "Dear God . . . dear God in heaven," Blue moaned as they turned a corner and the dust parted.

They rode on a street of dead men. Bloated corpses, three and four days old, lying in twisted configurations, choked the street. Riddled, cut, gouged and dismembered, the decomposing figures had been caught in the act of attacking, crawling, cradling friends and comrades. In their midst black · ravens and dun-colored vultures feasted as far as the eye could see. Glutted, too sluggish to fly away, the carrion eaters waddled out of the path of the Studebaker.

There was no choice but to go on. Knuckles white, eyes straight ahead, Maguire kept to the center of the street. The car bounced over one body after another. Bloated abdomens exploded with soft pops. Bones snapped. Mouths burst open and released trapped air in marrow-chilling sighs.

The mind reeled. Maguire, Blue and Corinne united in a silent scream of incomprehension.

Find a way out!

The hideous groaning, the stench of escaping gas.

Rigid jaws jerking open.

The clutching, pecking, waddling, sated birds.

The accusatory sighing, worst of all.

The limousine lumbered past and over the final barricade of slain *federales*, the wreckage of machine guns and scattered rifles. With luck, the worst was over. Once through the jumble of a wrecked marketplace, they would hit the Avenue of the Virgin of Guadalupe and a straight road out of the city. Maguire pulled out the throttle, swerved around a demolished cart and avoided a dead horse. Another two hundred yards . . .

Rifle fire, and the blasting roar of a shotgun. "Keep an eye out!" Maguire yelled to Blue.

The all-too-familiar figure of Riciotti Lucca emerged from a hidden corridor of broken stalls and carts, danced through a hail of ricocheting bullets and ran toward the car. Behind him, a dozen *rurales*, led by Jesus Fuentes, followed on horseback.

"Shoot, damn it!" Maguire shouted. Blue poked his head through the window, sat on the door and fired over the top of the car. The limousine squealed around a corner, sped up.

"Aren't you going to stop for him?" Corinne yelled from the back.

"Bullshit!" Maguire roared. "Aim for Fuentes. Shoot the son-of-a-bitch!"

A weight hit the side of the car. Maguire glanced over his shoulder. One arm hooked around the doorpost, Lucca was standing on the running board. "What the hell are you doing here?" Maguire yelled.

"I started back to *El Madronito* and ran into Fuentes." He threw his shotgun into the rear seat. "Give me your gun."

"The hell you say!"

"They're getting closer, Maguire."

He glanced in the rear-view mirror. Fuentes had recognized the Studebaker and was closing the gap. Cutting across corners, jumping debris, *Los Serpientes* converged from all sides. Maguire jerked the Le Mat from its holster and handed it through the window to Lucca.

The .45 roared and one *rurale* tumbled from his horse. The Studebaker smashed through an empty stall. Boards flew in all directions and a strip of canvas caught on the hood ornament and nearly covered the windshield. Maguire reached across the car and caught Blue's belt. Face bleeding where a board had struck him, Blue slumped in his seat. Wasting no time, Maguire enlarged the bullet hole in the windshield with his fist, reached through and jerked free the canvas.

Fuentes and his *rurales* had closed to within fifty feet when the Studebaker finally hit an open stretch. Slugs thudded into the luggage compartment, smashed through the rear window. Barely heard over the din, Fuentes screamed for Maguire to stop and fight. Then the shotgun bellowed. Maguire craned his neck to look into the rear seat. Corinne had shot through the rear window and the recoil from the Parker-Hale had knocked her to the floor. Behind them, not wishing to face another blast from a twelve-gauge, Fuentes's men were scattering. Lucca cheered. A grim-faced Corinne climbed onto the seat, and massaged her shoulder. Blue, exhausted, unbuttoned his shirt, sat back and let the wind dry the sweat from his chest.

Maguire concentrated on the road ahead.

They rumbled to a halt high on a pine-covered slope overlooking the war-torn city. Fires raged, purging entire blocks. The rattle of gunfire, made almost innocent by distance, testified to the continued death throes of the capital. Like an illustration in a book depicting the tortures of hell, purple clouds linked the great volcanic crests rising high above the valley floor.

Maguire stood alone, facing the past and all he had left behind. *El Madronito*, undoubtedly wrecked by now. Du Clerc, as dead as Payton no doubt. Aurora, Dauphine and countless others—he knew from experience that he might never see any of them again.

Too near for comfort, Corinne waited by his side. "What are you looking at?" she finally asked.

"Ashes," he said.

And out of them, resolve. Maguire turned and walked to the car. There was a good hour of daylight left. And his son waited.

North.

17

Patrick Henry Blue had seen sights he hoped never to see again. He had killed a man and shamed himself twice in front of Maguire. The *New York Times* had never seemed farther away.

He watched Corinne tending the fire. Maguire and Lucca were off in the woods somewhere. Mercifully Maguire hadn't mentioned Blue's moments of weakness. Blue rubbed his eyes, lay back on soft pine needles and tried to sort out the last few hours. He'd killed a man. Killed. He'd pulled a trigger, a gun had jumped in his hand. A man lay dead, crumpled against the courtyard wall of *El Madronito*. That was horrible. And yet there was more than just that awful realization at work. Much more. The Browning had leaped into his hand as if it belonged there as much as a pen. And in that moment, in the very struggle for his life, the aversion to violence was replaced by a

209

fierce elation that frightened him more than anything he could remember.

The late afternoon sky overhead glowed with a metallic sheen. Lucca slung the shotgun over his back, drew a knife from his boot top and picked his way through the pine and oak. Maguire hadn't said two words to him since the running battle in the marketplace. Hadn't acted for a second as if anything out of the ordinary had happened. But the man was thinking. Mulling over what to do next. He had to be.

Got to find him before he sees me, Lucca thought, thankful he'd worn the dun-colored *serape* over his white shirt. Trouble was, Maguire would be hell to see in that damn black sweater. That Maguire. He was . . .

The audible click of a hammer thumbed back snapped the stillness.

. . . a crafty one.

"You wanted me to hear that," Lucca said, careful not to move. "So you must want to talk." The Italian shoved his stiletto back into the boot sheath. Maguire rose from behind a low shrub. The Le Mat was still holstered. Lucca grinned at the bluff. "That's a dangerous game, my friend. I might have tried you."

Maguire shook his head. "You have the utmost regard for the sanctity of human life," he said, and began picking up pieces of dry wood for the fire.

Lucca unslung the shotgun, leaned it against a tree and helped with the firewood. "That was very unkind of you, Maguire. Those washers and that newspaper were a terrible trick."

"So was stealing them."

"I only did what you expected me to do." The Italian tossed a handful of sticks on the growing pile. "Where is the wrong in fulfilling the expectations of others?"

"Ricco, you have an intriguing set of values."

"Of course. Am I not descended from the Caesars?"

"I thought it was Garibaldi."

Lucca shrugged. "Him, too."

They worked in silence broken only by the snap of wood being gathered. Lucca kept glancing at Maguire, but neither man said anything. Finally, when they'd gathered enough to last the night, Maguire signaled a halt and sat on a piece of rock. The sun was almost down and the western sky blazed with orange-pink mackerel clouds. Lucca sat by him, pulled out his stiletto and picked a piece of broken bark from under his fingernail.

"Okay, Maguire. You want me to talk first so I will. What's your proposition?" No answer. Lucca sucked the blood from under his nail. "On second thought, let me guess. You need me, eh? The woman will stand but she is a woman. *Señor* Blue is just a pup. So you need help."

"That's right. Are you available?"

"Ah, you are tricky, Maguire. How do I know if I am available until you tell me how much you will pay and where we are going?"

"North," Maguire said. "To take back Mrs. Van Allen's son."

Maguire was being slippery again, leaving something out. "Take him back from who?" Lucca asked suspiciously.

"Gregor Bortha."

"Ahhh!" Lucca exhaled slowly and scowled. "Our old *jefe*, eh? I don't know. Bortha's memory is long. Perhaps he still wants to hang me for breaking into his wine cellar. There would have to be much incentive for me to . . . "

"One fourth of twenty thousand. The fourth that's in gold."

Lucca looked dubious. "I don't know. Fuentes rides for Bortha. He saw us escape and will be following. If he catches us"—he clucked his tongue dolefully—"that will be some fight."

"Half," said Maguire, getting up and dumping a load of wood into the Italian's arms. "My final offer."

"*Compadre!*" Lucca beamed.

Maguire slung Lucca's shotgun across his back, picked up the other half of the woodpile and started back to camp. "Just don't get any fancy ideas. The money's hidden."

"Hidden!" Lucca hurried to keep up with the taller man. "But suppose something happens to you, God forbid?" he asked, already checking the treetops for snipers.

"Oh, I don't think I have to worry. Not with you along to protect me—'old friend.' "

Walking into the smell of coffee, Maguire and Lucca joined Corinne who was alone in the dancing firelight. Kept at bay by the campfire, the chill night air stalked the camp and waited for the shadows to deepen.

Maguire had pushed for another fifteen miles, a distance he calculated was well beyond the endurance of Fuentes's already spent horses. Satisfied at last, he'd pulled off the road, bounced across an uneven meadow and parked on a hill, ready for a quick rolling start in the morning. The camp lay on the rear slope of a natural bowl. Above them, a semicircular ridge of stony ground, rimmed with stubby, windblown pines, protected them from the unceasing north wind. Below a thick mott of young oak kept them and the fire safe from prying eyes on the road. As extra insurance, a shallow hole scooped out of the thin topsoil and circled by easily gathered stones contained the firelight.

Corinne offered coffee and food. Lucca gratefully accepted a plate of beans and chunks of roast left over from the night before, sat cross-legged on the ground and began to eat. Maguire waved his aside and ambled upslope. Blue was leaning on the hood of the Studebaker and staring into the gathering darkness. Wind soughed through the pines. The motor ticked with steely pings as the mountain air sucked the last of the heat from the metal block. After the noise and horror of the city, the pristine emptiness of space rang in their ears. Maguire propped one foot on the bumper, rested his elbows on either side of the brass radiator cap.

The car was covered with a film of dust accumulated during their wild ride and escape into the mountains. Maguire rubbed a spot clean with his forearm. "I used to be able to shave in this," he said. Blue stared at the lusterless black paint, back up to the emerging stars. "Rough going back there," he continued in a soft voice. "You fought well when it counted."

Blue considered his hands. They looked pale in the starlight.

"Damn casino made me soft," Maguire ruminated, as much to himself as Blue. "The easy life has a way of sneaking up on you. First thing you know, bathing becomes a habit. That and three meals a day and a real bed at night." He patted his belly, grimaced and thought of the hard miles ahead. "Yeah. Too soft."

Blue stared at the line of trees, picked out Orion's belt. Orion was a hunter given immortality by Artemis. Why, he couldn't recall at the moment. A dead man lay in an alley and bloated corpses had whispered to him.

"There are two ways of coping with the fact you've killed a man," Maguire said bluntly, tired of pussyfooting around. "You can moon about, ask a thousand unanswerable questions, feel guilty and sorry for yourself and in the process be generally useless, or stand and keep on doing what needs to be done." He paused, not relishing the prospect but having to ask anyway, as much for Corinne and Lucca as for himself. "Life isn't going to get any easier for the next few days, and I have to know. Tonight. Which is it, Patrick Henry?"

For the first time Maguire had said Blue's name without derision.

"Know thyself," Blue said.

"What the hell kind of answer is that?"

"Solon of Athens. A Greek. Do you know about the Greeks, Maguire? I do. I studied them. They built cities

213

and a whole civilization dedicated to learning. Philosophy, art, political theory. A golden civilization. A golden age."

"And what happened to them?"

"Rome."

"Say what you mean," Maguire snapped. "Soldiers. Barbarians. Men like me destroyed them. Right?"

"You don't have much use for people like me, do you?" Blue said.

"That depends on who you are."

"And what the hell kind of answer is that?"

"The choice is yours."

"I don't know," Blue admitted in a weak and puzzled voice. His brain spun. "Do you remember the first man you killed?"

Silence then, between them as Maguire's own thoughts drifted into the past. "I was nineteen and camping out in mountains like these," he began. "A drifter came on my camp, tried to steal my food and my horse. If I'd let him, I would have died up there in the snow."

"So?"

"So I shot him." Maguire rubbed his palms on his thighs.

"And that was that?"

"No, that wasn't that," Maguire said, remembering he'd had to close the unknown man's eyes. That night, frightened of the dark and of his deed, he hadn't been able to sleep. "But it's not something I talk about a lot."

"Then you know what I mean," Blue said. "You see, it's something that can't be resolved in a hurry."

"On the contrary," Maguire answered icily. "Given the circumstances, a hurry is all you're allowed."

Maguire woke instantly when Lucca tapped him on the shoulder. The cold was numbing and the ground hard. Joints stiff, he rolled onto his belly and pushed to his feet. Lucca handed him a cup of coffee.

Maguire groaned, wrapping the blanket around him.

The coffee was very black and very bitter. "Thanks. Anything going on?"

"Quiet as death," Lucca said. "Except for an owl up on the ridge. Scared the shit out of me." He grinned. "Good to be out again though. Damn city was getting on my nerves."

"You'll be sore in the morning."

"That's fine with me." Lucca unwrapped Payton's bedroll and shook out the blanket. "Those people down there are crazy. I ran across one bunch. You know why the damn cannons were shooting all over the place?"

Maguire pulled on his gloves, checked one of the Winchesters. "No."

"Drunk *federales* having a good time. Shoot off a round, let the recoil bounce the cannon where it wanted and then load and fire again without aiming." He shook his head sadly. "That's no way to fight a war, Maguire. That's just crazy."

"Takes all kinds, Ricco." Maguire poured the last of the coffee into his cup, added some water and a handful of grounds to the pot and hung it back over the fire. "Wake you in the morning."

"Right." Lucca lay his shotgun on the pile of dry grass he'd fixed for a bed and rolled up in his blanket.

The fire popped. An ember flew out and landed next to Blue. Maguire dumped the dregs of his coffee on the glowing coal, rinsed his cup and hung it next to the other three. Lucca had been right about the quiet. After almost two years in town, the silence was unnerving. Maguire pulled the knit cap low over his ears, wrapped the blanket tighter around him and left the fire. Twenty feet away, next to the bed of pine boughs he'd made in the lee of a fallen oak, he stopped and knelt at Corinne's side.

Thirteen years. And still the left corner of her mouth drew up in a slight smile when she slept. Ever so gently, he pulled the cover up around her neck, arranged the tarp so the wind wouldn't find her head, and started to leave.

"Maguire?" she whispered.

"I thought you were asleep," he whispered. "We have a long day tomorrow."

"I want to know. Truth. What are our chances?"

"We have a chance. A good chance," he answered, clarifying himself for her benefit.

Corinne smiled, reached out and squeezed his hand, then stretched up and kissed him lightly. "Thank you for lying," she said.

"It was worth it," he replied, again tucking the cover around her. "Get some sleep."

"Okay, Maguire." Voice tiny, almost like a child. But not a child, Maguire knew. He gazed down at her and remembered. And then stalked uphill to check the car before he started remembering too much.

"Mexico City," Maguire said. The point of the twig marked an X in the dirt, traced a straight line in the cleared ground and scratched another X three feet away. "Bortha's *hacienda*, southeast of"—another mark a few inches farther along—"the city of Chihuahua."

"How far is that?" Blue asked.

Maguire glanced at Lucca. "Too far for the car. Around seven hundred miles as the crow flies. More by road. We'll never make it all the way."

"So what do we do?" Corinne asked impatiently.

"What few roads there are across the Central Highlands aren't good, but I think we can handle them. I'm acquainted with a few *hacendados* along the way who will sell us some gas."

"You hope," Corinne said.

"I know," Maguire said grimly. "Old favors," he added by way of explanation.

A new line starting from Mexico City arced to the left and rejoined the original line two-thirds of the way to their goal. "The railroad crosses our path in Lago Blanco, in the foothills of the Sierras, then runs north to

Chihuahua and on to the states. No trains are running out of Mexico City, we know, but the trouble shouldn't be affecting the schedules that far north. Especially since Lago Blanco is a health resort and mineral water spa catering to wealthy Europeans. There isn't a faction I can think of that's eager to disrupt or antagonize all that money."

"I wouldn't count on that," Lucca cautioned. "The way things are, we don't know who is doing what or where. Don't forget that craziness with the cannons I was telling you about."

"You have a point," Maguire agreed. "Even so, Lago Blanco and the train north from there is our best bet." The stick tapped the point that represented the resort. "Matter of fact, the way things look right now, it's our only bet."

"Lines drawn on the ground are one thing," Blue said grimly. "But that looks like a hell of a distance. Can we make it?"

Maguire flashed his most disarming, enthusiastic smile. "Easy," he said, smoothing over the crudely drawn map. "Easy as pie."

18

Studebaker "40"
" . . . the net result of more engineering experience than any other single car made . . . "
"Send for a copy of the MOTORIST'S LOG BOOK (with maps), giving the actual experience of a prominent motorist while touring France, Spain and Italy in a STUDEBAKER, . . . "

The left front fender was gone. So was the windshield and rear window. The hood latch, along with sundry other nuts and bolts, had been bounced loose and assorted rattles and clanks drowned out the sound of the motor. Trees and brush had chipped and gouged the paint and broken the right windshield support. The oil pan was leaking; only a gasket improvised from strips of Lucca's hat saved the motor from certain destruction.

The village they were approaching probably had a name, but nobody knew it or cared. They were all too tired.

The villagers heard the Studebaker before they saw it. Chickens craned their heads in alarm. Pigs scurried for cover. Curious dogs trotted down the road to investigate the strange noise. Mothers clutched their children and disappeared into dusty *jacals*. Fathers grabbed hoes and machetes and formed a brave line across the road.

A cloud of dust was the first visual hint that the noise was attached to a man-made contrivance. The men nervously licked their lips and told each other they were not afraid—until it came around the knob of the hill. Bravado disintegrated and the line faltered until Chaco, a young man who had been all the way to San Luis Potosi, a two day's walk to the north, stepped forward.

"This is the machine I told you of," he announced with great pride and the relief that accompanies vindication. No one had believed his tales of the machines that moved with great clamor and without horses or oxen to pull them. Chaco's eyes flicked to the third *jacal* on his left where he was certain he caught a glimpse of his girl watching him. His chest puffed out and he swaggered to the edge of the path the machine would have to take and folded his arms. The rest of the men, not wanting to seem afraid, stepped closer—but not as close as Chaco.

The machine traveled like the wind. Dust spewed out from under the wheels and hung in a long, thick cloud that stretched back down the road. The dogs turned tail and ran. The men held firm and gaped. The machine was as long as two oxen, taller than a man. Great eyes stared from the front of it and smoke rose from its nose. It was black as the devil himself and covered with dust.

Four *gringos* rode the beast. Two sat in front, two in the rear. The machine slowed as it approached. Someone pointed and nudged his neighbor. An excited whisper passed from man to man. A *gringa* sat behind a wheel. The wheel, when twisted, caused the machine to go from one side of the road to the other and so miss the deepest holes.

The three men passengers did not look rich. Bearded, eyes bleary, they slouched on luxurious seats of leather and dangled their feet out the windows. The one in the front seat was a bear of a man. Sound asleep, his mouth hung open and his head bounced up and down with each bump the machine hit. The ones in back looked very dangerous, though they feigned sleep. The villagers instinctively knew they were awake and watching.

Only Chaco dared stay close enough to touch the car, and in the process earn the grudging admiration of the whole village. Haughty and proud, he waited until the machine drew abreast. Then, as if the great clanking, snorting mass was no more than an ox, he reached out and let the curved metal pieces at the front and rear of the machine brush against his fingers. Little more was seen, for the cloud of dust enveloped him. When the dust settled, his girlfriend gazed at him with new respect.

That night, the village stayed awake until the moon was high. Over and over they told the story of Chaco's bravery, of how he did not fear the metal monster or flee from the large gun that pointed at him through the window. And, most marvelously of all, how the curly haired *gringo* with the ring through his ear smiled and winked at him, just as if they were the best of friends.

Chaco's girl came to his *jacal* later.

The trip had degenerated into a cursing, sweating, numbing ordeal. Such roads as existed were little more than trails for oxen and wagons between poverty-stricken towns. Occasionally a cleared stretch lasted five or six miles. More often the men were forced to chop away fallen trees or clear underbrush. Worst of all were the times all three strained against the rope to pull the heavy limousine up an impossible incline or, conversely, brake down equally insane slopes.

Miles and hours ceased to have meaning. But when

they neared San Luis Potosi they realized they were making progress. That night, eyes red and ears ringing with fatigue, they ate ravenously, drank too much tequila and tumbled into real beds that seemed uncomfortably soft after the cold, hard ground.

Lucca was in the worst shape the next morning. Several swallows of pulque helped, but it wasn't until three trips to the privy that he could function as a normal human being. By that time, Maguire had scrounged an extra tire and some gasket material. Blue and Corinne had the Studebaker loaded with food, fresh water and full gas tanks. "All downhill," Maguire announced as Lucca creaked into the rear seat and tried to find a comfortable position.

Blue tossed the last canteen onto the floor. Lucca winced. "Please," he whispered faintly, then cringed and held his temples as the motor sputtered into life.

They made good time out of town. Twenty miles and an hour later, the limousine struggled along the edge of a ridge where the road had undergone severe erosion. As they crossed a particularly worn stretch the land under the left wheels crumbled and gave way. Turning left down the steep bank, Maguire steered the bucking, careening automobile past boulders and jagged tree stumps, somehow managed to keep it upright as it skidded sideways, almost overturned and finally gained the valley floor. "That saved a lot of time," he called cheerfully over his shoulder. The bloodless, wide-eyed faces of his fellow travelers showed they were less than amused.

The desert highlands were a snap compared to the mountains. By the end of the first day, luckily for Lucca's hangover, the odometer showed they had covered almost ninety miles. That night they camped under an unrestricted dome of stars, surrounded by the haunting wails of coyotes. Morning dawned a dusky, gritty yellow. The wind had risen and blew stinging sand from the north to slow their progress. Before the day was out the motor was running roughly and they'd had to stop a half-dozen times to dig paths through the shifting, blocking sand before they could regain the proper road. A mule and a wagon, or even horses, would have posed fewer problems, Lucca grumbled, spitting out a mouthful of grit.

Six days into the trip, they crossed the railroad. In another car they might have been able to deflate the tires and ride the tracks, but the Studebaker was too wide. Stretching off to the northeast on a long arc that would bring it back to Ciudad Lerdo, the shining rails mocked the sweating, cursing men. Shortly after the crossing, the limousine suffered further damage. Lucca was driving and, feeling cocky, swerved to haze a wild-eyed bull. Bellowing with rage and looking for a fight, the old longhorn lumbered out of the way, then turned and charged. Corinne screamed. Maguire woke up with a start just as the bull ran full tilt into the rear door and fell back on his haunches, dazed but still angry. Maguire stared at the door hanging from the bull's horns. Lucca kept his eyes on the road and his mouth shut. Blue was about to comment, but a glance from Corinne convinced him silence was golden. When he dared look into the back seat a half hour later, Maguire was asleep again, one leg hooked over the jump seat so he wouldn't bounce out.

The gas generator for the headlights met a watery demise on the third crossing of the Rio Aguanaval. The left rear fender fell off on the rocky incline up the bank, at the top of which they had to stop to dry out the motor. The tires, patched and repatched, barely holding on to bent and dented rims, didn't look as if they'd hold up much longer. The oil was black as coal and full of sand. Maguire added the last quart and hoped they'd make it. Gasping and wheezing, the Studebaker traversed the pine-covered and gradually rising land and stumbled onto the main road into Ciudad Lerdo.

"Lago Blanco here we come," Lucca croaked.

"Be there by noon," Maguire said, looking back at Corinne. "I told you we'd make it."

That they had was a minor miracle, testified to by the looks in the eyes of the startled inhabitants of Ciudad Lerdo. Never before had such a rare quartet of *gringos* ridden out of the desert to the south. Maguire sat stiffly erect and guided the bedraggled limousine down the narrow streets lined with gawkers. Corinne sat next to him. In the rear seat, Blue and Lucca kept wary eyes on the crowd.

Palacio Gomez, nine miles down a decent road, was no different. Finally, just out of town, they turned right on the road to Lago Blanco. A mile up the long slope, the road was cut by a stretch of mud. Maguire stopped and slid out of the car. Corinne slipped behind the wheel. Blue opened his door and stepped out. Lucca didn't have a door to open. By force of habit all three lay their shoulders to the rear of the car and pushed it through the mud. Corinne stopped. Less than a mile ahead, a fairy-tale village waited. "Lago Blanco!" Maguire announced. The Studebaker shivered and groaned. And died.

Blue staggered by and stopped in the middle of the road. "Jesus!" he said, shaking his head in disbelief.

"Nobody ever said it would be easy," Maguire snapped.

Blue's strength had proved invaluable on the journey. He'd been the draft horse who had pulled the auto out of one impossible situation after another. Now he looked gaunt. His face and arms had been burned by sun and wind. His clothes were torn and covered with mud. Head and shoulders thrust forward, he turned and fixed Maguire with a murderous stare. "Yes, they did," he snorted in disgust, and started walking toward the town.

Maguire's feelings were hurt. His knowledge of the country had brought them through. His car had been ruined. He was as tired as everyone else. "Who?" he asked Lucca.

"You," the Italian wheezed, wiping a gob of mud from his cheek. "We going to leave this here?"

They managed to start the engine after a maximum of coaxing. The limousine rolled protestingly forward, lurching like a drunken man on its battered wheels. When they caught up with Blue, he grudgingly stepped onto the running board, which promptly detached itself from the car.

The limousine stopped fifty feet down the road. Three heads turned in unison. Behind them, a forlorn Blue stood on the useless piece of metal. Maguire put the Studebaker in reverse and backed up. Blue just stood there, staring dully at his feet and the broken running board.

"Blue?" Corinne asked.

"Huh?"

"Get in. Let's go."

Blue looked at Maguire. "Your running board fell off," he said.

"Get in," Maguire growled. Exaggerating his movements, Blue stepped off the running board, carefully climbed into the rear of the car and, with infinite caution, closed the remaining door behind him.

Maguire sighed.

The stationmaster was as curtly officious as his moustache was flamboyant. He stared with disdain at Maguire's haggard, bearded face, at the gaping holes in his black sweater and his worn, muddy and torn Levis. The strangest creatures appeared in days of unrest and the stationmaster, in the time-honored manner of pompous minor officials the world over, had pegged this newest arrival as one not worth his time. Luckily for him Maguire had left the shoulder holster with Corinne and the others, out of sight around a newly painted warehouse.

"The next train, señor?" the stationmaster asked in the precise English he reserved for the gringos who had never bothered to learn Spanish. "The first train from Mexico City since the troubles." His voice oozed with contempt.

"Troubles?" Maguire asked innocently, glancing at the wall calendar. The last circled date was February 23, eight days since they'd fled the city. Eight long, hard, exhausting days, Maguire thought, suddenly tiring of the stationmaster's arrogance.

"Yes. Now did you want a ticket?"

Maguire placed his hands flat on the counter and leaned forward slightly. His eyes glittered dangerously from under dusty eyebrows and his voice was edged with a new hardness. "I asked, my friend, what troubles?"

The stationmaster cleared his throat. One never knew with *gringos*. This one looked as if he could cause trouble of his own. "You have not heard?" he asked, taking comfort in Maguire's ignorance. "Why, General Victoriano Huerta resides in the presidential place. It was he who put an end to the ten tragic days of looting and killing."

"And President Madero?"

"*Ex*-President Madero is dead," the stationmaster announced, wondering why the *gringo* should care and trying to read an answer in his eyes. "We have heard conflicting reports. One says bandits attacked his car as he was being taken to prison; another says he tried to flee and was shot." He looked Maguire up and down once. "It is said Huerta will put the country in order again," he added, in a manner that showed how pleased he'd been when the uncultured had been reassigned their proper places.

Francisco Madero, the gentle dreamer, was dead. Maguire forced himself to remain unmoved. "And the first train north from the city arrives tomorrow?"

"That is what I said," the stationmaster repeated impatiently. "And now, *señor*, I am a busy man. If you want information, I am sure you . . ."

Maguire pulled a thick roll of peso notes from his pocket and peeled off the outside four. "Four first-class tickets," he said, tossing the bills onto the counter and stuffing the rest into his shirt pocket. "To Presidio."

The stationmaster stared at the bills, at Maguire and back to the bills. His moustache twitched nervously and he sat up straight. Whatever his appearance, this was certainly a man of wealth. Perhaps he had had an accident. "Yes, sir," he said respectfully. "Four?"

"That is what I said," Maguire answered in Spanish.

The stationmaster produced four tickets and fumbled with the change. Inside he seethed with fury at the inconsiderate nature of the rich, who treated those of lesser fortune in such a peremptory manner. Outside he smiled politely. "Will there be anything else, sir?"

"Yeah. I want to send a wire to Chihuahua."

"Your pardon, *señor,* but I am afraid that is impossible. Only yesterday were the lines to Mexico City repaired. Those to the north—" He sagged demonstratively. "What can I say? Our village has fallen on hard times. A rascal of a bandit rides the hills, cutting the lines and causing much consternation. *Señor* Broussaria's guests have been unable to leave or communicate with their families. Most are angry and upset."

"Bandit?" Maguire asked.

"*Si, señor.* One called *la Halcón.*"

"The hawk—a woman bandit, eh?"

"A bloodthirsty, vicious *soldadera, señor,* with no compassion in her heart." He turned and gestured out the window. "Our poor village. What will we do when the wealthy Europeans flee? You can see for yourself . . . " He turned back to the room and realized he was alone. The *gringo* had disappeared down the street. The stationmaster tugged at his moustache and began to grumble anew at the inconsiderate rich.

Broussaria's was a regal resort hotel and mineral water spa in the grand European tradition. Monsieur Antone Broussaria, world traveler and hotelier, coming upon the thermal springs only eight years earlier, had recognized a veritable gold mine. The physical setting alone was enough to make the heart leap. Far to the west, the Sierra Madres rose in breathtaking leaps to snow-crowned peaks. The springs themselves, set around the six-thousand-foot level, bubbled through white limestone into a series of jewel-like small pools which overflowed into a larger lake some hundred feet below, on a level with the hotel. The water in the pools, which emerged at a precise one hundred and ten degrees, was said to have curative and restorative powers. By the time it flowed into the larger lake it had cooled to an invigorating sixty to seventy degrees. Most marvelous of all, the lake emptied over a natural dam where the water fell for thirty-seven feet, there to form a pool again and to flow in a swift, clear stream that disappeared under a massive boulder just above the village of Lago Blanco.

The hotel M. Broussaria had built was a credit to the natural beauty of the spot. Within two years of his discovery, a gingerbread château, looking for all the world as if it had been lifted intact from the Swiss Alps, rose adjacent to the lake. Cedar walkways interconnected the major springs and the lake below. For those whose hearts were too weak, or whose bodies were too corpulent, a two-car funicular railway clanked up and down the slope between the hotel and the springs. Colorfully painted, donkey-drawn carts traveled the gravel road between hotel and the village below. The donkey carts were the extra stroke that made the difference between success and failure, for Broussaria knew his clientele. Nothing could be more pleasing to the monied patrons than to walk the primitive streets, haggle for trinkets in the tiny shops and mingle with the charming and quaintly unsullied natives. The natives, for their part, gladly accepted the easy money that trickled down the mountainside, treated the guests with deference, smiled profusely and kept their streets clean and their children dressed.

American dollars and a strong hint of mystery gained the four travelers acceptance and rooms overlooking the valley. A half hour later Corinne was deep in a tub full of scented water. At her side, the hotel seamstress displayed dresses hurriedly carried up from the hotel dress shop. Assured a simple but elegant eggshell cotton gown would be ready by dinnertime, Corinne waved away the seamstress and slipped into bed, to fall asleep immediately.

Three rooms down, Blue rinsed off, wrapped a towel around his waist and padded onto the balcony. Dry, thin air cooled by shading pines wafted against his chest and legs. Strange, how a person ended up in unlikely places, he thought. Barely a month before he'd been trudging a dusty road in Texas looking for a story. Now he was part of a story. He looked at his arms, browned as a result of the eight-day journey. He'd always been strong, but now he was tough as well, lean and hard as the rocks they'd traversed. Not many men had pulled and pushed a ton of Studebaker limousine over five or six hundred miles of mountains and desert. The accomplishment left him feeling almost exuberant.

And strangely lonely, too. Maguire was impossible to decipher. Lucca he thought he understood, and consequently considered unreliable. As for Corinne—he frowned. She was a mysterious lady in many ways. Outgoing one moment, reclusive the next, she seemed alternately intrigued and repelled by Maguire. Blue tried to swallow his jealousy and concentrated on the job at hand. A story would come out of all this. His story, under his byline, Patrick Henry Blue.

The mountain breeze held him at the balcony, and fluttered the empty pages of his notebook, lying open and long neglected on a nearby table.

Lucca wriggled his toes above the soapsuds and thumped the white-gray ash of his Havana into a Ming vase set by the tub. He watched Maguire spread their weapons, smuggled in a rolled *serape* past Monsieur Broussaria himself, on the meticulously designed hand-woven bedspread. Of more interest to Lucca was the money roll Maguire had flaunted and then managed to hide again. Lucca damned himself for not being more observant. He sipped Bacardi, considered the implications of so much money and planned his questions. "Tell me, my friend," he asked after an appropriate interval. "Does Broussaria's bill come out of your half or mine?"

"You would prefer beds with lice and dinners of boiled dog and pulque?" Maguire asked, emptying the first bandolier. The bullets were covered with grit. Each would have to be cleaned. "We are both paying, *compañero*. After all, we are two generous men," Maguire finished.

"Too generous, I'd say," Lucca snorted, and then began to laugh. "Ah, Maguire. You are a sly old fox, you know? But listen. Next time I would prefer to be consulted, eh? After all, half that money is mine."

"Not yet it isn't," Maguire replied tersely. "We've a way to go yet." He began to field strip the first Winchester. "Meanwhile you might heave your ass out of there and help with these. That is," he added sarcastically, "if it wouldn't be too much trouble."

"But that will take all afternoon," Lucca protested, realizing the importance of what Maguire said and yet groaning at the prospect.

"At least," Maguire agreed, blowing a grain of sand out of the firing pin spring. A gun coated with grit jammed, and these days, a jammed gun was the easiest way he knew to die. An afternoon was a cheap price to pay for a life. Especially his own.

19

The most astute observer never would have guessed a revolution had just been fought, or that bandits roamed the mountains. Broussaria's was a world unto itself. In the main dining room, exquisitely dressed ladies accompanied by portly, tuxedoed husbands or slim, dashing traveling companions, gossiped in cultured French and German. Silent waiters served at damask- and silver-covered tables. Glittering crystal chandeliers sparkled brightly and shimmered off a thousand precious jewels to add to the air of expectancy that charged the room with electric excitement.

The train was coming! Tomorrow, most of the diners would be on their way to the United States, away from troubled Mexico. Not that anyone mentioned the fact. That would have been a breach of the stern etiquette that required the true aristocrat to rise above the vicissitudes of daily life. In any case, the revolution did not concern them any more than the clouds of war gathering over their own continent.

A faint buzz of curiosity followed Maguire, Corinne, Lucca and Blue as the *maître d'* escorted them to an out-of-the-way corner table. Determined to be cheerful, Maguire ordered a sparkling burgundy, glared at the occupants of the next table and thanked his lucky stars Lucca's back was to the rest of the room. Beans, rice, tortillas and fried meat had been their fare for the past eight days. The feast that followed was sumptuous beyond the ability of their tongues to appreciate. A delicate cheese soup lightened with beer, spiced with a dash of tabasco and garnished with flakes of parsley served as the appetizer. Next came a small trout baked whole and topped with a white sauce, the secret of which resided in M. Broussaria's head. For the entré milk-fed veal had been sliced paper thin and laid on a bed of baby onions and delicate French cut green beans, all ringed about with chestnut-sized unpeeled baby potatoes. Translucently thin sugar cookies accompanied by a frosted dish of lime sherbet acted as a dessert, followed by cheeses and fruits, coffee and liqueurs.

Lucca made joking pretense to be confused by the profusion of forks and knives and spoons. Blue acted embarrassed by the Italian's comments, followed Corinne's every example and in the end secretly wished he'd had twice as much of everything. Maguire ate quietly, rarely speaking, preoccupied with the coming journey and disturbed by the presence of Corinne, who sat across from him and chattered animatedly throughout the meal.

Evenings at Broussaria's often ended with the men grouped in select circles in the billiard and smoking room, and the women in the salon. On festive occasions a recital or dancing brought the two groups together. This night, however, a subtle change, triggered by the early exit of the strange party of Americans, could be felt throughout the dining room. The current of fear struck even the most blasé, and one by one, the subdued diners rose and hurried past a distraught Monsieur Broussaria.

Night and the crisp music of dancing flames lulled Corinne into dreamy semiconsciousness. Eight days of dust and heat and cold, thirst and gnawing hunger, were behind her. Within the next twelve hours she would be on her way north again, closer to Christopher. Maguire would rescue him, she was sure. Bring him back home. Maguire. Her eyes closed and she was with him again after thirteen years of separation. Together . . .

Her head jerked and she blinked her eyes. "Mustn't think of Maguire," she mumbled, trying to get comfortable in the soft, wide bed. "Get some sleep . . . "

The fire beckoned. The bed was too soft. Hardly thinking, Corinne rolled out of the bed and threw the goose-down comforter, folded twice, on the rug in front of the hearth. Outside the wind moaned through pines and whistled through the decorative gingerbread, reinforcing the wonderful sensation of protected seclusion. Yawning, she wriggled out of her slip, let it drop to the floor. The glowing coals bathed the tawny muscles of her thighs and hips with radiant warmth. Light gleamed on the golden wealth of her hair. She had slept that afternoon because she had been exhausted. Now, bathed, rested and full, she was delightfully sleepy. Stretching, she sank onto the comforter and let the warmth rush across her belly. "Perfect," she whispered. "Perfect."

Except for one thing Corinne would not admit. And he was only a room away. Strangely, silently sad, she dozed, and slept at last.

She dreamed of strong but gentle hands kneading her shoulders and neck, running down her back. Lightly the hands floated across her buttocks and stroked her flanks.

Purring. Content. Corinne stirred and rolled over. Fingers brushed her temples, touched her eyes and caressed her lips, which she moistened with her tongue. Still asleep, she moaned as the hands pressed up against her breasts. At the same time, something moist plucked gently at one nipple, then the other.

The hands ran down her belly, pressed fleetingly above the soft mound where her legs met and moved on. Involuntarily her legs parted slightly in response to the insistent pressure on the inside of her thighs. The lightest of touches, a tantalizing breeze, played against her most private parts.

Eyes widening, startled, she awoke.

"Beware of unlocked doors," Maguire said throatily. "They are an invitation. Did I frighten you?"

"No. Yes."

He stood, pulled off his shirt. Her eyes slitted as he stepped out of his trousers and stood over her, rising out of the firelight into shadow. When Corinne reached upward, Maguire sank to his knees by her side, shivered slightly as she ran her hands along his length and whispered his name.

"And now?"

"Now," she said, guiding him between her legs. "I frighten myself." And rose to meet his weight. And cried out once, as at last they were joined.

She padded back from the bathroom, knelt by his side and handed him a warm towel. "What about the others? Did they see you leave?"

"Probably," Maguire said, stretching and enjoying the lulling, languid minutes after.

"So they know about us?"

"Does it bother you?"

"It should." His cheek pressed against the flat of her stomach. "It should bother us both."

Maguire grunted. "Not me." Playfully he wiggled his jaw, kissed the underside of her breasts.

"Your moustache tickles," Corinne giggled.

"You don't like it?" Maguire asked, rubbing her breasts with his cheek.

"Mmmmm."

"What's that supposed to mean?"

"It means you're vain and arrogant."

"And you want me to stop," he mumbled.

Her nipples hardened at the touch of his lips. "Not that," she said, pulling him to her. "Not that at all."

Their eyes met. Hungrily, side by side, their bodies stretched to touch along their lengths. What started as a playful kiss exploded into frenzy as their tongues met and probed. When they parted, Corinne lay atop him, felt him rising between her legs. Deftly she slid down, breasts tracing twinned lines of fire on his chest and stomach, then enfolding the hardening flesh.

"Maguire, Maguire," she whispered, guiding him to her. She settled slowly, watching him slide into her, feeling him fill her. Their eyes locked. His hips rose and he moved inside her, touching her with flame, binding her to him until, at last, muscles shrieking, the surging convulsions caught them both and held them, a single, melting statue against the fireplace.

Thirteen years. Thirteen missing years . . .

The fire was a dull ashen memory. Their lovemaking was not. Maguire lay quietly, thinking about the small picture in his shirt pocket. A son. His own flesh. Funny how he'd never contemplated leaving part of him behind. That wasn't true though. He had considered the idea before, but rejected it as inappropriate. A son didn't fit into the kind of life he lived.

A man's mind is capable of strange journeys, especially in early morning hours when the earth is still. Suddenly the old reservations disappeared. Things did change, after all. Hell, he was almost forty-one. Old enough to put away the guns, forget all that nonsense and settle down. Corinne could even have another kid or two. A farm or ranch would be the best place for them to live. A few years of honest work would do him good. He'd probably even learn to like it after awhile. At least he'd have something to show for all the years. Something to pass on to his son. Not like DuClerc, who'd left only a watch, for God's sake. That was no way to leave the world.

He knew if he stood to look out the window, the valley and village below would be bathed in the first emerald light of dawn. The prospect was exciting. Dawn. A new day. A notion he would have dismissed with a cynical shrug even a day ago had become acceptable, even desirable. Hell yes, Maguire could have a son. And a wife, too.

"What are you thinking?" Corinne asked, stirring in the crook of his arm. "Regrets?"

"Pretending to sleep," Maguire said, pulling her closer to him. "That's no fair."

"Which answers my question not at all."

"Tell me about the boy. My son." Corinne stiffened, rolled to the left and got to her feet. Naked, body gleaming in the half-light filtering through the curtains, she padded to the bed and gathered her clothes. "Corinne?"

She stopped, shoulders rigid, cheeks flushed. Of course he'd ask about Christopher instead of her. Thirteen years ago, Lee or no, she would have left with him if he'd asked. But a woman wasn't reason enough to overcome his scruples. A son was. Did he have to be so obvious, damn him? "He's very much like his father," she said evenly. "Never backs down. Stubborn. Oh, yes, stubborn and opinionated. His way is the only way."

Confused by her abrupt change in attitude, Maguire got up, crossed to her and touched her shoulder. Corinne jerked away from him, scooped his clothes off the floor and tossed them at him. Her eyes glistened. "Get out!"

Maguire dropped his clothes on the bed, caught her arms. "Corinne, we . . . "

"Let me go!" she hissed, trying to free herself.

"Not until you tell me what's bothering you."

"Just leave now. Please."

"No. I've been thinking. I want you, Corinne."

"You want Christopher. You want a son."

"All right. I want my son. But you, too. I want us together. We'll find a place, get married . . . "

"Stop it!"

"Is that so wrong? So terrible?"

"You're too late, Maguire." She jerked her arms free and turned her back on him. "I'm already married. I have a family. A husband and a son."

"My son," he insisted.

"Not any more! You gave him up when you took that train without me."

"And now?" Maguire asked roughly. She looked so vulnerable. Tiny, almost. Naked and tiny and vulnerable. He wanted to touch her but didn't dare because tenderness might be construed as pleading. "You know I'm right, Corinne. Last night proved it."

Corinne turned to face him. Maguire thought for a moment she was going to slap him. He had never seen her look so intent. "We crippled him once," she whispered hoarsely. "Would you do it again?"

"Guilt won't work, Corinne. Not now."

"We crippled him!"

"You don't love him."

"I never said that," she snapped, eyes flashing. "Not once. I do love him. As I did you."

Maguire looked at her as if he'd never seen her before. She stood erect, shoulders straight, eyes staring into his. She was sure of herself, but he was surer. He would win, and knew it, as he knew how their bodies fit together. "You've decided then," he said simply, already planning a campaign to change her mind.

Corinne turned and walked around the bed to the window. "Time decided for us, Maguire," she finally said, and pulled open the curtains to let in the morning light.

20

Rumor said the train, which was scheduled to arrive at six, would arrive at nine. Broussaria's was a beehive of activity by seven. M. Broussaria himself tried to be everywhere, exhorting his guests not to panic. The trouble in the south would not affect them. They would be safe. His pleading was in vain. The more he talked the more determined were the looks on the faces of his patrons. By eight a steady stream of donkey carts laden with trunks and suitcases rolled down the half-mile gravel path to the town below.

Maguire, Corinne, Blue and Lucca were among the first to leave. They carried little. Dressed in the clothes they wore when they arrived in Lago Blanco—clean and mended overnight by the hotel seamstress—they stood out in sharp contrast to the rest of the guests. They carried only bedrolls containing the new clothes they had bought the day before, and the cleaned and oiled weapons.

The plaza and train station were packed. Vendors hawked food and trinkets with little success to the irritated travelers who lined the platform and stared down the tracks. Maguire gazed wistfully toward the storage shed where the Studebaker was parked. He wished there was a way to bring the car with him, but that, in addition to a monstrous repair bill, would be prohibitively expensive, even if room could be found. So it had to be left behind. *El Madronito* and now the Studebaker. He was losing everything. Except Harvard's cane, which he had sworn he would never lose. He checked Corinne's bedroll, where the silver panther head peeked out of one end.

The shrill whistle of the train sent a charge of excitement through the crowd. Maguire looked around. "What happened to Blue?" he asked, concerned.

"Here." The youth wedged between a pair of argumentative Frenchmen. "I got to thinking," he said, handing each of the other three a *serape*. "If Fuentes has one of his men on the train, we might want these. Sort of blend in the crowd a little better."

"Good idea," Maguire agreed. "Put them on. I didn't figure on such a crowd. Let's work our way down the track." The whistle blew again and the crowd moved even closer to the tracks as the engine appeared around the bend. "Grab my belt," Maguire shouted to Corinne. "Don't get lost."

Eight passenger cars and four boxcars. "Try for the rear," Maguire shouted over the crowd's noise. The passenger cars would have little room to spare in any case. The boxcars might be their only chance. The way was blocked by a growing throng of brown-skinned girls with baskets of wares, old men come to see the first train since the new revolution, buxom matrons with children in tow. Barking dogs and crates of squawking chickens added to the din. The indignant wealthy, unaccustomed to being pushed, shoved, mauled and ignored, voiced complaints in cultured English, crisp German and flowing French.

"Oh, shit!" Maguire grabbed Blue's shoulder, turned him around. Corinne and Lucca stopped behind them. The train was squealing to a halt. At the same time, the boxcar doors slid open and armed men leaped to the ground to stretch their legs and toss pesos into outstretched hands that offered neatly stacked, steaming corn tortillas in return.

Los Serpientes! Maguire grabbed a young girl selling *sombreros*. "How much?" he asked quickly.

"*Tres pesos, señor. Son sombreros de mas alte calidad. Tres . . .* "

"Never mind," he cut her off with a handful of coins. "*Quatro. Dame quatro.* Put these on before they spot us," he said, switching back to English and trying to figure what their next move would be.

A thicket of hands waved from the windows as hungry passengers tried to buy food. Villagers surging forward to supply them vied for space with Broussaria's guests, who were becoming panic-stricken. A familiar figure wearing a glittering eyepatch stepped onto the platform of the last car and gestured to one of his men. Maguire's hand crept beneath the *serape* that draped him front and back and hung to his knees.

"Head for the lead car," he said, as the *Serpientes* began to fan out and mingle with the crowd. "Walk slow and stay together. It's our only . . . Where's Lucca?"

"He was right here a second ago," Blue said from beneath his *sombrero*. He was walking awkwardly, knees bent so his height wouldn't give them away.

"Maguire!" Corinne hissed.

Maguire lowered the brim of his hat as one of the *rurales* pushed through the crowd, stopped and spun around. The barrel of the Le Mat poked through the *serape* and touched the man's stomach. "It's a good day to die, Chino," Maguire said.

241

The *rurale* stiffened. He and Maguire had fought for the same side in the old days, so he knew how dangerous Maguire could be. Carefully he held out his palms to show his hands were free of any weapon. "There is no such thing," he answered, cursing the distance between him and his friends. Of course, with the *gringo*'s gun where it was, and his freedom to move restricted by all the people around him, friends hardly counted. Chino realized he was the most alone man in the world. The scar on his cheek turned upward as he forced a grin. "You are making a bad mistake, *amigo*."

"Don't you make one," Maguire said, deftly pulling Chino's .45 from its holster and passing it back to Blue. The *serape* muffled the click of the Le Mat's hammer being pulled back, but Chino heard. The corners of his mouth dropped.

"Turn around carefully and start toward the front of the train," Maguire ordered. Chino obeyed the nudging barrel. Corinne and Blue followed as unobtrusively as possible.

"What about Lucca?" Blue whispered.

What everyone took for a shot sounded in the shed where the Studebaker was parked. Before Maguire could respond, the throaty roar of an automobile cut through the noise of the crowd. A second later the limousine appeared, and horn blaring, cut across the plaza, smashed through a rail and bounced onto the station platform. A woman screamed. People began to fall back and a ragged path opened in front of the battered, jouncing car.

"It's them!" a voice roared in Spanish. The burly shape of Adolfo Suarez battered his way through the milling throng.

The Studebaker swerved toward a knot of *Serpientes*. Lucca pumped a load of buckshot into the midst of more *rurales*. Men howled and fell to the ground. Women screamed and snatched up their children. Vendors dropped their wares and ran, thoughts of profit not nearly as important as self-preservation. A chicken crate flew into a dozen pieces and a cloud of feathers filled the air. Leaving a wake of crushed valises and ruined food, the limousine bumped across the tracks, sped around a corner and into the town.

Pandemonium reigned. Women screamed, children bawled. Men shouted orders, cursed and struggled to keep their families from being crushed. Unnoticed at first in the commotion, the boxcar doors were opened to their full width in order to unload already saddled horses. Fuentes was first in the saddle. Suarez bludgeoned his way through innocent *peones* and wealthy vacationers alike, grabbed the nearest horse and joined the chase. A huge fat woman collided with Maguire, separating him from his captive. *Serpientes* on rearing, plunging mounts trampled anyone in their path in their haste to follow the Studebaker.

"To the engine!" Maguire shouted, pushing Blue ahead and dragging Corinne behind him. The frequent reports of rifles in the town told him Lucca was leading the *Serpientes* on a merry chase, but Chino was bound to attract attention and rally those behind. They had little time to spare.

Maguire's boots crunched on gravel. The machete scabbard on his back slapped him with each jolting step. The three ran past the first-class coaches where the faces of the fortunate rich stared at the near riot surrounding them. Maguire caught an iron rung and swung up into the cab of the locomotive. The engineer, a *Norteamericano*, glared at him in hostile surprise. "No one allowed in here, bub."

"We have tickets," Maguire said, hauling Corinne into the cab.

"Don't get funny with me," the lank, overall-clad trainman growled.

"Get this thing moving." The engineer's eyes widened

at the sight of the Le Mat. As he shrank back, Maguire snapped the gun up and fired once as one of Fuentes's *Serpientes* leaped from the lead coach onto the tender.

The *rurale* jerked, flung away his Springfield, clawed for his sidearm and died in motion. Maguire brought the revolver to bear on the engineer. "Now!"

"I need a fireman. I ain't got no fireman!"

"Let me worry about that. Blue!" Corinne stepped out of Blue's way as he climbed abroad. "The man needs steam. Feed it," he ordered.

Blue stared. "Feed it? Where's the automatic stoker? What the hell kind of engine is this?"

"Ain't my fault," the trainman stammered. "It's old, is all."

The engineer released the brake lever. Maguire kicked open the boiler door and spun Blue toward the coal piled near the boiler. "Shovel, damn it!"

The train slowly eased forward. Blue hurled a shovelful of coal into the fiery box. Then another, and another. His movements seemed lethargic at first, but soon speeded up. Shouts and cries of alarm sounded from the tracks to their rear, but the train gathered speed. Maguire yanked a rifle from his bedroll and handed it to Corinne. "If he tries to stop this thing, shoot him here," he said, indicating the engineer's crotch. "She will, too," he added by way of parting, and climbed back into the tender.

A well-placed nudge sent the *rurale*'s gray-clad corpse tumbling over the side. Maguire settled behind a hillock of lumpy coal and peered over the tender roof. He thumbed the hammer, set the gun to fire the underneath barrel. They came as he expected, two *Serpientes* left behind by Fuentes, running along the narrow walkway on the roofs of the cars.

Chino was in the lead. A second one followed. Maguire waited until they were midway along the closest passenger car, then stood, gripping the Le Mat with

244

both hands. Chino stopped abruptly and clawed at his rifle. The man behind him, not seeing Maguire and not expecting Chino to stop, collided with him and knocked him off balance. The Le Mat roared. Buckshot ripped into the *rurales'* flesh and hurled them backward. Holding his leg, Chino rolled down the slanting roof, his screams lost, ground beneath the pounding iron wheels. The young one, his chest pumping pink froth, lay spread-eagled on the walkway, staring into the blue-white beauty of the sky, trying to remember the faint, clear cold taste of wind in the pines.

"What happened?" Blue called from below.

Maguire began transferring coal to the locomotive cab floor. "Two more," he said.

"Maguire!" Corinne shouted, pointing to a limestone overhang ahead.

Maguire looked up to see Lucca waving to him from the edge of the precipice. He pointed behind him and, obviously anxious, motioned the train forward. Maguire frantically shoveled coal to make a more or less even landing place, then jumped out of Lucca's way and into the cab. Beside him, the engineer kept the throttle full open and an apprehensive eye on Corinne. Maguire stripped off his *serape* and poised on the edge of the tender, ready to jump back in and help Lucca.

The shadow of the leading edge of the cliff passed. Lucca, shotgun in hand, was in the air. He hit feet first, arms flailing wildly, shotgun flying. Maguire grabbed the gun, tossed it into the corner with one motion. Lucca's feet slipped on the coal and his shoulder slammed into the side of the tender. Maguire caught his arm and jerked him bodily onto the more stable platform of the cab. Lucca staggered backward, held onto an upright steel bar for support and, as if expecting applause, bowed graciously to Corinne.

"You're getting old," Maguire said.

"Old?" Lucca wiped the back of his hand across his

245

mouth. It came away bloody from where he'd bit his lip. "What's old? I made it, didn't I?"

"You used to land on your feet," Maguire replied. "What the hell happened? Where are they?"

Lucca pointed. Fuentes and a score of *Serpientes* lined the edge of the cliff and watched in frustration as the train pulled out of range. There was no way they could continue the chase. Maguire waved to them. "Pretty neat trick," he said.

"That ain't all, *amigo*," Lucca said, pointing to a mushroom of oily smoke rising over the treetops. "Your car." He grinned, joyfully twisting in the barb. "Wheel collapsed. I ran into a rock wall."

"Figures," Maguire mumbled, and to hide his disappointment, climbed into the tender and started shoveling coal down to Blue. Within moments his black sweater was wet with sweat and his shoulders began to ache. Nevertheless there was no way to avoid seeing the greasy, curling cloud that marked the final resting place of the Studebaker. It hung in the air like a tombstone, on which was engraved in dark letters the tale of simpler, easier days.

21

The engine's six great driving wheels stood the height of a man. In front of them a pair of smaller trailing truck wheels supported the weight of the driving pistons and helped steady the front of the locomotive. A large glass and brass acetylene lantern gleamed brightly in contrast to the rusty black of the boiler plate behind it. The huge diamond-head smokestack, painted red and green, jutted high in the air in front of the three belled steam chambers atop the boiler.

"She was built in 1881. Mogul 2-6-0's her number," the engineer had told them earlier. "Baldwin built." Since that made no impression, Jory decided not to tell them of the Mogul's distinguished service in the States or its ten dependable years on the Mexico City-Chihuahua-Presidio run after it had been purchased by the Mexican government.

Maguire sat behind and above the locomotive, perched on an unstable platform of coal and leaning back against the side of the tender. From there he commanded a view not only of the interior of the cab, but of the countryside, too. So far the trip had gone well. No one had tried to storm them from behind; no one had tried to shoot at them from along the tracks. Below, Corinne rested in the brakeman's seat and Blue fed the boiler. Blue's hands were chafed and raw, his face blistered, yet he hadn't complained once.

Too bad they'd had to flee Lago Blanco so suddenly, Maguire reflected. They could get along without a brakeman, but the loss of the fireman meant extra work for them all. Jory had grudgingly revealed his name, at the same time promising his complaints would reach all the way to the governor. Of Texas, he emphasized. He didn't trust Mexicans.

Movement along the top of the train. Maguire turned, checked his rifle and relaxed. Lucca leaped from the lead car to the stubby tender roof. Surefooted as a goat, he jumped down to the piled coal and joined Maguire. "You going to keep him at it?" he asked, nodding toward Blue. The roar of the engine made it impossible for their voices to carry to those in the locomotive. "He's not a bad kid."

"I know," Maguire said with a grin. "You can spell him in a few minutes."

Lucca blanched. "I fight," he said.

"So?"

"A man should know his limits. You know that."

He did. Maguire smiled, remembering words said to him long ago. Knowing one's own limits was an important part of the philosophy of men who followed wars and sold their services to the highest-paying faction. A man who didn't frequently took on more than he could handle and became as dangerous to himself and his companions as a jammed gun. In this case, hours of heaving coal would dull Lucca's fighting edge. And Maguire's too, for he would take his turn again. Still there was nothing to be done about it if they wanted to get to Chihuahua. Blue couldn't last the trip without help. They'd simply have to share the task at hand.

"Tell me about the rest of the train," Maguire said, clearing his mind.

Lucca drew a knife from his boot and began paring his nails. Thin strips of fingernail curled in front of the razor sharp blade. "I walked all the cars. None of Fuentes's men are aboard. The one you left above, I helped off."

"The rest of the passengers?"

"Just that. Passengers. Most of them are rich, high-tailing it from Mexico until things calm down. They still don't know what happened back there," he snorted in derision. "The rich never do. Too bad we're not bandits, eh?"

"What about the boxcars?" Maguire asked.

"Empty."

"Damn!"

"Except for the last one," Lucca said impishly. Maguire brightened considerably. "I counted eleven horses."

Cutting like a machete through the stillness of the desert, the rumble along the rails preceded them and spread over the empty land. The train creaked across rickety bridges spanning dry boulder-strewn riverbeds, highballed across vast stretches of sand and cactus. Twice they stopped in tiny towns and took on water. During those times, Maguire posed as a brakeman while Corinne, Lucca and Blue stayed out of sight in the tender. By one in the afternoon they'd started to climb into steeper hills and old Baldwin Mogul labored under the strain.

"Gets prettier the higher we go," Maguire shouted, pointing ahead and shouting over the thunder of released energy. Shirtless, his torso was streaked with coal

249

dust and soot. Emulating Lucca, he had tied a sweat-band around his head. "Another hundred or so miles, we'll be close enough for Ricco and me to head out on our own."

Corinne pushed a strand of hair out of her eyes. "That ought to make Mr. Jory happy."

"I doubt it. He'll stay in a sour temper until he gets to Chihuahua and replaces the bottle of whiskey Lucca stole from him."

Taking a breather from the insatiable maw of the firebox, Blue dodged Lucca's shovel and joined Maguire and Corinne by the window. A sheen of blackened sweat covered his chest, back and arms. He smiled, genuinely happy despite the exhausting nature of his labor.

"You look like pirates," Corinne laughed.

"That's because we are," Maguire said, looking fierce for her benefit. "First time I've ever stolen a train, though."

"Maguire!" Lucca yelled from the tender.

"Keep an eye on Jory," Maguire shouted, bolting out of the cab and scrambling up the coal pile. The climb was harder than it had been a couple of hours earlier. Ten years ago, at thirty, he wouldn't have noticed the difference. "What is it?"

Lucca pointed to a distant pine crowned hill. "There."

Maguire shielded his eyes, caught a brief but sharp glimmer of flashing sunlight. Once, twice, three times. And then repeated. "Looks like a mirror," he said. "What do you think?"

The two men peered into the distance ahead, but the way was too tortuous. Pine, oak and manzanita covered ridges severely limited their vision.

"It's a signal all right," Lucca growled, "but it can't be Fuentes. Men of Bortha's *hacienda*? We come that far already?"

"Bandits, more likely. Probably *la Halcón*'s bunch." Maguire stood and jumped onto the tender roof. The chill mountain air buffeted him. The train lurched from side to side but he rode easily, knees loose and flexing. Black smoke from the stack streamed past above him in a long roiling cloud. "The stationmaster said there might be trouble, and this stretch is her haunt. She'll know the train is packed with rich people getting out of Mexico City. Probably waiting in force. Lord knows they'll never find better pickings."

Lucca wiped the knife across his pants' leg and jammed it into his boot. "Looks like we're in the middle of things again," he said, grinning wolfishly. "Just like old times."

"Not if I can help it," Maguire said, recalling with a twinge the way he used to welcome a good fight.

Bert Jory bit off the end of the one cigar Lucca had left him and hoped he'd get it started before the Italian changed his mind and took it back. Lucca flashed a good-natured smile and kicked a live coal toward the engineer. Jory stooped, picked it up with a pair of pliers, lit the cigar and tossed the coal into the firebox. His practiced eye scanned the gauges. The pressure in the boiler was nearing the red line. Automatically he reached for the release valve knob. In response, Lucca raised the barrel of his gun and swung it to cover him.

"I got to do this or she'll blow," Jory shouted, twisting the handle. White steam hissed from the side of the locomotive. The shotgun didn't move. Jory wiped a burly forearm across his chin and glared at Lucca. "If you didn't have that shotgun . . . " His gloved hands clenched into fists.

"I'd have something else," Lucca said, glancing over his shoulder to see Maguire lead a sorrel mare alongside the cab. Corinne and Blue, each leading an extra pair of horses, waited near the center of the train.

"Let him go, Ricco," Maguire called over the noise of the steam.

"Go?" Jory wailed. "How the hell am I supposed to drive this thing and feed it, too?"

"Give me a minute and I'll send you some help," Maguire said.

"Drive your train, Mr. Jory," Lucca said, pausing before mounting the sorrel. "And be glad you are not as dangerous a man as you think you are." Lucca touched his fingers to the scarlet handkerchief around his head and vaulted into the saddle.

The two men turned their horses and cantered back along the train. At the second car, a gentleman in a frock coat, bowler hat and pin-striped trousers stepped down from the platform. "I say there," he began, removing a pince-nez from the bridge of his very proper nose. "You men. Just what the devil is going on here?"

Marguire tipped his *sombrero* in mock deference. "Bandits, sir."

"Good God!"

A woman appeared on the top step of the platform. Two younger men in fashionable suits made way for her. "What is it, Cecil?"

"Bandits," the Englishman replied.

"Dear me!" the woman exclaimed, clutching the hem of her skirt and scurrying back to the safety of the car.

"We're going on ahead," Maguire explained.

"That's a good man," Cecil nodded in approval. "Scout the way."

Maguire eyed the two younger men, who continued to stare suspiciously at him. He nodded in the direction of the locomotive. "Engineer needs someone to ride shotgun," he lied. "We'll be busy up ahead. Think you can help him out? Knew you would." Without waiting for an answer he joined Lucca, Blue and Corinne, and disappeared up the wooded slope.

Coats flapping in the breeze that whistled through the narrow cut, the pair walked along the track to the locomotive. "Man said you needed some help," the first one said in a thick Yankee accent.

"What?" Jory asked, distracted from his valves. He looked the pair over as they climbed into the cab. "Volunteers, eh?" A broad smile lit his face. Their suits would be ruined, but at least they'd get to Chihuahua.

"The man said to 'ride shotgun,'" the second chimed in, looking around for the promised weapons.

"Shotgun?" Jory asked, perplexed. "Shotgun, hell. If you ever want to see the good old U.S. of A. again, you'll shuck those coats, roll up your sleeves and begin shoveling coal."

"You're kidding!" the first one said, astonished at being asked to do such a menial chore.

"No, he's not," a third voice with a decidedly Germanic accent added. Elrecht brushed a piece of boxcar straw from his long stringy blond hair and leveled a heavy barreled Springfield at the three men. "We're heading back. Off with your coats and get to work. You." The gun stabbed in the engineer's direction. "Reverse. We're going back to Lago Blanco."

Bert Jory glanced at the controls, at the gun, at distant vistas and the painfully bright sky overhead. And beyond that to whatever prankish gods were at play with his fate. "Not even Job," he sighed, throwing a lever and craning to see behind the train. "Not even Job."

Maguire rested the rifle barrel in a notch in the *trinchera*, a moss-covered low stone wall put in place by some long-forgotten builder. Lucca crawled to his side and slid the shotgun over the stone. He'd replaced the buckshot with solid slugs, which, at the range involved, made the Parker-Hale twelve-gauge as effective as Maguire's Winchester. "Easy," Maguire whispered.

Lucca ducked his head below the wall and removed the scarlet headband. "Where is he?"

"Let him move."

The men waited patiently. To their rear heavy oaks harbored acorn woodpeckers whose black, white and red plumage could be seen flashing through the branches like bolts of raw, crackling energy. Mexican jays complained bitterly with raucous cries. Gray squirrels chittered and scolded: the intruders were too near a precious hoard of nuts.

Fifty yards away on the opposite side of the ravine, the vegetation was completely different. Once thick top-soil had, over the years, washed away to reveal a harsh pink and brown volcanic substrata that retained little water. Torrey yucca, spiny lechuguilla and stubby paddles of prickly pear vied for space. Clumps of chino grama grass offered forage enough for such goats as happened to pass that way. Little else other than tiny desert animals adapted to dryness, intense heat and cold, lived there.

Maguire guessed the ravine lay some fifteen to twenty miles south of Ciudad Camargo. Careful to stay well east of the railroad, he had led them a good ten miles north before stopping to make camp for the night. Unless something unforeseen happened, he planned to ride into Camargo the next day. There they would leave Corinne and Blue to wait for another train while he and Lucca cut across the desert to the hills south of Chihuahua, where Bortha's *hacienda* lay.

Lucca elbowed Maguire. A man clad in baggy white cotton shirt and trousers followed a goat trail that slanted up the opposite slope. His features were little more than a dark patch in the shadow beneath the wide brim of his *sombrero*.

"No," Maguire said.

"Not over seventy-five yards," Lucca whispered. "An easy shot and a quick death. Better than what he'd get from the *federales*. Better than what he'd give us."

"No."

Lucca sighed, ran a hand through thinning curls and watched the bandit skyline himself and then disappear over the ridge. "If you're afraid of the noise, there's still time for me to catch him," he said, running his thumb across his throat for effect. "If he cuts across our tracks, we'll be in for it. Better now with the odds in our favor."

"We still may run into his friends before we reach Bortha's. Killing him might kill whatever chances we have."

Lucca grinned. "Well. I suppose I might have missed."

"I doubt it," Maguire said dryly. "Not with that cannon. C'mon. We'd better get back."

Their camp was in a small glade surrounded by a wide-spread cluster of manzanita shrubs. Directly to the north, a madrone tree, reminiscent of the one Maguire had liked so much in his courtyard in Mexico City, guided the two men to the hidden camp. All was peaceful. The horses grazed quietly to one side. Blue had gathered dry broken mesquite and oak and was wisely waiting for everyone's return before starting the fire. He was alone.

"Where's Corinne?" Maguire asked, not liking the feeling of her being absent from the clearing.

"Filling the canteens. Find anything?"

"No. One man, but he didn't see us." Maguire stopped, puzzled, looked around. Everything looked all right, yet something bothered him, tugged at the back of his mind. If he could only . . . "What?" he asked, suddenly worried. "Where?"

Blue pointed toward a huge sycamore at the base of a nearby overhang. "Over there."

"Stay here," Maguire ordered. Boots digging into sand and broken shale, he broke into a run. Branches whipped across his cheeks. Shouldn't have left her, he thought angrily. Should have scouted the area more thoroughly first. Should have checked . . .

He leaped the gnarled, twisted trunk of a fallen oak and glimpsed her leaning back, tilting the canteen to her lips. He sprang the remaining yards and swatted the canteen from her hands. Corinne yelped and fell backwards, eyes wide with panic before she realized it was Maguire.

"Congratulations," she said when she'd caught her breath. "You scared me half to death."

"Good. We're even then. How much did you drink?" he asked, kneeling by the little pool. Spring water glimmered, mirrorlike and clear as glass. Patches of golden leaves covered the bottom, inches beneath the surface.

"A pint or so. I was thirsty." She touched her throat apprehensively. "Why?"

"It's no good," he said, touching his tongue to a handful and then spitting.

He was treating her like a child, and Corinne responded with anger. "I know good water, Maguire. It tasted fine."

"Right." Maguire reached across the pool and touched a peculiarly ashen vine armed with thorns fully two inches long. "The people in these mountains call it Devil's Dagger. It taints the water it grows in."

Anger gave way to fear. "You mean I'm poisoned?"

"I mean you'll probably be sick." He pointed to the sycamore. "Go on over there and throw it up."

"What? I . . . "

"Unless you want me to stand here and watch, get over there and get rid of as much of it as you can."

Corinne stared at him a second, then ran for the tree. Maguire emptied the tainted water from the canteen, listened approvingly as Corinne purged herself. Five minutes later, face white and hands shaking, she reappeared. When she came to him, Maguire held her in his arms. "Will it be bad?" she asked in a tiny voice.

"I don't know. Was that all you drank? When I first found you?"

"A little more a few minutes earlier."

"You probably got rid of most of it. I doubt you'll be too sick. Depends on how much your body absorbed. Come on. Let's get back to camp before Ricco gets worried."

Slowly, Maguire's arm around her, they walked down the long slope. "Isn't there anything I can do?" Corinne asked weakly. "Isn't there anything?"

"Wait."

Lucca and Blue sat by the campfire and, waiting for signs of the illness, watched Corinne. At last, convinced she was asleep, their attention drifted back to the fire and the lonely voices of the wind. "Why doesn't he come down here where it's warm?" Blue finally asked, whispering so he wouldn't waken Corinne.

Lucca shrugged. "He is worried about the bandits. And the train backing up. That surprised him." He spat out a piece of grass he'd been chewing. "Me, too. The engineer acted like there was a fire in his boiler, and the sooner he crossed into Texas the quicker he'd douse it."

"Do you think he returned to Lago Blanco to pick up Fuentes?"

"Could be," Lucca said, minimizing what he feared to be a certainty.

"This Fuentes. Why does he hate Maguire so?"

"Questions, questions, questions." Lucca stood, shook out his blanket and wrapped it around him before lying down. "That is always the way with young pups."

"Young pup, hell! I could break you in two."

"Only if I let you get close enough. Which I wouldn't." Ricco pulled a knit cap over his head and lay back, his saddle for a pillow. "Sleep now, eh? We need the rest." Blue looked like he wanted to press the point, but Lucca glared at him a moment, wriggled around to get one last stone out from under his hip and settled in for some sleep. He'd have to stand his turn on watch in a few hours. But the memories wouldn't let him sleep. And he was a tale teller unable to resist the past.

"It happened a little over two years ago," he began, his voice a low rumble in the darkness. "Maguire and

I were fighting with the *Maderistas*, as was Fuentes. Life was hard. Little food, bad water for the most part. Tempers ran thin among those of us who were fighting more for money than freedom. Anyway, that particular week we drove the *Porfiristas* from a little village by the name of Mapini. The people there were *pacificos*, or peaceful ones. They were farmers; poor people who raised barely enough to feed their children and keep themselves in rags. Somehow, during all the bad years, they had kept their land and wanted no part of the war.

"Fuentes was furious because they had harbored the *Porfirista* army and would not pledge themselves to fight with *Maderistas*. But what could they do, I ask you? No guns, outnumbered, gentle men and women . . . Fuentes chose nine of the villagers and the outlaw priest who led them. The rest of the villagers he set to work digging great pits in a large field just outside the town. When the pits were finished, he had the chosen ten buried up to their necks. Still the villagers, heeding the cry of the priest, would not budge.

"They were herded like animals to watch the slaughter of their own. Fuentes was preparing to gallop his *serpientes* over the unfortunate ten when Maguire and I arrived. We and a dozen others, all *peones*, had been rounding up stray cattle for the *Maderista* army. When Maguire saw what was about to happen, he rode his horse between Fuentes and the buried men, stopped and dismounted."

Lucca paused, remembering, and chuckled. "Ah, my friend, that was one glorious sight. Maguire and Fuentes, face to face. They quarreled, of course, and when the Captain of *Los Serpientes* pulled his machete and rode at Maguire, Maguire stepped aside and struck with his bullwhip. The tip caught Fuentes across the eye."

"And what happened then?" Blue asked.

"Nothing. It was over like that." Lucca snapped his

fingers. "The rest of Madero's army entered the village, and Francisco Madero himself turned the first shovelful of dirt to free the imprisoned ones. For which he was much acclaimed. As for Fuentes, everytime he looks in a mirror, stoops to drink from a quiet spring or passes a window, he sees himself. And recalls his humiliation."

Ricco Lucca pulled the blanket up to his chin. "One day those two will have to settle this," he yawned. "That will be some fight. I hope I am there to watch."

Blue listened, heard only a second, wider yawn, and then deep breathing. Ready for sleep himself, he slid closer to the bed of coals and pulled his own blanket tighter about him. Soundlessly he visualized a blank sheet of paper waiting for the quill of his imagination and formed the first page of a novel.

Four came riding into the kingdom of the hawk, the killing ground of the cougar, the unquestioned territory of the silvertip grizzly, invincible lord of the mountains . . .

The page shimmered, dissolved, and Blue slept.

A snapping twig, a rolling stone, alerted Maguire. Noiselessly, finger curled around the trigger, he raised the Winchester and peered from between the broken rocks. A quarter moon transformed Corinne's hair into a mantle of ghostly silver. "Here," he whispered, placing the rifle to one side.

Corinne traced the sound of his voice to a cul de sac hidden in a jumbled pile of boulders. From his vantage point Maguire could watch over the camp and the approaches to it. "Is there room?" she asked.

"Yes. Barely. Come on in," he replied, making room for her beside him. "Don't burn yourself."

She hadn't seen the fire until she was inside. Mostly coals, the heat from it was captured by the rocks and distributed evenly. In fact, Corinne decided the protected nook was almost cozy—in comparison to the outside, at least. "I thought I'd tell you I'm still alive," she quipped.

"That's not funny. You'll be sick for a few days, is all."

"I know. I'm sorry. But at least it proves you're worried about me." Wrapped in her own, she lay on Maguire's blanket. "I love this," she said, looking at the stars. "Did you know that babies think they are close enough to touch the moon? They reach and reach . . . "

She could feel her breasts rising and falling under the blanket, feel his eyes staring into hers. Slowly, her fingers moved, undid the buttons of her shirt and opened it. The wool was harsh and scratchy on her breasts. Twisting she undid her pants, slid them off into a small heap near her feet. At last Maguire rose and undressed until he stood naked, a light shadow blocking the stars.

"You'll freeze," she said, opening the blanket.

Shivering, he spread his coat over her feet and crawled under her blanket beside her. His flesh was icy cold, but Corinne held him close as she lay wrapped in his arms. Her breasts crushed the matted hair on his chest. His thigh, heavy between her legs, pressed against her. "This may be the last time for us," she whispered. "I want it to be as friends. No obligations, no remorse. Like it used to be—like we used to be—together."

They kissed, gently at first, then harder. In the dark shadows between the stones, little could be seen. A glimmer of flesh, a flash of moonlight on hair. They were thirteen years younger. Lost in the indefinable time between past and present. His arms and belly sinewy and lean, in the darkness. Her breasts full, in the darkness. Her hands found him, guided him between her legs as he hardened. The years fell away, slipped unseen from under the blanket. What time had made of them, how it had changed them, no longer mattered, for the rhythm of love was not subject to time.

Softly at first, tentatively, as if the night before had been a prelude, roving hands were impelled to rediscover every curve and plane of flesh. Gentle and slow the entrance, the acceptance. They lay on their sides, not moving, filled with wonder at the joining that made them one being. Eyes locked, there was no need for words. Corinne reached out and touched Maguire's face. Her fingers ran across his forehead, traced his eyebrows, remembered the slope of his cheekbone and chin. Together they waited, letting the pressure and the need to move build. Who did so first was impossible to say. Perhaps only the fire or the boulders knew.

To be together necessitates prior separation. To fill requires prior emptiness. Maguire shuddered. Corinne's eyes widened, then closed as he drove inward. With the exquisite agony of flesh in flesh, flesh surrounding flesh, male and female locked, one body within the other, Maguire rolled atop her and Corinne's legs wrapped about his waist. The blankets had slipped off them but they'd forgotten the cold, and sweat gleamed on the soft skin between her breasts.

Motion, then, sped by internal fires that raged higher and higher, crescendoing in the silence until they reached the peak and froze, held motionless again in the grip of roaring, climactic surges.

"Maguire," she said, the name a long, drawn-out hiss between clenched teeth.

He did not answer; instead he slumped forward, spent.

Above, corridors of starlight swept the sky and outlined a night hawk. While Corinne watched, the bird was changed into an incandescent spirit that spiraled upward and carried with it all the weeping and laughter of earth to heaven.

She tried to summon it back.

Tried . . .

The cold found them and reclaimed the warmth of the dying fire and the tenuous heat generated by their coupling. Corinne woke to gray dawn. Maguire, his elbows on a rocky ledge, was watching the campsite and scanning the valley through which they'd traveled. Corinne dressed in silence, shivering as she pulled on the night damp clothes.

"We'd better head back down," Maguire said, kicking sand over the dead fire. "Time to move."

"Maguire . . . " Corinne's teeth were chattering so hard she couldn't finish the sentence. Curse the cold, she thought.

He turned to look at her. "Yeah?"

Corinne's face was pale against the blanket she'd wrapped around her shoulders. "Never mind," she said, clenching her teeth to keep them from rattling. The angle of the slope was funny. She steadied herself in an attempt to correct it, but couldn't.

"Better let me give you a hand," Maguire said, concerned.

She waved aside his hand. "I came up alone," she slurred. "I don't need . . . " And fell forward, collapsing into his arms.

22

The old man moved through the cracked and rubble-strewn patio. Skin stretched like leathery bats' wings across the angular bony planes of his body. The years had left him sallow, like the soil and rocks themselves. His legs were spindly and his gait cautious, but his back was straight and his head erect, for he was one of those who do not surrender easily to time. No one knew his age, not even the buzzards who had given up on him save for an occasional pass over the centuries-old *hacienda*. They didn't care that his knees and elbows were bulbous and hard, that his shoulder blades stuck out from his back, brittle and tasteless. One day they would rend away what protein there was, and be satisfied.

Don Memo—the villagers who lived deeper in the valley to the east called him *viejo*—avoided the darkness because he disliked it and because he would know timeless cold soon enough. To breathe is to be warm, he might have said, were there someone to whom he might speak, and were he a talkative sort. This morning, though, the voices had told him he must rise in darkness so he could walk to meet the sun. When the voices spoke he did not hesitate nor question, for he had learned long ago the folly of such disrespect. That was what, he sometimes thought, made an old man wise and a young man foolish. An old man had learned to listen.

A scrawny, brown-spotted goat trotted through the crumbled opening into the patio, stopped and waited. *El viejo* looked at the dusty little animal, who lowered its head in a gesture of determination.

"So you heard too, and would follow me, *Señor* Maximilio?"

The animal bleated in reply and pretended to charge, stopping just short of collison to present a pair of nubby horns in the hope of a scratch or two.

"Very well then. Come. It will be morning soon and I appreciate the company." Together they walked out through the ragged stone walls and into the skyward slanting, yellowed radiance of approaching dawn.

To his right the sun would soon spin upward over the black hills which rimmed the valley. To his left, more miles away than a young man could walk in two days, the peaks of the Sierra Madre Occidental cut the edge of the sky in bold serrations. There, indistinguishable in the distance, great evergreens held dominance amid plentiful springs. It was not to these, though, that he turned, but to the north and west, toward *Los Estados Unidas*. There, between his own home in the foothills and the great river, the land rose and fell in arid, sandy convolutions. Desert country. Kingdom of the *ocotillo* and savage spiked *cholla*, each with its own jealously guarded space. Nothing gentle or promising. For that one must journey to the south or west to plentiful water and wealth and an easier existence.

"But no visions," Don Memo muttered, at last speaking his thoughts. Shaking his head, he continued with measured steps up a gently rising bluff to stand at the edge of a cliff. *Señor* Maximilio touched his leg, and Don Memo drew the bright sliver of steel, all that remained of his machete after a thousand sharpenings. A deft flick of the blade severed a frost-blackened prickly pear fruit from its mother plant. The old man rolled it in the dust to remove the barbs, then picked it up, peeled it and gave it to *Señor* Maximilio to feast upon. Duty done, the old man turned undimmed eyes to the purple blue of the High Lonesome.

His attention was drawn to one peak more noticeable than any of its companion heights. The harsh rock resembled a tremendous, crudely chiseled arrowhead thrust base first into the desert landscape and rising over five hundred meters to a mitered point. The side facing him had been smoothed by countless rock slides. It was to this sight his restlessness, and the voices, had brought the old man. He knew the peak, and the abandoned ruins at its base.

Nothing happened at first, but his was an unhurried vigil. He continued to watch, patient in *serape* and homespun clothes, gifts from a woman who lived in the village and called herself his daughter. Of this he was none too sure, but the woman was not one to be disputed lightly. *Señor* Maximilio nudged his leg again. "Be patient, *mi emporer*. A little longer. Ah! See? There. *La lanza del herimiento de Jesu Cristo.* Do you see?" The mitered peak, called the Sword of Christ's Wounding, had captured the light from a still invisible rising sun and it glowed with a radiance mined from heaven. Golden, fierce, painful to look upon. Above it, three bright stars dappled the lessening night sky with their fading light.

"Ah!" the old man sighed, his eyes unshielded against the distant beauty. Months had passed since he had last made the trek to the cliff's edge. Suddenly, *el viejo* caught his breath, crossed himself rapidly three times and said a hurried prayer to the Blessed Mother. The gold was undergoing a metamorphosis, changing color before his eyes. "Truly, this is the Spear of Christ's Wounding," he muttered aloud, frightened and exhilarated at the same moment. Such a sign was not given to every man to see.

The peak slowly washed crimson in the growing light and burned with the luster of spilling blood. Deepening. Slowly deepening, the red darkened, as if drying. How much time passed, Don Memo could not tell, but when he thought to stir and look about, the burned peak had blended into the bleak range. He knew that if he asked, his voices would tell him it was time to go home. He had seen what he had been sent to see. What it meant he did not yet know.

"Don Memo."

The old man knew the voice. He did not respond, but continued to roll the *puros*, the tiny cigars that were his only vice, and set them to dry on the flat rock. A shadow fell across them.

"Don Memo. Why don't you answer when I call? For all I know, your spirit had fled the world, leaving your poor body to shrivel in the sun like one of your cigars." A white man's tanned hand reached down and selected the dryest of the sticks on the rock.

El viejo followed hand and cigar to a face set with pale blue eyes that glinted with experience and a touch of amusement. Shaggy salt-and-pepper hair and moustache. Jaw and cheeks darkened with a thick black stubble of day-old beard. He knew this one. And the small, evil-looking one with the shotgun rounding the corner wall. The *gringo* with flames for hair and the slumped, exhausted woman tied to a horse were strangers. Don Memo shrugged. "Such worries are mine alone, *gallito*."

Maguire patted the dust from his faded Levis, dug in his pocket to produce a kitchen match which he scraped along the sole of his boot. When the *puro* finally caught, he exhaled a blue-gray cloud of smoke. "Ah. The best. The very best."

Don Memo struggled to his feet. His knees tended to lock in place when he squatted too long. "Tell me, young rooster, why grace my home with your presence?"

"I'm no longer so young, Don Memo."

The old man's laugh was high and tinkling. "To me everyone is young."

"Why do I ever come?" Maguire asked, hands held out, palms upward. "To rest in the shade of *el viejo*'s walls and drink his water: water that is the coolest and sweetest in all these hills. As you see, I bring friends also. The woman is sick. We must stay until she is well."

Don Memo wagged his head. The vision that morning took on sudden meaning with Maguire's unexpected arrival. Blood would follow, without a doubt. It was too much. Especially for an old man who had seen enough blood shed in his lifetime. "You cannot stay here, Maguire. Rest, yes. Drink? Likewise. Food? That, too. I will share with you what I have, but you cannot remain."

Maguire puffed on the cigar, looked around and noted the many horse tracks. The old man had had visitors, was perhaps expecting more—or the same ones to return. "You have never turned me away before, Don Memo."

The old man hunched his scrawny shoulders. It was too bad the woman was sick, but what could he do? She would have to find help in Camargo, even if it was a hard day's ride. "You have been gone more than two years, Maguire. There is a new face in these mountains. One who has less respect for an old man, and a great hatred for *norteamericanos* who have allied themselves with the powerful. And especially those who fight with no allegiance except to gold."

Which explained the hoofprints. "The *soldadera* who calls herself *la Halcón?*" Maguire asked.

"Yes."

"Do you really think Maguire is afraid of a woman bandit?"

Don Memo shrugged. "I have not spoken of fear. I am speaking of prudence. You are only three. They outnumber you, and do not fear *gringos*. Should you, a man who fought for the *Señor* Bortha . . . "

"That was another time, another war," Maguire explained patiently.

El viejo chuckled. "In these hills, Maguire, time stands still. And the war has never ended." Picking up his cigars, he shuffled across the courtyard to a two-roomed hut propped against the crumbled adobe wall of the ancient *hacienda*.

Maguire looked back along the empty trail they'd followed, ahead to the austere mountains that lined the trail north. Against the mottled blacks and browns the spindly branches of distant ledge-top trees fractured the sunlight. Twisting the butt of the cigar under his heel, he moved toward the horses. "Let's get her down and under cover," he said flatly. "We're staying."

They rode in from the northwest, having followed a different trail in order to leave some of their number on tiny farms hacked out of the desert. The path from the barricade they'd built to stop the train was long and tortuous. Deprived of their prize, a trainload of wealthy foreigners, the journey had been tiresome and depressing.

Eleven horses trudged up the long incline, at the end of which lay the ancient *hacienda* with its well full of sweet water. The riders, used to long hours in the saddle, sat easily. Dust covered, eyes half closed against the bright light, they paid little attention to the old man sitting in the sunlit courtyard.

Maguire watched and waited inside the old man's hut. He knew these men he would have to face, not by name, of course, but by reputation. To the *peones* fighting for land to live on with dignity and a measure of security, they were patriots. To others, those who wielded power in this harsh section of Mexico, they were simply bandits, vermin to be wiped off the face of the earth. Whichever, they differed little from brave men everywhere. Above all else they required and respected bravery in those they faced. The time had come for him to demonstrate he did not fear them.

Face blank, step decisive, Maguire walked from Don Memo's hut and stood in full view. He held an *olla*, a dried gourd, filled with water that he sipped slowly. A tiny gust of wind kicked up the dust at his feet. The horsemen stopped. Eyes wary now, they watched the single white man who seemed so at ease. And so alone.

A whisper passed among them and, cautious but not afraid, they nudged their horses forward across the empty ground. Maguire waited until they reached the center of the courtyard, then set the clay jug on a rickety table at his side. On this signal, Lucca appeared in the doorway of the shattered ruins of what had once been a chapel. Two pistols jutted from his belt and the shotgun, cocked and ready, rested easily on his shoulder. The riders had no sooner swung their heads to inspect him than the sound of a boot heel on planking diverted their attention to the other side of the courtyard. Campaign hat squarely on his head, Winchester in his hand and a look of sober determination on his face, Blue stood next to a dilapidated two-wheeled cart.

Three to one odds. Unless the *gringo* held a fourth—or more—in reserve. A flurry of soft words drifted through the dust of their arrival. Almost casually three of the bandits wheeled their horses to face the rear while three more to either side concentrated on Lucca and Blue. The two left walked their horses to within twenty paces of Maguire. The first, slightly in the lead, was a sober, grim-faced Tarahumara Indian, his skin burned almost black by the sun. Next to him, a smooth-faced boy, draped in a *serape* and protected from the sun by a large *sombrero*, snapped closed the bolt of his captured Springfield.

"You are from Bortha?" the Indian said without the slightest trace of emotion. The youngster stared at the holstered Le Mat, but the Indian's eyes didn't waver from Maguire's.

"From Bortha?" Maguire spat. "I've come to kill Bortha."

Not a muscle in the Indian's face twitched. "How do you know we are not Bortha's men?" he asked. "How do you know we will not kill you, now that we know?"

Maguire smiled. "Because *la Halcón*, wherever she is, would not like it if her men killed an ally. Even if that ally were *gringos*, like me and my friends."

The black death's head visage split into a wide, toothy grin. At the same time, the youth at his side flipped off his *sombrero* and shook his head. Long jet curls flew out to either side and settled like a black waterfall that hung almost waist length. Light brown features surrounded dark brown eyes as unfathomable as the earth itself. With a swift movement, she pushed the *serape* over her head and let it fall back onto the rump of her horse. Underneath it she wore a khaki shirt open at the neck.

"I am Estrellada," she said, rising in her stirrups. Her voice was low and musical, yet throbbing with confidence and power. "I am *la Halcón*!"

Blue gaped in amazement. My God, he thought. She's beautiful! His mind raced, forgetting the seriousness of their predicament. The few pictures of *soldaderas* he'd seen portrayed blunt, earthy, masculine-looking women. This one was a different as . . . as . . . No comparison came to mind.

Maguire nodded in a perfunctory manner. "And I am Maguire," he countered flatly. "Now, *Señorita Halcón*, which is it to be? Guns or water? I haven't all afternoon."

Estrellada caught a glimpse of movement off to her side. Turning, she caught sight of Don Memo stepping from the sun and trying to cross unobtrusively to a mammoth cone-shaped jar, fully eight feet high. "I see you, old man," she shouted in Spanish. "Trying like a mouse to scurry away from my anger."

Señor Maximilio bleated and hurried on to hide behind the storage bin. Don Memo stopped and turned to face her. "A grandchild who does not show respect for her great-grandfather cannot expect the Christ child to smile upon her."

"I have no need for smiles, old one. From the Christ child or anyone else. Bullets and guns, yes. Sturdy horses, of course. I would burn candles in the church all week if God would give me these. But not smiles. Where do you run to?" she asked, trying to watch Maguire and her grandfather at the same time.

"I run for beans," *el viejo* said softly. "And corn for tortillas. You two will talk, try to frighten one another into surrender while I begin to cook." He looked at them and then around to each face planted warlike in the courtyard. "I know you both, great-granddaughter. You and Maguire. To frighten is impossible, so you will tire and decide not to kill each other. Then you will make camp together and soon be complaining to an old man that your bellies are empty and asking why there is no food and what is taking such an ancient one so long to bring *tortillas, frijoles* and *café*." He straightened, turned to leave and paused for a parting shot. "I am too old for such child's games."

Neither Maguire nor Estrellada spoke. The Tarahumara Indian sat like a statue. Finally Maguire reached over and picked up the *olla*, ignoring the Indian who lowered his worn-and nicked Winchester. "The old one makes a lot of sense," he said. "And like I said, I don't have all afternoon."

Corinne stirred and woke at his touch. Maguire wiped a dampened bandana across her sweat-slick brow. "I . . . I didn't know it would be like this," Corinne said, shivering.

"It always is. The fever has to run its course."

"How long?" She struggled weakly to sit up.

Maguire slipped his hand behind her back to support her and pushed a straw-filled pillow behind her. "A few more days," he said gently. "I brought you a cool drink."

"Can't," she whispered.

"Got to," he said, holding a cup to her lips. "You have to get liquid in you with all that sweating. Drink."

She took two or three sips, twisted her head to one side. "Can't stay. Can't wait too long, Maguire."

"Come on. Drink."

Another three sips. "You go alone. I'll stay here."

"I wouldn't do that. Come on, drink some more. Give you strength."

Corinne gulped, made a face and waved away the cup. "You're a liar." The cool liquid felt good in her stomach and made her sleepy again. "I can tell. You were thinking . . . " Her eyes blinked and she took a deep breath. " . . . the same thing."

Maguire put aside the cup and rearranged the blankets so she'd stay warm. The more she slept the faster she'd recover. "Think you know me pretty well, don't you, lady?" he said, taking her hand in his.

"Yes," she breathed, her lips moving but no sound coming out. Smiling, enjoying the last word, she closed her eyes. Maguire watched her for a moment. When he was sure she was asleep, he refolded the wet bandana and laid it across her forehead. Then, moving the candle away from the straw bedding, he slipped out the door and closed it behind him.

Night chill draped the dry mountain air. As Don

Memo had said, Estrellada's men had camped and eaten. Now Estrellada and her great-grandfather rested alone next to a crackling fire that gave off a pool of warmth. Neither had spoken for almost an hour when Estrellada suddenly sat up. "I thought you butchered the last of your herd," she said.

"I did," *el viejo* nodded. "All but *Señor* Maximilio."

"I heard sheep in the hills."

"It was the wind."

Estrellada shook her head. "No. I can tell the difference between the wind and goats."

"Ha. Even I who am far wiser than you, often cannot tell the difference."

"What do I do with this Maguire and his companions?" Estrellada asked, finally speaking what had been on her mind since her arrival that afternoon. "Can they be trusted? I am tired, *viejo*." Her proud, youthful face suddenly looked haggard. "Sometimes I feel . . . very lost."

The night makes men humble, the old man said to himself. Overconfident, cocky young great-granddaughters, too. Silent moments passed while the stars slid past the moon and Estrellada waited for an answer. Only once did she look at the old man, and then firelight bathed Don Memo's wrinkled, friendly face in a crimson mask that so closely resembled an awful wound that she looked away again. Her eyelids grew heavy, then blinked open as the old man handed her a cup of heavily sweetened coffee. "Tomorrow," he said, pulling his *serape* tightly about his frail shoulders, "you must go into the mountains with your men."

"Why?"

"To see if the panthers have made off with the wind." He chuckled at that, thinking it very funny. Uncomfortable because she had displayed weakness, Estrellada sipped the coffee. "The mountains are full of paths," her great-grandfather said cryptically, as he stood up.

"And Maguire can be trusted. Stand aside. Let him wreak what havoc he will. You will not be harmed by this if you stand aside." Advice given, he disappeared into the shadows. It was time for an old man to sleep.

Estrellada curled her hands around the tin cup and stared into the coffee. "Stand aside," her great-grandfather had said. But could she? The mountains through which Maguire would ride were a trust. She looked over them with fierce pride. Whatever he was up to—especially if it truly involved killing Bortha—was her business. The old one might be right, but she wasn't at all sure she could or should take his advice.

Footsteps crunched on the stone and Estrellada looked up. The rest of the men, including Lucca, sat quietly around a second fire in a far corner of the courtyard. From time to time a voice raised to emphasize a point floated to her. Holstered automatic slapping against his thigh, the one called Blue had left that group and was approaching. Without invitation, he poured himself a cup of coffee.

"Mind if I join you?" he asked, chancing a smile.

"*Sientate,*" Estrellada said, using the personal pronoun as one would with a child or a servant. The insult was lost, though, for it was obvious Blue had only understood that she had asked him to sit.

He placed his campaign hat to one side, crossed his legs and sat, tin cup secure in both hands. The coffee was strong and oily tasting but warm in the gut where it counted. Smallish breasts straining against her shirt, the girl leaned forward, took a burning twig from the fire and started playing with a scorpion that had wandered too near. Mercilessly she drove the confused arachnid deep into a chink in the stones, then speared it with the flaming twig.

Blue cleared his throat. Eyes burning with the reflected light of the fire, Estrellada glared at him. Embarrassed for some reason, Blue looked down. Her

274

ankles were the color of light clay freshly dug from the earth. Her trousers were soft, worn smooth to her body. The fact she could be so cruel bothered him; that she could be so cruel and beautiful at the same time confused him. He cleared his throat again. "Tell me, Estrellada," he began, stumbling over her name and struggling with the Spanish.

"I am called *la Halcón*," she answered forcefully in broken English.

"You speak English?" Blue asked, surprised.

"Many of us do. The weak always have to learn the language of the strong," she said, biting off the words.

"Yes. I suppose so," Blue mumbled. He grinned self-consciously. "It's not that I haven't been trying. In college I learned Latin, but that was just reading and there was time to sort out all the endings. Talking and listening are different, though." He screwed his face around. "My tongue gets confused. Living in Connecticut and New York doesn't exactly prepare you for Mexico."

Estrellada laughed, then eyed him intently. "You lived in *Nueva York?*"

"Sure. Went to college there."

"Aiaee! To have an education! If my people . . . " she waved her arm in an all-encompassing circle. "They do not even let us learn how to read and write. Do you know why?"

"Well, probably because—"

"—they are afraid of us. And because they look on us as animals." She spat into the fire. "I spit on them. Pigs. Tell me about *Nueva York.*"

"Well," he started, trying to figure out where to begin.

"You haven't been there," she accused.

"I have, too." It was his turn to lean forward, excited. "People. More people than you can imagine. Cars. Trolleys, electric lights on every street. Buildings, big as mountains—yes, that's true. And museums and theaters and restaurants and ships and factories . . .

You should see it." Estrellada's eyes were closed, as if she were trying to do just that. Blue watched her. She was so tiny, so diminutive, yet so full of spirit. And strength, he reasoned, in order to be able to lead the desperate-looking men he'd met that afternoon.

"I don't understand," he said quietly.

Her eyes friendly, she looked at him. "Eh?"

"I mean, how does a girl only seventeen years old leave her father's house to become a bandit?"

The friendliness disappeared, replaced by cold anger. "When the girl's father is murdered by *federales* in the very fields he made green with his own labor. The fields of his father and his father's father. When the girl's mother dies in the burning ruins of her house because she cannot run because she is sick because she has too little food because she is only a *peon* and *peones* don't need food.

"When the girl is taken to the *hacienda* of General Gregor Bortha and given to his men for their filthy pleasure, over and over again until she escapes. Then the girl learns; learns, for instance, to slit a *rurale*'s throat while he voids himself in the shadows outside of his camp. In this way a *girl* becomes a leader of bandits."

Blue examined the contents of his coffee cup. He examined the dirt encrusted in the seams of his boots, the grit underneath his fingernails. Finally he looked at her. "I'm sorry," he said, hoping that the feeling of friendship that had started to grow between them was not lost.

Estrellada cocked her head and peered at him. He was a big man, handsome in a light-skinned way. Not a blusterer or braggart like most who came from the north. Like it or not, she found herself drawn to the *gringo*. The thought disturbed her. *Gringos* were no better than *gachupines*. They looked down their noses at *peones*, distrusted those who fought for the land. "Sorry is very little," she said scornfully.

276

"What do you want me to do?" Blue retorted sharply. "Go back and change my parents? It's not my fault, you know."

"It never is." Pensive, Estrellada chewed on her knuckle and looked toward the fire where Lucca, on his feet, was dramatizing one of his many exploits. A burst of laughter rose from the bandit spectators. Estrellada pointed to Lucca. "Him I understand. He is like us; like the wind in the mountain deserts. He is unpredictable, but hot or cold, always strong. Maguire, the one who leads you? He is not so easy to understand, but I know his kind. He is *muy macho*, dangerous as a cornered *tigre* when he is against you, but a good friend if you are lucky."

"And me?" Blue asked.

He looked so intent, so serious that Estrellada had difficulty keeping a straight face. "I don't know," she deadpanned. "You are *simpatico*, but you ride with Maguire. You carry a gun, yet I think you do not wish to use it. And one thing more." Blue leaned forward. "You are too serious. I think you must die very soon— from looking so sour!"

Blue jerked back in surprise. Estrellada rocked back on her haunches and laughed loudly, her voice echoing through the courtyard. Across the way, the bandits at the other fire joined in out of habit. Blue grinned weakly, embarrassed at being made fun of.

"Keep laughing." Both Estrellada and Blue looked up to see Maguire standing behind them. He had rolled a tortilla around a scoop of refried beans and was munching contentedly.

A chill was in the air. The laughter at the other fire died abruptly. "Why?" Estrellada asked guardedly.

"I have a plan that will have Gregor Bortha welcome me with open arms. And it involves you."

23

Maguire woke when the stars started to fade. Four-thirty, he estimated, from the position of Orion. Time to be getting up and starting. Briefly he ran over the plan he'd invented. It was simple, really. He and Lucca would take the girl to Bortha's, give her to him as a gesture of goodwill and offer to join up with him again. Once inside they would locate Christopher and then figure out how to neutralize Bortha and his men. A signal to *la Halcón*'s men waiting outside would bring them running to the rescue, and they'd all celebrate a happy ending.

Simple. So simple a thousand things could go wrong. The sound of horses leaving the courtyard assured him somewhat. The men assigned to head back to the railroad were on their way, which meant that the wires would be cut in at least a dozen new places. Word from Fuentes to Bortha would not get through. As added insurance, the same men would remove a few sections of track. Which left only the wily Bortha to worry about. That was enough.

A piece of gravel crunched to his left. Maguire's hand moved beneath the blanket and grasped the Le Mat. "No need. I came to talk," a guttural voice said in *poblano*. The Tarahumara whom Estrellada called Trigo squatted to one side, his Winchester balanced across his knees. His hand gripped the stock. He wouldn't be able to fire quickly from that position, but could use the rifle as a club with deadly efficiency. Maguire didn't let go of his own gun: Trigo had been the most vociferous opponent of his scheme.

"I do not like you, Maguire," the Indian finally said.

"That doesn't really matter one way or the other," Maguire responded dryly.

Trigo nodded in acknowledgment. "*La Halcón* has decided to accept your plan. It is dangerous, but she has never feared danger."

"Why do you come to tell me what I already know?" Maguire asked.

"I came to tell you something you did *not* know," the Indian went on.

"Oh?"

"Yes. Now *I* accept it."

Maguire took a chance, brought his hand out from underneath the blanket. "Then I can sleep with both eyes shut," he said, thinking he struck an amused chord somewhere behind the implaccable, stone-carved face.

"But if anything goes wrong," Trigo warned, "if *la Halcón* is harmed—," His stare hardened.

"—you'll hunt me down and cut out my heart."

Trigo grimaced distastefully. "No. Just shoot you in the head." A semblance of a laugh rumbled deep in his chest. "I'm civilized." He patted the worn stock of the rifle, then used it to support his weight and help him to his feet. Sandals padding quietly across the courtyard, he moved with bulky grace to join his companions.

Maguire lay still for a while longer while the sounds of men breaking camp increased. A loud yawn. A throaty laugh. A grunt, followed by the slap of a saddle being thrown on a horse. Someone poured a bucket of water into a pot. The pot clinked against stone as it was set on the fire. A hammer tapped, the sound changing as a new nail went through a horseshoe and into a hoof. Tack jangled. Someone farted. Everyone laughed.

So much for sleep, Maguire told himself. Up and at 'em, as the old sergeant used to say. Grunting, he rolled to one side, got to his knees and stretched out the kinks. Should have slept outside the walls, he groaned. Damned packed dirt is hard. Grumbling, he stood, reached for his canteen and rinsed the taste of sleep out of his mouth.

Breaking camp was a routine he was well used to. Within moments his blanket was rolled and tied, his gear assembled. The smell of beans cooking floated across the morning air. Stomach grumbling, he headed for the fire, only to be intercepted by Blue, coming out of Don Memo's hut. "You're up and about early enough," Maguire grumbled. "Somebody make coffee?"

"The old man has some inside," Blue answered. "I was saying good-bye to Corinne. She wants to see you. I'll get the horses ready."

"Wait a minute." Maguire caught Blue by the elbow. "Not so fast." Damn, he wondered to himself. Did I look that fresh at five in the morning when I was twenty? Shouldn't be allowed. "Look. I'm grateful for your help, but no one's going to think the less of you for staying behind and keeping her company." Blue looked down at his arm. Maguire let go. "Matter of fact, it would probably be a good idea," he added quickly. "If we don't get back, she'll need someone to help her to the border."

"The three men *la Halcón* is leaving behind will see to that," Blue said. "Corinne will be safe here." He cast a hurried glance toward Estrellada as she swing onto her horse. She was so smooth. So lithe and capable. "I guess

281

I'll come along," he said. "Your horse will be ready when you are."

Maguire watched him go. "I'll be damned," he finally said under his breath, suspecting Blue's ulterior motives. Thoroughly awake and shaking his head in disbelief, he wandered inside. A pot of coffee spread a thick aroma through the room. "Good morning, *viejo*. I see you have coffee ready."

Don Memo didn't answer. Maguire sniffed appreciatively, poured a cup and squatted in front of the old man. "Estrellada will be all right," he said. "I promise you she'll be all right. I'll be in there, too, and won't let anything happen to her."

"General Bortha is not an easy man," Don Memo finally said.

"I know. Neither am I." Maguire stood. "I'll see to Estrellada. You'll watch over Corinne for me?" he asked, gesturing to the inner room.

"I'll watch over her for her. Not for you."

Not prepared to waste more time trying to ease the old man's mind, Maguire stepped into the back room. A new candle burned on the table and gray morning light seeped through the unframed hole that served as a window. Corinne had propped herself against the rear wall. She had managed to run a broken comb through her hair, which curled along the sides of her face. Still her eyes were hollow and her cheeks pale. Maguire entered and sat on the wooden stool near the bed. "You look better. Maybe I should wait another hour or two."

Corinne smiled wanly. "Lying this early in the morning? I'm weak, and the old man says I will be for another day at least."

Maguire put his hand on her forehead. "The fever's gone down some."

"I don't want you to wait, Maguire. Christopher is too much like you. He'll keep trying to escape until he drives Bortha to the breaking point, and then keep on trying."

"Or succeed," Maguire ammended, trying to drive from his mind the image of a small boy facing, alone, the terrible rigors of the Chihuahuan desert in the winter.

Corinne reached out and brushed the tips of her fingers over the sleeve of his ragged sweater. "I'll mend that for you when this is over," she said.

Maguire searched her expression for an unspoken commitment even though, under the circumstances, none could be expected. After all he might be dead in a few days. But what the hell? Who guaranteed the next two minutes, much less two days? And why suddenly start worrying about it? He was alive this moment. That had always been enough.

"Maguire!" The bandit leader's voice echoed through the wind-worn remains of the broken buildings.

Corinne grasped his hand. Outside a horse whinnied and shod hooves clattered on stone. Maguire leaned forward and gently kissed Corinne on the lips. Then, without hesitating, the mercenary rose, brushed past the old man and was gone.

The ancient Mogul puffed to a stop in front of the barricade left by *la Halcón*'s bandits. His face black with fury, Fuentes ordered his men out to clear the tracks. A half hour later, the last timber and boulder thrown aside, they jumped back aboard as the train lumbered past.

And stopped around the next bend.

"Won't run without rails, Captain," Jory said, shrinking back against the wall of the cab.

Apoplectic, Fuentes jumped from the cab and ran forward to inspect the railbed. Sure enough a length of track had been removed and, in all probability, thrown into the canyon to his left. He peered over the edge, but could see nothing but the tops of trees and stretches of rock. They could waste another whole day searching.

Stiff-legged, he stalked back to the cab and climbed in. "Reverse," he told the engineer. "Back to where you left off the others."

Jory swore silently and got busy. If he ever crossed the Rio Grande with his skin in one piece, he'd damn well find another line of work rather than set foot south of the border again. Slowly, puff by puff, the steam drove the six giant wheels into motion, back down the track.

Fuentes stood motionless. Past anger now, he calculated times and distances. Having to travel in reverse and at night had slowed Elrecht and the train hadn't arrived in Lago Blanco until early morning of the day after it was stolen. That whole day had been spent rounding up enough coal—Lago Blanco was not a regular coaling stop—and getting it loaded aboard. Finally, near sundown, they'd started out only to stop twenty miles outside of town with a stuck valve that took the engineer three hours of cursing, sweating labor to repair.

The original plan had been to reach Chihuahua as rapidly as possible and then ride the twenty miles southwest to Bortha's *hacienda*. The removed rail changed that. Nor could they simply start riding, for a gorge cut across their path a mile ahead. No horse could cross the bridge of ties, and the cliff face was impossible for men on horseback to descend. Their best chance lay in following Maguire's tracks.

"Elrecht!"

"Yes, sir." The German stepped forward.

"If you value your manhood, you will not miss the exact spot where they left the train."

Elrecht's expression did not change. "Two bends," he said crisply. "We'll be able to see where their horses went up the slope."

Fuentes rapped Jory on the shoulder with the flat of his machete. "Slow down."

The engineer backed off the steam, touched the air brakes. Two bends later, precisely as Elrecht had said, the men caught sight of the trail made by Maguire's eight horses. Even as the train was stopping, Elrecht was running down the length of the train. With the final squeal of brakes, *Los Serpientes* were piling from the cars and unloading the horses.

Single-eye fearsome, Fuentes leaned toward the engineer. "You will not allow this train to budge one inch until my men and horses are clear. Is that understood?"

"Yes, sir," Jory gulped, thinking he would do almost anything to get that machete-wielding madman out of his cab.

Fuentes leaned out and called for his horse. "Oh, yes," he said with an exaggerated smile. "Have a nice trip— back to Lago Blanco." Jory groaned. It would be morning before they could get back. And lord knew how long before the telegraph lines were fixed and tracks repaired and he could get coal. "You may tell the passengers that Captain Jesus Fuentes apologizes for the delay." Bowing, Fuentes slipped his machete in its sheath. Seconds later, Diego, his orderly, rode up leading his sorrel stallion.

Fuentes mounted gracefully. Twenty-three men—the campaign in Mexico City and the fiasco in Lago Blanco had been costly—followed suit. Sharply aware of each one's weaknesses and strengths, their captain cantered past them. "Look at them, Diego," he said. "Only the best are left. Let Huerta rule in Mexico City. Here in Chihuahua, Fuentes is king."

"And Bortha?" Diego dutifully asked.

Fuentes reined in his horse. A faint wind soughed among the pines towering over the pass. A wind out of the north. "Perhaps our general's days are numbered," he said in a quiet, ominous voice.

"But first Maguire?"

The musical piping of snow geese winging homeward from distant fields was a beauty wasted on the single-minded purpose of the revenger, Jesus Fuentes. "First Maguire."

24

Tlaloc, the Old Grandfather God, stood amid a pantheon of lesser deities, stared blankly as the intruders filed through the low eastern pass, paused momentarily and entered the approaches to the sacred Avenue of the Dead. If he saw them he gave no indication. Men had come before; men would come again. Small, insignificant creatures of flesh who moved too rapidly for him to consider seriously. Of deeper significance were the mountains stretching before him and the desert beyond. There the eastern sky was beginning to slide beneath a mantle of lengthening shadows as the sun balanced on the massive, barren ridges far behind him. His back splitting the light, Tlaloc, deliverer of the corn-ripening rain, sat and waited.

Sunlight divided by eroding rock formed corridors of almost palpable brilliance through which the travelers rode. As mortals had for centuries, the band stopped on the rim of the valley of the ancients and beheld in awe its magnificence. Before them stretched the Avenue of the Dead. A hundred yards wide and a half-mile long, the time-emptied way was lined with low hills on which sprawled the ruins of houses and temples. Slowly, almost as if they did not wish to disturb the silence, the band walked their horses along the level, man-made plain.

"We'll camp here." The sound of Maguire's voice came as a shock. Each of Estrellada's men, Blue noticed, crossed himself hastily to ward off the sleeping spirits.

At their feet lay a hundred-foot-long rectangular depression, the sunken courtyard of a ceremonial building or temple that had disappeared centuries before. Some trick of the wind, no doubt, had kept it from filling with sand. Estrellada's men, happy to get out of the open, led their horses down a narrow ramp into the depression and began making camp.

Blue sat stock still, staring at a huge pyramid that blocked the western end of the valley some two hundred and fifty yards away. Overpowering in its magnificence, crowned with jutting stones silhouetted against the late afternoon sky, the pyramid rose more than two hundred feet into the air.

"The House of Dawn," Maguire said. "We can walk to the top if you want. There won't be time in the morning."

Mesmerized, Blue nudged his horse forward, around the sunken courtyard and to the broad base of the pyramid. There he looped the reins over a *maguey* and, heart beating with the excitement of being in the presence of something older and grander than he'd ever seen, began to climb. Worn by centuries of blowing sand in the summer and digging fingers of ice in the winter, the steps were precariously shallow, offering support to only the front half of his feet. He kept on doggedly, though, until he reached a level spot at least ten feet deep that appeared to run around the whole pyramid. Lungs burning, grateful for a rest, he leaned against the next rising wall and looked about. A hundred feet below the bandits were invisible in the deep shadows. A hundred feet above, a solid wall of cut rock reached to the sky. To his left, in the center of the face of the pyramid, a massive stone slab divided in two equal parts by an inches deep trough extended into empty air.

A sound behind him startled Blue. He turned to see Maguire scrambling up the remaining steps. For a moment the two men stood silently. "Be dark soon," Maguire said. His voice sounded small, so high in the air. "Better keep going."

Ten minutes later, panting and sucking in oxygen, they climbed the last step and leaned aginst one of the giant stones. When he got his breath, Blue stepped back and inspected the stone figure that towered ten feet taller than himself, then looked around at eleven more ringing the plateau at the top of the pyramid. Not even the Greeks or the Egyptians had built anything to compare with what he saw. "They're statues," he said. The primitive figures were covered with strange writing and carved representations of animals. "Who are they supposed to be?"

Maguire shrugged. "Gods of some sort. No one knows."

"But why'd they leave? I mean, this place must have been green and bustling with lots of people. Unless the Spaniards killed them all, or they ran out of water."

"They were gone a long time before Columbus even thought of sailing. And there's plenty of good spring water in a well that never dries up. But no one with any Indian blood will stay here for more than one night at a time. This whole place,"—his gesture included the valley and the ruins that made up the Avenue of the Dead—"is a mystery. Archaeologists haven't made it here yet. Suspect they will, one day."

The conversation was interrupted by the arrival of Estrellada, who appeared over the edge of the plateau and walked past the exhausted men. Younger and lighter, she seemed totally immune to the exertions required by the climb. Maguire and Blue exchanged glances, then followed the girl to the center of the windswept summit. There, Estrellada stood in the shadow of an awesome image of fierce expression and massive black bulk. By its size and grandeur, and by its location, it was evident this was the lord of the lesser gods.

"Tlaloc," the bandit leader said, her voice subdued.

Maguire nodded and gestured to the surrounding columnar deities. Each figure was topped with a broad, flat crown of stone. "Met a man once, expert artillery-man working for the *Porfiristas*. He told me these once served to support the ceiling of a great temple. And that no matter what the time of year, first light always strikes Tlaloc before any of the others—the House of Dawn."

Blue walked to the edge of the pyramid. Far below, in the ruins of the palace where the bandits were setting up camp, they had built a pair of fires to ward off the chill. Whether it was his imagination or the clarity of the air Blue could not tell, but it seemed the fires were brighter than usual. He couldn't blame the bandits. He was a rational, college-educated man, and the place had him spooked. How much more would the ancient stone gods affect simple farmers whose lives were filled with superstition?

Suddenly he was aware that Estrellada had joined him. All day he had mulled over the notion of dropping back to ride with her, but had sensed an aloofness and indifference on her part that made him keep his distance. "The slab makes a good place to rest on the ascent," he said, making small talk. "I can see the priests standing there and looking over the valley and their people."

"The slab was an altar," Estrellada said. "There, over the cup in the center of the stone, the high priests offered in sacrifice the hearts of girls chosen to be the handmaidens of Tlaloc. This my great-grandfather told me. It happened many centuries ago, yet you can see the stone is still stained dark where the blood collected and ran like a river to spill down the face of the pyramid." Eyes twinkling mischievously, she looked up at him. "Only virgins were used, of course, so a prudent girl could take precautions."

The wind gusted, sent Estrellada's long black hair streaming around her cheeks and full lips. A faint wailing, lost and remote, rose from the Avenue of the Dead. Blue tensed, made himself relax. "Wind, I guess," he said with a forced laugh.

"Tlaloc," corrected Estrellada. "Come on. We'd better get down before dark." Not waiting, she stepped over the edge and, as casually as if she were walking down a terraced garden walk, began the descent down the treacherous incline.

"Better be careful of that one," Maguire cautioned, coming up behind him.

"What's that supposed to mean?" Blue snapped defensively. "I can take care of myself."

"Not when a girl like that sets her hat for you."

"*La Halcón?* Hell, she'd slit my throat if I so much as touched her."

"Yeah. Well, some women have a funny way of showing affection."

"And if Bortha doesn't believe you?" Trigo scowled. The question, in guttural *poblano,* sounded more ominous than it would have in either English or Spanish. "How will we know?"

His booted feet square in the middle of the plan he'd outlined in the sand, Maguire leaned against the wall and remained silent. To one side Lucca worked the slide of the Parker-Hale, ejected and caught a shell in midair. "You'll know, my friend. It won't be a secret."

"You'll have to decide on your own," Maguire said. "We'll raise all the hell we can, but what happens beyond that will be up to you."

Trigo glanced at his companions, one of whom muttered, "We ride in." He spoke for all of them.

"Good enough," Maguire agreed. "*If* we fail. Otherwise, if we take Bortha during the day, which I hope doesn't happen, one of us will fire four times; two shots, a pause and two more shots. Get there fast because it'll be an emergency. If we take him at night though, the way I planned it, one of us will signal with a pair of lanterns swung in opposite circles. As soon as it's dark enough that the guards can't see someone in the bell tower, you'll need to get one of your men up there. Come in on foot and quietly, unless you see one of the lanterns thrown, in which case get there as fast and as noisy as you can. Got it?"

Trigo nodded. "I will have one man watching at dusk every day."

"You're certain of the people in the village?" Lucca asked.

"We'll ride in one or two at a time," Trigo explained. "Those who might talk will suspect nothing. The man who will hide us is my mother's father."

"Who is as old as the old church he watches over," another bandit joked. "And his roof needs as much repair."

The men laughed. Trigo did not join them. "He has no love for Bortha. And he is not afraid. As for the old church, no one goes there anymore and the front porch of the *hacienda* is visible from the bell tower. It will be safe."

"What about *la Halcón*?" Lucca enquired. "Shouldn't she hear any of this?"

"*La Halcón* trusts us," Trigo answered, "and cares to know only one thing. When Bortha will be delivered to her. At gun point."

"To us all," said another. "I myself once had two brothers. He has yet to pay for their lives."

"You'll stay in El Tule with the others," Blue muttered sarcastically, mimicking Maguire. He kicked a stone, heard it ricochet off another and plop into water. Moving carefully over the uneven ground, he felt his way through the ancient corridor Lucca had described to him. Three feet above, light from the waning moon brightened the black stone. On the ground the shadows were ink-black.

At last the corner. Blue stepped out of the blackness and stopped. He was in what at one time was evidently a huge room. The ceiling, as all ceilings in the valley, had long since caved in and disappeared, leaving only tall and crumbling walls. Ahead, in the center, lay the silted remnant of the valley's water supply. Once it must have been immaculately cared for, probably even tiled. Now only a small pond remained. Perhaps ten feet in diameter, the edges sloped sharply with blown sand barren of any growth. On the east side, a statue spewed a steady stream of water from exaggerated lips carved of stone.

Blue kneeled at the water's edge, touched the moon-mirrored surface. The water was warm compared to the surrounding air. It must have come from some deep, artesian well, he conjectured. Where it went and why nothing grew around it, he could not guess.

"No wonder they think it's haunted," he said aloud. Not even Lucca would accompany him there in the dark. Blue looked around apprehensively. The constant tinkling splash of water had a hollow quality that in the otherwise utter silence was unnerving. "Bullshit," he added. "No such thing as haunted. Superstition." Sitting, he undid his bedroll, pulled out clean clothes, then unlaced and peeled off his boots. Socks, shirt and trousers followed. The air was icy cold. Carefully he felt his way step by step into the water.

At least it was warm. Sighing, he leaned back, thrust his chest upward and floated. The water was a balm that eased the saddle soreness out of his legs. "I did as

293

much as any of them," he said aloud to the sliver of moon left in the sky, recalling the frustration and feeling of uselessness that had sent him stumbling angrily from the camp. "I've earned the right to be trusted, damn it."

"That's the water we drink, you know."

Blue thrashed about wildly and stood upright, the tips of his toes barely touching the bottom. Estrellada stood at the edge of the pond. Legs apart, she straddled his bundled clothes. "What are you doing here?" Blue asked, having to bounce to keep the water from pouring into his mouth. "Place is supposed to be haunted."

Her laughter sounded as hollow as the falling water. "Do you really believe that all Mexicans are superstitious primitives, *gringo*?" she asked scornfully. "I'm more interested in the purity of the water than I am of ghosts."

"The water coming out the spout is clean," Blue said, pointing, "but if it's that important to you, I'll get out."

"Good," Estrellada said, at the same time nudging his clothes toward the water.

"Hey, what are you doing?"

"Hurrying you along, *gringo*." She pushed them again.

Blue hopped through the water until he could stand flat-footed, walked forward until he was only waist deep and then hesitated. "Why don't you turn around. Or step behind the fountain."

"Better hurry." Estrellada smiled sweetly and pushed his boots toward the edge. "Wet boots are hard to walk in."

"Wait!"

His clothes were almost in the water. Another few minutes . . .

"Damn it to hell!" Blue exploded, charging from the pond. He grabbed his clothes and tossed them away from the edge.

Eyes lit with growing interest and appreciation, Estrellada stepped backward for a better look. "Now I know why your mother was so fond of you," she said.

His hands were gripping her shoulders before she

finished the sentence. Lips parted, Estrellada tilted her head back and let herself be drawn to him. To her surprise, she felt herself lifted bodily and hurled into the pond. She emerged a sputtering, irate tigress, clawing her way to shore while Blue laughed. "Turn about's fair play, Estrellada."

"*La Halcón,*" she hissed, diving for the Browning automatic on the ground. Blue caught her before she could take it from the holster, picked her up again by the back of her shirt and the seat of her pants and effortlessly returned her to the pond. Drenched, spitting, thoroughly bedraggled, she stumbled ashore again.

"Stinking son of a one-eyed . . . "

Blue started for her. Estrellada swallowed the curse, and coughing, waved her hands to plead an end to hostilities. Panting, she sank to the ground and tugged at one boot. The wet leather proved impossible. "Well?" she asked. Blue stood over her, took her foot and jerked. The boot came off with a comical sucking sound that amused them both. The next one followed quickly.

Estrellada stood. They were no longer laughing. She undid her belt and slid her soaked trousers over rounded buttocks and down her legs. Almost losing her balance, she caught Blue's arm for support and wriggled her feet free of the clinging material.

They stood face to face, neither feeling the cold air. When Blue reached for her, Estrellada shook her head no and started unbuttoning her shirt. Aroused, Blue watched as the thin cotton molded so tightly to her breasts opened and fell away, and Estrellada leaned forward to wring the water from her hair. At last she straightened and flipped her hair over her shoulder.

The severity of the line of her hair softened her face. Her eyes were soft and dark, almost glowing, he thought. Her mouth, lips parted slightly, waited the touch of his. Her breasts were small and perfectly shaped. Her nipples, extended, hardened in the cold air. Her waist swelled out into rounded, low-slung hips.

She moved closer to him. Towering head and shoulders over her, he was bigger than any man she had ever known. Tentatively she touched him. Drops of water fell from him and light, fine hair sprang out in ringlets on the bulging muscles of his chest. Hairless, his stomach rippled with more muscles, and lower yet, the hardening shaft of his manhood sprang from dark red curls.

The air grew warmer. Blue could hardly breathe. His hands moved up, cupped her face and tilted back her head. Slowly he leaned down until their lips touched. As if that were the signal, their bodies met.

The sand cushioned them as they knelt. The air swirled with an all-pervasive muskiness. Body tan as sand, Estrellada blended with the earth. An insistent animal moan sounded deep in her throat as Blue's kisses traced an intricate pattern across her breasts and stomach. She pulled him to her. Blue sucked in his breath. The night, the desert, the lurking fear of the morrow, heightened his senses. The touch of her, the nearness of her, the scalding breathless moment of their becoming one was more than he could bear. Every muscle of Blue's body turned rigid. Suddenly Estrellada shuddered. In the same instant Blue clenched his teeth and threw back his head as the tension that had built to such unbearable heights was loosed. Overhead the stars and moon coalesced into one blazing, blinding light that, he thought, would never dim.

Dark hair tangled about his thighs. Still in a half daze, Blue stirred, propped himself on his elbows and looked down at her. Her head on his stomach, Estrellada lay curled in a tiny ball near his side. Her eyes caught the moonlight as she looked up at him. Catlike, she reached and stroked the hair on his chest. "Your hair is like sunshine," she said.

"Yours is like midnight."

She laughed, low and throaty, stretched to her full length and raised her arms high over her head. Estrellada shivered. "It's cold."

"My bedroll's here someplace," he said, groping for and finding his blanket. Awkwardly he unfolded it and pulled it over them.

Her voice muffled, Estrellada protested, crawled upward and lay atop him. He could feel her breasts pushing against his ribs. They lay that way for a half hour, warm with each other, content to be close. Blue couldn't help feeling that perhaps Estrellada was what he'd been searching for. With her at his side he would write anything he wanted. Go anywhere, do anything. His fingers touched her hair, traced a long strand lying down her back. "Estrellada?"

"Mmmm."

"You awake?"

"Mm-hmmm."

"I been thinking. About you coming with me."

"I do not understand you. We are here."

"No. I mean after we . . . after . . . "

She rolled away abruptly, sat upright. "Where would you take me?"

"New York to begin with. We could be together. There's so much to see. So much I could show you."

Estrellada's voice was tight, a little strident. "To show your ignorant little *puta?*"

"I didn't mean anything of the sort and you know it."

She spun on him. "You think Estrellada can just leave while the fighting continues?"

"Fighting is men's work."

"Ha! You are all alike. Men's work!" She spat. "Imbecile. The women and children suffer as much as any man. Maybe even more. The men are not raped. It is our fight, too. It is for us also to kill or be killed."

"But look at you. Having to grub around like an animal. You should be married. Raising kids."

"Married, pfah! You want to see me wearing pretty clothes and cooking tortillas while others starve and die? No! I fight for my freedom first, *gringo!*"

"Oh, come on, Estrellada. One regime's like another. They're all the same."

"Which is why we fight." Furious with Blue, and for having allowed herself to become tender even for a short time, Estrellada hurriedly began to dress. Blue tried to touch her, but she moved out of reach. "No!"

"What is it? What's the matter?"

How could she tell him? In her heart, where the galling truth hammered away at her resolve, Estrellada knew that to stay longer with Blue invited caring and warmth and love. And there was no time.

"But what about us? Doesn't any of this have any meaning for you?" She caught up her shirt, shook the sand out of it and started to leave. "Answer me," Blue said, jumping up and grabbing her arm.

Estrellada twisted away. "Meaning? But of course, *gringo*. I let you pleasure me. It was good. That's all." Angry at the tears spilling down her cheeks, grateful for the concealing night, she ran from him then.

Blue turned to the still pond, to the rumpled blanket on the sand. "Well, damn," he blurted. The walls caught his voice and played with it in the darkness, bounced it around as a child a rubber ball. " . . . damn . . . " they said. " . . . damn . . . damn . . . damn . . . . "

Estrellada paused in the shadows outside the camp. "Damn him," she whispered, alternately hugging herself and flapping her arms in order to keep warm. "Damn all *gringos* who don't understand!" Gradually her temper calmed and, in spite of the lure of the warmth of the fire, she considered going back to him. They could make love until the sun rose and it was time to leave for Bortha's *hacienda*. The thought of Bortha cut through cold and desire. *La Halcón* would not go back. Going back was a softness she could not afford. Not with Bortha waiting. Hardness was what she needed most. Hardness and implacable resolve. And hate.

Maguire and Lucca were sitting apart from the main fire. Thankful for as much distance as possible between Estrellada and himself, Blue joined them. Their conversation died as he approached. "Don't let me interrupt anything," he growled.

"The water was warm enough?" Lucca asked mischievously.

"What's that supposed to mean?" Blue said, fists clenching at his side.

The Italian mercenary winked at Maguire, cocked his head to one side and pulled on the gold ring in his earlobe. "You leave, the girl leaves. The girl returns wet, you return wet. I have always said baths are more fun than bed. With the right woman, of course."

"Why don't you shut your filthy mouth," Blue snarled.

"Ricco!" Maguire warned, too late to stop the smaller man from drawing his stiletto and springing to his feet. A ham-sized fist shot from Blue's side, buried itself in Lucca's stomach and lifted him completely off the gound.

The knife flew to one side. Lucca collapsed, groaning. Blue spun toward Maguire. "I've come this far. I'm going to Bortha's."

Maguire set down his coffee cup. "No, you're not," he said, slowly and distinctly.

"The hell you say!"

"You're that desperate for a story?"

"Screw the story." Blue's anger suddenly drained. His fists and shoulders relaxed. "It's more than that now."

"Maybe it always has been," Maguire said calmly, still keeping an eye on him. "But you still aren't going in."

Blue took a step forward. Maguire held him with his eyes. "Sit down." Unsure of himself, not knowing whether to fight or obey, Blue gave in and sat. "It's not because you don't look the part," Maguire said evenly, "or because you can't act it. That we know you can do, right Ricco?"

The slumped figure by the fire groaned.

"Ricco agrees."

"But why not, damn it? I—"

"Because if anything happens to us, you're the only one left to see that Corinne makes it safely across the border." He held out a folded sheet of yellow paper. "That's a map of Chihuahua. And if the trains aren't running or if there's other, unforeseen trouble, beyond to the border. It isn't accurate or completely to scale, but it should do."

Blue took the paper, unfolded it and held it so he could see. Everything seemed clear enough. He refolded the map and stuffed it in his shirt pocket. "This is for real?" he asked. "You're not just trying to make me feel good?"

"I don't want anything to happen to her," Maguire said.

Blue considered. "I'll see to it," he finally said, once convinced Maguire wasn't lying, then got to his feet, went over to the other fire and helped himself to a plate of beans. Estrellada lay huddled in her blanket away from the fire. Blue's cheeks began to burn and he swung around, his back to the bubbling cast iron pot. A few feet away, Trigo had materialized and was staring at him. Blue returned his scrutiny, finished his beans and walked back to the other fire.

Lucca sat up and glared at him as he approached, but when Blue didn't waver, the Italian flashed a broad grin and held out his hand. Surprised and not a little cautious, Blue took the extra three steps and shook it, then stood awkwardly as Lucca mater-of-factly lay back down and rolled up in his blanket.

Maguire was asleep. Quietly Blue stretched out and pulled his blanket over himself. He remembered how Trigo and the others had looked at him. Let them wonder, Blue thought. They'll see tomorrow what I can do. His legs ached from too many hours in the saddle. Confused by Estrellada's actions, his mind reeled. He tried to sort everything out and put his thoughts in order, but nothing made sense. And then it didn't really matter, for he was asleep.

25

El Tule, the town that had grown up outside the walls of Bortha's *hacienda,* lay sleeping beneath a high, burning noonday sun. "As close as we come, for now," Maguire announced, dismounting.

"Trigo, Antonio, Cirilio. Start. Do not enter until after sundown," Estrellada said in *poblano*. The three riders grunted in assent and urged their horses down a side arroyo. By late afternoon they would have circled the town in order to ride in from the north as night fell. The rest of the band dismounted and tied their horses. Maguire, Lucca, Blue and Estrellada crawled to the top of the low ridge that sheltered them.

"There it is," Maguire said.

To his left, Estrellada spat into the sand. Her memories of El Tule and the men who lived within Bortha's *hacienda* were bitter.

"Trigo's grandfather is caretaker of the church. The last padre died a couple of years ago and no other has been appointed. The man's name is Armedo," Maguire said to Blue specifically. "He speaks no English, so you'll have to listen closely. Do whatever he says."

The church in question, once whitewashed, was now a dingy, gray squat rectangle topped with a small dome, a bell tower and a crucifix. A cluster of single- and two-story adobe houses and mud-dabbed mesquite *jacals* sprawled along the widening circumferences of a multi-rimmed imaginary wheel with the church as a hub. To the west, the village flattened and butted up against a dull stone wall.

As they watched, an automobile of undetermined make sped down the road from Chihuahua and entered the town. Orange brown dust billowed in its wake. "Bortha," Estrellada hissed, her eyes blazing with hatred. Arched gates opened in the wall and the automobile disappeared inside.

"Take it easy," Maguire said. "You'll get your chance. Come on. We might as well be comfortable." Careful not to raise dust, the four crawled back down off the ridge.

The day had dawned bright and sunny as the last of the clouds had been driven to the north by a damp, southern wind. When the wind would shift to the north again, no one could tell. Not for a few days, Maguire hoped, for the combination of dry, cold wind from the arctic and damp, warm wind from the south could trigger a desert storm that would slow them considerably. For a moment, though, the weather was pleasantly cool in the protected arroyo. The horses, free of saddles, switched their tails and, desert-wise, carefully nibbled the barb-free bases of prickly pears. The men and Estrellada looked for soft spots where they could lie down. None knew when next he would rest.

Blue couldn't sleep. He kept picturing the town and the surrounding countryside. Getting in would be no problem, he thought. Getting out again . . . Footsteps. He peered out from under his hat. Estrellada stood but a yard away, and as he watched, she shook out and spread her blanket close to his. She looked strikingly pretty, he thought, and surprisingly girlish. Why she had flown off the handle the night before was still a mystery to him, but perhaps that didn't matter anymore. She sat abruptly, and he turned his head so he could see her as she lay down. Blue wasn't sure, but he thought she had smiled. Feeling good again, he grinned and pulled the hat back over his eyes. A moment later he was asleep.

Maguire watched Blue and Estrellada and marveled at the ability of the young to put themselves into impossible situations. And not only the young, he thought ruefully. Suddenly uneasy, he took the photograph from his shirt pocket. The knowledge that Bortha waited just over the hill, no more than a mile away, drove home the realization that, for the first time in over twenty years, there was something more than gold at stake.

A son. *His* son. And though Maguire wouldn't have admitted it to another soul, the truth of the matter rang clear with each battering-ram pulsing of his heart.

He was afraid.

The first step was the worst. The world pitched and bucked like a storm at sea. Corinne determined not to give up. Don Memo and the men left to guard her had promised to leave without delay once she had demonstrated she was well enough to ride.

Somehow avoiding all of them, she made it outside the walls and headed for the ravine where, one of the guards had pointed out, a stream sped downhill. A stone slipped beneath her foot. She almost grabbed a barrel cactus for support, but thankfully managed to stifle that reflex. The noon sun was warm, but she shivered beneath the heavy poncho she'd found in Don Memo's room.

The old man's ruins were completely out of sight by the time she reached the edge of the ravine. Resting a moment, she surveyed a path through fallen trees and tumbled boulders. A helping hand and strong shoulder would have been in order but there was no one. Determined, she started down, slipping and sliding to the bottom of the ravine.

Oak, cypress and cottonwood cloaked the stream bed in deep purple shadows. Corinne tasted the water, found it far too alkaline to drink. It did feel good on her hands though, so she knelt, scooped up double handfuls and laved her face and neck. The water was ice cold. Shivering, she pulled up a corner of the poncho and wiped the water from her eyes.

"Refreshed, *señora*?" a voice asked.

"Why, yes," she answered, looking up in surprise as she realized the question had been asked in English. The man on the opposite bank, not six feet away, doffed his *sombrero*. Sunlight glinted off his richly embroidered black trousers and short black jacket. And, when he straightened, off a mock golden eye.

Corinne stood abruptly and the blood drained from her head. The trees spun and the world tilted. On fear alone, she clawed hand over hand up the side of the ravine. Thorns pierced her flesh and plucked at her clothes. Laughter followed her, whipped her along.

"Memo!" she gasped, her voice a tortured gasp. The steep slope climbed upward forever. Laughter chased her. At last, barely able to stand, she gained level ground and blindly started running toward the walls of the *hacienda*. A horse loomed on the periphery of her vision. She tried to stop but couldn't. The horse, ridden by a gray-clad rider and dragging at rope's end one of the bandits left on guard, struck her a glancing blow. Her shrieks faded as the horseman headed for a rock-strewn field where two more riders dragged similarly grisly, bouncing bundles of broken bone and torn flesh.

Three other men now appeared. All clad in the same foreboding gray, they gathered in a ring and hemmed her in until the man by the stream approached. "Permit me, *señora*. I am Captain Jesus Fuentes," he said formally. "These are my men. They are called *serpientes* because they are very dangerous men."

"Where is Don Memo?"

Fuentes shrugged. "Who can guess? Hiding somewhere. Others are looking. They will find him. And your friends?" he gestured lazily toward the distant horsemen. "Food for the *zopilotes*."

"No," Corinne whispered. "You couldn't have."

"Ah, but I did, *señora*." He stepped closer to her, raised her chin with his hand so she was forced to look at his face. "You are going to be worth a great deal of gold to me, *Señora* Van Allen."

Corinne's expression paled as she pushed away his hand. "I know no one by that name," she said. "You are making a terrible mistake."

Fuentes adjusted his eye patch. His single eye glowed sardonically. "Take her," he said, switching to Spanish.

The men howled gleefully and rushed forward. Corinne tried to resist, but hands grasped her arms, gripped her legs and tore at her clothes. A knee slammed into her forehead. Rough, foul lips covered her mouth. Then the crowding, brutish men fell back. Fuentes squatted beside her. "I will ask once more, *gringa*. Your name is? . . . "

Unable to accept the consequences of defiance, Corinne lowered her eyes and began to sob. "You know my name," she said. "I am Corinne Van Allen."

26

A scruffy liver and white dog with red eyes, one torn ear and an intense dislike for horses followed them through El Tule. Short hair bristling, the dog dodged between the legs of the unconcerned animals. Lucca eventually persuaded the mutt to keep its distance by giving it a healthy swat alongside the muzzle with the stock of his shotgun. Maguire ignored the diversion and kept his eye on the shuttered windows of the houses that they passed. Estrellada, appropriately unarmed, rode a few paces ahead of her supposed captors.

Giving no indication whether or not they recognized *la Halcón*, several of El Tule's more daring residents poked their heads out of doorways to watch the brief procession pass. Maguire took note of each one, then spurred forward to turn Estrellada onto the wide, dusty road that led to the gate in the wall surrounding the *hacienda.* Silently the trio rode between a motley collection of dilapidated *jacals, pulquerias,* shops and austere adobe houses.

A pair of *rurales* appeared on the fortresslike walls and gave the alarm as they approached. Maguire congratulated himself for remembering to switch horses with two of Estrellada's men. It wouldn't have done at all to arrive on mounts and saddles obviously belonging to *Los Serpientes.*

"Hey, Maguire. Now that we're maybe gonna get killed, how about you pay me my money. I don't want to die poor," Lucca cracked.

Maguire shrugged, slipped a bandolier over his head and handed it to Lucca, who began to chuckle. "Ah, you are the fox. All this time I am looking for a hidden pouch or belt and you are wearing my money right in front." The Italian dug his fingers into the cleverly sewn pockets behind the cartridges. "But these are so narrow." He found one empty, a few pesos in another. "How can you possibly carry all that money in this?"

"I didn't."

Lucca quit digging and glanced over at his companion. "I think I am not going to like what you are about to say."

"I only brought enough with me to cover expenses. I buried the rest."

"Buried?"

"Don't worry. No one will find it."

"But where?"

"El Madronito."

Lucca shook his head in disbelief. "Buried," he moaned. "Buried. You bastard. You lied to me. You promised me money. Riciotti Lucca works for pay, not promises. Gold."

"I never said I wouldn't pay you," Maguire replied.

"Yes. But how?"

"Simple. After we're finished here, we ride back to Mexico City, dig up the money, split it and there you are."

"There I am. Buried with the money, you mean." Lucca slapped his forehead with his palm. "Back to Mexico City, he says. Maguire, you should be torn to pieces by dogs with broken teeth and bad bowels. Why do you do this to me? For some woman and a boy who are nothing to me?"

"I needed help, Lucca. And what the hell. No one asked you to jump aboard my car back there when Fuentes was chasing you."

"That is unfair," Lucca blustered. "I had no choice."

"Neither did I," Maguire countered. Lucca's eyes narrowed. "The boy is my son."

Lucca drew himself up indignantly. "Oh, come on, Maguire. This is Ricco Lucca. You can't . . ." But Maguire's expression said he wasn't lying. Lucca sighed, reached across the short space between them and returned the bandolier. "Okay, Maguire. This one time, for your son, I will fight on credit."

As they entered the shadow of the wall, a guttural voice from above ordered them to stop and identify themselves. Maguire told the guard his name and that he had come to see General Bortha. The man on the wall told them to wait at the gate. Slow minutes passed. The horses stood quietly, switching their tails, from time to time tossing their heads. Lucca smiled reassuringly at Estrellada, but the girl ignored him. Her jaw was clamped shut in an obvious attempt to keep her emotions in total control. Neither of the men could blame her. They were taking a risk, true, but she was sticking her head in a noose.

"Hey, Maguire," Lucca cracked, trying to alleviate the tension. "I was just thinking. If this doesn't work out, you think Blue will write about us?"

"Probably."

"What do you think he'll write?"

Hinges creaking, the gate groaned open. "That we rode tall in the saddle," Maguire said sarcastically. Taking him seriously Lucca nodded and assumed a truly heroic seat as Maguire led them through the entrance and into the courtyard.

The house of El Tule's master stood approximately seventy-five yards from and directly ahead of the gate. It presented an imposing façade. The adobe walls would be virtually impregnable. Arched iron porticos complete with massive gates sealed off the front porch. The windows were protected by ornamental—and highly efficient—grillework. The red clay tile roof was highly sloped, and slippery. To the left, along the south wall surrounding the courtyard, stood a long barracks. To the immediate right of the gate, a large corral built to hold at least fifty horses occupied the northeast corner of the walled-in space. Behind it and running along the north wall, a long shed served as a tack room, barn and smithy. Still farther along that wall stood a smaller barracks and adjoining storerooms. Barely visible around the corner of the house was the first of a dozen or so randomly placed *jacals* used by the few men who had wives. Not seen, but all important, El Tule's most dependable water well lay directly behind the house.

The *hacienda* was lavishly handsome and efficient, as it would have to be for a man of Bortha's prestige. The Boer possessed a high degree of self-esteem and saw to it everyone in his employ shared that appraisal. There had been a time . . .

The past. Don't reflect on the past, Maguire warned himself. Reflection breeds inattention, and inattention can kill.

He counted the guards. Two atop the gate, two below. Two leading the procession across the baked clay courtyard. Three men visible in the shed, another standing in the doorway of the storeroom. One, two, three walking the walls. Thirteen in sight. How many in the barracks and in the private *jacals* behind the house? No telling. Assume another twenty—at a minimum.

The sound of an automobile being started echoed off the walls and bounced around the courtyard.

The front doors of the *hacienda* opened. The two riders escorting Maguire's small party veered to one side, leaving the trio to go on alone. Maguire stopped twenty feet from the steps and waited, knowing full well Bortha wouldn't simply appear without some show of force preceding him.

Sure enough the sound of the automobile increased and a dusty Model T Ford appeared around the corner. The vehicle had undergone a peculiar customizing. The whole top had been removed and the back seat replaced with an iron tripod mounting for a Lewis gun. The car braked to a stop off to one side and the man in the back swung the heavy cylindrical barrel of the machine gun to cover the newcomers. These two, driver and gunner, were the only men Maguire had seen who displayed a modicum of efficiency, which was a point worth noting. He filed it along with rapidly forming, tentative escape routes.

To impress upon them the great man's station, they were forced to wait again. Five minutes passed. Ten. The horses grew restless. At last, with the sound of hard leather heels clicking militarily on the tile, Bortha appeared.

Five feet ten inches. Gone to fat. Bullet bald head, in keeping with his image of himself as a no-nonsense officer. Small, steel gray eyes. Soft and manicured, pudgy hands. Once they had been hard as adobe bricks. Three rows of medals gleamed on his chest.

"You look well, Gregor," Maguire said.

"For a man of sixty," Bortha shrugged. "And you? Tsk tsk. The last two years have been unkind, Mr. Maguire. Is that gray I see in your hair?"

"I worry too much," Maguire said, calculating the pounds Bortha had put on since they'd last met. At least thirty. Which meant he was getting complacent, sure of himself.

"Ah. Worrying. About coming here, perhaps?" Bortha asked, with an amused chuckle. "Our parting was less than cordial, if I remember correctly. Your cursed temper, Maguire. That was ever your downfall. Kept you from being a first-class soldier."

"I never had the energy for perfection, Gregor."

"Judging by the condition of your clothes, I agree with the observation." He paused, raised his eyebrows in mock surprise. "But who do you have with you? Is that Ricco?" The Italian shifted uncomfortably in his saddle as Bortha squinted at him. "By my faith, it is. We have unfinished business, do we not?"

"I hoped you'd forgotten that, General," Lucca said, trying his most winning smile.

"Theft, I believe," Bortha said, his voice ringing. He pulled a handkerchief from his belt and dabbed at his mottled, bald scalp. "I become more and more intrigued." His brows knotted. "You are still Madero's men, eh?"

Maguire would not be rattled. "I'm sure you know what I've been doing for the last year and a half."

"Madero is dead," Lucca said. Maguire had to force himself not to tense as he watched. If Bortha knew of the president's death, word of Maguire's reason for coming might have reached him, too. If he knew that, they'd better start shooting quickly and hope for the best.

"Oh?" Bortha asked, unable to hide his surprise. Maguire sighed. "How?"

"Revolution," Maguire said offhandedly.

"A pity." The general didn't look or sound overly distraught. "And who . . . ?"

"Victoriano Huerta is the new president of Mexico."

"Ah." Bortha mulled that over a moment. If the news distressed or gladdened him, he gave no indication. "I suppose there'll have to be certain . . . ah . . . adjustments made, but life goes on, eh?"

"I suppose," Maguire said dryly. "At any rate we've

come to join you. And to show our good faith, have brought you a gift."

Bortha pretended to notice Estrellada for the first time. "I have women," he replied. "Who wear skirts as women should."

"But you do not have *la Halcón*." Again, he watched Bortha's face closely. Only a slight reddening of his neck betrayed the general's hatred of Estrellada. "She had set up a barricade to stop the train we were on. We caught wind of it, sent the train back to Lago Blanco, followed her and her men until they dispersed and then took her. Thought you might like to have her, since she was in your territory."

Bortha had not moved. "You were right," he finally admitted, snapping his fingers. Two soldiers appeared in the front door behind him, stepped smartly to Estrellada and dragged her from the saddle. She offered no protest. "Take her to the cells."

Maguire unobtrusively shifted the Winchester so it pointed at the Boer's medal-bedecked chest. Whether Bortha noticed or not hardly mattered, for he waved at the men in the Model T. The automobile kicked into gear and backed out of sight. Bortha waited until the soldiers who had taken Estrellada disappeared around the corner of the house, then held out his arms in a gesture of greeting. "I admit she is a good gift. Come, my capable friends. Have wine with me," he said, and reentered the house.

Maguire and Lucca dismounted and handed the reins of their horses to the *rurales* still stationed nearby. "Looks like it worked," Lucca whispered. "I said . . . "

But Maguire wasn't listening. He was looking at a small, black-haired boy standing in the doorway. He was looking at his son.

27

Casting back two years to the time when Bortha had first taken over the *hacienda,* Maguire tried to recall enough to draw a mental map of the house. A wide set of stairs rose from the back of the foyer to the upstairs. There the closed hall that ran around a central patio opened onto bedrooms on one side and an open balcony on the other. Downstairs, to the left of the entrance, was a formal sitting room; behind it an equally formal dining room. To the right was a large, informal sitting room dominated by a huge fireplace. Opening off the den was a small, private dining room. Beyond that, Bortha's offices. The rear of the house was given to kitchen, pantry, servants' quarters and work space.

The three men turned right. "You'll join me in something to drink?" Bortha asked, and went to the side-

board where a bar was set up. Lucca gazed around, ill at
ease in spite of the general's hospitality. Maguire stood
with his back to the fireplace and took stock of the room.
The walls were lined with trophy heads and weapons,
most of which came from Africa. The room was definitely
Bortha's own, and reflected his personality in both its
lavishness and overpowering sense of masculinity.

"Why did you not have her bound?" Bortha's question
and the proffered glass of bourbon whiskey dangling before his face broke Maguire's chain of thought. He was
about to speak when Bortha, sensing his guest was preoccupied, turned to see what had claimed Maguire's
attention and noticed the boy standing in the doorway.
"Ah. You may enter if you promise to behave."

The boy hesitated only briefly, then entered and inspected Maguire and Lucca. Bortha himself paused before handing his guests their drinks. Uncanny, he couldn't
help thinking, the two bore an amazing resemblance to
each other. The same clumpy dark hair. Blue eyes
alternately bemused and insolent. Even their chins were
the same—hard, flat lines that bespoke determination and
a willingness to buck all odds. That both could be stubborn
and intransigent the general had learned from firsthand
experience.

"What's your name, boy?" Maguire asked gently.

Narrow, wiry shoulders tense, the set of his thin, tough
frame a portrait of defiance, the boy stood his ground and
glowered at Maguire, then Lucca—whose height he
matched—then back to Maguire. Without warning he
slapped the glass from Maguire's hand. The glass shattered on the hearth. Bourbon transformed the grout lines
into amber canals.

"Insolence!" Bortha snorted, grabbing a riding crop
from a nearby table and swinging it at the boy. A black
hickory cane blocked the blow inches from the
boy's hunched shoulders. Bortha blinked in amazement

and turned his anger on Maguire. "I'm disappointed in you," he snapped. "Only ten minutes a guest in my house and already a confrontation."

"A minor one, General. I took enough whippings when I was a kid. I wouldn't relish seeing the same inflicted on him. Or anyone else, for that matter."

"Leave," Bortha ordered sharply. The boy lost no time in obeying, pausing at the door only long enough to look back questioningly at Maguire.

The tension ebbed quickly. Bortha tugged on a bell pull by the fireplace, settled back in his easy chair and watched Maguire pour himself another bourbon. A pair of voluptuous young girls, the plainness of their faces more than offset by rounded, wondrously endowed bodies, entered the adjacent dining room and began setting the table. Giggling softly between themselves, they glanced invitingly at the guests whenever their master wasn't watching.

"You are very sure of yourself, Maguire," the general said as Maguire returned to the fireplace.

"One of my more endearing qualities, Gregor," came the laconic reply.

Lucca shrank down in his chair. This baiting of the general made him nervous. He understood it was Maguire's way of testing a situation, but understanding didn't leave him any happier. Especially when it came to men like Bortha.

"Está listo, señor." One of the girls stood in the doorway and curtsied. Bortha sighed, unbuttoned the top three brass buttons of his uniform coat and gestured for Maguire and Lucca to precede him to the table.

Individual loaves of bread, side dishes and wine had been set at each of the three places. A huge china bowl of spicy beef stew steamed on the sideboard. "I had to teach them to make something other than those damned tortillas," Bortha said proudly. "Took awhile, but they've

317

become fair cooks. Exceptional, if a man's hungry. Shall we begin?" At his signal, the girl nearest him collected the dinner plates, held them while her companion ladled the stew, and returned them to the table.

No ladies present, and the day having been long, little time was wasted on conversation. By the time they were finished, the fire in the living room had been lit and coffee, brandy and cigars were waiting. Pleasantly full, Lucca and Maguire settled in deep chairs flanking Bortha's, stared into the fire and lit their cigars.

"Who's the boy?" Maguire finally asked after the girls had finished clearing the table and left.

"His name is Christopher Van Allen," Bortha said, pleased with himself. "I arranged for him to 'visit' me here."

"*The* Van Allen?" Lucca asked, taking his cue from Maguire.

Bortha nodded. "None other."

"The Van Allen family has enough money to buy you a world of trouble," Maguire ventured.

"Maybe, maybe not. Mr. Van Allen tried once and failed."

Maguire puffed on his cigar, blew a smoke ring. "Which means?"

Gregor Bortha milked the moment for all it was worth. "Follow me," he grunted, rising from the deep, soft chair.

The general led them from the den into the foyer and to a door beneath the main stairs. The door opened to reveal a flight of narrow stone steps leading down. "Hadn't discovered this the last time you were here, Maguire." Bortha chuckled, and winked in Lucca's direction. "Just as well, too, I'd say." Bathed every few feet in amber halos of guttering candles, the men descended into a large cellar. "We're under the patio now," their host continued, his voice sounding curiously flat and muffled in the still, close air. Spider web arches joined stone pillars that held up the ceiling. Cockroaches scuttled from under-foot. A slight wavering of the candles gave evidence of a hidden vent leading to the outside. Four sturdy wooden doors set in the opposite wall drew Maguire and Lucca's attention. Bortha stood in front of the nearest one and slid back a rectangular viewing port.

"La Halcón," he said, closing the panel again immediately. "I've waited a long time to get her in here." Eyes twinkling, he moved to the next door. "See for yourself."

Maguire ducked his head under a rafter and peered into the cell. A gaunt, scruffy *norteamericano* sat motionless on a built-in plank cot, the only piece of furniture in the cell. The man's shoulders were like rounded knobs as he hunched forward. Thin brown hair matched the scraggly growth on his chin. The light was poor, but Maguire could see his nose had been broken once long ago. Aware he was being watched, the man stood and started to limp toward the door.

Maguire slapped closed the panel and rejoined Lucca and his host. "Who is it?" he asked, his expression bland in spite of instant recognition.

Gregor Bortha beamed. "Lee Van Allen," he said. "The boy's father."

The logs had caught and the fire settled down to the serious business of heating the room. Bortha pulled back the drapes on one of the windows opening onto the compound. All appeared peaceful, even serene. A pair of sentries paced the wall. The horses in the corral were quiet. The last of the month's moon, a thin sliver whose light was scattered by a high haze, cast weak shadows over the night.

Very similar to Africa, Bortha had decided. An armed compound beyond the borders of civilization. An inhospitable climate. Shifty, lazy natives who couldn't be trusted much less taught anything beyond the barest rudiments. Land to be held and defended. He ran the palm of his hand over his hairless, smooth scalp and sighed. On the whole, Africa had been better. But the Orange Free State where he'd carved out and lost a niche was an infinitely far place and time removed.

Bortha's reflection in the window moved, letting the curtain fall closed so he wouldn't have to see the newly formed paunch straining his crisp, white shirt. As Lucca returned from the bar with brandy, Bortha undid the last buttons of his uniform. "And so. Van Allen came down here with some native hirelings. Fuentes killed them all, of course." He shook his head in dismay. "Quality in men of our profession is sadly lacking these days, I'm afraid. At any rate, I immediately sent word to Mrs. Van Allen informing her that if one hundred thousand dollars was too much to pay for a son, perhaps it would not be too much to pay for a son and a husband. I was prepared, in other words, to let her have both for the price of one out of the goodness of my heart."

He left the window, crossed to the fire and eased himself into his chair. "Unfortunately she didn't respond."

"Oh?" Maguire prompted.

"My man returned bearing the unwelcome news that she had disappeared. Gone south, evidently, in the company of a young man. What that meant he wasn't able to determine, but I don't like it. She has, I am afraid, something up her sleeve."

"Which means?"

"Without Fuentes here, I am shorthanded. And forced to admit I need you both."

Lucca looked over the rim of his glass. "The pay?" he asked.

"I'm certain we'll agree on a sum—with the usual bonuses if there are problems. But we can discuss that tomorrow. And so!" Bortha clapped his hands sharply.

"In the meantime I'll have Pia show you your rooms. They will be on the opposite side of the patio from mine. I trust you'll find them satisfactory."

Maguire finished his drink, set the empty glass on the table. "I'm sure we will. We've had a hard few days," he said, rising and taking Lucca's glass from him.

"Good for you," Bortha laughed. "Toughen you up after life in the big city. Ah, Pia." An elderly retainer stood in the doorway. "If you'll show my friends to their rooms, please? The two south of Captain Fuentes's room should do nicely. I hope you sleep well, gentlemen."

"Thank you," Maguire said, leading the way to the door.

"Ah! One thing more." Maguire stopped in the doorway. Bortha finished pouring himself a fresh brandy. "The bad blood between you and Jesus Fuentes. I will not permit it to affect the performance of your duties. The captain is due back any day now. When he arrives, I expect you to settle your differences." He looked at Maguire and a thin, cold smile crossed his face. "Once and for all."

Le Mat, Winchester and machete, side by side on the bed. Maguire turned down his lantern as far as it would go, tapped on the door connecting his room to Lucca's and entered. The Italian was busy propping a chair under the knob of the door leading to the hall. He too had laid out his weapons. The Parker-Hale was propped against his bed. A pair of stilettos rested on the night table next to a .45 caliber revolver liberated from a deceased *serpiente*. "Well, we're in," Lucca snorted, flopping down on the bed. His boots left a line of brown dirt and sand on the *serape* spread. "So now what?"

"Mingle with the men tomorrow. Talk to them. We'll find out all we can, then try to run a bluff. No shooting, if we can help it."

"Never did like the idea of going up against a Lewis

gun," Lucca agreed, checking the .45 and stuffing it under his pillow.

"We'll know more tomorrow."

"That's a cheery thought. Maybe I'll feel better about it after I've had some sleep," Lucca answered pointedly.

Maguire took the hint, blew out the lantern and went back to his own room. The *hacienda* was quiet. Outside a rooster waked, crowed and went back to sleep. Pensive, Maguire pulled off his boots and socks and lay back on the bed to ponder the variables. He guessed that Christopher slept downstairs, locked in one of the workrooms at the back of the house. Lee and Estrellada were in the cellar. Bortha's men surrounded the place. Fuentes was due back . . .

He couldn't sleep. Rising, Maguire prowled the room and, searching for something to do, at last resorted to unrolling and hanging up the clothes he'd bought at Broussaria's. Still tense and wide awake, he washed out his socks in the basin, hung them on the windowsill to dry. When someone moved across the compound below, he quickly blew out the lantern.

Bortha, alone in the otherwise empty compound, was making his own rounds. That meant he was worried, Maguire hoped it was about what Corinne Van Allen was up to. The more Bortha looked to the outside, the less likely he was to suspect that the danger came from within, that those he had reason to fear slept in his own house.

Feeling better, Maguire stripped off his shirt and Levis and climbed into bed. Images whirled in his mind. Fuentes. Bortha. Corinne. Was she well? On her way? Safe? Christopher. He had to find the time—and a chance—to be alone with his son. Lee too, if at all possible. Damn! Why here and now? He twisted, trying to get comfortable. Lee, Christopher, Corinne. Guilt, love and dreams. The irony of it all.

He loved her, damn it. No longer even tried to deny

it. The two of them and Christopher could make a good life together. There had to be an honorable way. Had to be. Except for one obstacle. First he had to save the man who stood between them. The one man who could take her away from him.

28

Wind rattling the shutters woke the boy. The light was cold and gray and Christopher thought he must have waked early. Why he wasn't sure, because he always woke up at the same time. At least since he'd been brought to the *hacienda*. One thought keyed another. He and Gus, his father's foreman, had been riding under a cold winter gunmetal-blue Texas sky. Ostensibly checking fences, Gus had spent the day recounting the tales of blue northers, blizzards, gunfights and trail drives—the adventurous west that was, and would never be again.

Without warning, a puff of dust flew from Gus's chest. He tumbled over the rump of his horse and, already dead, hit the ground with a sickening thud. The sound of a gunshot, frightfully close and fracturing the dry air, reverberated off the bluffs behind them. By the time Christopher leaped off his horse and ran to Gus, a half-dozen horsemen emerged from a nearby gully and surrounded him.

The bolt on the outside of his door rattled, then slid back. Had it been a little later, Christopher would have expected Pia, the woman who always brought him hot bread and coffee sweetened with honey. But it was barely light. Too early. He grabbed the heavy clay candlestick from the table and, ready to defend himself, crouched in the middle of the floor. To his surprise, the door opened only far enough to admit a hand holding a red bandanna.

"It isn't white, but all I could come up with in a pinch. Truce?"

"What do you want?" Christopher whispered loudly, backing away as the man who had saved him from a beating the night before slipped into the room and closed the door behind him.

"They lock you up every night?"

"What of it?"

"Must be pretty dangerous."

Christopher shrugged. "They know I'll try to escape." His shoulders squared. "Almost made it once."

"What happened?" Maguire managed to close the gap between them.

"I got lost in the desert. They found me and brought me back."

"Mind if I sit?" Maguire asked, pointing to a stool against the wall.

Careful not to be taken in, Christopher eyed him closely. "I don't know your name."

"Maguire." He stuck out his hand. "I'm a friend."

The candlestick was getting heavy. Christopher placed it beside him on the table and shook Maguire's hand. "Christopher Van Allen. You can sit if you want."

"Thanks."

Christopher pulled on a shirt and tucked it into the trousers he'd slept in. Maguire looked mean as sin, but evidently didn't intend any harm. "You stopped the general from whipping me," Christopher finally said. "How come?"

"I had my reasons. The desert's a pretty stout undertaking for a boy."

"I'm twelve years old."

"How long ago did you try?"

"Ten days ago. I ain't been much in the mood since then."

Maguire smiled. "Give up?"

The boy's dark eyes flashed with fire and his cheeks flushed. He ran one hand through grimy black hair. The knuckles on his other hand were white where he gripped the table. "Not hardly."

A boy in gentler times, adversity had brought him to the brink of manhood. At the age of twelve. He was a boy who would never cry unless assured he was away from prying eyes. "Must be trying to figure a way to take your father with you," Maguire probed.

Christopher grabbed the candlestick but Maguire was too quick for him. The cane he carried whipped out and rapped the boy's wrist. The candlestick thudded back onto the table. Undeterred, Christopher spun and slammed his fist into the soft spot between Maguire's belt line and his shoulder holster. Maguire grunted, reached out and stopped a left headed for his chest. Afraid of being overheard, he jerked Christopher off balance, picked him up and threw him face down on the bed.

Silence. Maguire listened for footsteps, kept a close eye on the boy. When nothing happened, he leaned back against the table and rubbed his side. "Okay. You tried. Ready to talk again for a minute?"

Sullen, Christopher worked his way around until he was sitting up, then froze, staring at Maguire's feet. Maguire glanced down to see that the photograph Corinne had given him had fallen to the ground. "Where'd you get that?" Christopher asked in a choked voice.

'Your mother gave it to me."

"My mother!" He looked dubious, and ready to do battle again.

"I told her I'd get you out of here and bring you home."

Fists clenched at his side, Christopher stood and stared at Maguire. Whether or not he believed what he'd heard was debatable, but that he wanted to believe was obvious. "You looked awful friendly with the general. How do I know?"

"You'll just have to take my word for it." Maguire bent to pick up the photograph and winced. "Whew! You throw a pretty mean right."

"My father taught me to fight."

"Good. You may have to do some more of it before this is over. Are you game?"

"Yes, *sir!*"

"Good. Stay in here as much as you can so we can find you when we need you. The man with me last night is named Ricco Lucca. He's on our side. If I don't come for you, he will. Between the two of us, we'll get you out of here."

"And my father?" Christopher's eyes were wide, alive with hope and relief at no longer being alone. "I'm not leavin' without him."

Maguire's throat tightened. The room was too damned stuffy. Lack of ventilation made it hard to breathe. "Wouldn't expect you to," he agreed with forced heartiness.

"We go together or not at all."

Maguire cracked open the door. The corridor was empty. Except for the melodic chatter of women coming from the kitchen, the house still appeared to be asleep. "Mr. Maguire?" Christopher asked, coming up behind him. Maguire turned. Christopher's hand was extended. "Thanks. I . . . well, just thanks."

"It's what I get paid for," Maguire said bluntly, shaking his son's hand, then slipping out and bolting the door behind him.

That was his son, all right. A good handshake and one hell of a right. Spunk. Fire in his eyes and grit in his maw. It took no little courage to attempt a desert crossing alone. A son, his son. Find a place with Corinne and Christopher, build a home. Raise a few cattle. Or horses, maybe. Have another kid or two. Give Christopher some responsibility. Almost a man, by God. Almost a home.

Maguire entered his own room again. Everything was as he'd left it. He checked the Winchester. The noise of the action, the smell of gun oil and the touch of cool deadly metal soured the dream and he sagged onto the bed. You're a fool, Maguire, the refrain continued. Forty years old and haven't learned a thing. He looked down at his hand wrapped so competently around the grip of the rifle. Corinne his woman? Christopher his son? They had a home already. Corinne knew that and, while she had tried, had been unable to make him understand. Unable to make him listen or see.

"You lose, Maguire," he said softly. "Men like you always lose."

Christopher Van Allen had a father. One he loved. And Corinne had a husband. One she loved, too. Or claimed she loved, which amounted to the same thing.

"Quit thinking, damn it," he told himself. Do your job. The bitter words came back at him. "It's what you get paid for."

"My name is Arturo." That was his last thought. Conscripted into the service of General Gregor Bortha, he had been delighted to have steady food and a dry, warm place to sleep. Because of this he'd worked hard and faithfully, at last earning a most favored position: personal bodyguard to the general, which included the honor of being responsible for the Lewis gun mounted on the Ford.

Yes, life was beautiful, when he thought of it. The *peones* in El Tule respected and feared him. He had been

329

praised for his efficiency by Captain Fuentes, who had hinted of a place in *Los Serpientes*. His *querida* in the village would soon accept him into her bed on a permanent basis. And when the new padre arrived . . .

But the double-edged stiletto sinking between his ribs ended flights of fancy. Notions of a handsome uniform and a beautiful wife faded. His feet beat against the dirt floor. A south wind whistled through the slatted walls. Four stalls down a mare whinnied and snorted as some atavistic sense told her that death was nearby. She was the only witness.

The blade sank home a second time and found Arturo's heart. Lucca twisted once, expertly. The struggling *federale* gasped and went limp. Lucca dragged him to the farthest stall and covered him with straw and sacks of grain. Quickly, he retraced his steps, covering the trail of blood and erasing all signs of his presence. Finally he plunged the blade of the stiletto into the dirt until it came out clean.

"Ricco, what the hell? . . . " Lucca came to his feet, body crouched and stiletto ready. When he saw Maguire, he sighed in relief and sheathed the knife. Maguire looked around, figured out what had happened. "Oh, Christ," he muttered.

"You said the only ones we really had to worry about were the two in the car," Lucca said indignantly. "This one was the gunner. If we're lucky, none of the others will know how to use it."

"Yeah. And if we're not lucky, he'll be missed. If he's found before tonight, we'll—"

"He won't be. No one saw me enter and the body is well hidden. I'm telling you, this was the one to worry about. The others can be bluffed like you said."

Still not totally convinced, Maguire prowled about the barn, double checking to make sure all traces of the dead man had been obliterated. "Maybe you're right," he finally agreed. "I've been roaming about. Our count was long. There's only fifteen here, not counting Bortha and the women."

Lucca threw up his hands. "Fifteen! And you are angry because I lessen the odds?"

"Not by that much. From the looks of them, the rest will do whatever Bortha says. And if Fuentes shows, we'll have a bitch of a time just getting out of here alive. The way I see it, we'd better make our try tonight—just after supper, say. When it's getting dark and everybody is full and relaxed."

"All right with me," Lucca said, picking up his shotgun and patting the stock. "The sooner I get out of here, the happier I'll be."

Maguire stabbed a thumb in the direction of the hidden body. "You just keep an eye on his buddy. And stay sober."

The rumble of an approaching automobile cut short Lucca's protest that the notion of imbibing had never entered his mind. He and Maguire walked to the barn door in time to see a bright yellow Model T speedster roll through the gate and enter the compound. The auto stopped in front of the *hacienda* and two men in dusters and goggles jumped out to be greeted by a medal-bedecked Bortha.

"Who the hell are they?" Lucca asked nervously.

"Guests for dinner tonight," Maguire said. "A handy diversion. I hope."

Hunched in the saddle and accompanied by the youthful bandit whose name he still hadn't been able to catch —he was too embarrassed to ask for it a third time—Blue had been the last to arrive. The night that followed was full of noises that kept him awake. The horses stabled in the foyer of the deserted chapel munched fitfully at the scraps of straw swept into the corner for their benefit. The chittering of bats swooping close to his head as they prowled for flying insects rasped on his nerves. The thought of being trapped in an unsympathetic town and surrounded by God knows how many *federales* was appalling.

The day that followed wasn't much better. The interior of the chapel grew hot and stuffy. He was exhausted, sweat-streaked and dirty. At last he dozed fitfully, waking over and over again to imagined alarms. Sometime in the middle of the day a girl sent by Trigo's grandfather arrived with food and fresh water. The food and drink refreshed and relaxed him, and at last Blue slept.

He woke in the late afternoon. Sun slanted through the western windows and filled the abused sanctuary with soft yellow light. Blue lay quietly, listening, picking out phrases, gradually beginning to see Estrellada and her men from a different perspective. The wrongs committed against them by Bortha and Fuentes—indeed, by the long line of preceding governors—had pushed them to the limits of endurance. Common men though they were, they had finally struck back, seeking justice in the only court left open to them—armed rebellion.

As the sun sank lower, the time came to post the watch in the tower. The small group of bandits broke up. One man headed up the decrepit stairs. Trigo crossed the sanctuary and squatted next to Blue who, rifle in his lap, was leaning against the altar rail. "I wonder, *señor*," he began, speaking slowly so Blue would understand. "You never take your hand away from your rifle. Perhaps you think we will sneak up to you and—" He ran his thumb across his throat.

"No."

Trigo's laugh was deep and a little sad. "Ah, but you lie. I see you, like the other *gringos*. You think we are thieves and murderers."

"That is not true," Blue said in halting Spanish.

"Am I a thief because I take what is mine?" Trigo persisted. "Am I a murderer because I kill the men who took my father and brothers and sold them into slavery in the Yucatan?"

"No. I never said—"

Feet pounded on the stairs from the bell tower. Trigo jumped up and the rest of the bandits grabbed for their weapons and gathered about the man who had been sent to watch. The mixture of Spanish and *poblano* was nonstop and poured out so rapidly Blue found it impossible to decipher. Something was afoot, though. He hurried forward. "Is it the signal?" he asked.

The conversation stopped and the men stared at him. Trigo's look was belligerent and threatening. "The *federales* are building a gallows inside the walls. Your *gringo* friends have failed us."

"You don't know that," Blue said, frightened.

"We have been betrayed!" one of the men to Blue's right exclaimed, leaping toward him.

Blue twisted to one side, grabbed the attacker's arm, and, using his own momentum, hurled him into the others. Three men went sprawling over pews. Blue cocked and leveled his Winchester. Trigo slowly slid his machete back inside its sheath.

"I don't know what is happening," Blue said, "but if the scaffold isn't finished, they won't hang her before morning. It's almost dark. I say we wait for the signal."

"And if it doesn't come before morning?"

"I'll ride with you," Blue said, full of bravado that surprised even him. "All the way."

"*Señores!*" The girl who had brought them food earlier burst into the chapel. Distraught, she hurried to Trigo's side.

"What is it?" the Tarahumara asked.

"One rides this way from the mountains. Don Anselmo saw him as he came through the pass."

"So?"

"He wears the gray of *Los Serpientes!*"

333

Trigo stalked to the window. Someone flailed a horse almost white with lather toward the town. "Get ready," he said, turning to his companions and ignoring the threat of Blue's gun. "We go in after dark."

29

The ruffled front of Maguire's shirt added a dash of elegance to his attire.

"Everything's ready," Lucca said, coming into the room. "Soon as dinner's started, I'll light the lanterns and call in Trigo and then get back to the boy." He stopped. A huge grin split his face. "Ah, Maguire! You are beautiful. A little rumpled, but beautiful."

"Cut it out, Ricco," Maguire growled.

"Too beautiful to fight. You sure you want to—"

"Just make sure the boy's all right. Or I'll have your ass." The hall clock had chimed seven, the hour appointed for dinner, and Bortha didn't excuse tardiness lightly.

"You're forgetting this," Lucca pointed out, holding the shoulder holster.

Maguire checked himself in the mirror. Short black coat, charro trousers and ruffled shirt left little room for the Le Mat, which would be far too obvious. "I think it would make Bortha nervous."

"Make me even more nervous. While I'm playing signal corps you'll be in there unarmed—and unable to help if I get in trouble. Here. Turn around." Not waiting, he circled Maguire and tucked the Le Mat in his belt at the small of his back. "Okay?"

"Damn!" Maguire winced. "You better not take too long." Grabbing his cane and trying to walk as naturally as possible, he left the room, turned right at the bottom of the stairs and headed for the formal dining room and the sound of men's voices. Pausing just before the door, he made a tiny adjustment so the Le Mat didn't dig in quite so painfully, then entered. Bortha and his guests were already seated.

"Ah, Maguire. You're late. I've been extolling the marvels of Chihuahua to my guests."

"Your pardon, General." Two men, both middle-aged and bullish-faced, rose. Bortha had told him they represented a mining outfit, but Maguire thought they looked more like politicians. He inclined his head politely. "And yours, too, gentlemen."

Bortha stood. The bodyguard, the *federale* who drove the Lewis-rigged Ford, pulled out his master's chair. If his partner's absence bothered him—or Bortha—no one showed it. "Have a seat," Bortha said, indicating the empty place to right. "Gentlemen, an old colleague and my right-hand man, Captain Maguire, newly returned from Mexico City.

"Captain, this is Mr. Cole"— The shorter of the two men shook hands with Maguire—"and his assistant, Mr. Travis." Travis nodded and muttered a greeting. "Mr. Cole has come to us from Colorado to evaluate the feasibility of expanding his mining company's operations to our Chihuahuan mountains."

The proper amenities exchanged, the four men sat again. Bortha snapped his fingers and one of the serving girls circled the table, refilling wineglasses. "Maguire is the one I spoke of," Bortha went on. "I myself must return to the city on other business tomorrow, but I leave you in extremely competent hands. No white man knows these hills better than Maguire." Leaning forward, his polished metals tinkling, the general picked up and shook a tiny crystal bell.

Cole was talking, but Maguire, though he appeared to be listening, was checking out the room. He faced the front of the house, which was good. The door to the kitchen was behind him, which wasn't so good. The bodyguard was dressed in an impeccably tailored uniform and carried a sidearm. Impressive, Maguire thought, and a very real problem. The bodyguard would have to go first.

The door behind him opened and a servant entered. Arms shaking from the strain, she placed a huge sterling silver tureen in the center of the table. Behind her, a second girl carried a platter piled with small, round, single-serving loaves of bread. Cole, at the end of the table opposite Bortha, leaned forward with interest as the girl filled a china bowl with black bean soup and placed it before him. Travis, across from Maguire, thrust his beaklike nose toward the center of the table and sniffed. "By God, but that smells delightful," he said.

Cole nodded in agreement. "Bone china, sterling silver, vintage French wine. I'm impressed. You live well, General. I must admit to a certain degree of surprise."

"I try, Mr. Cole," Bortha said, silently reminding himself that, uncouth or not, Cole meant profits which he meant to have. He took a tentative sip of the soup and his face lit up. "Ah, perfect," the general sighed, changing the subject. "Black beans are looked down upon in some circles, but I've never underestimated them, especially in a soup. This is my own recipe, by the way. The girls are good at following instructions, as I trust you'll learn in the course of time."

"You mean cooking, of course," Travis said, chuckling at his own innuendo.

"My *every* instruction," Bortha stressed, his eyes twinkling.

The businessmen laughed. Maguire remembered to laugh also, at the same time listening for telltale sounds, tasting black bean soup, feeling the presence of the man with a gun strategically placed behind Bortha. Too many variables, he couldn't help thinking. The body in the stables, just waiting to be found. Christopher, eager to get out and see his father rescued. Lucca, alone in the compound, facing the problem of giving the signal and unlocking the gates. Trigo and his men . . . The Le Mat dug into his spine.

"General Bortha has been telling us he has quite a day lined up tomorrow," Mr. Cole said, forcing Maguire to concentrate on those in the room again.

"General Bortha has a knack for entertainment, as you'll no doubt learn," Maguire responded. And Fuentes, he added silently. Where the hell was Fuentes?

"First the hanging of an outlaw," Travis broke in, tearing apart one of the small loaves. "Symbolizes the end of lawlessness and the growth of modern industry in northern Mexico. Our company appreciates that, General."

"That calls for a toast," Cole said, rising. The oil lamps leant a peculiar amber luster to his carefully trimmed, graying hair.

Mind racing, wondering what was taking Lucca so long, Maguire stood with the others.

"To General Gregor Bortha," Cole said, holding out his glass, "and a prosperous future for—"

A commotion at the front door interrupted him. Excited voices rose in volume. From his vantage point facing the front of the house, Maguire could see a bedraggled figure push past the servants and literally drag the two *federales* who had been on duty at the front door through the living room. Gray jacket and trousers thick with dust, black *sombrero* a ruin, the new arrival burst into the dining room and stopped abruptly, staring at Maguire.

"What is the meaning of this?" Bortha roared, his face and scalp mottled with anger at the intrusion.

The tableau held, seconds long. Beneath the grime and dust, Maguire recognized the man even as he was recognized. And then everything happened at once.

Elrecht! The *rurale* clawed at his holster flap. Maguire threw his wine into Bortha's face. A gun roared and Lucca charged in the front door and attacked the startled *federales* from the rear. Bortha's bodyguard pulled his sidearm, ducking a handful of silverware Maguire had hurled at his face. Coming out of nowhere the heavy silver panther head struck the underside of the bodyguard's jaw.

Someone screamed. Maguire threw himself at the momentarily blinded Bortha and both men tumbled over a chair to the floor. The revolver dropping from his limp fingers, the bodyguard slid down the wall.

Two more shots, blending into one. Too late Elrecht realized Lucca was behind him. By the time he tried to react, the Italian was only a step away. Elrecht ducked, but not fast enough. The butt of the shotgun slammed into his head and he went down.

Maguire kicked aside the revolver dropped by the bodyguard and pulled the Le Mat from his belt. Hauling the struggling Boer general to his feet and using him as a shield, he backed into a corner. Mr. Cole had disappeared beneath the table. Mr. Travis was still standing, frozen in place. Lucca disarmed the unconscious Elrecht and hurried to Maguire. "You all right?"

"Yes."

Bortha struggled. Maguire jammed the Le Mat into the side of his neck. "Sixty caliber shotgun shell, General. If you try anything, I'll take off your head." Turning to Lucca, Maguire asked, "You give the signal?"

"Barely. And then that one came riding in and all hell broke loose. The whole place is up in arms and the gate's still locked, as far as I can tell."

"The general and I will take care of that. You check on Christopher and then cover my rear. I don't want two or three of these sons-of-bitches surprising me from behind."

"Right." Lucca ran out the back door of the dining room.

"Now, General—"

"You bastard, Maguire. You double-faced, lying, treasonous bastard. I'll see you cut to pieces. I'll make sure you—"

The Le Mat jabbed deeper into the soft skin of Bortha's neck. "That'll be enough, Gregor. Let's go out front."

"So help me—"

"Now!" Maguire pushed the general toward the door, stopped when a pair of *federales*, rifles at ready, rushed through the foyer and into the living room. "Hold it!" Maguire shouted.

Spotting the revolver placed against their general's neck, the *federales* stopped. Maguire grabbed Bortha's collar and twisted. "Tell them to throw down their arms. No bargains, no stalling, no tricks. I count to three and then put your brains on the wall. One . . . two . . . "

"Put down your guns!" Bortha wheezed. "Put them down. It is an order."

The soldiers, unsure of what to do, stared in confusion at each other and Maguire.

"Now! I command you!" Bortha repeated frantically. The *federales* hurriedly did as they were told.

"My God," Mr. Cole wailed from beneath the table.

"Oh, dear God," Mr. Travis groaned as he watched his own blood drip on the white linen cloth. His arms buckled and he collapsed forward, overturning the tureen and spilling the still steaming black bean soup onto the table and floor.

Voices shouted outside. Maguire pushed Bortha toward the front of the house. "You two," Maguire ordered the *federales.* "In front of us. Out the door." Moving slowly, intensely aware of the pistol jammed into Bortha's neck, they crossed the living room and foyer, and went out the main door. "Tell them—all of them—to throw down their guns and open the gates."

"The hell you say, Maguire." Men rushed toward them from the barracks, stopped only when they saw their general at gunpoint. "I wouldn't—"

"Your choice," Maguire snapped. "One . . . two . . . "

"Open the gates!"

His faith in professionalism was shattered. Stunned and angry, Bortha stared at the ground between his feet. He'd watched his men disarmed and marched into their barracks to be locked up. A pair of bandits stood guard on his walls. Three more strutted through his *hacienda,* no doubt looting his laboriously collected treasures while he sat shackled to a chair with his own leg irons. He would be the laughingstock of all Mexico when word of his ignominious treatment got around. Worst of all, *la Halcón* would be free. He didn't want to even predict what retribution she would seek.

Maguire stood in front of him, held out a glass of brandy. Bortha looked away. "Better take it, General. They'll be bringing up *la Halcón* in a minute. You might need it."

"I prefer a firing squad," Bortha growled.

"Sorry, Gregor. I'm not going to let them kill you. Whether or not they realize it, you're the only ace they have in this game."

Bortha's eyes fixed Maguire's in a murderous stare. "You're more of a damned fool than I thought then. If our paths ever cross again, I won't hesitate to kill you."

"No, I don't imagine so," Maguire said, offering the brandy again.

The general took the glass, held it in mock salute. "Here's to generosity." He tossed back the brandy. "I'll not make that mistake again."

A door slammed and footsteps sounded in the hallway. "Where is he?" they could hear Estrellada ask.

"On the patio."

Captured Springfield in hand, *la Halcón* walked up to Bortha and stood in front of him. Bortha stared at her with morbid fascination. The look in *la Halcón's* eyes was of pure hatred. Suddenly she spat in his face. "Pig!" she hissed. "Now it is your turn to be the animal!" Again she spat. "What do you say now, eh?"

Spittle ran down Bortha's cheek. He remained silent.

"Okay, Estrellada, that's—"

"*Halcón!* I am *la Halcón!*"

"Okay. *La Halcón.* That's enough for now."

"No!" Her hands a blur, she worked the bolt and aimed the rifle point-blank at Bortha's face.

Maguire knocked aside the rifle with his cane. The bullet chipped adobe behind him. Estrellada worked the bolt again. "I said that's enough," Maguire repeated.

"I will kill him."

"Not while he's my prisoner."

Estrellada stepped around him and brought the Springfield to bear. Maguire wrenched it away and tossed it to Trigo. Estrellada proceeded to attack Bortha with her hands, but Maguire grabbed her and shoved her away. "You want a war? It can begin right here, but I promise it will cost what you've just won," Maguire shouted angrily, looking to Trigo for support.

"*La Halcón,*" Trigo said, trying to calm her down.

She spun away from Maguire. "Kill him, Trigo. Kill them both!"

The Tarahumara shook his head. "We must use him for more than his death. And not fight among ourselves."

Color slowly returned to Estrellada's face, normalcy to her eyes. "Very well," she finally said. "I will wait." Pausing only long enough to retrieve her rifle from Trigo, she stalked through the patio doors, ignoring Blue who passed her on his way in.

Blue watched Estrellada leave, then turned to Maguire. "Mr. Van Allen is in the den. He wants to see you."

Maguire nodded. "Is the boy with him?"

"Yes, sir."

"What about Cole and Travis?"

"Mr. Travis is dead. Mr. Cole wants to get back to Chihuahua, but Lucca told him he was going to have to wait. He's pretty upset."

"Can't say as I blame him. Lucca was right though. See he gets fed and give him a room. Tell him he can go in a few days. Last thing we need is a whole regiment of *federales* showing up." Maguire turned to Trigo. "As for the general, put him where *la Halcón* was. Give him a taste of his own medicine. But watch him closely. He's slippery."

A wide, broken-toothed grin spread across the Indian's face as he pulled Bortha's hands behind his back and tied him before removing the leg irons. "Do not worry," he said slowly. "The general won't go anywhere. Not while Trigo watches."

"And you can bet on that," Maguire told Blue on their way out. "You better also be damned happy that Indian is on our side."

"There you are," Lucca said, catching sight of Maguire as he and Blue came through the foyer. "The German wants to talk. You better get in there quick. *Halcón's* boys roughed him up a little and I don't think he'll last long."

"Tell Van Allen I'll be with him in a minute," Maguire said to Blue. "Let's go, Ricco."

Elrecht had been bound securely to one of the dining

343

room chairs. Left alone by Maguire and Lucca while the rest of Bortha's stronghold was being secured, the hated *serpiente* had fared badly at the hands of the bandits. His face was bruised and blood ran from the corners of his mouth. His hands had been tied tight and were swollen to almost the bursting point. Blood seeped through his pants where he'd been shot in the right knee.

Maguire gazed dispassionately at him, took a glass of water from the table and dashed it in his face. The German moaned and lifted his head. "Please," he mumbled. "No more."

"What's your name?" Maguire asked.

"Elrecht. Hermann Elrecht."

"How's it feel to get what you've been giving, Elrecht. Like it?"

"Please."

"Have a way of biting back, don't they? Can't say as I blame them. What about you?"

"Please." Elrecht's head sagged forward again.

Maguire grabbed his hair, snapped his head upright. "I'll tell you what, Elrecht. I don't like you or any of your *compadres*, so I may very well just give you back to *Halcón*. The only thing stopping me is what you might have to say, and it wouldn't take much to make me forget that. Do you understand?"

"Yes," Elrecht replied weakly. He tried to focus on Maguire, but his eyes didn't seem to be functioning properly.

"Good. So what is it?"

"Get me out of here. I can take you to her."

Maguire paled. "Who?" he asked.

"Please. My hands—"

"Who, goddamn it?"

"The woman." He licked his lips nervously, tried to enunciate clearly. "The three you left behind fought and were killed. We captured the woman. Fuentes has her. I can take—"

344

"You son-of-a-bitch!" Maguire grabbed his hair again, held his head up. "Is she harmed?"

"No. I swear it. Fuentes knew who she was—and why she'd come."

"What about the old man?" Maguire asked, his mind racing.

"We could not find him, but he must have poisoned the well because all except me took sick. I did not drink, so Fuentes sent me ahead to warn the general."

"And?"

Elrecht breathed deeply, tried to forget the pain in his knee. "That is all. I rode here. The others will follow soon."

Maguire waited. Fuentes had Corinne. Damn, but he shouldn't have left her behind. Should have known better. "What else, damn your soul?" Maguire suddenly shouted in Elrecht's face.

"Nothing! I swear it. Please. My hands . . ."

"*Halcón*! Trigo! Cirillo! *Ven por aca!*"

"No! Don't call them back, please!" Elrecht was near tears. "There is nothing else! I swear nothing else!"

"*Que quiere?*" Cirillo, one of the bandits, lounged in the rear doorway.

"What do I want?" Maguire asked. "Tell them what I want, Elrecht."

Elrecht looked like he was going to faint. "No. Please," he whispered.

"You were in Mexico City, weren't you? You were the one who brought me the little girl's dress." His voice choked with emotion. "And then you went back and stood in line with the rest, right?"

"Only because Fuentes told me—"

Maguire could see Remedios stretched out on the bed. See her blackened hands and feet, her blood-streaked body. "Bullshit!"

The room fell silent and the rage that had enveloped him subsided. Drained, Maguire let Elrecht's head drop and looked toward the door. A second and third bandit had joined Cirillo there. "Take him," he said flatly. "Hang the son-of-a-bitch the way he is. Chair and all."

Blue, his face pale, stood in the entrance to the living room. Lucca, shotgun cradled in his lap, lay on the couch. "Ricco, take Patrick Henry and check the prisoners. Stay away from the gallows. I'll be out when I finish with Van Allen."

Lucca rose lazily from the couch and snared a bottle of rum he'd found in the den. Maguire pretended not to notice, but his cane flicked out. The silver panther head struck the bottle, which broke apart, leaving Lucca holding the neck. The Italian looked mortally stricken. "Stay sober," Maguire said, and stalked out of the room.

Pausing in the hall to compose himself, Maguire crossed the hall to the den. Lee Van Allen lay on a couch that had been pulled in front of the fireplace. Christopher sat next to him and, Maguire noted with a pang of jealousy, held his father's hand.

Eyes hollow, skin pale and tight around a square-cut chin half hidden by a scraggly beard, Lee touched the patchy hairs covering his face. "I never could grow a good beard," he said.

"From the look of things, it's not from a lack of trying." Maguire tried to keep his tone light, but knew he sounded strained.

"This is the man, Father," Christopher said.

"Yes." Lee took a sip of brandy. "This is the man."

"You want to leave us alone for a minute, Christopher?" Maguire asked in the silence that followed.

Christopher looked to his father. "It's all right, Chris. Mr. Maguire and I need to talk."

The youth looked disappointed; he didn't want to be left out.

"Tell you what," Maguire said. "Your father looks like he could use some food. There ought to be a kettle of bean soup out there in the kitchen someplace. Why don't you find some bread to go with it and fix him up a tray."

"Sure. I mean, yes, sir."

They watched him go, and then were alone with. a hundred things to say and as many more to avoid. Perhaps, given time, they would have figured out how to broach the years and the ugliness that still separated them, but there was no time. Lee peered over the rim of his glass and sipped his brandy. Maguire pulled up an easy chair and sat. "They have Corinne," he finally said.

Lee's eyes flickered and his lips tightened. "Who?"

"Fuentes. You know him?" Lee shut his eyes, let his head hang back. His adam's apple was a sharp point that bobbed, once, as he swallowed. "I have a plan," Maguire continued. "It isn't much, but the only thing I can come up with." Lee didn't move. "I'll take Bortha and trade him for her."

"You're right. It isn't much of a plan," Lee said. "When Fuentes captured me, I gathered he wasn't too enamored of Bortha. Said some harsh words about him. He just might be real pleased to have you do his dirty work for him."

"Then I'll just have to sweeten the pot. Jesus Fuentes would kiss the hind end of the devil almighty to get his hands on me."

Lee's laugh was brittle, caustic. "My oh my. A hero. That's a new cut of cloth for you, isn't it, Maguire?"

There was no point playing the whipping boy, however righteous Lee's anger. Maguire pushed back his chair and stood.

"She still loves you," Lee said, the words burning his throat.

"She *stayed* with you," Maguire said, his hand on the doorknob.

"Out of guilt. Not love."

"She stayed."

"It isn't the same, damn it! Of her own free choice. That would have meant something."

Maguire almost repeated what Corinne had told him about Lee's intransigence and how he had built a wall between them. A wall she had tried to break down but couldn't. The time and place were wrong though. Would always be wrong. "If I'm not back in two days, *la Halcón* and her men will see you and Christopher safely across country to Presidio. Wait there. If I can't bring Corinne, my partner will. I'll promise him some of your money."

Lee was forced to accept the change of subject. "All right, Maguire. You win. I'm in no shape to do anything. *La Halcón's* a bandit, isn't she?"

"That's right."

"If you trust her, I guess I can, too."

"You can. Her price will be guns and bullets. She'll need them, too, after this."

"She'll have them. She has my word."

"Good."

"Maguire!"

The soldier of fortune turned in the doorway. Lee Van Allen's mouth framed soundless syllables. At last, helpless and at a loss, he shook his head and sighed. "It's been a while, Maguire. Been a long while."

"It has that, Lee." The door creaked. "See you." And clicked shut.

30

Face wan and pale, skin drawn parchment tight over fevered cheeks, only Fuentes's single, undeterred will had kept the men in check, held the woman inviolate, untouched. Only the unsleeping eye that saw in the dark, penetrating fire dance and rock shadow, protected her from harm. For the sickness did not still lust. Not in *Los Serpientes*.

Corinne rolled up her blanket and sat across the fire from him. Fuentes smiled absentmindedly at her as one would an obedient animal. Working slowly, he removed the cartridges from the cylinder of his .45 and placed them in a row on a flat stone. Then, one by one, he set each on another stone in front of him and scored the tip with a tiny x. Next, laying his knife edge down over the guiding marks and using his revolver like a hammer, he struck the back of the blade once, gently. Twice per cartridge. Times six.

"The bullet, on contact, expands explosively. It makes a very big hole in a man."

"Or woman or child," Corinne said, letting her contempt for her captor show.

Fuentes shrugged, immune to her venom, and started replacing the cartridges in the cylinder. "Only when necessary, *señora*."

"That kind of death is never necessary."

The cylinder snapped into place, clicked smoothly as Fuentes spun it. "In a perfect world, madam, no kind of death is necessary. As you may have noticed, however, we do not live in such a world, and many kinds of death are necessary."

The shadowy bulk of Sergeant Suarez lumbered into the firelight. Huge and chunky, wrapped in his blanket, he looked like a boulder that had found legs and learned how to walk. Fuentes glanced up briefly, indicated with a nod of his head that Suarez should sit and started removing rifle catridges from a bandolier. "Are the others awake?" he asked sharply.

"Yes, sir. They are saddling the horses." Suarez squatted next to Corinne by the fire. He, too, looked tired, as if he hadn't slept all night. His eyes were pouched from sleeplessness and his skin was slightly grayish, the same symptoms Corinne had exhibited during her bout with the illness brought on by tainted water. "They grumble because they have no coffee," the sergeant went on, wagging his head in appreciation as Fuentes pulled his knife and began scoring the new cartridges. "I told them they would feel better when the sun came up."

Fuentes nodded in agreement, glanced to the east and resumed his deadly chore. "And the old man?"

"No sign. It is still very dark."

Corinne hid a tiny smile. Those capable of riding or walking had scoured the nearby arroyos and ridges for

Don Memo the day before, but the ancient will-of-the-wisp had eluded the searchers. They had not been able to find even his goat. The only discovery worth mentioning had been the bundle of roots and curious thorned vines dangling deep in the well.

The eastern sky was graying when an orderly approached. Corinne remembered hearing Fuentes address him as Diego. "There are still five who are very ill, Captain."

"They must ride with us," Fuentes said, jamming cartridges back into the bandolier. His eye patch glittered. Diego looked away. "We have no more water," the captain continued. "Waiting will not help, and I can wait no longer."

"A long, hot ride," Suarez groaned. He leaned over to one side, reached out to catch Corinne's leg above the knee and slid his hand along her Levis toward her upper thigh. When she slapped his hand aside, he chuckled and heaved to his feet. "I will tell them," he said. "They will ride."

Fuentes slid his machete from its sheath. Taking the whetstone from the pouch on his belt, he began to hone the blade. Corinne gritted her teeth at the sound.

"Tell them this, too," Fuentes said. "There will be water to slake their thirst under the sands of *rio Benito Gordo*, then water enough for coffee when we camp for the night at the House of Dawn." His teeth glimmered in the new light. "And gold when we have found Maguire."

Blue searched the corral for a horse big enough to carry him, found a gray gelding a full seventeen hands tall and led him into the stables to saddle up.

Tap.

He spun around. Maguire sat on a stool next to an anvil. He place a .45 cartridge base down on the anvil and notched the lead nose of the bullet.

Tap.

351

Blue squared his shoulders. "Lucca told me your plan. I'm going with you." Maguire ignored him, concentrated on the bullets. "You hear me?"

"I heard you. No. You're not."

"Do we have to go through this again?"

"Evidently. You're not going. Not this time."

"You can use the help. The German said—"

"I know what the German said, Patrick Henry, and I still say you're not going. I'm not about to have your death on my hands—not to speak of my conscience." He started pushing cartridges into the Le Mat. "Stay here with Estrellada and court her. At least *that* story has a chance for a happy ending." He spun the cylinder, returned the Le Mat to its holster and got up to leave.

Blue grabbed Maguire's shoulder and spun him around. Maguire's fist shot out and clipped the side of Blue's jaw. The youth grimaced and sent Maguire reeling with a well-placed right to the midriff. The mercenary bounded off a wall and slid to a sitting position. "Oh, shit," Maguire groaned, rubbing his side.

Applause sounded from the doorway as Estrellada and Lucca rounded the corner. "Ah, the energy of youth," Lucca laughed, walking over to Maguire and helping him to his feet. "Did I not tell you he had the strength of a mule? And you laughed when it was my turn."

"I did not." Maguire bent over, massaged his stomach. "I didn't say a thing."

"You laughed secretly. What happened?"

"Patrick Henry here was trying to convince me to take him with us."

Lucca winked broadly. "He can go in my place," he suggested brightly. "I'll be glad to stay behind and keep an eye on things."

"Won't work, Ricco," Maguire said, picking straw from his sweater.

"I'm going with you," Blue repeated defiantly.

"They rode tall in the saddle," Lucca said, recalling Maguire's words and earning a sour look.

"I'll be ready in five minutes." Turning, Blue walked to the gelding and tossed a blanket on its back.

The kid was determined enough, Maguire thought. And he and Lucca admittedly could use another hand. But damn it, he didn't want another dead kid on his conscience. Remedios, of the Street of the Owls, was enough. A boy-faced giant would be one straw too many. "Look, Patrick Henry, this is just—"

"Three is better odds than two," Blue said, throwing a saddle on the gray's back.

"But we know what we're getting into, damn it!"

Blue turned. One hand on the saddle, he faced Maguire confidently. "So do I," he finally said, in a quiet voice.

In that moment, Maguire saw a man behind the boyish expression. And a man had to go his own way, make his own decisions. Maguire had lived by that code: Patrick Henry Blue would have to also. Strange, the fleeting, tingling chill that ran up his spine, though. Pride, Maguire guessed, and a hint of loss. Much the way he'd probably feel if he had a son, in that moment when he realized . . .

But he did have a son . . . "Five minutes," Maguire said harshly, suddenly angry. "If you're not ready then, we leave without you." Motioning for Lucca to follow, he strode out of the barn.

Obviously puzzled, Estrellada waited until Maguire and Lucca were gone, then walked over to Blue. "You want so much to die?" she asked, trying to read his mind and failing.

"Not going to die," Blue corrected her, hauling on the cinch. When nothing happened, he gave the gelding a swift kick in the belly, driving out the air the animal had inhaled to keep the saddle loose.

"Then you do this to impress Estrellada." She stood close to him, reached out to touch him and, because she was afraid he would think she was trying to trick him, drew back her hand.

"You're wrong, but suit yourself," Blue said, concentrating on tying the cinch strap tightly. Moving quickly— Estrellada had to step clear in order not to be knocked aside—he retrieved his Winchester from where it lay on a bale of hay and jammed it into the saddle scabbard. All the while he tried not to notice Estrellada, or remember the hour they had spent together. All emotion carefully kept from his face, he swung into the saddle.

"Well, you don't impress me, *campeon*." Estrellada, her face twisted into a scowl so he wouldn't see she cared, stood a half-dozen paces in front of the gelding. "*Campeon*? Ha! You are *loco*, you hear? *Loco!*"

Blue spurred his mount forward, reached down and caught Estrellada in one arm. Before she could think to struggle, he lifted her to him and kissed her. Estrellada started to throw her arms around his neck, but suddenly found herself dropped into a pile of hay. Head thrown back, Blue roared with laughter and, immensely pleased with himself, spurred the gelding into a gallop and disappeared out the door, leaving *la Halcón*'s fuming, invectives boiling the early morning air in his wake.

31

A warming sun hung lemon-drop yellow against the afternoon sky. The south wind, gusting, swept desert sand over the hills that protected the valley, from either side of which the ruin tumbled ground reared symetrically upward as if furrowed by a giant's hand. Maguire stood atop the House of Dawn and surveyed the scene.

They had been lucky, Maguire knew. Far below in the sunken ruins where they'd rested three nights earlier, Blue had set up camp and with Bortha's coerced assistance was gathering brush for a bonfire as per Maguire's instructions. Lucca was out of sight on the north slope. Fuentes, short of water and coming from the southeast, would be forced to stop in the valley, if not that evening, the next. Using binoculars taken from Bortha to check, Maguire saw no sign of Fuentes so far. To the north a thin line of dark blue indicated that a norther was on the way. Except for the coming change in weather, the situ-·

ation was as controlled as possible. Three to twenty, Maguire thought with a grin, might not turn out as disastrously as it sounded.

A final three-hundred-and-sixty-degree scan showing nothing, Maguire dropped the glasses back in the case and started down the long, precipitous ramp of narrow steps. Another three hours and it would be dark. Two hours after that they'd know if Fuentes was going to show up that night. Lucca appeared from behind a pile of rubble on the north slope as Maguire reached the bottom of the pyramid. The Italian scurried down the incline and trotted across the flat avenue to meet Maguire. He wiped the sweat from his face with a soiled bandanna, then retied it around his forehead. "She's set," he said grimly. "We'll come down those hills like Huns. What if Fuentes shows before dark?"

"You put brush over it?"

"Sure. It's hid. Nice smooth path all the way down, too."

"Dark or not, we've no choice. The plan stays the same."

Lucca took a revolver from his sash and spun the cylinder. He did not look happy, but Maguire was used to that. "I hope Mr. Van Allen is more generous than you."

Maguire laughed and clapped Lucca on the shoulder. "Ricco, you're the most pessimistic, morose son-of-a-bitch I ever met. Believe me. It'll work. Besides, what are you complaining about? You'll be getting paid twice for one job."

"That's too much luck for me. It's unlucky."

They'd had essentially the same conversation a dozen times in the past. For one who loved to fight, Lucca always spent an inordinate amount of time grousing. Still and all, Maguire thought as they trudged the last few yards to their campsite, he's the best. A man never had to worry when Riciotti Lucca was fighting beside him.

The bonfire was ready to go. Blue had even strung a

tarp over one corner of the camp in case the norther brought rain. By force of habit, they spent the next hour field stripping and cleaning all their weapons while a small fire heated the meat, beans and coffee they'd brought with them. At last there was nothing to do but watch and wait.

Maguire took off his boots, lay back against the pile of canteens and studied the late afternoon sky. Unprompted, his thoughts turned to Christopher, who had run alongside him, reached up and touched his arm as they rode out of El Tule. "Be careful, Mr. Maguire," he'd said, and then fell back as the horse broke into a gallop. A man needs to have a son. A man needs to be called father once in his life.

"He will kill you." Maguire started, looked up to see Bortha standing in front of him. So engrossed had he been, he hadn't even heard the general's leg irons clanking as he approached. "He'll kill the three of you and I won't lift a finger."

Maguire scowled, sat up and pulled on his boots. Nearby, Blue squatted by the fire, his rifle across his lap. Lucca stood a few feet away, drinking coffee. "If I go, you'll go, too," Maguire growled, suddenly in a bad mood.

"I can show mercy. I can be forgiving," Bortha said, his voice high-pitched. A nervous tic had begun above his right eye. His medals needed polishing and his once immaculate white uniform coat was torn and soiled. "Very well then. You are a dead man. So be it. I wash my hands of you. Unreason is your undoing."

"Why don't you be quiet?" Blue said, slowly and clearly. "Why don't you just shut the hell up?"

Bortha looked at him in astonishment. "I am General Gregor Bortha," he proclaimed indignantly. "Who do you think you are to talk to me in that manner?"

Blue looked at him, smiled politely. "I'm the man with the gun," he answered.

Lucca slapped his leg and began to laugh. Bortha, completely flustered, turned red and, chains clanking, stomped away from the fire. "You're learning, Patrick Henry," Maguire said. The black mood had dissolved as rapidly as it had appeared and he realized that he, too, was laughing. "You're by God learning."

Blue grinned sheepishly. He wished he could laugh, too, but the truth was he was simply too scared.

Dusk came prematurely. The heavy air stilled as the barometric pressure dropped and the southern wind failed. The norther was almost on them. The line of dark blue clouds and dust filled the sky over the rim of hills.

Suddenly Maguire spun, the Le Mat materializing in his hand as the figure of a man appeared from behind a shaggy yucca. "I made much noise so you would hear me and not shoot," a voice said.

Don Memo! Embarrassed by having been caught dozing, Maguire holstered the Le Mat. "My mind was elsewhere," he replied by way of apology.

"Best it were in this time and place," the old man said, stepping closer. "Fuentes comes. I meant to warn you earlier, but the journey was too difficult for old bones." He shook his head. "Not so many years ago, I could have walked this far in a day." He looked past Maguire to the fire and the horses. "I see my journey was wasted."

"We took one of his men prisoner."

The old man nodded. "I watched him ride off. Then you know of the woman."

"Is she unharmed?"

Don Memo shrugged, cocked his head to one side. "Who is unharmed in this world? I could not wait close by to see, but I do not think One Eye will allow his men to harm her until he knows it is safe to do so. You wait for him?"

"Yes. I assumed he would have to come here for water. For that I have you to thank. Because he was slowed, I owe my life to you again. Will you come to the fire? There is coffee," Maguire said, nodding toward the small blaze built in the sunken temple floor fifty yards away. "The wind will change any minute now. There are blankets."

"I am too old to fight. Old men can only watch and bury the dead. I will find a sheltered spot"—he gestured to the ruins above them on the southern rim of the valley—"and return to my home when it is safe."

Maguire almost cursed *el viejo* for his plodding manner. "Fuentes is that close?" he asked harshly.

Don Memo pointed toward the eastern pass. "He will come very soon. With many men. Twenty *serpientes*. Too many for you alone, Maguire."

"We'll see," the mercenary replied. "I am not alone."

The goat herder started climbing back up the rubble-strewn slope. "Sit with us and share our coffee in the morning, *viejo!*" Maguire called.

"We shall see," came the bemused answer from the shadows. *"Vaya con Dios."*

An ill-fitting benediction, Maguire thought, in this valley of long-dead gods. Which one? There had been so many. Quickly he started across the open ground to the sunken campsite. Damn! A hell of a time for Fuentes to show. A storm about to hit . . .

"He's on his way in," he shouted, leaping down into the pit. "Give me a hand and get out of here." Working swiftly while Blue restrained Bortha, Maguire and Lucca threw blankets and saddles on the gelding Blue had ridden and a well-trained sorrel mare Maguire had picked.

Halfway through the chore, the wind stopped completely. For a minute, the stillness hung over them like a cloud. Then with a roar, the norther tore into the valley. Dust, sand and debris carried by the wind filled the air. "Shit!" Lucca yelled, jerking off his bandanna and retying it over his face.

The horses whinnied, plunged about restlessly. Maguire angled against the wind, cut through the flying sand to Blue. "Bring him on over and let's get him on the horse," he shouted over the wind. "Then cover your face and get your coat on. It's going to get cold fast."

Grabbing the reluctant Bortha, they propelled him toward the gelding, unlocked one shackle and helped him aboard. "You are insane!" Bortha screeched. "You won't be able to see! I urge you—"

A bolt of lightning followed by the immediate crack of thunder drowned out the rest of his sentence. Maguire reached under the gray's belly, caught the free leg iron, pulled it back under the horse and clamped it shut around Bortha's left ankle. Lucca tapped him on the shoulder. "He's right," he said, his mouth close to Maguire's ear, his voice muffled by the bandanna. "Seeing anything is going to be a bitch."

"For them, too," Maguire yelled in return. The temperature had already dropped a good ten degrees. "Besides, it'll slack off after a few minutes. You ready?"

"As I ever will be."

"Good luck, *compadre*," Maguire shouted, shaking Lucca's hand. "Remember that gold, you son-of-a-bitch, and keep an eye on my back!"

"Like a Hun. I never forgot gold yet." Another flash of lightning illuminated Lucca's grin. Now that the fight was close, his pessimism had vanished, replaced by the exhilaration of his first love—battle. "Shoot straight," *cabron*." Turning, he motioned for Blue to follow, grabbed two of the extra horses they'd brought and started for the north hills.

Maguire caught up with Blue just as he left the fire. "Scared?"

"Yes."

"It'll go away. You'll do fine. See you."

"Right."

"Hey, Patrick Henry!" Blue stopped. "If we get rain with this, it'll be slicker'n owl shit, so be careful."

Blue laughed, caught the last three horses, led them up the ramp and away from the sunken campsite. He hadn't been lying when he'd said he was afraid, but Maguire had eased the tension. The fear that remained was a healthy kind, he imagined. A fear that cooled his blood and washed away extraneous distractions. Calming the nervous horses, he leaped aboard one and led the other two along the path Lucca had taken across the level avenue and up behind a jumble of rectangular stones. There he ground-tethered them securely before climbing the smooth wagon-worn path that angled up the slope.

Shivering—the temperature continued to drop—Blue clutched the coat Maguire had insisted he bring along. Lucca was already in place. Using a block of cut granite as a bench, the Italian was busy checking the action of the Parker-Hale. When he finished, he wrapped the action and stock in a piece of cloth and handed the pump gun to Blue. The massive gun appeared properly proportioned at last. "Keep that rag on it until it's time to start shooting," Lucca yelled into Blue's ear. "Don't want sand in it."

"Won't you need it?" Blue yelled back.

"I'll have my hands full!"

Blue nodded. The Parker-Hale felt solidly reassuring in his hands. Suddenly he realized the significance of what had just happened. Lucca had given him his gun! Accepted him, that meant. The past two weeks flashed before his eyes. Mexico City was a lifetime ago.

The wind pushed against him. A single raindrop splashed on his face. He breathed deeply through the bandanna tied over his nose and mouth. Strangely, perhaps because death could well be near, he had never felt so alive.

32

Maguire could see them, a knot of individually indistinguishable horsemen illuminated briefly in a flash of lightning. The wind had died off as he'd predicted, now blew steadily from left to right, from north to south, across the open plain that the ancients had named the Avenue of the Dead. Moving slowly but surely, wolf's pace, Maguire lit the shielded torch he'd built and stuck it in the ground near the ramp out of the pit.

"You're going through with this?" Bortha asked as Maguire untied the horses. "Van Allen must have promised a great deal."

Maguire wrapped the reins to Bortha's horse around the pommel of his own saddle and climbed aboard. "Well, you know what they say, General," he replied, reaching down and grabbing the torch as they rode out of the pit. "The devil dances in an empty pocket."

Twenty yards to the waiting pile of brush. Maguire spurred the mare toward it, thrust in the torch and circled to the right rear. As the flames rose, they would hide him and make an accurate shot difficult. Fuentes was damned sure going to have to work hard for revenge, twenty men or no.

The wind caught the flames, pushed them through the piled wood. The twigs and small stuff caught rapidly, burst into flame and heated the larger pieces they'd brought with them. Maguire tried to imagine what Fuentes would think, how he would react.

And then he saw them. Corinne rode next to Fuentes, the reins of her horse in his hands as they entered the circle of light.

"That's far enough!" Maguire shouted against the wind.

Fuentes rode another three or four paces and stopped. Behind him, in a tight clump, his men sat uneasily on their horses. Fuentes looked tired, but capable as always. His men, roughly twenty as the old man had said, presented a formidable array of firepower.

Look closer, damn it, Maguire told himself. Find an edge. They are all tired, and some of them are still sick. Predictably, Fuentes had pushed them hard, knowing they had to have fresh water. Whether or not they were capable of fighting well was moot. He'd find out soon enough though.

Fuentes raised his hand and gestured. Not a word yet. The bunched *rurales* began to drift apart to either side of the fire. Maguire didn't dare let them surround him completely. The men were tired, hungry, thirsty, unsure of what was happening. Their horses were skittish from the thunder and the fire, and half wild with thirst. How the hell was he going to get Corinne out alive? They'd be shooting at him, of course, but uncertain because of Bortha. A straight-out charge, maybe. Under the circumstances . . .

Slowly Maguire sidestepped the mare so Fuentes could see him past the flames.

"So you've finally stopped running!" Fuentes yelled. "You never cease to amaze me. Or amuse me. It's been a long time, Maguire. Too long. I thought the little present I left you in Mexico City would speed things up. You are a patient man."

Maguire stiffened at the reference to Remedios, but suppressed his anger and let it seep into his limbs where, he knew, it would explode into action when needed. Corinne's horse stirred. Suarez reached over and gripped the animal's mane to steady it, then moved his hand from the horse to Corinne's waist and shirt front. Maguire nudged the mare forward. The crackle of the flames at his side, the wind strong and unrelenting, the weight of the revolver and the reassuring touch of the machete scabbarded on his back. All fit into place like the pieces of a puzzle Maguire had lived with for twenty years. "I am here to make a trade," he called across the yards separating them. "Bortha for the girl."

Fuentes laughed openly.

"I'll kill him," Maguire threatened.

Fuentes shrugged. "Even generals sometimes die in battle. When they do, they become great heroes," the leader of the *Serpientes* said. "Who am I to deny—"

"Now you listen to me, Captain Fuentes!" Bortha yelled.

"Shut up!" Maguire said.

"Run, Maguire!" Corinne screamed. "He doesn't care about Bortha!"

Suarez slapped her across the face. "Kill her if she speaks again," Fuentes ordered.

Arranged in pairs, *Los Serpientes* stopped in a wide semicircle. Rifles ready, some faced Maguire, others the surrounding darkness. Suddenly the one farthest from Fuentes on the north heard a noise in the hills and

warned his companions to beware. The word ran around
the arc of men, who shifted nervously on their mounts.
To their consternation, the noise continued, a dragging,
slouching sound borne on the wind. One man muttered,
"Spirits!" That too ran around the circle. Holding their
reins tightly, the men crossed themselves.

Maguire fiddled with a leather thong looped around
his saddle horn, and held out a string of canteens tied
together. "Well, if you won't trade for the general, how
about for water?"

"There is plenty of water at the spring, Maguire. Do
you think I am stupid?"

The sound was still undecipherable, but louder. The
horses were getting harder to control. One of the men
called to Fuentes, who stilled him with a curt gesture.

"Sorry about that, Fuentes. I brought a two-day-old
carcass of a mule with me from El Tule and dumped it
in the spring."

Angry complaints erupted from the *rurales*. After illness and a long ride, they needed water desperately.

The sound came closer. A rumbling sound, like me-
chanical thunder echoing through the valley. A flash of
lightning revealed . . .

"Maguire!" Corinne screamed.

. . . a monstrous black beast coming toward them
down the hill. The men on the northern wing of the semicircle shouted in terror.

Maguire threw the canteens into the fire, then slapped
Bortha's mount across the rump. The animal leaped forward. "Get the canteens!" Fuentes shouted. Diego and
two others rushed the fire in hopes of saving the precious
water. To the side, the black beast grew four blazing,
baleful eyes and emitted a horrendous blaring roar. The
combined effect of lights and horns produced blind panic
in the men. Their mounts, eyes rolling, bucked and
sawed the air.

Overlooked in the confusion spawned by the diversion,

Maguire spurred the mare forward, leaped for Corinne and pulled her to the ground as he fell. The canteens, filled not with water but powder and buckshot, exploded. Shrapnel, shot and flaming embers flew through the air.

The screams of wounded horses vied with the wind. Rifles fired indiscriminately as order and discipline disintegrated. Bortha collided with Fuentes, knocking the captain from his horse. Several nearby *rurales*, thinking the general part of the ruse, opened up on him. Bortha screamed in agony as slugs from the heavy Springfields tore through him. Tied and helpless, riddled with bullets, the general slid off the saddle and hung, head down, under the horse. And then a new sound rose from the black monster that swept down the hill and onto the avenue: the thudding, battering insistency of a Lewis machine gun.

A bullet stung Maguire's shoulder and he rolled, the Le Mat bucking in his hand. The scored slug flattened as it hit Suarez in the jaw and reduced his head to a red mist that was blown away by the wind. Maguire caught the dead man's horse, shoved the bloated, headless body from the saddle. Grabbing Corinne and using the horse for cover, he ran toward the sunken temple.

Almost there, the horse buckled and collapsed. Maguire pulled Corinne out of the way, shoved her over the edge and dived in after her. Bortha's Model T, machine gun firing short bursts, sped by dangerously close. A bolt of lightning flared through the leaden sky. Maguire could see Lucca at the Lewis gun outlined against the rain.

Rain! Damn. Hugh drops pelted his face and chest. Corinne clawed awkwardly through the downpour, held out her bound hands. Maguire pulled his machete from its scabbard and cut the ropes. Corinne threw her arms around him. "Christopher?" she shouted against his ear. Thunder crashed.

"Safe with Lee," he shouted back. As fast as it had started, the rainsquall stopped. But there was no time to

367

notice, because a cluster of terror-stricken horses and riders were bearing down on them.

Blue spun the steering wheel and the Ford skidded. He swung the wheel in the opposite direction and kept the throttle wide open. Lucca held on tight to the Lewis gun, keeping his finger curled around the trigger as the automobile's momentum slung him from one side to the other. It didn't matter to him. He'd told Blue to keep moving. They'd be a harder target to hit that way. Besides, there were men all around him, and each was fair game.

As it was, rifle fire stabbed at them and .30 caliber slugs dug holes in the metal and whined off into the gloom. Those who had not fled were fighting back, but for every round aimed in the car's direction, the Lewis gun answered fourfold.

Wet sand spattered the windshield. Blue spun the wheel again, slid across the mud-slick valley floor. Behind him the heavy cylindrical barrel shuddered as flame issued from its muzzle. The big ninety-five-cartridge drum revolved slowly as Lucca spaced his shots. Steaming brass casings littered the floor underfoot and rolled from side to side with each swerve of the car.

A movement to the left. Lucca swung the gun. To the right. A quick burst. A rifle flew into the air and, brightly lit as the lights passed over him, a man danced a grisly jig.

One of the headlights had gone in the first fusillade. Another followed. The two extra Lucca had rigged remained, but were more for effect than illumination. Oily black smoke gushed from the engine. Blue couldn't have cared less. The world had gone mad and, howling war shrieks to match Lucca's, he with it. A man appeared in a lightning flash. Blue ducked to one side as the small windshield exploded. Something white hot seared his cheek, but he hardly noticed. The *rurale* grew larger in the headlights, tried to work another cartridge into the chamber, then threw up his arms and turned to run. The front of the car struck him square in the back. Screaming, the man rolled over the hood and dropped off to the side, spilling like a torn rag doll to the earth.

Once again, Blue turned, spun the wheel and, trying to turn again, jammed on the brakes. Too late. The earth fell away and the Ford was flying through the air.

Maddened with fright, the horses stampeded across the open ground. The sunken temple didn't even slow them down. Never missing a stride, they jumped to the temple floor and, racing full out, leaped a tumbled pile of stone gods and jumped out the other side. Still caught in the frenzy that had set them running aimlessly, they pounded along the avenue and, spooked by something new, disappeared up the southern slope.

Maguire and Corinne rolled out from between the stones, then scrambled back to cover as the Ford, throttle wide open and motor revved to a screaming pitch, dropped nose first into the temple ruins. The jarring stop sent Lucca tumbling head over heels over Blue and the hood and into the sand and slippery muck.

Maguire pulled a spare automatic from beneath his sweater and handed it to Corinne as they ran toward the smoking auto. The rear wheels still on the avenue, the car tilted at a forty-five-degree angle. In the driver's seat, Blue slumped forward against the steering wheel. Maguire pushed him back. He was conscious, but groggy. His nose sat at a crooked angle to his face and spurted blood. "Get out," Maguire shouted, tugging and pulling.

"Sha-gumph," Blue mumbled, spitting blood. A bullet glanced off the left fender.

"Hurry. They'll be all over us in a minute!" The Le Mat roared twice. A gray-clad *rurale* ducked back behind a rock.

Blue's hand closed around the stock of the Parker-

369

Hale. "Shotgun . . . " he repeated, shrugging off Corinne's help.

"Come on!" Maguire shouted, grabbing his arm as he stepped from the car and shoved him toward the center of the ruins.

The unexpected fall and rough landing had knocked the wind out of Lucca. Chest heaving spasmodically, fighting the suffocating feeling, he staggered to his feet. Maguire caught him by the scruff of his collar and pushed him after Blue. Together all four ran toward the make-shift redoubt of stone-carved sculptures of bird gods and jaguar gods and snake gods.

They gained cover at the same moment three *rurales*, survivors of the Lewis gun, stumbled down the ramp and headed for the shelter. Pushing Lucca to one side, Maguire fired the Le Mat's load of buckshot. Rock chips stung his face. He thumbed back the hammer and fired the upper barrel. A figure moved to his right. Trying for a clean shot, he leaped to another rock and, boot slipping on the mud slick surface, slipped and went down.

His bearing lost, Maguire shook his head, tried to concentrate. To his left a man with a machete bore down on him. He squeezed the trigger. Nothing! Heart beating wildly, he rolled to his right and, knowing there wasn't enough time, reached for the hilt of his own machete. Suddenly Corinne was next to him, on her knees, firing, unable to stop. The *rurale* corpse had ceased twitching before she emptied the clip.

"Where are the others?" Maguire gasped.

"Over there. To your left," Corinne said, guiding him around a stone jaguar god.

"Try to keep together. There can't be too many left . . . Lucca!"

"I need a gun," the Italian shouted over his shoulder as he staggered away from the protective statues. He ran stooped over, zigzagging toward the Model T.

"Lucca!" Blue called.

Maguire looked behind him. Blue stood there, frozen, the Parker-Hale held over his head. By the time Maguire turned back, the Italian was searching the front seat, then clawing his way up the side of the car to get to the Lewis gun. A jagged gash of lightning lit the sky and Fuentes, arm extended, rose out of the very earth. Lucca didn't see him.

"Ricco! Behind you!" Maguire shouted, running into the open. Beside him, Blue matched him stride for stride. The Italian stared at them, waved and pulled back the bolt on the machine gun. "Ricco! Down!"

Fuentes fired.

Lucca spun. His finger squeezing convulsively, he sent the remaining slugs screaming along the avenue and across the temple floor. Maguire and Blue hit the ground, rolled clear and were up and running again instantly. Fuentes had disappeared.

They found Lucca sprawled in the back of the car, right hand held high, finger caught in the trigger guard, left hand hanging limp over the side. Blue could have thrust his doubled fist through the hole torn by the exiting slug. Lucca stared down at the gaping wound in his chest, shook his head in disgust, and died.

Blue snapped. Leaping onto the avenue, he methodically shoved shells into the shotgun. Maguire left Lucca and tried the pull the crazed giant back, only to be brushed aside. Slowly, howling his rage, Blue stalked through the night, pumping shots into anything that moved.

Someone leaped at him but he battered the man aside and shot him where he lay. Fired again and again, reloaded, emptied five more and reloaded again. A form stirred. He shot it. A man tried to run. He shot him, reloaded and searched for another target.

Maguire finally caught up to him. Blue tried to push the mercenary away, but this time Maguire was ready, ducked and slapped Blue twice across the face. The youth's eyes cleared and he stood, trembling, tears streaming down his cheeks.

"Go back to Corinne," Maguire said gently.

Blue looked around. "No."

"Do as I say, Patrick Henry."

"But . . . "

"They're gone. They've had enough. Fuentes is the one we have to worry about. He won't run."

"He killed . . . " Blue couldn't finish the sentence. "I'll help find him."

"No. He and I have to settle this alone, and Corinne needs someone with her." The matter settled as far as Maguire was concerned, he dug the remaining three shells out of his belt, fitted them in the Le Mat and closed the cylinder. "Don't worry. If he kills me, you'll have your chance. He'll come after you."

"You can't be certain—"

A shot rang out and a shrill voice called over the wind. "Maguire . . . Maguire . . . " It was Fuentes.

The stairs that ascended the House of Dawn were covered with dust that the brief rain had wet. Before Maguire had climbed ten steps, he found himself wishing the rain had continued and washed away the glistening, treacherous veneer of mud that was far slippier than ice. Moving slowly he placed each step with infinite care and twisted the ball of his foot to cut through to hard stone before transferring his weight. Once, when a slug spattered the rocks to his left, he instinctively leaned forward and plastered himself to the face of the pyramid. The reflex almost cost him his life, for his feet slipped and he bounced and slid down a half-dozen steps before, clawing and scratching, he caught himself.

"Slow and easy," he chanted silently, making himself concentrate on each step. Fuentes was above him somewhere in the dark. A quarter of the way up, in the dim glow of a distant bolt of lightning, Maguire thought he saw the outline of a crouching man, took a chance and fired. When the form didn't move, he traversed the steps anyway and found a clump of creosote clinging to the rocks. Panting, numbed by the cold, he snapped off a twig and chomped down on it to keep his teeth from chattering. And then started to climb again. His muscles cramped, a sure sign of his growing exhaustion.

Step, twist, transfer weight, shove up. The wind blew. His clothes, wet with rain and sweat and mud, felt like a second, frigid skin. Step, twist, transfer weight, shove up. With each step the machete thumped against his back and reassured him. "Slow and easy." Step. "One at a time." Twist. "Remedios." Transfer weight. "And Lucca." Shove up.

At last his groping hand felt nothing. "Halfway there," he told himself, rolling across the flat space until he ran into the wall of rock reaching high above him. Still alone, he crawled to the outthrust altar. Water seeping down the upper face of the pyramid collected in the bowl, and turned the trough into a miniature canal that emptied onto the long drop below. Maguire lay flat in the lee of the altar stone and gathered strength before the final assault.

How Fuentes, supposedly weakened from the debilitating effects of the poisoned water, was able to make the climb, Maguire couldn't imagine. Madness, perhaps. The years made a difference, too. Forty-one was too old for adventures. Maguire began to climb again. Should have waited below. Let Fuentes come to him in the morning. Crazy, Maguire. Emptiness . . .

He was there. The top. With Fuentes waiting? Slowly he worked his way to the far left side of the steps, crouched on the next to the last. His fingers searched through the darkness, but couldn't find a loose piece of stone. Giving up, he extracted one of his spent cartridges and tossed it as far to the right as he could. When it hit, he leaped and hit rolling, rolling over the mud damp and sandy plateau until one of the pillars stopped him.

Wind sound defining silence. No Fuentes. Not even by the dim light of lightning that accompanied the now distant storm. Only the pillars, godlike guardians of high places, dark ghosts barely distinguishable from the clouds. In the center, Tlaloc, waiting to decide who should live and who should die. For a moment, Maguire didn't really care.

Too tired and cold to hunt or fight. Hands clawing, he scooped a deep hollow in the sand drifted in the lee of one of the pillars. Should have settled this long ago, he thought, crouching out of the wind. Lee . . . Christoper . . . Corinne . . . Too tired to think any longer.

Corinne . . . Corinne . . . Corinne . . .

Silence woke him. No wind. The sky was clear, the norther having pushed the last clouds far to the south. The big dipper hung low in the northern sky. Slate gray light tinged the eastern horizon. Cold. Bitter, numbing cold. At least he was dry. Heart pumping, Maguire poked his head up and looked around. No Fuentes. He must have slept, too. Funny, in a way. Ironic. Two men determined to kill each other and, by mutual, unstated agreement, forced by exhaustion to sleep instead. But not forever. Not yet, forever.

. He checked the cylinder of the Le Mat. Two unspent shells remained. A measure of his exhaustion, Maguire though ruefully. Should have reloaded before nodding off. He patted his pockets and found two more good cartridges. Four would have to be enough. Four and the machete.

Easing the machete from its scabbard, he stood and leaned against the stone pillar for support. Nothing moved. For a moment he wondered if Fuentes was even there, if he had been chasing a chimera. No. Tracks led from the edge to the center of the plateau. Not his tracks, he knew. Fuentes was there—waiting.

Breathing quietly, letting his blood warm, Maguire looked down. One thing was evident. The Avenue of the Dead was aptly named. Diminutive figures of dead horses and men were scattered near its center where the fight had taken place. Swirling around them, he could make out the tracks of the now useless Model T crisscrossing those of the *Serpientes*. The energy they'd spent snaking the machine along the sometimes narrow trail to bring it with them had been a small price to pay, for the car and Lewis gun had meant the difference between success and annihilation. As for the crumpled form in the rear of the car . . . Maguire looked elsewhere, searched for Bortha and spied the general's lifeless body, still manacled to his horse, near the remains of the fire. Blue and Corinne were nowhere to be seen. Just as well, he thought.

Machete in left hand, Le Mat in right, he began the hunt. Each pillar was suspect. The hairs on the back of his neck prickled. The silence was awesome. Slowly, careful not to kick a rock or pebble, he inched toward the next pillar, plastered himself against it and then, pistol ready, jumped around the corner.

Nothing. He shut his eyes for a second and forced his heart back down his throat.

Think, Maguire.

Survive.

The tracks lead to the center. Get it over with. Calmer, he strode toward the massive stone god. Behind him the sun rose through the eastern pass. The first rays struck the ancient face of Tlaloc.

And Fuentes! The machete sliced the still air and clanged off the barrel of the Le Mat, knocking it from Maguire's grasp. Maguire stabbed with his own machete but Fuentes danced to momentary safety. At last they faced each other. Alone.

"Ah, Maguire, this is how it should be, eh? Death for one of us. The old ways are the best. *Mano a mano*."

Hand to hand. Fuentes beamed and his clean, aristocratic features lit with satisfaction. Bedraggled as he was, he cut a splendid figure. And a confident one. Machete to machete, he knew no man could match him. Smiling, he feinted and moved forward to prove the point.

A duel with machetes was not the ringing of steel, but the sibilant rush and retreat of razor-sharp blades cutting empty space. Occasionally meeting, they were quickly disengaged, for without hilts each man's fingers and hand was vulnerable should his opponent's blade slide along his own. More evenly matched than Fuentes imagined, the fight turned into grim, meticulous work. Butcher's work.

The front of Maguire's sweater had been ripped twice. Each foot-long gash oozed crimson over the black knit fabric. Fuentes limped where his thigh had been opened. They moved back and forth, each trying to put the sun in the other's eyes, gradually working away from Tlaloc and the center of the plateau.

Maguire swung, notched his blade on the pillar that had protected him during the night and now Fuentes in the morning. Fuentes ducked, rammed his blade upward toward Maguire's heart, felt it sink in and howled a cry of triumph that turned into a curse as Maguire stepped away, untouched save for a mutilated shoulder holster.

They stopped, panting, resting. Beyond Fuentes the hills were draped in blue shadows, still and infinitely beautiful. The sun had cleared the horizon and was climbing into the sky. Fuentes touched his eye patch. The flesh beneath ached. But wouldn't once Maguire was dead, he knew. Life would be sweet then. He would be revenged. It would have to be fast though, for he was tiring.

Without warning, he threw his machete. Taken completely by surprise, Maguire stuck his blade in front of him. The spinning machete struck his and caught him, handle first, in the forehead. Staggered and dazed, he fell to his hands and knees.

Fool fool fool! The word ran through his brain, dumbly repeating itself. Vision blurred, he saw Fuentes race toward him, grab the machete he'd thrown. Maguire tried to stand, but couldn't. Machete held aloft, blade pointed to the sky, Fuentes roared in triumph and stepped forward to deliver his killing blow.

Maguire lunged upward, fell to the side in the same motion and swung his own battered blade in a two-handed stroke that sliced through Fuentes's abdomen. A hideous crescent wound exploded, gushed fluid and viscera. A soundless scream distorting his face, Fuentes slammed into Maguire and staggered stiff-legged to the edge of the plateau. Hands trying to stem the emptying of his belly, Fuentes plunged over the lip of stone, hit and bounced and hit again. A horrid wail of agony echoed off the face of the pyramid. A line of crimson marked his descent.

Slowly, ever so slowly. Maguire lay on his back and stared at the sky. It was blue and clean and clear, and hurt his eyes. When he could breathe again, he rolled over slowly, pushed himself onto his hands and knees and crawled to the edge.

Fuentes had landed on the altar. Splayed across it, mercifully face down, he lay motionless. As Maguire watched, blood mingled with the rain water flowing through the trough in the stone. The red line lengthened, and at last, spilled over and washed the face of the pyramid.

It was over. Maguire lay back in the sunlight flooding the House of Dawn. Morning shimmered and danced around the feet of Tlaloc, Old Grandfather God, and bathed him in radiance.

33

Presidio, town of dun-colored buildings and frame houses, stretched along the Rio Grande. A train waited on the tracks that cut the town in two. Patience came easily to iron and steam. Lee found Maguire standing at the end of the platform staring off into the long distance.

"Maguire." Rest and plenty of food had filled out Lee's gaunt form and brought color to his cheeks. Even his limp seemed less noticeable, though he still needed a cane. Christopher left the depot and walked along the platform to stand beside Lee.

"Corinne will be out to say good-bye. I wanted to . . . " Lee faltered. "*We* wanted to thank you."

Maguire looked at him, glanced down at Lee's hand resting on Christopher's shoulder. Maguire held out his hand. His face sober with adult solemnity, Christopher shook it. "Take care of yourself, boy." Maguire paused, forced himself to go on. "Take care of your father, too."

Was that a look of relief in Lee Van Allen's eyes? Then he knew. He knew and still loved the boy.

The train sighed and shuddered. Maguire stared at the locomotive, coughed nervously. "Have a good trip, Lee. You and your son, both. A safe trip."

Lee started to speak, found himself without a thing to say. "Let's go, Father." Christopher said, tugging Lee's arm. Father and son started toward the coach that would take them north to the ranch. Maguire turned back, headed for the stables. He'd bought a horse, gear and provisions. He didn't need to see the train pull out.

Corinne stood in the shadow of the open barn door. The spun finery of her hair hung like flax about her shoulders. Maguire stopped in front of her. "I always liked the smell of straw," he said.

She wiped a line of moisture from her cheek. "Do you hate me for going back with him?"

"Lee needs you," Maguire said, trying to keep his voice light.

"What happened . . . This . . . Everything . . . He's changed, Maguire."

"There's no need to explain."

Silence between them. "What will you do?" she finally asked.

The train whistled shrilly, shattering the interlude with urgency. "Go home, Corinne," Maguire said gently.

Her lips touched his. "I won't ever see you again, will I," she said.

"Life is long . . . "

She shook her head. "You're wrong, you know. It's too short."

"I stand corrected."

Corinne reached out, touched his hand, then stepped past him and ran out of his world, forever.

The train was a ghostly echo floating over the desert when Maguire led his new gelding from the stable. He fitted the Le Mat into his patched shoulder holster, touched the bandage on his forehead and sighed. Just what he needed. Another scar.

A familiar figure, a big bulky giant of a man he assumed had taken the train suddenly cantered up on a huge mule. His rumpled campaign hat was set at a jaunty angle. A bronze growth of beard outlined once smooth cheeks. Patrick Henry reined the mule alongside Maguire's gelding. He carried a Parker-Hale shotgun slung over his shoulder. "Only thing I could find big enough," he said, grinning self-consciously and slapping the mule affectionately on the neck.

"I thought you'd left," Maguire said.

"I thought I had, too. And then I thought I'd tag along south with you."

"South?"

"All the way to Mexico City. Figured you might like some company."

"And you might just find Estrellada again," Maguire said, swinging into his saddle.

Blue checked the watch hanging on the gold chain dangling from his vest. "May be. You ready?"

"And just what makes you think I'd chance Mexico City?" Maguire wanted to know.

"Well, the gold you buried at *El Madronito*, for starters."

Maguire booted his horse in the side. A grin slowly spread across his face. "You're learning, Patrick Henry. You're learning."

Historical Romance

Sparkling novels of love and conquest against the colorful background of historical England. Here are books you will savor word by word, page by spellbinding page.

☐ AFTER THE STORM—Williams	23081-3	$1.50
☐ ALTHEA—Robins	23268-9	$1.50
☐ AMETHYST LOVE—Danton	23400-2	$1.50
☐ AN AFFAIR OF THE HEART Smith	23092-9	$1.50
☐ AUNT SOPHIE'S DIAMONDS Smith	23378-2	$1.50
☐ A BANBURY TALE—MacKeever	23174-7	$1.50
☐ CLARISSA—Arnett	22893-2	$1.50
☐ DEVIL'S BRIDE—Edwards	23176-3	$1.50
☐ ESCAPADE—Smith	23232-8	$1.50
☐ A FAMILY AFFAIR—Mellow	22967-X	$1.50
☐ THE FORTUNE SEEKER Greenlea	23301-4	$1.50
☐ THE FINE AND HANDSOME CAPTAIN—Lynch	23269-7	$1.50
☐ FIRE OPALS—Danton	23112-7	$1.50
☐ THE FORTUNATE MARRIAGE Trevor	23137-2	$1.50
☐ THE GLASS PALACE—Gibbs	23063-5	$1.50
☐ GRANBOROUGH'S FILLY Blanshard	23210-7	$1.50
☐ HARRIET—Mellows	23209-3	$1.50
☐ HORATIA—Gibbs	23175-5	$1.50

Buy them at your local bookstores or use this handy coupon for ordering:

FAWCETT BOOKS GROUP
P.O. Box C730, 524 Myrtle Ave., Pratt Station, Brooklyn, N.Y. 11205

Please send me the books I have checked above. Orders for less than 5 books must include 75¢ for the first book and 25¢ for each additional book to cover mailing and handling. I enclose $_____ in check or money order.

Name_____

Address_____

City_____State/Zip_____

Please allow 4 to 5 weeks for delivery.

Victoria Holt

Here are the stories you love best. Tales about love, intrigue, wealth, power and of course romance. Books that will keep you turning the pages deep into the night.

☐ BRIDE OF PENDORRIC	23280-8	$1.95
☐ THE CURSE OF THE KINGS	23284-0	$1.95
☐ THE HOUSE OF A THOUSAND. LANTERNS	23685-4	$1.95
☐ THE KING OF THE CASTLE	23587-4	$1.95
☐ KIRKLAND REVELS	23920-9	$1.95
☐ LEGEND OF THE SEVENTH VIRGIN	23281-6	$1.95
☐ LORD OF THE FAR ISLAND	22874-6	$1.95
☐ MENFREYA IN THE MORNING	23757-5	$1.95
☐ MISTRESS OF MELLYN	23924-1	$1.95
☐ ON THE NIGHT OF THE SEVENTH MOON	23568-0	$1.95
☐ THE PRIDE OF THE PEACOCK	23198-4	$1.95
☐ THE QUEEN'S CONFESSION	23213-1	$1.95
☐ THE SECRET WOMAN	23283-2	$1.95
☐ SHADOW OF THE LYNX	23278-6	$1.95
☐ THE SHIVERING SANDS	23282-4	$1.95

Sylvia Thorpe

Romantic tales of adventure, intrigue, and gallantry.